UNTETHERED

UNTETHERED

RUTH RAKOFF

Cormorant Books

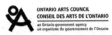

We acknowledge financial support for our publishing activities: the Government
of Canada, through the Canada Book Fund and The Canada Council for the
Arts; the Government of Ontario, through the Ontario Arts Council, Ontario
Creates, and the Ontario Book Publishing Tax Credit. We acknowledge
additional funding provided by the Government of Ontario and the Ontario Arts
Council to address the adverse effects of the novel coronavirus pandemic.

LIBRARY AND ARCHIVES CANADA CATALOGUING IN PUBLICATION

Title: Untethered / a novel by Ruth Rakoff.
Names: Rakoff, Ruth, author.
Identifiers: Canadiana (print) 20230215351 | Canadiana (ebook) 20230215416 |
ISBN 9781770867017 (softcover) | ISBN 9781770867024 (HTML)
Classification: LCC PS8635.A4565 U58 2023 | DDC C813/.6—dc23

United States Library of Congress Control Number: 2023935159

Cover design: Angel Guerra / Archetype
Interior text design: Marijke Friesen
Manufactured by Friesens in Altona, Manitoba in July, 2023.

Printed using paper from a responsible and sustainable resource,
including a mix of virgin fibres and recycled materials.

Printed and bound in Canada.

CORMORANT BOOKS INC.
260 ISHPADINAA (SPADINA) AVENUE, SUITE 502,
TKARONTO (TORONTO), ON M5T 2E4

www.cormorantbooks.com

In loving memory of my brother Davey

I.

LIBERATION FROM MONTHS of built-up stress had left Petal with a tension-release migraine that throbbed so hard behind her left eye she knew she was about to vomit. She made the obligatory pass to shake hands with each member of her thesis committee and excused herself. Three steps down the echoey hallway of NYU, Petal barfed in the miraculously convenient garbage can.

Celebration's never been my strong suit, she thought.

Benjamin was waiting in her lobby with a bottle of chilled champagne and a bouquet of flowers. Petal squinted her left eye and pointed to her temple.

"Dr. Wolffe, I presume?" Benjamin said, handing her his gifts.

Petal kissed him on the cheek, muttered a barely audible, "Thanks," and took the elevator up to her apartment to sleep off her good-news migraine. Tomorrow, she would revel in her success. Tomorrow, she would call Der.

PETAL WOKE FEELING human. She pulled on her jeans, sniffed the armpits of the closest T-shirt, brushed the night off her teeth, and headed out to meet Benjamin. Her phone purred inside the kangaroo pocket of her oversized hoodie as she locked the door behind her. *I will not let anything interfere with this day,* she thought, placing the key on top of the doorframe. Benjamin had warned her against this reckless practice in New York City, but she prided herself on having nothing worth stealing in her five hundred

1

square feet other than the two-ton Murphy bed he had forced her to buy. Petal wasn't good at ownership.

"You cannot continue to live in this place!" Benjamin had decreed the first time he'd visited her previous apartment, a dingy studio with a bathtub in the kitchen. "This 'Joad abode' is a straight shot to razor blade land! I must find you something better!" He'd made it his mission. He'd practically camped out in the lobby of the building across the street from his Tudor City apartment when he heard about a vacancy, accosting the building manager and forcing a cash deposit into his fist.

Petal moved in with nothing but her two duffel bags of old clothes and books. Benjamin was appalled. "A bed! A chair! A plate that doesn't come from the thrift store, complete with some-one else's scars and stains!"

He took her shopping. Petal hated shopping.

They lay side by side on the Princess and the Pea model at Manhattan Murphy Beds.

"You need to live like an adult. You need to believe you are worthy of owning two thousand pounds of stuff! And you can't underestimate the importance of back support," Benjamin encouraged.

Petal sighed deeply. The salesman rolled his eyes. "It comes in white and grey. Glossy or matte."

"We'll take it," Benjamin said.

"We'll?" Petal said. "Does that mean you're going to pay the ridiculous price for this bed?"

"You know I would give you anything, Pet, but I'm afraid that would defeat the purpose of this particular purchase. Don't think of it as paying for a bed. Think of it as buying roots."

Petal bought the Murphy bed, spending endless wakeful hours between the time of purchase and delivery contemplating how she could have so much inherited proverbial baggage but no actual baggage.

PETAL CHECKED HER back pocket for a lighter.

She checked her watch: 8:43. It always said 8:43. Petal found its consistency reassuring.

Her phone buzzed again. She tried not to check but then thought she should since it might be Der.

"I knew it!" she said out loud to nobody, her sister's number glowing. She pocketed the phone and took the elevator down.

The beautiful spring weather meant she would meet Benjamin across the road in the small courtyard behind his building instead of under the sheltered front awning of 325 East 41st Street.

For four years, they had been meeting every morning no matter the weather at exactly 8:45 a.m. Benjamin brought strong black coffee in ironically garish mugs, Petal brought two cigarettes, and together they shared what they referred to as their "morning motivator." When the weather was at its worst, Benjamin would leave the coffee on the large table in the Tudor-style lobby of his building while they cowered under the awning by the front door, smoking their one-a-day. They would drink their coffee at the theatrical table where Benjamin liked to pretend to be a medieval knight, showcasing his impeccable comic timing and acting talent. Petal always squirmed with self-conscious embarrassment when he nudged her to play along.

"Sir Codswallop, has your pillaging been profitable of late?" he would prompt.

Petal would blush, nestling her face as far into her coffee mug as she could.

"I say, my dear man, have the wenches on your travels been as ample of bosom as you are of bottom?" he'd prod.

"I really have to play this game every time we sit at this table? I hate make believe. I'm no good at it."

"Do as you wish, but I will not skirmish for you if you upset our lord the king."

And so it would go, never more than a few minutes, just long enough for Benjamin to cajole a good-natured, character-worthy response from Petal. He liked coaxing her out of her default drive of heavy oppression toward silliness. For that she loved him. For that and more, she needed him. She also knew, without a shadow of a doubt, that skirmish he would for her.

Normally, by 9:30 they would each be at their respective writing. Most days that happened, though occasionally, rather than motivating one another, they did precisely the opposite and enabled mutual slacking and lack of productivity. Today, there would be no writing.

Petal crossed the threshold of the wrought iron fence into the garden as Benjamin exited the back door of his building. They met at their bench. Petal pulled two cigarettes from the kangaroo pocket of her sweatshirt, put both into her own mouth, retrieved the lighter from the back pocket of her loose, faded blue jeans, fired the cigarettes up, inhaled deeply, removed them both, placed one between Benjamin's lips, and relieved him of one of his cups of coffee in a series of well-rehearsed motions.

"Let's not be us today!" she said, exhaling a cloud of smoke.

"Okay, sweetie, who shall we be? Knights?" he teased.

"Anybody but knights! Today I feel I could be anybody." Petal flung her arms away from her body as though preparing for flight, snagging her wild brown curls on the articulated band of her grandfather's ever-constant watch.

"If anybody, then why not us? I sense an anybody good, not an anybody bad, in your constitution this morning, Pet. What's up?"

Her phone buzzed inside her pocket.

"That!" she said, clapping her hand over her ringing abdomen. "She's called at least three times this morning! I will not let her fuck up this day!"

"Today is yours. You don't have to answer the phone, but you shouldn't feel you must be someone else to enjoy it. You worked damn hard for today. You deserve to celebrate it, Dr. Wolffe!" Benjamin cradled Petal's shoulder. "Doctor! Can you believe it's finally official?"

"Not really. That's why I don't want to answer. I'm terrified my sister's drama will steal my thunder again." Petal dropped her cigarette butt on the ground, crushing it with the toe of her sneaker, and bent to pick it up.

Petal and Benjamin would often invent thematic motifs to give direction to their wanderings. To celebrate her hard-won doctorate, Petal and Benjamin had decided to spend the day roaming Alphabet City and the East Village in pursuit of things to eat in alphabetical order. It seemed an appropriate place to fete almost five years of research about literacy education and comprehension.

Walking down 2nd Avenue, they stopped at a fruit cart in front of Gristedes and bought an apple and a banana they shared while ambling downtown. It felt strange to amble. New Yorkers do not, as a rule, amble. Benjamin prided himself on being able to walk faster than a city bus, covering two street blocks in one minute. He could calculate very precisely how long it would take him to walk from one place to another and found immense self-satisfaction in being absolutely on time for everything, almost as much as he found in calling himself a New Yorker.

Petal's phone rang incessantly.

"If you're not going to answer it, maybe turn it off," Benjamin suggested.

"I'm going to give Der a quick call. He'll be waiting to hear how yesterday went."

"Here's to family-by-choice!" Benjamin held his hand high in anticipation of Petal's high five, which she didn't return.

"You, my dear Benjamin, are my FBC. Der, not so much. By the time I was born, he had been my grandparent for more than twenty years. When I was little, I thought everyone had a Der — like uncles and aunts and Ders. Only I didn't have uncles or cousins or anything other than Der. Did I ever tell you about my first-grade teacher going on holiday?"

"Do tell," Benjamin encouraged.

"I told my bubby my teacher was going to her Ami for Christmas. Since we didn't have any family, I figured that when she said she was going to Miami, an Ami was just something else I didn't have."

"You are too much! We should all be so lucky to have a Der like yours," Benjamin said.

"Ain't it the truth!" Petal dialled her Der. "The last answering machine on the planet," she said, holding up one finger and waiting for the beep. "Hey, Der, I guess you aren't home. Just wanted to let you know that yesterday went very well. I'm relieved. Spending the day with Benjamin. I love you forever and for always. Talk later," she added before hanging up.

"Done," she said, switching her phone to vibrate. Standing in line for coffee, Petal noted almost triumphantly that she had ignored seven calls from her sister. Ignoring her sister had never been easy.

"Why's she calling so much? What could possibly be so important?" Benjamin said. "It's not likely she's calling to congratulate you."

Petal snorted.

"She needs money for Passover next week," Petal said. "This

happens every year. She only calls when she needs something. It's always been like that."

"Why is Passover different than other days?" Benjamin asked.

Benjamin, a Jew by birth, self-identified as Jewish but was entirely non-practising. He knew just enough to be intrinsically burdened by the historic plight of his people. In other words, he liked to blame a lot of his neuroticism on his membership in the tribe but knew little about the details of the faith.

"They go overboard even for them and their religious wackiness at Passover. They throw away perfectly good food in order to replace it with the same stuff that has been labelled kosher for Passover by some rabbi. They live in abject poverty with their way-too-many kids and insufficient income and have no problem throwing away food!"

"Let's get doughnuts," Benjamin said, redirecting Petal away from her aggravation and toward their shared mission.

"And egg tarts," Petal added.

"Does pho count as 'F' food?" Petal asked Benjamin as they passed a Vietnamese restaurant at the corner of 2nd Avenue and 23rd.

"Oh, look at little miss literacy — I mean doctor literacy! Absolutely not! If you want pho, you'll have to wait till we get to 'P,'" Benjamin said, turning east on 23rd. "Or should we go along Fourteenth to First?" he asked.

"Either way," Petal said, following him. She knew he liked to walk through StuyTown so he could tell her about its checkered history. Benjamin liked nothing better than to play New York tour guide, spouting obscure facts only someone who had worked hard to know everything about New York could know. Stuyvesant Town was like the bonus round of NYC trivia. Anyone could wax philosophical about where the homeless used to dwell before Mayor Giuliani sanitized the city beyond recognition or tell you where they had been on 9/11, but for Benjamin, the beauty was in the obscure details of the city. And for Petal, the beauty was in the obscure details of Benjamin.

"You know, this isn't actually StuyTown," Benjamin said. "It's Peter Cooper Village until about Fourteenth Street."

"Really?" Petal said. "You know, you've never told me that before. Except for every time we come this way."

"I'll make it up to you. When we get down to Fourteenth, we'll double back and stop at Trader Joe's."

"Excellent! Then we can get freeze-dried mangosteen for 'F.'"

"I don't know why you like those. They taste like Styrofoam packing peanuts with an ungenerous dusting of fructose."

"Exactly! That's what I love about them. When we were kids, my sister and I would play this game. I'd get her to think of the most disappointing things in life. I know it's weird, but I tried to get Rosie to understand how I felt sometimes. Anyhow, one of my most disappointing things was that Styrofoam wasn't edible."

"You're a total nutbar!"

"Think about it. It has the most wonderful texture, makes incredible sounds when you break it or bite into it — yes, I would bite it on occasion — it begs to be eaten! But obviously it isn't for eating. When I found freeze-dried mangosteen, I felt a piece of life's significant disappointments was eliminated. That's a pretty big deal. That's probably thousands of therapy dollars and countless hours saved. The only thing that would make it better is if it came in slabs."

"Aren't rice cakes like slabs of Styrofoam?"

"Yes, but they're also deprivation food, which, as you well know, makes me sad. They're what you eat when you don't have any choice. No one ever says, 'I prefer rice cakes to chips.'"

"You really are loopy, my Pet."

Petal's phone vibrated in her pocket. She reached in to touch it.

"Answer it or leave it alone," Benjamin said.

"She makes me crazy!" she said, stomping her foot too gently.

"You let her. You are here. She is there. You know what she wants. Answer the phone and get it over with. Don't let her control you," Benjamin said, sounding exactly like Dr. Farmer.

NOT SURPRISING THAT Benjamin could mimic the doctor so accurately. He'd been a patient of Farmer's for years. Long before Petal had even set foot in the office of their mutual therapist, Benjamin's ass had worn a divot in the doctor's aubergine velvet couch. That is in fact where the two of them had met. Not in the couch divot but at the office in the 16th Street brownstone, where said couch and divot resided. Petal had gotten a referral to Dr. Farmer following a brief hospitalization her first year in the city.

It had been a difficult time for Petal for many reasons. She knew enough to recognize the edge of the cliff she was on, having stood there before. She walked herself from NYU over to Bellevue and asked to be admitted to psych. After three days, she was released from hospital with a referral to Dr. Farmer.

Petal began seeing him once a week on Tuesdays at noon. It was a quick scoot across 4th Street and up 3rd Avenue to 16th Street from the university, and on a good day Petal could make it in about twelve minutes. Exactly enough time to get her full forty-five-minute session in and be back at her desk before anyone noticed she was gone. Not that anyone would have either noticed or cared that a graduate student was not at her desk for months on end let alone a little over an hour once a week. After she moved out of her depression-inducing studio into her Tudor City apartment, Petal mostly worked from home, venturing to the university only on Tuesdays.

Dr. Farmer's office was on the third floor of a beautiful (but perpetually in need of a good dusting) walk-up that was reached via a once-grand glossy black staircase with a smooth handrail and generous treads with worn black carpeting that felt beneath her feet as though it might have once upon a time been expensive. His office, in what was actually a parcelled-off piece of a former apartment, was entered through what must have been a servants' closet of some sort, dark and tiny. Dr. Farmer had tried to make it comfortable with a small, exquisitely embroidered chair and a designer floor lamp, but despite its costume, it was an awkward alcove that required passing patients practically rub up against one another upon arrival and departure. The inner sanctum of his office gave Petal an almost instant sense of warmth and uncharacteristic calm, with its rich, jewel-toned furnishings, hardwood floor scattered with kilims, wall of books, and subdued lighting — the kind of place that felt as if a fireplace roared and warm drinks were being served, though neither actually existed.

At first, she found it somewhat disconcerting that he would eat his lunch while she was with him, but to be fair, he always asked if she minded, and she always said she didn't. Eventually, she actually didn't mind and occasionally brought her own lunch with her, though usually she grabbed something greasy from a food truck on her way from or back to the university. Dr. Farmer was not Petal's first therapist, but he was the first one she'd grown to genuinely like. That was partly to Benjamin's credit and partly because Dr. Farmer was a good practitioner.

Benjamin had the appointment before Petal, and weekly they would cross paths in the waiting area outside Dr. Farmer's office. Benjamin always said, "Hello, lovely lady," which Petal found both unnerving and enchanting. Benjamin was devastatingly handsome, but she was on her way in to see her shrink. She would smile sheepishly and lower her chin to her chest like a shy child, but week after week he greeted her in this way as the close quarters necessitated some acknowledgement.

One Tuesday, when Petal had been seeing Dr. Farmer (and Benjamin) for some months, Benjamin opened the door between the office and the antechamber and introduced himself.

"Hello, I'm Benjamin Vessel," he said, offering his hand formally. He then proffered a wad of bills. "Dr. Farmer would like to apologize, but he has been called away on an emergency. He asked me to either give you this money so you can go for lunch on him — he feels really bad — or he wants me to take you to lunch. Either way, he's paying."

Petal was so shocked she said nothing.

"I'm not hitting on you. I swear, Farmer asked me to. I promise I'm a card-carrying homosexual with no agenda other than helping out a man who has helped me immeasurably over the years."

"Years?" Petal said.

Benjamin laughed. "Yes, years. I'm pretty fucked up, but not nearly as fucked up as I used to be. So, would you like to have lunch? Union Square Café? He's picking up the tab." And before Petal could answer, Benjamin hooked his arm into hers and started walking and talking.

"Let's start with your name," he said as they descended the swooping staircase out to the street.

"Petal," she said. "He asked you to take me to lunch and didn't tell you my name? Doesn't that seem a bit odd to you?"

"Yes, a bit, but that doctor-patient confidentiality thing. He is nothing if not a gentleman. If you cancelled on him, he would charge you. He felt it only right that he compensate you in some way for cancelling at the last minute. He's rather old fashioned and thought you might not feel comfortable dining alone. So, you got me. Unless, of course, you would rather just pocket the cash and be done with it."

"Union Square Café it is," Petal said.

Petal felt beautiful, almost buoyant, walking with Benjamin. It was not like her to feel beautiful, and weightlessness was even more alien to her. Benjamin had fair skin, larger-than-life features, light-reflecting green-grey eyes, glossy black hair, and perfect posture. He carried himself like he was perpetually looking over the crowd for a lost friend, yet he managed to be entirely with her. Walking across Union Square arm in arm with Benjamin felt to Petal like how confidence might feel if she were ever to find any.

Benjamin listened as though he genuinely cared. He spoke poetry and swore with equal aplomb, which made Petal feel stupid until she got used to it and realized it was just the way he spoke. He was humble and self-deprecating, but Petal had a hard time believing his insecurity was genuine. From her perspective, he was overflowing with God-given gifts. From his perspective, his flaws overshadowed any minimal talents he had. The world disagreed with Benjamin's assessment of himself. So did Petal.

Benjamin was a twenty-first-century Renaissance man. He'd begun his time in the city doing improv theatre. "You know why the improv group is called Second City?" he asked Petal early in their friendship.

"Because it originated in Chicago — the second city," she said.

"Wrong. It's the second lowest form of performance art, playing a close second to mime. It's bullshit. It's what people who are afraid to be real actors or writers do until they give up the arts completely with full-fledged self-loathing or grow a pair of balls and try to create something real."

"Didn't a lot of really famous people start in improv?" Petal asked.

"Not nearly as many famous people as complete ne'er-do-wells."

Later, Petal learned that Benjamin had been on the cusp of being one of those famous people who got their start in improv.

Before he gained notoriety from his writing, he had been offered a spot on *Saturday Night Live*. The timing was wrong, and that is always a fatal flaw in comedy.

"It was the eighties. It was a devastating time in the gay community. Everyone was scared. There was a cancer on the loose that was targeting us. The Christian evangelists were right. It was the fucking fires of hell."

Petal and Benjamin had been friends for almost two full years before she learned about Scott, the love of Benjamin's life. When he'd died in 1988, he was thirty-five years old. It wasn't until ten years later, when Benjamin reached the age of thirty-five himself, still alive (much to his own amazement and in spite of his very risky behaviours), that he sought counselling for the first time.

"Even with AIDS everywhere in the gay community, you still had unprotected, anonymous sex?" Petal said, not disclosing her own high-risk conduct of that time. Perhaps, even years later, she was not ready to acknowledge that as a straight woman, the risk was as real to her as to anyone.

"We were pretty sure we all had it anyhow. I mean, my life partner died of it, and we had been having unprotected sex for years. You have to understand that until AIDS, condoms were not a product gay men bought. By the time HIV and AIDS had names, we all figured we were goners. I was grieving and angry and self-destructive as hell. We were young, beautiful, and immortal one second and dying hideous, messy deaths the next.

"He wanted to die at home. No heroic measures. We agreed on comfort care. By then, so many of us had died that the community had mobilized. There were care teams who came, put in an IV, brought meds, made it possible to die with whatever dignity remained. We had learned how much morphine we could administer without crossing any technically illegal lines. All of us had already helped too many friends die. Truth was, the hospitals were

more than happy for us to stay away. Even healthcare profession-
als still believed you could catch it by breathing the same air!

"Scott was estranged from his family, but near the end I asked
him if he wanted me to call them. They didn't know he had AIDS,
let alone that he was dying. I don't know what I was thinking.
Maybe just that it was the right thing to do. He agreed. I called.
His parents showed up from Connecticut at an awful moment.
He was in respiratory distress from the lesions in his trachea. It was
horrifying to watch him struggle for breath, but I had seen it before
and knew the end was near.

"Without asking, his mother called 911. I was shut out. In
every way other than statutory, he was my husband, I was his
family, but as soon as the ambulance came, his mother claimed
him. Fucking homophobic bitch hadn't spoken to him since he
came out, and all of a sudden, she's calling the shots. They took
him to hospital and intubated him. Nothing I said mattered. I had
no legal status or documents giving me power of attorney. I didn't
think I would need any. The doctors knew he was palliative, but
his mother insisted on interventions. He was tortured with everything he didn't want at the end.

"I wasn't welcome at his funeral. He wanted to be cremated,
but they didn't care. They buried him in the family plot in
Connecticut."

"Holy crap, Benjamin! That's horrible," Petal said.

"Horrible, but far from unique for the times. In so many ways,
we were denied our right to grieve. That'll fuck with your head
but good!"

"No shit!"

"When I turned thirty-five, I threw a party. The theme was 'Still
Alive at 35!' Pretty fucking morose, huh?" Benjamin grimaced.

"Kind of funny in retrospect," Petal said.

"But we weren't laughing yet. We were still too in it. It was a 'fuck you' to destiny, but inside, despite still being HIV negative, or maybe because I had dodged the AIDS bullet, I was closer to death than I cared to admit. The invitations were so smug and cynical. I told guests that in lieu of gifts they could make contributions to my therapy fund. We had decorated jars all over the place with labels on them like 'For Benjamin's Psychosis,' 'For Benjamin's Neurosis,' or 'Benjamin Has Homosexual Tendencies,' all covered in pictures of Freud and Jung and cigars."

"Cute idea," Petal said. "We should have done that for birthday parties when we were kids. Think of how much further ahead the crazy Wolffe twins would be today. I might even be over the trauma of my never-acknowledged birthday." Petal snorted.

"Everybody thought it was so funny. All night, people were shoving money in the jars. At the end of the party, when I counted it up, there was a couple grand in the therapy fund. I figured I was being given a pretty clear message, if not by some higher power, then at least by my friends. Doc Farmer saved my life."

PETAL CONTINUED TO ignore her vibrating telephone as they left Trader Joe's with assorted freeze-dried fruits, guava roll, and a small package of chocolate halva. They headed toward Union Square.

"I've been talking your ear off for months with my thesis crap; I feel like I barely know where things are at with your work."

"Oh, you know, it's all shit! I thought I was liking the novel for a bit, but I'm pretty sure I was momentarily deluded. It feels stale and trite. Like I don't have anything new to say, and I fucking hate my main character. She's a total narcissistic bitch, and no matter how hard I try to get her to do anything compassionate or humane, she betrays my efforts."

While Petal found Benjamin's diatribes about his writing fascinating — the lack of control he claimed to have over the fictitious characters and situations he created — she never really believed him when he lamented his literary shortcomings. It wasn't that she was unsympathetic to the woes of writing, but his brilliance and success were so evident in everything she had ever read or seen or heard from his oeuvre that it seemed suspect that anything he was working on was less than stellar. Nonetheless, she recognized that just because he always managed to eventually produce plays that got rave reviews, screenplays that got nominated for awards (though thus far hadn't won anything big), and a couple of high-brow novels, each of which had had brief appearances on the bestseller list, he struggled with the process and fought demons of angst and self-doubt every step of the way. Maybe that was why his writing was so good. He was never satisfied.

"Maybe if you introduce a nasty friend or a bitchy mother, she'll look good in comparison," Petal offered. "Like you're friends with me because I make you seem super well-adjusted."

She pushed her arm through his and clung to his bicep as though it were a life jacket.

Benjamin chuckled. "What now?"

"Like, right now? Or now that I'm finished my dissertation and defence?"

"Both," Benjamin said.

Petal stopped and thought for a moment. "I can't eat another thing, and we're only at 'I.' If we walk down through Washington Square Park and into the Village, I might be able to work up to something savoury and some juice. After that, maybe we can just name foods that begin with the rest of the alphabet instead of eating them."

"You're a lightweight. You talk a good game, but you haven't got what it takes to eat the alphabet," Benjamin said.

Petal smiled. "As far as the other now, I hope to do as much of nothing as humanly possible until my teaching term starts in September."

"So, you just want to lie around in feathered silks and eat bonbons?"

"Correct! I best run out and buy me some feathered silks!"

"You best run out and buy yourself some decent professorial clothing for the fall, Dr. Wolffe," he said, gently tugging on the hood of her sweatshirt.

They walked the full circumference of the park; standing underneath the arch in Washington Square, Petal was feeling both preternaturally optimistic and a bit peckish. The city was at its zenith of perfection. The weather was warm but not humid, the sun was bright but not oppressively so, the trees were in bud but the allergens were nonexistent, and the park buzzed with the springtime activity of people released from months of indoor incarceration. "I love New York" was never truer than on a day like this one.

"All the vibrating against my belly has activated my digestion," Petal said. "Let's get Indian food truck dosas."

"First call your sister. This is supposed to be our day, and I feel like I'm sharing you with some kind of mythological siren beckoning you to her island. Just call her and get it over with."

They sat on the sun-warmed slats of a park bench. Reluctantly, Petal reached into her pocket and took a deep breath, mentally preparing to dial her sister in Toronto. But the vibrating phone beat her to the punch.

"Hey, Rosie," Petal said, answering.

"Mrs. Wolffe?" said a man.

"Who is this? Who are you looking for?" Covering the mouthpiece, she stage-whispered to Benjamin, "Some guy."

"Is this Mrs. Wolffe?" he asked again.

"This is Petal Wolffe," she said over Benjamin's correction of "Dr. Wolffe" in the background. "Dr. Wolffe," she corrected.

"Are you the sister of Mrs. Hirsch?" the man asked with a heavy Brooklyn accent.

"I'm Rosie's sister. Who are you?" Petal asked again.

"Mrs. Wolffe," he said.

"Doctor," Petal corrected, pricklier than before.

"Dr. Wolffe, I am a friend of the family. I do not have good news."

"What's wrong!" Petal grabbed Benjamin's arm. "Something's wrong! My sister? The kids?"

"Dr. Wolffe, I think your sister is not well," said the still unidentified caller.

"What do you mean, you think my sister is not well? Who are you? What the hell is going on?"

"My name is Rabbi Glisserman," the man said. "I study with your brother-in-law, Schmeil. I know him well. I'm the one they call when there is trouble in a family."

Rosie was *chozeret te'shuva* — someone who had found their way back to religion, not raised Orthodox from birth. This fact was not exactly hidden so much as kept close and quiet within her adopted family and community. That Petal was a doctor should have perhaps been a clue that she herself was not ultra-Orthodox, though it wasn't an entirely dead giveaway, for she might have been a more modern Orthodox. Nonetheless, Orthodox or ortho-dox Orthodox, Petal might have understood that Rabbi Glisser-man was the sort of man who might be called upon "when there is trouble in the family." But since he only knew the world he lived in, it didn't occur to him that Petal wouldn't understand. And since she knew very little of his world, the notion of a guy who gets called when there is trouble in the family was completely foreign. She pictured a plumber, but that image quickly changed to an electrician. Even the un-handiest of Jews could plunge a toilet, but electrical work required a phone call, though to be fair, there were in fact Jewish electricians.

Petal stood up. She squinted in the sun and turned her back on Benjamin, who also stood up so he could continue to overhear her conversation.

"Rabbi Glisserman, is someone sick?" Petal tried as best she could to parse her confusion.

"You could say so," he replied.

"Could you please explain, *clearly*, what is going on there?" Petal said, foot pumping the asphalt. "I don't really understand my sister's religious life, so you need to spell it out for me if it has anything to do with God or the laws or anything like that."

"My apologies. These things are not common in our community. When they happen, people don't talk about them so much. It's a struggle both to keep secrets and to admit when the secrets should not be kept. I try to help. I have no official title, no education in this regard, but I have a reputation for discretion and, I suppose, an intuition about matters of emotional well-being."

"Rabbi, tell me quickly, like you're ripping off a bandage, is everyone all right?"

"Your sister seems to have had a breakdown of some kind. She's here. We are with her — me and Schmeil. The children are in school, but we think you should come."

"Come to Toronto? You know I'm in New York, right? Like a mental breakdown?" Petal sat down again on the bench. Benjamin sat down next to her, put a hand on her knee, and leaned in close, his left ear tilted toward her right ear.

"I know where you are. Your sister is asking for you, and, in my opinion, she needs you. She needs family."

Petal sighed, her head falling backward as though it had become unhinged from her neck. She used her left hand to push the back of her head into its upright position. "Can I speak to her?"

"That's not possible. She's sedated. It's best you should come. How soon before you can be here?" Rabbi Glisserman asked.

"Can I speak to Schmeil? Surely he'll speak with me in a crisis!" Petal had no interest in speaking with her brother-in-law at the best of times, which worked well because he seemed to believe that he could not engage in conversation with a woman who was not his wife. He didn't seem to be concerned with the fact that, according to all the sources Petal had consulted (she was nothing if not a thorough researcher), there were no laws restricting his communication with his sister-in-law. Nonetheless, they never spoke. Ever. In fact, in the twenty-plus years that Schmeil and Rosie had been married, they had rarely been in the same room together.

"This situation is very trying, Mrs. Wolffe. Let me be the go-between in the meantime. Let's agree to simplify rather than complicate, as much as possible. Okay?"

Rabbi Glisserman sounded remarkably sensible to Petal despite the myriad of prejudices she had against the whole encompassing paradigm of her sister's life.

"Okay," she agreed. "So, you think I need to get on the next flight out and show up at Rosie's door?"

"As soon as possible. I'll pick you up at the airport. It'll give me a chance to fill you in. We'll work from there. There's a lot to discuss and consider."

"I guess I'll be in touch."

Rabbi Glisserman hung up without saying goodbye.

"You're not going, are you?" said Benjamin.

"I have to." Petal stood and then sat right back down again, overcome with dizziness. "I think I'm going to barf." She folded herself head between knees.

"Oh, sweet Pet." Benjamin placed a firm hand on the back of her neck.

Despite the closeness of their friendship, most of what Benjamin knew about Petal's sister had been extrapolated from complaints about the crazy, needy, parasitic twin who lived north of the border but may as well have been living on another planet, given the extent that their lives did not overlap or correlate.

What Benjamin did not know, or perhaps did not understand, much as Petal herself did not understand it, was that Petal needed Rosie and Rosie needed Petal and that was that. It did not occur to Benjamin that Petal would entertain trekking to Canada to save her sister. For Petal, once crisis was declared, it was not something she needed to think about for even a second.

Petal carried a heavy existential load made up of the sum of her parts, but her fraught relationship with her sister, her sense of responsibility to her, her resentment toward her, and her complicated feelings of betrayal and abandonment were all overridden by her inexplicable love for, need of, and yearning to be needed by Rosie. They were bound together.

PETAL SAT IN the middle of her rumpled bed contemplating packing a suitcase, knowing full well that she had neither a suitcase nor the will to pack. *This wasn't the plan*, she thought, falling onto her back as though pushed by the pressure in her chest.

"Knock, knock." Benjamin entered Petal's mayhem holding a small celadon-green bowl and spoon, pulling a carry-on bag.

"It's not as bad as it looks." Petal sat up and looked around. "The clothes are all clean, just not folded, and the papers can all be tossed now that I'm done my defence."

"I didn't say a word. 'I' is for ice cream," he said, handing her the bowl.

"Pretty pink and green," she said, slipping a spoonful of strawberry ice cream into her mouth. "Where's your ice cream?"

"Don't you fret. I scarfed down the bulk of that tub before I came over."

"I thought you didn't like strawberry?"

"I'm an equal opportunity consumer of frozen treats. It's not my favourite, but today was supposed to be your day, so your favourite it was. What time is your flight?"

"Not till one," she said, checking her watch. 8:43. "I could have gotten an earlier flight, but as it is, I'll have to get up at the crack of dawn to get the train to Newark."

"Why would you take the train? The shuttle is so much easier. It's literally around the corner. You're not going to schlep all the way to Penn Station."

"It's more expensive, and my last-minute plane ticket already set me back."

"Well, in that case, why don't you take the #62 and save yourself another fifteen bucks?" Benjamin pulled out his phone, thumbs flying on keyboard.

"Are you checking bus schedules?" asked Petal, mistaking sarcasm for suggestion.

"I just booked two tickets for the 9:45 airport express shuttle tomorrow morning."

"You're crazy! You're going to ride there and back just to prove that the shuttle is worth the expense?"

"Uh-huh." Benjamin smirked his naughty-boy smirk. Petal laughed. "See, worth it already. Let's get you packed." He opened the suitcase.

AT 8:43 A.M., Petal wheeled her bag across the road and met Benjamin at their bench.

"All set?" he said, handing her a coffee in exchange for a lit cigarette.

"As set as I'll be." Petal exhaled a puff of smoke.

"Passport? Ticket? Toothbrush? Clean underwear? The burden of familial obligation?" Benjamin chided.

Petal bumped shoulders with Benjamin, shoving him a tad harder than she had intended. "Sorry," she said.

"No, that's okay. Get your shots in before you walk into your role as underappreciated younger sibling."

"I'm older."

"I just assumed she was older. You know, all the kids and the husband and the trappings of conventional adulthood, but you don't really talk about your sister much."

"Well, Rosie has a way of stealing the show even when she isn't around, so I do my best not to give her too much airtime."

PETAL WAS NOT being unkind in her assessment of her sister's capacity to upstage. It really was undeniable. From the moment she was born, Rosie had been the unexpected to Petal's grounded. They were two of a very rare type of fraternal twin known as "post-conception gestational twins," conceived through superfetation. It was probably not as rare as documented, because it likely went undiagnosed — if *diagnosed* was the right term — more often than not. Twins are born. One is significantly bigger than the other. Oh well, these things happen. But in the case of Petal (née Daisy on April 28, 1968, but renamed Petal at about a month old), her twin sister, Rose, was not born until almost three weeks after her on May 17, 1968.

The girls' mother, Chavie, was what in those days was known as "a bit wild" but these days is called bipolar. At age nineteen, she had been on a manic high for an indeterminate period of time. It was 1967, and everybody who had the sense to get in on the fun was enjoying the Summer of Love. It was hard to tell who was high, who was crazy, who needed to be institutionalized, and who was just having a good time.

In the fall of that year, Chavie, having been away from home for the better part of four months — causing her anxious, immigrant, Holocaust survivor parents a summer of torment and worry — returned. Estie and Irving Wolffe were so relieved to have their daughter home they didn't give too much weight to some of the things that might otherwise have been cause for concern.

Estie shrieked with unbridled relief when Chavie appeared grimy and dishevelled at the foot of her bed. Leaping out of bed, Estie threw both arms tightly around her daughter's neck, ignoring both the pungent smell and Chavie's rebuffs.

It should be noted that as a survivor of the Second World War and Hitler's death camps, Irving had a pretty good grip on the much later introduced concept of "not sweating the small stuff." Their daughter was away with friends; he worried but figured she was probably okay, given the climate of the times. Or perhaps he needed to believe as much. Estie, despite their daughter's many and frequent disappearances, didn't cope as well. But with their daughter home where they could see her, what could possibly be wrong. Right?

Chavie arrived at their Toronto apartment weighing less than one hundred pounds fully clothed. She took a shower — something she hadn't done in a good deal longer than a sane person might consider reasonable — forced down an obligatory bowl of her mother's kasha with bow ties, and got into bed. When she got up some months later, she was pregnant. Very, very pregnant.

By the early spring of 1968, Chavie was so big that she looked like she had swallowed the girl who had shown up and gotten into her bed months before. By the time she got to a doctor, she was practically in labour, and there wasn't much doubt that she was going to have a baby. Unsurprisingly, she did just that on April 28.

Chavie did not take to mothering naturally, and Estie supposed she just needed some time to recover from what had been a difficult delivery. Until such a time, Estie took care of Chavie and her new granddaughter, Daisy. In fact, for those first two and a half weeks, her biggest concern was that the name the child had been given by her mother was not a good fit. She couldn't bring herself to express the real reason out loud, which was that it was a name she thought of as too *Goyish* — too Gentile by far — for her granddaughter, so instead she said things like, "To me, she doesn't so much look like a Daisy" or "To me a Daisy should be blond hair" or "Such a *schvartzinke* like a Bedouin qveen. Ent brown, brown eyes. Vouldn't Daisy be a gut name for a girl mit maybe blue, maybe green eyes?"

To this, Irving shrugged one shoulder. He was a man of few words, but she understood what his shrug meant. It meant don't worry about things you do not control. It meant this should be your biggest *tsureh*. It meant leave it alone.

On the sixteenth of May, Chavie was not well. Estie tried to get her to nurse the baby, but she refused. Estie worried that something was wrong between Chavie and her baby, but in those days, they didn't have the vocabulary for things like bonding or postpartum depression. But a mother too sick to feed her own baby! That was a terrible and serious thing.

Then, according to Estie, a miracle happened. Chavie began to vomit.

To Estie, this meant things would get better between baby and mother. But Chavie's vomiting grew violent, and her abdominal pain got so bad she was screeching and thrashing about on the floor. Irving, who was less alarmist but sometimes more practical than Estie, decided a trip to the hospital was necessary.

The emergency room doctor declared that Chavie was in labour and fully dilated, which, needless to say, confused a number of people.

Estie screamed as she held Daisy up and waved her about frantically as indisputable evidence that the baby was already born.

Born or not, there was another one on the way, and the doctors were concerned about the speed with which this baby was coming. Chavie was wheeled off to the delivery room while a somewhat frazzled intern sat with the very bewildered Wolffe family and explained the rare phenomenon that was taking place. Chavie was having twins. Twins conceived in the same menstrual cycle but at different times. It happened — rarely. Usually, they were born at the same time, but occasionally not. Even the intern had learned that that could be possible only minutes before he was tasked with explaining to the family that it was a good thing. That it meant the second baby — likely the younger of the two — would be better developed than it might have been a few weeks earlier, making it healthier and stronger.

As Estie tried to understand, it dawned upon her that if two conception dates were possible, so were two different fathers, but when she asked, Irving shrugged one shoulder, which Estie understood meant it wasn't important.

The birth of the second baby recalibrated Chavie, and she slipped out of her depression straight into a brand-new mania.

People marvelled at how much energy this young mother had. How well she was coping as a single parent with newborn twins. And in some ways, she was, but to a watchful eye, the pass she was given as a single mother of newborn twins allowed for a whole lot of crazy to go unnoticed for quite a while.

With the coming of the second baby came a name change for the first. Daisy became Petal, an accessory to the star of the show, Rosie.

"BENJAMIN, CAN YOU please ..." Petal said, trying to hoist her suitcase onto the overhead rack. "I'm not sure why it feels so fucking heavy. There's nothing in it."

"Baggage?" Benjamin said, raising his eyebrow as he effortlessly swung the bag up.

The ride to the airport was just about an hour long, and as silly as it was that Benjamin had come just to prove a point, she was glad he was there. She knew that he knew that she needed him at that moment, so he'd found an excuse that allowed her to nestle in his protective love.

"How come you never told me about being born three weeks before your twin sister? That is seriously cool! You can't make that shit up in a novel. No one would believe it."

"I guess it's not something I like to talk about. It was hard enough being Rosie's twin growing up. All I needed was another feather to add to our circus-freak family cap."

"I hear you, but I can't promise I won't steal it. I've warned you that writers are vultures," Benjamin said, pushing his arm through hers.

"I thought you said no one would believe it if you wrote it."

"Yeah, but I love the idea of readers looking up the science to see if it's true."

"You're a cheeky one! I hereby gift the story of my unusual birth to you. Do with it what you will. It's one of the only things I actually know about my family history. It might as well be told by someone."

"There's something liberating about telling secret stories, even if they're someone else's. Secrets have too much power."

Petal knew this too well to reply.

About five minutes before they got to the airport terminal, Benjamin pulled a brown paper bag from his satchel and handed it to Petal.

"What's this?" Petal asked.

"J, K, L," he said, "for the plane. But eat it before you get there. 'J' for *jambon* — ham and cheese on a croissant. 'K' is for massaged kale salad with bacon vinaigrette, and 'L' is for licorice allsorts."

"You still owe me half an edible alphabet," she, said trying to smartass her way out of deep emotion.

"No, you still owe me consumption of half an alphabet," he said, putting the suitcase in the aisle ahead of her.

"Don't be a hero, Pet. If it gets too real, don't surrender. Retreat! Come home! And whatever you do, don't kiss the rabbi with your bacon breath!"

"I love you," she said. "Don't have fun without me."

"I couldn't possibly, my love. Call."

PETAL ALWAYS CHOSE a window seat. She liked to lean her head against the cool glass and feel the hum of the engines as the airplane ascended. It didn't matter where she was going, that feeling of flight felt almost spiritual to her. Gravity be damned! She could soar, even if only briefly. But once altitude was reached, the momentary breach between earth and space faded, and her thoughts returned to mortal matters and ill-fated flights both taken and not taken. *On my way to outer space*, she thought.

Petal had often said, when speaking of her sister's life, "If I were to visit Mars, it couldn't possibly be more foreign to me than my sister's world." So, for the most part, she stayed away.

Rosie — or Raizel, as she chose to be called — lived with her husband, Schmeil, and their eight children, who ranged in age from nineteen to three years old, in a small, decrepit bungalow near Lawrence and Bathurst in the heart of Toronto's ultra-Orthodox Jewish community. It was all of five blocks from where the girls had grown up, but it might as well have been another planet.

That the two women's lives had become so opposite was not as peculiar as one might imagine. They were so different from one another that it was easy to speculate that in utero they had simply divided the available options for everything from the physical to the metaphysical.

Petal got dark features, café au lait skin, curly hair, an old, burdened soul, and a propensity for bouts of debilitating depression. Rose was fair and freckled with hair so fine it levitated in the presence of even the slightest hint of electricity and an innocence born of what must have been a first time around the incarnation wheel. Rose was always up for a good time, a party, or an adventure. Petal was resistant to fun — not opposed to or incapable of but standoffish and suspicious of mirth and merriment. They were polar opposites. Together, they were whole.

As children, they had been so close. Their grandmother believed that they were conjoined twins accidentally separated before birth.

"A Siamese mistake just," Estie said more than once.

"That's just a regular twin, Ma," Chavie would say when she was still in their lives.

"No, I'm tellink someting differen. Helf a whole. Dis is someting, dis so close."

The girls slept in the same bed until they graduated high school. It was only partly a choice. Their apartment was small for five people. Zaideh Irving refused to put bunk beds in their room. There was no talk of the Holocaust or the camps in the Wolffe household, but bunk beds were called *Nazishe tenementen*, and they were not welcome in their home. So when the girls grew out of their shared crib, a second twin bed was put in the room. They pushed them together to make space for games and for a long time slept together on one half of the available space, leaving room for their mother, should she happen to show up, which, by the time they were seven years old, she never again did, leaving another cavernous void of things that were never discussed in their family.

When they grew out of the kind of play that required real estate, they kept their beds together out of habit and probably need. They shared a loss that bound them together as though they were one another's exoskeletons — an extra layer of protection against the realities of life that they were much too young to know yet old enough to have suffered. Perhaps these days, one might call it codependence, but then their need to cling to one another literally and figuratively was dismissed as "a twin thing." But the gossamer webbing that bound them together was made not of silk but of fine steel threads, forcing each girl to carry not only her own weight but the weight of her sister and all their collective history.

As twins, naturally they celebrated their birthdays together. Mostly, Petal didn't mind that it was always on Rosie's day. Who had the energy for two birthday parties three weeks apart? Rosie loved parties and Petal was reticent about them, so the unspoken agreement made sense. But the truth was, Petal was compliant and undemanding. Rose was unpredictable. It was easier for everyone, including Petal, to appease Rose and avoid fallout.

Rosie was popular. She got invited to all the parties and always took Petal along despite the need to beg and plead with her sister each time. "It'll be fun," Rose would say, never learning, no matter how old they got, that to Petal fun was a deterrent, not an incentive.

"You say that like it's a good thing. I am the fun sucker. I am the party killer," Petal would say.

But it wasn't true. She could be a lot of fun, and from an early age. Rosie was on a mission to prove that to her and to the world. It was a challenge made somewhat more complicated by Rosie's extraordinarily magnetic personality. She was sociable and outgoing. Where Petal was shy and insecure, Rosie was confident and flamboyant. If Petal was in black and white, then Rosie was not only in Technicolor, she was neon!

"My sister is a gas!" Rosie would tell her friends.

"A gas bag," they would mock.

"A gas chamber," they would say, crossing a line they didn't know existed.

But it was Petal who got Rosie through school. She was a strong enough student to drag reluctant Rosie across the finish line with distinction — not her own high distinction, but recognition nonetheless for a job well done.

Rosie was certainly as smart as Petal, but she lacked focus. Occasionally, she would become obsessed with something in particular and really excel, but mostly she was a perpetual motion machine that sprayed streamers and confetti in its wake. The Rosie show was a going concern, and Petal was lucky to be in the front row. Most of the time, she knew it. Occasionally, she cursed the burden of being Rosie's sister, but given the rest of their family, it was a gift.

Theirs was a complicated family, and against all odds they made it through high school because of one another and in spite of all else. And shortly thereafter, they parted ways — sort of.

2.

IRVING AND ESTIE met in a displaced persons camp in Marseille around 1947 at a time when everyone was broken and no one had any expectations of ever being fixed.

Petal knew of a few families who talked about being survivors, about the camps and the death marches and the smell of straw from the gas chambers and being hungry. Her own family, however, never spoke about such things, and what she knew of their lives before or during the war was almost nonexistent.

When they were about nine years old, Petal and Rosie had one of the very few actual fights they ever had as children, not including the usual bickering that siblings engage in regularly. The girls attended Jewish school on Sundays, which for a long time they were indifferent to; eventually, they grew to hate it and refused to go. But at age nine, they were still going regularly, and from time to time they seemed to learn something.

They had never discussed the Holocaust before then — not at home, not in school. It simply hadn't come up. When it did on one particular Sunday, and the teacher asked if any of the children knew anyone who had been through the Holocaust, Petal raised her hand.

"My grandparents are Holocaust survivors," Petal said.

"It's not true!" Rosie screamed, turning a bright crimson hue. "Petal's a damn liar."

"No, I'm not. It's true," Petal said. "Why do you think they talk so funny? It's because they come from Poland, Rosie. Why do you think they have numbers on their arms?"

"*No!* It's because they are old, stupid," Rose insisted. "We'll get our numbers when we're older, dummy."

When Irving and Estie came to pick them up, Petal asked the question.

"Zaideh, are you a Holocaust survivor?"

Estie answered. "From vhere is comink such qvestions? *Mentor nischt zogen.* Ve shouldn't speak from such tinks."

"We were learning about the Holocaust today. I said you were in the Holocaust, and Rosie called me a liar."

"Rosie, you think it's nice to call your sister a liar?" Irving deflected.

Rosie didn't answer. In fact, Rosie didn't talk to Petal at all for three days.

Petal knew this was not a topic open for conversation, but she needed to know. She went to Irving and asked again. "Zaideh, is it true? Were you there?"

"It's true," Irving said.

"And Bubby? Was she there?"

"She was there."

"Were you there together?"

"No. Not together."

In time, Petal learned that if she asked her zaideh the right questions, she could glean fragments of information.

"Zaideh, who do you love the most?"

"Mamaleh, I love you each the most," he said.

"No, Zaideh, I mean Bubby. Do you love Bubby the most of anyone you ever loved?"

Irving shrugged one shoulder.

"You don't? You love someone more than Bubby?"

Little by very little, one tiny drip of information at a time, which was all Irving could manage, Petal cobbled together a highly redacted version of "the truth." At best, it was a thin scrim of porous record.

She never knew when either of them had arrived at the DP camp in Marseille; she only knew that was where they'd met. Irving, then called Yitzchak, was older by almost six years — an old man of twenty-five. Estie, who went by Esther, was younger — a child of nineteen. For Irving, there had been a wife and a child. For Estie, there had been a mother, a sister, a father, a brother. Their broken parts and missing pieces fit together well. When they eventually arrived in Palestine by ship, they presented themselves as a couple in order to not be settled separately. Petal yearned to know more. At some point, she resigned herself to incomplete information, which left holes in her history and in her soul.

Somehow, her friendship with Benjamin helped fill in her holes. He seemed to understand her, perhaps because he too had experience with unspoken truth.

AS A HIGH school graduation present for their granddaughters, Irving and Estie signed them up for a six-week summer trip to Israel. Irving, a tailor for a furrier, and Estie, a part-time book-keeper, earned modestly. They saved to have the money for what they thought was a very special gift.

"You tell, Yitz!" Estie said, so excited she couldn't get the words out.

"No, Estelleh, you tell."

"Tell what?" Rosie asked.

"Is it good or bad?" Petal wanted to know.

"It's good, it's good. I'll tell," Estie said, slapping her hand over her gaping mouth, overcome with glee.

"So *nu!* Tell them already!"

"We signed you up for a trip to Israel! A gift before university!"

Petal was caught off guard. "For a tour? With a group?"

Rosie grabbed her sister's shoulders and attempted to engage her in a hora-like do-si-do around the living room. Petal brushed her away.

Petal, aware of how ungrateful she sounded, reacted. "When you hinted, I thought it would be me and Rosie — our own adventure."

But Irving was smarter than that. And Estie was far too anxious to ever let the girls venture off on their own. She had never recovered from either the grief or the guilt of Chavie's disappearance eleven years earlier. Even the idea of the girls going away, let alone so far away, had required not insignificant coaching from Irving and Der to reach agreement.

"Don't be ridiculous!" Estie said. "You'll love more mit a group from youngsters!"

Petal tried to speak with her zaideh alone. "You know I'm not really much of a joiner. It's easier for Rosie. She makes friends in a second. I don't want to have my first experience of Israel poisoned by the stress of having to make friends with a whole bunch of new people! Can't we just go on our own and travel together? We'll be with each other."

Every ounce of freedom the girls had stolen growing up cost untold fortunes to Estie's mental health, and they knew it. So, they learned to do what for other children might have been considered lying but for them was necessary fabrication to facilitate some semblance of independence. "We'll be together," they would say even when they were going their separate ways. "Of course, her parents will be home," they would answer when the truth was an entirely different story. "We're just going to Lawrence Plaza" became code for not going to be anywhere near the plaza close to home. And Petal got used to covering for and inventing excuses for Rosie. It seemed easier than the truth.

"Mamaleh, you, I'm sure of. Your sister, less," Irving said.

Petal understood that her zaideh was protecting her from the responsibility of Rosie's "possibilities." It was the unpredictability of her sparkle that often led to disaster, and Petal didn't need reminding of numerous incidents where she had not been able to rein in Rosie's exuberance. "You're gonna be so proud of what I can do, Pet!" was usually how misadventures began. Petal had physical reminders of times Rosie's unbridled enthusiasm and search for approval had broken too free.

There was the small scar that ran through Petal's right eyebrow. Rosie had come up with a plan to put on an ice-skating show in the back alley after an ice storm left everything coated in a layer of crystalline magic. Rosie convinced Petal to strap on her skates at the back of the apartment building for a front row seat to the show, which would of course star the incredible Rosie. That neither of the girls could skate with any proficiency was immaterial. Rosie pulled a skirt up to her armpits so it looked like a skating dress. She fashioned a sparkly top from a fancy pair of multicoloured striped tights by cutting off the feet and pulling the tights onto her arms like a shrug. This particular act of creativity left Estie in tears.

"Dis is vhat you make from perfuctly gut? You break perfuctly gut?" Estie wept.

The skating surface was not nearly as smooth as it appeared through the window, and within seconds, Petal's skate caught an edge, and she face-planted into the ice-covered asphalt, landing her in Sick Kids emergency with a face covered in blood and six stitches above her right eye. In Petal's memory, the ruined tights got more airtime in the aftermath of the day's misadventure than the gash over her eye, which was never mentioned.

The back alley and winter were a dangerous combination for the girls. One time, the snow had fallen so deep that Rosie and

Petal could climb on the roofs of the garages without any help. A jubilant game of follow-the-leader left Petal chasing Rosie in energetic leaps from one roof to the next, until Petal missed, fell, and — one broken ankle later — returned from the hospital with a cumbersome plaster cast. Estie made Der paint a picture of a shoe on the cast.

"So now all is gut," Estie declared as though the ankle was miraculously healed by the camouflage of the picture. "Now, kasha and bow ties for you." Kasha and bow ties was Estie's magic potion to render bad things innocuous, or at least invisible.

The Wolffe twins were raised on a strange recipe of adult phobic anxiety, benign neglect, denial, make-believe security and well-being, the best of intentions, and love. Maintaining the ruse that held the precarious concoction aloft demanded a great deal of willful ignorance. Once an event passed, it was prudent to leave it be, unless you had a craving for overcooked buckwheat groats and mushy bow tie pasta.

Despite her better judgment, Petal sometimes got sucked into the Rosie vortex. By the time she realized things had gotten away from good sense, she was being stitched up or put in a cast or pumped out. "It's all fun and games until someone gets hurt" was a cliché coined by Rosie's imaginings and anointed by Petal's blood and tears.

"JUST BECAUSE SHE can't be trusted, I have to suffer," Petal lamented to Der over a bowl of split pea soup.

Rarely, and only ever in private to Der, did Petal express resentment toward her sister. There was no room anywhere else in their family.

"Being responsible for your sister is a burden you must bear," Der said, "but also a blessing. Rosie can be a handful, but I'm pretty sure your life is more fun because of her."

It was true. Petal was responsible. Rose was fun.

Petal hid her exasperation behind the steam from the soup.

"It's perhaps not what you envisioned, but it can hardly be thought of as suffering," Der said. "I think I might have been better off had I had the opportunity to go to Israel with a group when I was your age. But that was then and this is now."

They both knew the subject was not open for discussion and that Petal would comply, as she always did.

AFTER A THREE-WEEK stint living and working on a kibbutz in the southern Negev, the group of teens hit all the usual highlights of an Israel tour: a pre-dawn hike up the Roman snake path of Masada, their efforts rewarded with a spectacular sunrise at the summit; a float in the Dead Sea commencing in awe of the sci-fi buoyancy the water provided and ending with a mad dash for the barely trickling sweet-water showers to stop excruciating genital and anal burning from the salt; a tour of the beautiful Báha'i gardens in Haifa; compulsory song and dance routines on the stage of the old Roman amphitheatre of Caesarea; consumption of the otherworldly hummus and fūl in the old city of Akko; and, of course, Jerusalem. Days packed full of touring and evenings of freedom to roam and explore independently helped offset Petal's resistance to groupdom. It also helped to be Rosie's sister. Everybody loved Rose, and, by extension, Petal gained social cachet that made her feel cautiously secure some of the time.

They stayed in Jerusalem for three nights at a dormitory in the north end of Talpiot, a little distance from the centre of town. The un–air conditioned, dirty city bus back to the dorm from Ben Yehuda Street in the evening felt so authentic to Petal that she was tempted to sleep in and miss the tour bus the next morning. She didn't.

Their second day in Jerusalem, they were let loose in the Arab market of the Old City with instructions to make their way to the

Western Wall in the Jewish Quarter for dusk and the coming of the Sabbath. Holding hands, Petal and Rose walked through the Jaffa Gate, past the imposing ramparts of ancient stone scarred with the markings of battles long done, into the Old City. They stumbled down the worn-smooth cobblestones of white and grey and amber rock that descended into the heart of the market. Colourful shawls and clothing hung from awnings and open metal shutters, creating a rainbow canopy of fabric that lined the passageway. Arab men cowered from the heat in the shade of their hanging wares, standing or sitting at the entries of their shops. Stores teeming with silver jewellery sparkled, and spices perfumed the air; there were dried fruit, and leather goods that smelled like camels and tanning oil, Bedouin embroidery in pinks and reds on black backgrounds, olive wood carvings of praying hands and inlaid backgammon boards. The atmosphere was exotic and unfamiliar to North American city girls. Arabic music swirled and lilted from invisible sources, overdubbed with the sounds of conversation and transaction. Noisily clattering three-wheeled carts that hauled canvas sacks of lentils and copper cauldrons were steered precariously through the crowds, accompanied by the clattering, bumping, barely controlled navigation and shouts of, "Allo, allo, allo!"

They were aware of the leering eyes of the shopkeepers upon them. They were used to it. At least Rosie was used to it, and Petal was used to being next to it with Rosie. She was beautiful at the worst of times, but at eighteen she was particularly striking with her sun-kissed freckles, her strawberry-blond silken hair, and her short shorts that emphasized her long, tanned legs. It was no surprise that people stared. The surprise was that on this occasion, it was not Rosie who was being stared at.

"*Aintibah*," the men started chirping from the market stalls, like a warrior warning shouted to alert the troops. Guttural phrases echoed the length and width of the ancient street. "*Ma alhimar!*" Had the girls understood, they might have heard, "Heads up, boys! Nice ass headed your way!"

"Hey, baby, you've got groovy eyes," said the young Arab man selling leather hassocks. "Only sixty-nine shekels." It seemed that everything in the market was "only sixty-nine."

Rosie giggled and covered her eyes with her hand.

"Not you," he said, and he pointed at Petal, raising his eyebrows and moving his hands in the universal sign for a woman with curves.

Petal did not look like the girls in the magazines — at least not the magazines she knew. She was the dark to Rosie's fair, the curl to Rosie's straight, the zaftig to Rosie's skinny, and the short to Rosie's long. But at eighteen, it was undeniable that her rear end was unequalled.

"I can give your father many camels for your love," another shopkeeper shouted, holding up a wild, woolly sheepskin coat. "Come try it on."

Rosie spun around, but the man was pointing at Petal.

Petal grabbed Rosie's hand, and, as quickly as the crowds would allow, they pushed past, deeper into the market. A little further down, a merchant selling silver rings encouraged them to view his wares.

"Come into my shop," he said. "Looking is free."

The girls approached cautiously, knowing well enough not to go too far into the back of the shop where they could not be seen by the eyes of the market. Some boys from their group passed by with hookahs they had bought. Rosie motioned them over.

"It's all right. They are safe with me. I treat all my wives with respect," the merchant said to the boys with a treacly grin, lifting

Petal's hand and pushing a silver ring inlaid with turquoise and coral onto her middle finger. "I only want to see how beautiful my work looks on your perfect hand."

Petal quickly pulled the ring from her finger, and the girls dashed from the shop, grabbing the boys at the entrance, moving on, giggling and shrieking.

"Pet!" shrieked Rosie.

"Ro!" shrieked Petal. "Is this what it's like for you? How gross and creepy!"

Rosie giggled and snorted. "You've got groovy eyes," she screeched.

With escalating hysteria, they made their way through the narrow alleyways to the Jewish Quarter, which only heightened the attention Petal was drawing.

Catcalls followed. Gripping one another, laughing, they slipped through the smells of sesame, *za'atar*, and rosewater seeping from the market into the private world only they shared.

"I'm gonna pish myself," Rosie squealed as they rounded the corner, following the signs to the Western Wall.

Rosie stopped short, catching sight of the concourse, the stone wall bathed in late afternoon sunlight — Jerusalem of Gold — her eyes reflecting rapture.

"What?" Petal said.

Rosie didn't answer. She let go of Petal's arm and, as though led by an invisible force, floated down the stairs. Petal followed her into the throngs of people, but they seemed to be moving with different velocities. Rose moved smoothly like a fish swimming downstream, as though her path was unobstructed. Petal jostled and bounced like a ball bearing in a pinball machine, flipping hither and thither on the pointy elbows of the masses. For a few moments, Petal could see Rosie's copper hair glimmering amid the sea of black, but she lost sight of her sister, who disappeared into the crowd.

ON SUNDAY MORNING, Rosie, who hadn't been seen since Friday afternoon, didn't show up for the bus. Petal got off the bus. *What the fuck, Rosie!* she thought.

But that was not what she said. With false confidence, she assured the ill-equipped twenty-something group leader that she would find her sister and meet the group in Tel Aviv. The bus driver closed the doors and drove away, which surprised Petal. For six weeks, they had been closely chaperoned, and suddenly there was no hesitation about abandoning her in Jerusalem.

Petal assumed Rosie had accepted an offer of hospitality from a family or a yeshiva and spent the Sabbath somewhere in the new Jewish Quarter of the ancient city. She had also been approached and invited, but she knew stories of seemingly benign invitations.

A boy two years ahead of them at school had been found naked and unconscious in a bathtub full of beer bottles at a legendary house party. The police broke down the bathroom door so the paramedics could step over an equally naked, vomit-covered girl (she liked to pretend it hadn't been her sister) and pull him out of the tub to resuscitate him. His parents decided to send him to Israel to settle down. Petal couldn't understand why on earth they'd thought it was a good idea to send him halfway around the world when he was obviously in trouble. Nonetheless, it seemed to be common practice for well-to-do North American families to send their troubled teens to Israel, as though Israel needed other people's problems on top of their own.

He, along with a number of other formerly handsome, previously popular, erstwhile athletic, too-wild-for-their-own-good boys from her high school, was blissfully ensconced in a yeshiva, happily shuckling and swaying his way to marriage, the blessing of many children, and rabbi-hood, all stemming from an innocuous invitation proffered at the Western Wall to spend Shabbat with an Orthodox family and "experience something new!"

But what had never crossed her mind was a girl leaving secular life to reinvent herself as an Orthodox woman, burdened by the restrictions and obligations of religious life behind the pink-and-gold walls of the city. In fact, it hadn't occurred to Petal that Rosie had disappeared anywhere other than to a social event that had caught her momentary attention. She was Rosie, after all. She'd probably lost track of time. Petal just needed to find her sister and give her a little push back onto the path she was meant to be on.

WHEN ESTIE AND Irving took the girls out as children, they always had the same conversation before getting out of the car.

"Hold hents," Estie said anxiously.

"Hold hands," the girls repeated in unison, knowing their echo was required to complete the incantation.

"Stay togeder," Estie said.

"Stay together," the girls repeated.

"Ent ..." Estie prompted.

"And go back to the beginning if you get lost," they said like preprogrammed robots.

"And go back to the beginning," Irving repeated before letting them all out of the car.

More often than not, excursions ended when Rosie disappeared into a crowd. Estie panicked. Irving managed Estie's agitation. The day's activity abruptly ended with the grown-ups clutching Petal's hands as though life depended upon this fierce corporeal connection, going back to the car to wait until Rosie appeared, unfazed and excited to recount her tale of adventure, completely oblivious to having caused any disruption. On these occasions, Petal unknowingly experienced cognitive dissonance. She was always relieved when Rosie returned, but she hated her for disappearing, for making Bubby nervous, and for ruining everything all the time. To this feeling she couldn't articulate, she attached a memory of smell and taste. This was what Petal called "kasha and bow ties." She hated it but knew she had to eat it, and, despite its musty, leaden, oppressive properties, it served as a comfortable realigning or levelling. It was the calm after the storm, or, perhaps more aptly, the resurrection.

So, Petal went back to the beginning to look for Rosie and feel kasha and bow ties. Rose was exactly where Petal expected her to be.

Wrapped in the pale-blue sheet she had been given to cover her immodest clothing, Petal approached as Rosie emerged from a throng of women huddled against the right-hand side of the Western Wall, as though their meeting had been scheduled for exactly that time and place. Rosie, last seen in shorts and a tank top, was wearing a denim skirt past her knees and a black T-shirt that covered her elbows and collarbones.

As though no time had passed since their hysteria in the Arab market, as though Petal's heart had not skipped even one beat of concern for her sister, Rosie grasped Petal by the shoulders and said, "I won!"

"What did you win? I hope to God you didn't win that outfit!" Petal said.

"I won the answer to the biggest question! The 'what will I be' question!"

"What are you going to be, Ro?" Petal asked.

"*Eshes chayil*, Pet! I'm going to be a Jewish woman of valour," Rosie said, winding herself into full-on spinning, arms out, head flung back — Maria the nun on an Austrian mountaintop, laughing with an exuberance and elation that worried Petal to her core.

When they were kids, Rosie would get so excited about things, or occasionally so frustrated or overwhelmed, that she would literally and figuratively spin out of control. Their bubby would say, "Don't make yourself a frenny, bubbaleh." This, one of Estie's many malapropisms, had the capacity to instantly catapult the girls into fits of laughter. Estie knew the word was *frenzy* but recognized a working redirect when she found one. So, *frenny* stuck in their family.

Petal stood in the bright glare of the sunshine, watching Rosie twirl without a care in the world as the weight of Petal's own responsibility to her sister sank in, cementing her in place. She folded herself, crouching, arms on her head, shield-like, as though an air raid siren had sounded and in this exposed plaza she was her own singular possibility of protection. But she knew the bomb had already exploded inside of her sister, and it was up to her to gather the fragmented pieces and try make order of the chaotic aftermath. The frenny was on, and it did not smell like kasha and bow ties at all.

Rosie refused to leave Yerushalayim, as she had taken to calling it. In the thirty-six hours since her disappearance, she had converted from Rose to Raizel and from good-time party girl to born-again Jew girl.

It was not the first time Rosie had insisted on a new name accompanied by a new persona. When they were seven years old, Rose had suddenly declared and insisted that she was Mr. Slipper, a character who spoke mostly in nonsensical rhymes and wouldn't respond unless addressed as such. Petal was distraught by Rosie's change.

"If she is Mr. Slipper, then who will be my sister?" Petal wept inconsolably on Estie's lap on the plastic-clad flowered couch in their oddly formal living room. Estie focused on Petal's grief over her sister, because to have tried to redirect the child might have shifted the ground enough to unearth the deeper sadness in their lives at that moment, the unspoken understanding that Chavie had disappeared for good. How the finality of this became clear was never discussed. It just was. Perhaps there was a change in grammar, as in, "Your mother loved you very much" instead of "Your mother loves you very much," a hollow mantra the girls heard on Chavie's absent behalf too often. Maybe it was a clandestine clearing of Chavie's things from the apartment. Maybe it was that any mention of Chavie stopped. Whatever it was, it was decidedly covert yet known, even to Petal and Rose.

"Rosie mit any udder name she's still Rosie, Mamaleh," Estie explained over and over. She gently caressed her granddaughter. "I call you Mamaleh, but you're Petal. Der calls you Tiggaleh, but still Petal. Tvitch is Der's name for Rosie, but she's still all Rosie."

"But Rosie always calls herself Rosie, which makes her all Rosie. If she calls herself Mr. Slipper, then Rosie is gone," Petal wailed, streaming tears and snot as though truly mourning the loss of her sister.

"Shh," Irving said. "I'll show you." He led Petal to the big oval mirror on the prim white vanity in the girls' bedroom and insisted that the two girls sit side by side on the pink, tufted bench in front of the mirror. "Estelleh, bring an old lipstick."

At the top of their reflections, directly on the mirror, Irving wrote their given names in frosted peach lipstick and asked each of them to read out their own names and then the name of the other twin. Under the reflection of their chins, he wrote, "Tabitha Twitchet" and "Mrs. Tiggy Winkle" and asked Petal, the stronger reader, to read the names out loud. At the left side of Petal's face, Irving wrote "Mamaleh" and then again at the right side of Rosie's face "Mamaleh," which he asked Rosie to sound out for him. On the other side of her face, he wrote "Mr. Slipper." And across the middle of each of their faces, he wrote the word "sister."

"Sister," he said. "No matter what anyone calls you, no matter what you call each other, no matter what you call yourselves, you will always be sisters. Rosie will always be Petal's only sister. Petal will always be Rosie's only sister. You will have other people in your lives. They will call you many things. You can even call yourselves many things. But nothing you call yourselves will change who you are to each other. Do you understand, Petal?"

Petal nodded and sniffed.

"Okay, Rosie?" he asked.

"Mr. Slipper, pister blister," Rosie said.

"Mr. Slipper, Petal's one and only sister, *farshteist du?*"

"Hey, it rhymes, chimes! Mr. Slipper has a sister!" Rosie rhymed.

"*Farshteist?*" Irving asked again gently demanding a response.

"*Farshteist*, to taste!" Rosie answered pushing her fingers into Petal's clenched fist.

The writing on the mirror remained for many years. Sometimes, the girls would sit on the bench in front of their slightly felted lipstick names and laugh about how small their faces and how big their sorrows had been.

But the real tragedy of that era remained in the volumes of unspoken stories in the family vault. "*Mentor nischt zogen.*" Don't say it. Don't speak of it.

"ALL RIGHT, 'RAIZEL,'" Petal said, miming air quotes, "you can hang here. I'm going to Tel Aviv. We can meet at the airport."

Petal was determined to feel it as no big deal.

Before Petal finished speaking, Rosie chased after a group of girls dressed identically to her.

"Rosie. The airport," Petal shouted after her sister. "Raizel!"

The airport, Rosie mouthed over her shoulder.

Petal knew she should not leave Rosie in Jerusalem, but life had taught her too well how to suppress her feelings. *Rosie will not derail my plans!* Petal silently decreed.

Petal found her way to the small, dark bus station. Standing in line, all hell broke loose. Shouting and pushing and people running in what seemed to be all directions, but it rapidly became clear there was only one direction and that direction was out!

"*Chafetz chashud! Yalla, achutza!*" commanded a skinny young woman in army fatigues, arms churning windmill-like toward the exit.

Petal didn't understand that the chaos was about an unattended knapsack, which in an Israeli bus station constituted a suspicious object requiring bomb squad mobilization. Forced by the collective movement of the crowd, Petal streamed out of the station onto the street and watched as Kevlar-clad soldiers, looking more like children in Halloween costumes than military personnel, led their sniffer dogs into the fray. It all happened so quickly. An embarrassed boy rushed in on the heels of the bomb squad, waving his arms and begging forgiveness for having forgotten his bag.

"*Idyot! Tembel! Mefager!*" Idiot! Moron! Retard! The inconvenienced commuters cursed as he shamefully retreated, eyes down, bag clutched close, a shield against the hostility of the crowd.

Her niggling anxiety about her sister supplanted by the excitement of Israeli reality, Petal bought a ticket to Tel Aviv and stifled any thoughts about Rose.

PERHAPS IT WAS freedom and independence that ignited something inside her. Maybe it was lifting the invisible veil of that "Israel the Good" Zionist promotion of organized touring that tousled her senses. Possibly it was the primal severing of some prenatal cord that still existed between her and her sister that sparked a visceral response in Petal. Or it could simply have been the heat and humidity, which hung viscously in the air. Whatever the origin, arriving in Tel Aviv, Petal felt something — something she couldn't define or name, but something undeniable, and for a moment, she thought she understood her sister's enchantment with Jerusalem. Only her rapture was not divine, it was the opposite. It was the unvarnished, insalubrious authenticity of Tel Aviv that made Petal's heart beat a little harder.

The chaotic specifics of the open-air market and bus station didn't register explicitly with Petal that first day in Tel Aviv. Rather, it was the overall bustle that fed something in her, and she wanted to taste it all.

Petal pulled the soiled paper itinerary from her satchel and unfolded it delicately, like an ancient document, so as not to tear the worn-thin seams of repeated foldings and unfoldings. She noted the group was scheduled to visit the Carmel Market that morning and the beach in the afternoon and decided her best bet was to follow in their footsteps and hope to track them down. Worst-case scenario, the itinerary listed their Tel Aviv lodgings as the Basel Hotel. She could find her way there. *How hard could it be?* she thought, uncharacteristically confident.

"You don't know where the Carmel Market is? It's the centre of town! *Kav Arba*," the woman said, holding up four fingers on her right hand, flipping her left hand skyward to indicate just how idiotic Petal's question was.

Petal had figured out that what seemed rude or aggressive was just a cultural style: Canadians were overly polite and apologetic; Israelis were blunt, straightforward, and entirely unapologetic.

She found her way to the bus, paid her fare, and took a seat. Grinning, Petal congratulated herself on her successful independent navigation.

The bus wound its way through streets laid out completely randomly — a map drawn by a toddler with a marker let loose on a swath of paper — crisscrossing, bisecting diagonally through intersections, along narrow streets with wide sidewalks, so unlike the orderly grid of Toronto. Petal felt a moment's anxiety. The embarrassingly loud singing of the bus driver — the radio broadcast his backup band, his true calling rock star and his bus driving entirely incidental — had a levitating effect on her. She watched through the window as the city spilled by, exhilarated by the normalcy of it all. It wasn't an ancient Roman ruin or an underground water cistern or a mountain in the desert or a sea choked with salt or a religious pilgrimage site or a military monument. It was just a city. And yet different, exotic, exciting, exposed.

"Shuk Ha'Carmel!" the driver shouted, and Petal rushed to get off, pushing her way through the crowd, elbows out, like she had seen the locals do.

At the entrance to the market off Allenby Street, the portal into the central laneway of the market beckoned, different than the touristy wares of the Jerusalem Arab market. Petal was thrilled by the domestic nature of the vendors' offerings. Smells of peanuts, sesame, warm bread, cigarette smoke and sweat, fresh mint, parsley, dill, rotting fermented fruit, garbage, and exotic spices wafted densely in the soupy air. Petal gulped in the fragrant with the repulsive. The pavement below was thick with accumulated black sludge, its gummy adhesiveness perceptible even beneath Petal's sandals, and from above, the sun shone down where the merchandise wasn't dense enough to filter it. Shoes, clothes, discount cosmetics, cheap jewellery, and a plague of undergarments laid out and hung on kiosks that lined the thoroughfare, interspersed with stalls selling fresh fruits and vegetables, flowers, stacks of sesame-encrusted bagels and spice-studded pita, bins of black, purple, brown, and green olives, pickles, bright-yellow turmeric-bathed cauliflower and deep-orange carrot slices redolent with vinegar, large rectangular gallon tins of olive oil, plastic

baskets and bundle buggies, enormous plaid shopping bags, blue
barrels filled with brooms and squeegees, cleaning products and
housewares, toys and candy in colourful piles of insurmountable
puerile seduction, blocks of white cheeses stacked in skyscraper
towers fragrant of fields and sour milk, American cigarettes, but-
tery baklava, knafeh, kadaif, sticky sweets laid out on trays in
geometric patterns of triangles and diamonds, golden filigree nests
of pastry threads stuffed with almonds and pistachios, Turkish
delight — green, pink, red, yellow — powdered with sugar and
perfumed with sweet rose blossoms, bricks of halva studded with
nuts and swirled with chocolate, pyramids of whole watermelons,
cookies and cakes like her bubby made with yeast dough and cinnamon and poppy seeds, sunflower seeds the size of small mice.
Her senses were on fire!

Reaching the bottom of the market, she noted the absence
of her fellow travellers. Her next step would be either the hotel,
where she would no doubt have to wait for them, or an attempt
to find them on the beach. Petal had no way of knowing that the
likelihood of stumbling across her friends on the Tel Aviv beach
was high. She did not know that the entire beachfront could be
walked from the south to the north end of the city in less than
forty-five minutes. She did not know that from where she stood,
she was less than a ten-minute walk to the sea. Nonetheless, she
opted for the "how hard could it be" approach.

"*Mayim?*" she asked the first passerby, who shrugged at her,
uncomprehending.

"*Mayim?*" she asked a friendlier-looking shopper, who replied,
"Cola?"

"No! Not to drink!" she said, pantomiming cup to mouth. She
paddled her arms in a freestyle windmill. "To swim."

"*L'yam!*" he said, pointing to the right.

Petal turned right and felt like an idiot. A few steps and

there was the sea in the distance. She walked along Daniel Street through the muggy, heavy heat that lay thickly on the asphalt. She mistakenly attributed the sweet smell of jasmine to the fiery flowers of the bougainvillea bushes that lined the sandy patches of dirt along the way. As she crossed Hakovshim Street, it felt as though a curtain had been parted and the atmosphere opened, the heat cut by a breeze of cool sea air and the blue-green water inviting her with an irresistible pull.

Petal crossed Hayarkon Street, noted that their hotel was along this same street, crossed a strip of dry, brown grass, pulled off her sandals, scorched her feet in the hot sand, and randomly but correctly headed north along the shore, the water lapping at her ankles.

A couple of days of sun and sand on the beaches of Tel Aviv was the perfect end to Petal's Israel adventure. *Rosie missed out,* she thought as their tour bus headed to Ben Gurion Airport.

Some of the kids were headed to Europe (mostly the Greek isles), some were headed home to Canada, and others were staying in Israel to visit with relatives. Rose and Petal were going back to their anxiously awaiting Bubby.

On the steamy sidewalk of the hot, humid night, Petal slung her backpack onto her shoulders and entered the terminal. She waited on the floor near the check-in for her sister. Departure time approached. Rosie didn't appear. Petal began to feel a familiar sense of dread. She closed her eyes, breathed deep, and consciously shoved against the encroaching panic and paralysis.

"What to do, what to do?" she said, conjuring a mantra of composure.

It was crystal clear to Petal that her absolute last resort would be to call Irving and Estie. She needed to fix this herself.

Petal approached the EL AL kiosk. "How much would it cost to change my flight?" she asked, pushing their passports and tickets toward the olive-skinned, gum-chewing beauty at the counter. Petal had taken responsibility for Rosie's documents. It hadn't occurred to her it might be the whole person who got lost.

The girl examined the ticket. "For serious? Your flight is just now?"

"Yes, for me and my sister," Petal said, entirely uncertain of her impulsive decision.

"Where your sister is?" the girl asked, looking away from Petal toward a cluster of soldiers.

"She was supposed to meet me, and she isn't here," Petal explained.

The girl turned to her colleague. "*Zot'hee rotzah l'shanot tisa. Achotah lo higiya. Yaysh efsharoot?*" He examined the ticket and passport.

"*B'chol ofen ha tisah b'overbooking,*" he said.

"I don't understand Hebrew," Petal said.

"You don't understand 'overbooking'?" He added, "When you want to switch?"

"Next week sometime?" she said, not having thought through her next step.

"Not possible," he said.

"What is possible?" Petal asked, trying to remember that he wasn't actually being rude or unhelpful, just Israeli.

"Just until September first," he said.

"Okay." She knew Rose wasn't coming. And in that second of choice, or lack thereof, with that *okay*, their worlds shimmied, and the course of their lives changed forever.

Petal found a telephone just outside the terminal building. She would make an excuse that Estie could tolerate like she always did.

But she didn't call her grandparents.

Der accepted the collect call.

"I fucked up," Petal said, bursting into tears. "I let go of Rosie for a second, and she didn't show up at the airport. I didn't want to cry. I changed our tickets. We're staying a couple of extra weeks."

"Tiggaleh, tell me the truth," Der said.

"It's the truth, Der. It's Rosie, and you know she can be ... unpredictable. She's in Jerusalem. She's fallen under its spell, and I just need to go drag her away. I never should have left her there. I need you to run a bit of interference with Bubby and Zaideh. Just until I find her."

"Not out of character for Rosie to succumb to the romantic rapture of Jerusalem. She certainly isn't the first. As soon as you find her you, call me. I'll handle Estie."

Petal was used to covering for Rose. Missed curfews, skipped classes, questionable social arrangements, and inappropriate boys were all part of the web of deceit in which Petal was complicit in the interest of protecting ... Rosie? Estie? Both? Petal had lost clarity on this particular issue long ago. Despite her never-abating discomfort with lying or glossing over truths, her intrinsic responsibility to protect weighed more than the momentary truth, or at least it often seemed to in the instant of circumstance.

THE GIRLS SAT in the cool darkness of an ancient stone dwelling reclaimed as a bohemian café. Don't Pass Me By was in an alleyway off the bottom of Ben Yehuda Street in Jerusalem. Petal had insisted they meet outside the Old City, hoping she might break the spell enchanting Rosie. Petal ate a piece of overly sweet banana cream pie. Rose refused to eat anything because the restaurant was not officially glatt kosher, something each girl had barely had any knowledge of two weeks before.

"We were supposed to be back home almost two weeks ago. You know I can't show up in Toronto without you, but I also can't drug you and put you on a plane. So, if you could help me out here, Ro ..."

"Stop being so dramatic, Pet. Lots of kids spend a year in Israel before they go to university. Just because we didn't plan it doesn't mean it's wrong. It's *beshert*!"

Petal clenched her fists and gritted her teeth.

"It means fate, Pet."

"I know what beshert means! What I don't know is how come you think it's my fate to spend the next year in Israel and my responsibility to break this batter of an unbaked plan to Bubby and Zaideh. Der already paid our first-term tuition!"

Rosie looked at Petal with the forlorn puppy dog eyes she had been using to corral her sister into complicity their whole lives. "You know they'll never let me stay without you, Pet. 'We're just going to the plaza. We'll be together.' You know that's how it has to be! I'm begging you, Pet. I know this is what I'm supposed to do. I need your help. Please."

Petal knew resistance was futile. Rosie was a force beyond reckoning, and the sooner she accepted that she would in fact stay in Israel to keep an eye on her sister — she would invent a persuasive argument, and with Der's help she would sell it to Irving and Estie — the better off she would be. Once again, Rosie wrote the show, and Petal spoke her lines.

Der was actually left to clean up the mess, as was often the case. Petal knew only Der could deliver bad news to Estie without her climbing into bed and remaining there for weeks.

Irving was prepped in advance. Der crossed the hall for tea as he often did. He sat down on the plastic-covered sofa, behind the tea tray with its delicate, mismatched teacups and the teapot with the pink-and-gold cabbage roses. Estie poured two cups of tea with milk and one without for Irving.

Der waited for Estie to put a sugar cube in her mouth and take a sip of tea before he began. He hoped her sweet tooth might lessen the blow. It did not.

Try as he might with Pollyanna positivity to deliver the news that the girls were staying in Israel to continue their adventure, Estie wasn't buying it

Abandoning her tea, sugar cubes, and favourite biscuits, Estie got into her bed.

Irving pleaded. Der mediated. Estie acquiesced.

Petal complied, agreeing to remain in Jerusalem to keep an eye on Rosie. Her path of least resistance was the *mechina*, a pre-university year at the Hebrew University, where she could take classes in English and do an Ulpan to learn Hebrew. She tried to see it as an unexpected opportunity, but blind optimism was never her default drive.

Rosie's enchantment with Yerushalayim, as she still insisted on calling it, much to Petal's irritation, verged on ecstatic. She was living and studying at a girls' seminary in the Old City. Exactly what she was studying was unclear because in Petal's opinion she was becoming more ignorant and less enlightened by the day.

While Rosie flourished in her adopted world, Petal's dorm room became increasingly dismal as winter approached. As other students feathered their nests with mementoes brought from home, photographs of loved ones taped to their walls, pretty sheets bought especially for their years abroad, no doubt by doting mothers, Petal became increasingly resentful of this situation she had found herself in, which she had neither planned nor wanted nor, as it turned out, accepted.

Petal circled the perimeter of the campus, trying to escape the oppressive closeness of her room. Looking down from Mount Scopus, she could see the terraced hillsides cut into the rock faces of the inhospitable geography, which her mood made her take personally. *Why the fuck does everybody want this obviously untenable land?* she thought.

The magnificent view down onto Jerusalem's Old City, the gleaming golden cupola of the Dome of the Rock like a beacon screaming, "We are here. As much as you, our holy of holies, right smack dab in the middle of your holy city's walls!" And less than fifty metres away in the other direction, East Jerusalem, Isawiyeh, desert, the Dead Sea, Jordan, laid out like a real-life bird's-eye map. Petal heard others rhapsodize about the beauty of it all, but she couldn't muster the same conviction. She recognized only too clearly the ivory tower status of her — of their — presence there. *Who am I to have any right to be here?*

Between worrying about and checking up on Rosie and her own propensities toward moroseness and sullenness, she found herself feeling isolated, lonely, and angry. Angry with Rosie, angry with her bubby and zaideh for expecting her to be the watchdog, and, for the first time in her life, furious with the mother she could barely remember.

PETAL'S MEMORIES OF Chavie were mostly fabricated from minimal snippets of virtual footage spliced from fact. Sometimes Chavie would appear with a man, never the same man, but always a man who made Petal feel unsafe. Those times felt too long, though Petal was sure they never lasted longer than a few hours or minutes. Long enough to bring a feeling over the house that Petal couldn't articulate until many years and hundreds of hours of therapy later. As a child, the chaos and conflict felt like fire in her belly that could only be dampened under the covers of her bubby's bed, clinging to her sister and eating jelly beans that Estie conjured from the folds of bedding and doled out one at a time to the girls until the maelstrom had subsided and Chavie was gone until she returned.

Mostly, Chavie appeared at home when she was crashing into a downward spiral of depression. In Petal's idealized recollections of her mother, Chavie would show up and take her two girls to bed with her, where they would cuddle endlessly. That was what Petal chose to believe, because the memory of trying to muster even the smallest amount of attention from the almost catatonic Chavie was too painful.

What Petal preferred to remember was Chavie before her frequent departures — excited, fun, adventurous, playful, the word *manic* never spoken. Chavie would emerge from her bed after weeks of hibernation, renewed and refreshed and ready to play. The truth was that Chavie took little interest in the girls as babies or toddlers, even on her good days. They bored her. Until they were old enough to participate in her games, she really had little use for them. But when she got out of bed, and the girls were old enough to play along, Chavie was the best cruise director in the whole world! Scavenger hunts and costume parties, baking and musical productions, all put in motion with excitement and grandiosity. Inevitably, though, Chavie would lose interest and take off before the prizes were given out or the cake was out of the oven or the audience was in their seats. Petal's true memories of her mother were of broken promises, disappointments, and disappearances, so mostly she didn't think about her at all, except in fairy-tale versions of reality.

In the weeks leading up to the girls' first day of junior kindergarten, Chavie was home and high. That is, after four or five weeks of near catatonia, she cycled up and embarked upon the epic preparations for the start of big-girl school. The planning of the Met Gala, had any of them known of it, might have paled in comparison to the elaborate machinations Chavie orchestrated with her girls. They shopped for book bags and lunch boxes they embellished with glitter and ribbons that would no doubt be the envy of kindergarten girls throughout the kingdom. They prepared decorations for Irving's car — tissue paper flowers of pink and purple for the hood of the car, streamers for the back, and voluminous pleated tulle curtains for the rear windows, also amply encrusted with enough glitter to rival Cinderella's carriage to the ball. It was clear to a watchful eye that the vast quantities of paper flowers and accompanying adornments could only have been achieved through far too many sleepless nights, but Chavie was home and happy; what could possibly be amiss?

Der discreetly let it be known to Yitzchak that what was going on under his roof was suspect, but Yitzchak picked his battles both with his wife and his daughter. How harmful could summer fun for the girls be?

"Come school," he said, "there will be enough structure. Now they can play. Now their mother can entertain for a while."

And there was no denying that the grandparents needed respite. The day-to-day of two small children wore on them. They did the best they could under the circumstances, but this was not their first trip to the preschool rodeo, and when the circus was in town in the form of the children's mother, they hoped for the best because all they had was hope.

First day of school hairdos were tried and perfected till Rosie had settled on ringlets of gold and Petal a beehive entirely inappropriate to both her age and the texture of her tight curls. It hurt when her mother pulled at her hair with a comb and teased it into submission, lacquering it with enough hairspray that Estie had to shampoo it three times on practice days. When Petal complained that it pulled at her scalp, Chavie said, "That's the fun of it!" completely indifferent to her daughter's pain.

The day before the start of the school year, Chavie used additional pink tulle to turn the skirts of the sensible school dresses Estie had bought for the girls into fairy princess gowns. Chavie couldn't sew, so she stapled the frothy adornments to the dresses in such chaotic quantity that each girl would have required a full retinue of attendants to carry the trains of their gowns into kindergarten.

That's when Irving realized it was time to tame Chavie's wild ideas and put his foot down gently.

"*Genug shoin!* Summer is over. They are going to school, not a party. They shouldn't look so special that others might be jealous or worse."

"Abba, it's just for fun!" Chavie said, giddy with excitement.

"Yitz, just fer fun," Estie parroted her daughter, afraid to upset the delicate balance between here and gone.

"Fun is fine, but this? It's immodest, Chavie, to treat your children like objects of envy, to make them stand out and draw too much attention; this is not a good thing. Let them be like all the other children," Irving implored.

At age four, Petal didn't know whose side she was on, or even that she had any say in the matter. All she knew was that something new was coming and her mother was here and paying attention to her. But even she could see that Chavie's bubble had been burst when chastised by her father, and the feeling in Petal's stomach turned from eager anticipation to watery cramps.

By the next morning, when the girls woke for the start of school, Chavie was gone. All the tulle and flowers, even the new school dresses, were shredded and strewn all over the apartment. Estie didn't get out of bed, and the girls didn't get to school that day.

"It's all Zaideh's fault," Rosie said, but Petal was angry with her mother, not her zaideh. Her mother broke promises. Her mother broke hearts. Each time, Petal replaced the sorrow with a version of events her psyche could tolerate. "Oh, what fun we had when Mama was around" felt better than "She always leaves."

But missing yet another first day of school, the day she was meant to have at the University of Toronto, not at the Hebrew University of Jerusalem, seemed to dissolve a lifetime of revisionist memory and unleash a torrent of truth and pain.

At first, Petal looked for comfort in the arms of the multitude of interchangeable, nondescript boys who were happy to be invited back to her room, never more than once. The sex was just that — sex. The more it hurt, the better. Hard, fast, violent fucking. Nothing like what the young innocents she used for her own self-harm expected from a nice Jewish girl in the Holy Land.

"You can get out of my room now," she said, turning away from her object the moment he was done, her disdain hanging heavily in the unkempt room. Petal recognized her behaviour was self-destructive, but she didn't care.

The forty-five minutes between Jerusalem and Tel Aviv might as well have been an interstellar flight given the dichotomy between the two cities and the difference Petal felt in each. Jerusalem was either Orthodox or Arab depending upon whether you examined it from the West or the East. Tel Aviv was mostly neither. Jerusalem was pink and gold. Tel Aviv was white and terracotta. Jerusalem had a walled city at its centre and was surrounded by hills. Tel Aviv either spilled into the Mediterranean or was born of it. Jerusalem was cold at night and rainy in the winter. In Tel Aviv, the sun shone bright and the nights hung humidly, warm or temperate most of the time. Jerusalem felt hostile. Tel Aviv, welcoming. At least to Petal.

So, from time to time, Petal got on the bus in Jerusalem, entombed in her khaki-green *dubbon*, the heavy cotton parka purchased at the Ha'Mashbir department store on King George

Street, hood on, zipper pulled up past her chin, eyes down, a cocoon against weather and world. The old busses worked their weight asthmatically up and down the terrain surrounding the city, the stifling closeness of the cedar- and olive-lined hills opening up as the road flattened out and they weaved their way toward the coast, the palm trees lining the road welcoming her like a receiving line of giant Sendakian Wild Things: "We'll eat you up, we love you so." And Petal wanted nothing other than to be consumed.

In the bustling chaos of the Tel Aviv bus station, she emerged from her quilted chrysalis into the vastly different climate and atmosphere. As though she could suddenly breathe the air on this planet without need of external apparatus, Petal shed her winter coat, shoved it into her empty knapsack, and started walking.

She knew nobody in Tel Aviv, felt responsible to no one, which was of course part of the allure. There was an excitement to the activity of the muddled disorganization of the city she could relate to on some primal level. She loved the storefronts that seemed to sell nothing in particular and everything one might want or need: a pyramid of chocolate bars, a mop, a bikini, cheap plastic toys and a transistor radio from God only knows what decade all displayed haphazardly behind the glass windows.

In Jerusalem, Petal never felt any compulsion to speak with strangers with whom she crossed paths, but in Tel Aviv, as she walked the back streets of the rundown neighbourhoods that branched off from the bus station, she felt a yearning to engage. She chatted with the furniture menders on the narrow sidewalks of Levinsky Street, testing out her halting, newly acquired Hebrew. She smiled at the smoked fish vendor in the market at Ha'Aliyah. She wondered who lived and worked and created behind the whitewashed walls burgeoning with papery bougainvillea in varied shades of flame and fuchsia in the red-roofed cottages of Neve

Tzedek and daydreamed about all she might have in common with them. Petal wandered aimlessly for hours, reclaiming herself in small pieces along her way, awakening her senses with smells she breathed deep, tastes that sparked memories of contentment, sights and sounds that soothed: the bakery ovens of Abu Laffia in Jaffa, spilling their nourishment into the street; the overripe fruit of the Carmel Market that felt like life in all its colour and abundance; Rothschild Boulevard, lined with trees carefully planted decades before by design, with intention; and the sea with its horizon of endless possibility.

"What's that?" she asked, pointing to fruits she had never seen before.

"What? You don't know pomelo?" the vendor said, digging his thumbs deep into the thick, leathery skin, unleashing the sharp citrus smell as he cleaned away peel and pith and membrane, offering her a cluster of jewel-like fruit capsules. "Taste."

And she did, and it felt new and fresh and good.

Petal usually ended up at the beach no matter the weather. She sat and watched the waves and felt the electric current that somehow failed to spark and run inside her in Jerusalem come back to life. It was not a subtle imagining but a tangible tingling that began in her fingers and — as though flicking switches along a path, like a Rube Goldberg machine inside her — turned on the parts that could feel until her heart beat and her blood ran warm.

When the sun set, she went back to the bus station, boarded the #405, pulled her dubbon from her backpack, draped it across her lap like a blanket, and felt the climb of the wheels as the landscape darkened and closed in on the hilly passageways, returning a heaviness to her as though she was pulling the bus with her heart, her guts, her soul up into the Jerusalem landscape. By the time the bus pulled into the station, Petal's mood had darkened, her heart had hardened, and her blood had congealed.

PETAL DID HER best to keep track of Rosie in Jerusalem, a task that had never been easy, even when they'd lived under the same protected roof. She switched course with abandon. She never hesitated to change plans, didn't show up at agreed-upon times and places, and never worried she might be putting anyone out. She was not malicious, she was simply suggestible, distractible, and very excited by the most of-the-moment things in her path. If, for example, one arranged to meet Rosie at a movie at a given time and place, it was fair to say that at the time of making the plan, she had every intention of being at the movie. But if, along the way, a puppy abandoned in the park caught her attention, she might be waylaid. Her sudden mission to get that puppy to a safe place would supersede any previous engagements. Or if, on the way to her scheduled appointment, a friend or acquaintance happened to cross Rosie's path and present an alternative plan, Rosie might switch gears, not because the found friend or new plan was more exciting or better but because it replaced the old plan in her frontal lobe. Immediate, now, this instant was Rosie's default. So, Petal learned to plan accordingly for the both of them. When heading out, leave the house together. Never, if avoidable, make plans for the future. And don't, under any circumstances, take Rosie's flightiness personally.

Making plans to see Rosie in Jerusalem was additionally complicated. Petal had a phone number for the dormitory where Rosie lived, but that was all. She did not know exactly where it was or what it was. She knew it was within the maze of pedestrian alleyways in the new Jewish Quarter of the Old City but had no idea how to find it. It seemed to have neither a name nor an address and was simply known as the *Bais Bonos* or Girls' House. On the rare occasions when Petal tried to track Rosie down by venturing into the Old City and asking to be pointed in the right direction, she was met with Alice-in-Wonderland non-answers and misdirection. Essentially, one had to be a member of the club to know where the secret hideout was.

"It has to be kept secret, or the girls wouldn't be safe," Rosie said, throwing pebbles over the fence into the Sultan's Pool as they walked the perimeter of the excavated gully. "Boys have no self-control, so it must be imposed upon them."

"What a load of horseshit!" Petal replied. "Everyone knows where it is, they just pretend not to, like some stupid, unwritten rule — it's the fucking emperor's clothes!"

"Please, Pet, don't swear," Rosie said, looking around to see who might be listening.

"Oh, Ro! Don't give me that holier-than-thou shit! Now you're too religious to swear? Did you also find your virginity behind those sacred walls, Rosie?"

"Raizel is pure of heart, Petal! Hashem knows!"

"Well then, let God be your keeper," Petal said, ending the visit in much the same way as most of their check-ins.

Petal would call; the phone would ring twenty or thirty times before some girl would answer from what sounded like the bottom of a lake.

"Can I please speak with Rosie Wolffe," Petal would say.

"Who?"

"Raizel. Is Raizel there?"

"I'll check."

Petal would wait, listening to the *clunk, clunk* of receiver against adjacent wall and the comings and goings of the resident girls. She would feed pierced asimonim tokens into the phone until either she ran out or the girl returned to say she couldn't find Raizel and offered to take a message that Petal knew would never be delivered or returned. Occasionally, Rosie herself would pick up.

At first, Petal made Rosie meet her outside the Old City because she held on to the possibility of deprogramming her sister; later, it was because she hated the Old City — well, not all of it, just the Jewish Quarter. They would make arrangements, and most of the time Rosie would actually show up, which did give Petal fleeting thoughts that perhaps Rosie's newfound affiliation with God was a good thing. In late November, Rosie pleaded with Petal to meet her in the Jewish Quarter.

"It's cold and raining, Pet! Please come meet me here?"

"It's cold and raining for me too, Ro," Petal said.

"But you have boots and a proper coat, Pet. Pleeeease," she pleaded.

"Rosie ..."

"Raizel," Rosie corrected.

"Raizel, come meet me in the city, and we'll buy you a coat and boots."

"Not today, Pet. Another day. When it's not raining. I promise. Today, come meet me at the top of the stairs at ten-fifteen." Without waiting for an answer, Raizel hung up.

It was a pain-in-the-ass meeting spot, particularly on a rainy day. The trip from Mount Scopus to the stairs took half an hour on a good day and closer to three quarters of an hour in the rain. By the time Petal walked the five minutes to the bus stop at the top of French Hill — traversing the rushing rivers of water in the gutters — and waited for the bus to arrive behind schedule, she was a soggy, shivering mess. The ride down the winding roads into the city — through the sloppy weather, past the square buildings of golden stone that took on the deep grey of the sky, past the old Arab dwellings along Derech Schem, past the American Colony, crossing the unmarked border between West and East Jerusalem and switching busses in the middle of

Christian Jerusalem — reminded Petal of everything she tangibly
hated about this city. She walked from the bus into the Old City
through the aptly named Dung Gate or, in Hebrew, Shaar Ha'Ash-
pot — Garbage Gate — and reached the top of the stairs in a foul,
frozen, sopping state. All she wanted was to grab Rosie and head
for the nearest coffee shop in the Arab market to warm up with
a cup of strong Turkish coffee and a piece of warm, sickly sweet
knafeh. But Rosie wasn't there.

Instead of her sister, two completely generic Orthodox girls
wearing identical navy-blue *dubbonim*, knee-length denim skirts,
and rubber boots approached Petal. Giggling, the girls asked,
"Are you Raizel's sister?"

"Yeah. Is she okay?"

"She asked us to give you this," they said, handing Petal a
damp piece of paper and disappearing into the maze of alleyways
with shrieks of laughter.

Petal backed into the nearest overhang and uncrumpled the
wet note.

It read: *Walk right. Make a left at the third alley.*

"You're fucking kidding me!" Petal said to nobody because
there was nobody out in the dreadful weather. "Today of all days
you want to play hide-and-seek!"

Petal considered leaving, but she didn't. She walked straight,
climbed the terraced steps of the passageways, trying to avoid
the rushing waters streaming down the cut stone troughs running
through the centre of the lane, and turned at the third alleyway.

From beneath a doorframe, Petal was ambushed by two different yet the same girls with another note, which she furiously
grabbed.

"Tell her I don't want to play!" Petal shouted at the retreating
backs of the girls as they rushed away, disappearing into the laby-

rinth. She followed the instructions, first right then right again then left and then right. *If Rosie isn't there, I'm leaving. Fuck her!* she thought as she trudged along the slick cobblestones, her anger mounting with each precarious step. By the time she was accosted by the third twosome of girls who asked again, "Are you Raizel's sister?" her answer was different.

"*No!* I am *not* Raizel's sister," she shouted, pushing by the girls, slipping as she stepped, landing hard on her hip and shoulder in the stream of water. Petal could feel her chest burning and her throat tightening. Struggling to her feet, she saw a hand reach out to help. From her vantage point, she saw rubber boots and the hem of a navy-blue skirt. She looked up into her sister's smiling face.

"Screw you, Rosie!" Petal said, bursting into tears and turning her back as she got to her feet.

"Don't be mad, Pet. It was supposed to be fun!"

"For who, Ro? Like everything, it was for you! What about me, Rosie? Do you ever think about me?" Petal pushed Rosie aside and rushed away.

"Pet," Rosie shouted at her back. "Don't be mad!" But Petal had disappeared into the maze of the Old City, and Rosie had been warned against venturing too far on her own, lest she find herself in the wrong part of town.

By the time Rosie arrived at the door of Petal's dorm room that evening clutching a moist bag of cinnamon raisin rugelach as a peace offering, Petal had had sex with a boy whose name she couldn't remember or hadn't known in the first place. He'd worn a crocheted kippah. The skullcap resembled a round slice of watermelon, with dark green, light green, and red concentric circles. Petal thought it was ridiculous and told him so when he removed it before hopping into her bed, and he forgot it when he left. When she heard the knock at the door, she assumed he was coming to retrieve it. She had no intention of opening the door.

"Pet, please open the door," Rosie said. "I'm sorry. I'd been planning it for so long, I didn't think about the weather. Please, I brought you a treat."

Rosie stood outside the door in the cinder block corridor for a long time, but Petal didn't answer. "I'm just going to leave this bag of rugelach out here for you, Pet. I'm really sorry." Rosie put the bag at the crevice between door and floor.

A few minutes passed. Petal opened the door to toss the watermelon skullcap into the hallway. Rosie was still there.

"Go away! I'm not in the mood for you," Petal said. Rosie blocked the door with her boot.

"Pet, I'm sorry. I'm an idiot. Please. I need to cuddle. I need you not to be mad at me." Rosie tilted her head down, pushed out her lower lip, and raised her eyebrows to open her puppy dog eyes.

Petal turned away, dropping back onto her unmade bed. Rosie picked up the bag of pastries and stepped into the room, dropped her coat on the floor, kicked off her boots, and lay down beside her sister. She unfurled the crumpled edge of the paper bag, pulled out two small, crescent-shaped pastries, put one between her own teeth, and placed another one on her sister's stomach. She held Petal's arm. Eventually, both girls fell asleep.

When Petal woke up, she recognized her own need for escape before she touched the floor and made quiet haste to get herself out of Jerusalem, even if only for a few hours. Rosie slept.

"*Ani cholah! Ani cholah!*" Petal said, elbowing her way to the front of the bus as it pulled into the Tel Aviv station. Stumbling down the steps onto the pavement, Petal crouched, vomiting against the wheel, sweating inside her heavy jacket. The convulsions of her stomach subsided. She stripped down to her T-shirt and felt miraculously better with the sun warming her back and shoulders. The bus station was particularly lively that day. Loud Mizrahi music emanated from kiosks selling cassette tapes and sunglasses. Shopkeepers shouted to attract buyers, each one louder, more insistent than the next.

"*Shalosh b'eser!* Three tapes for ten shekels! Pita, cham ve'tri, hot fresh pita, bagels, bourekas, garinim, pitsuchim," came the cries from the sellers of nuts and seeds and baked goods.

Petal bought a can of cola and drank it down in one long gulp.

She bought a second can, sipping it slowly, winding her way up and down the unknown side streets and alleyways that ran off the main thoroughfare of the bus station. Completely new territory was what she needed. She wandered in and out of shops that sold cheap clothing, T-shirts with meaningless English words, housewares, and cleaning products, slowly feeling more and more like Petal. She tried on dozens of pairs of shoes she had no intention of buying in equally as many shoe stores lining both sides of an entire street. She ate peanuts covered in hard, fried batter that made her teeth sound as though they might crack, and falafel she was sure would do her gut no good. Petal dawdled aimlessly through the rundown, grimy neighbourhood of Neve Sha'anan, up Levinsky Street, along Har Tzion Boulevard, and around Shapira, breathing deep the putrid, down-to-earth smells of feral cats and leaky cars. At sundown, having ventured no more than a few blocks from the station, Petal doubled back, bought herself a powdered jelly donut, and boarded a bus back to Jerusalem believing she felt better.

As the bus began its ascent to Jerusalem, her ease escaped into the darkness of the night. Dread hit her hard as the bus pulled into the station. For the first time in her life, but certainly not the last, Petal was mentally calculating the available options for suicide between the station and Mount Scopus.

Anonymous in her standard-issue jacket, she walked in the direction of the campus. All was dark. She had no plan. She had no feeling.

"*Hey, motek. Hey, chaticha. At levad?* Are you by yourself? You speak Hebrew? You wanna fuck me? I wanna fuck you."

Petal tuned in to the repeated catcalls behind her.

"Yeah, I wanna fuck you," she said, not looking back, walking just fast enough that her pursuer remained a few paces behind her.

"You wanna fuck me?"

Petal continued, the unseen man trailing close behind her — never turning around to look at him, hoping he might catch up, hoping he might kill her.

"Are you coming to fuck me?" she taunted.

"I'm coming to fuck you hard."

Petal allowed the man to follow her right into her dormitory without looking at him. She unlocked the door of her room, let him in, let the door slam shut. In the pitch dark, they groped and tore at one another. She hoped her guest was violent enough to release her from herself.

When she came to, one eye swollen shut, searing pain in her abdomen, pounding, throbbing head, the taste of carrion in her battered mouth, she had two thoughts in rapid succession: *Oh crap, I'm still alive … I think I'm in trouble.*

Petal didn't remember how she got to the Shalvata Hospital in Hod Hasharon. She had no memory of phoning Der nor of leaving Jerusalem. She could not, either at the time of the events or afterwards, recall any details or vagaries except that the hospital smelled of overcooked cruciferous vegetables. The staff were expecting her.

"Efshar la'azor? ... Tzricha mashehu?" said a young woman with thick, black kohl ringing her eyes.

Petal understood she was being asked how she could be helped and what she needed. She unbuckled one side of her faded blue canvas bag, rummaged for her dog-eared passport, and put it on the counter.

An olive-skinned man appeared. He wore a white lab coat over his jeans and an open-necked plaid shirt from which protruded a tuft of salt-and-pepper curls that matched the loose mop of curls on his head. "You are Petal Wolffe, yes?" Eyes crinkling, heavy accent, slight lisp, warm smile.

Petal nodded.

"I was waiting for you. Roie Boded. Dr. Boded or Roie. Whatever you like. Dr. Levy is a colleague and an old friend. He's a relative of you?"

"Dr. Levy?" Petal repeated. "Der?"

"Yes," Dr. Boded said, picking up Petal's passport and checking that he was in fact speaking with whom he thought he was. "You are coming from Jerusalem?"

"No, I'm Canadian," Petal said.

"Yes, of course, but just now from Jerusalem. No?"

Petal couldn't answer any more questions. She dropped onto her backpack as though whatever resources she had accessed to get herself there had run dry and all that remained was a thin trickle that seeped from the lower lids of her vacant eyes.

"We want to admit you," Dr. Boded explained. "You are from the wrong district for involuntary admission, so you must to agree. I'm making exception for my old friend."

Petal must have agreed, because she found herself sitting in a cramped, windowless room, wearing a hospital gown and slippers. There was a television with a picture but no sound and a ragtag group of gown-clad patients in varying stages of apparent distress.

Somebody brought a tray of bourekas, which were handed out on paper towels. Petal wasn't hungry. She wordlessly offered her boureka to the young woman next to her, who freaked out and threw it across the room.

"Where am I?" she asked her fellow inmates in the stark dormitory of the Shalvata Hospital emergency department. "How long have I been here?" she asked someone who looked official. "Where are my clothes? I want my clothes."

"You must earn that privilege," said a nurse.

"I just need to sleep." But at night, the patients ranted, and during the day, lying down was forbidden. Going outside was forbidden. Pills were handed out, and she was watched while she swallowed them. "What are these for? What am I taking?"

"Just take. Don't ask."

A young Ethiopian orderly came to take her upstairs to a ward bed.

"I'm locking your clothes in the cupboard," he said as though apologizing. "The nurses will decide when you can have them. Someone will come get you for lunch. You can wait here until then."

Petal lay down on the bed and fell into a drugged, heavy, uncomfortable sleep from which she couldn't rouse herself. When she woke, Der was there.

"Tiggaleh?" he said softly.

Petal cried. Her heart blocked the path from her lungs to her mouth. There was not enough air to get the words out, nor did she know what the words were.

"You've been sleeping a lot," Der said, reaching for her hand beneath the bedding. "You must be very tired."

Petal squeezed Der's dry, cold hand. "You're cold."

"A little. It's a dismal day," he said, lifting the blind, exposing the grey, rainy weather through the wind-rattling window.

Petal squinted into the glare of the muted gloom outside. "I thought it was sunny. Did I dream sunshine?"

"Perhaps yesterday was sunny."

Petal closed her eyes and opened them again, trying unsuccessfully to force her unresponsive pupils to constrict in the light.

"Do you want to keep sleeping?" Der asked. "Don't feel you have to wake up because I'm here."

"No ... Maybe ... Der ...?"

"Yes, Tiggaleh?"

"Der? How did I get here?"

Der looked at Petal, and the pain reflected in his face reminded her of what she couldn't see. Petal reached up to touch her face, feeling the cuts and bruises that were changing colour and scabbing over. "Oh ... So you came ...?"

"Oh, my Tiggaleh," Der said, unable to stop his own tears. Petal looked so small and wounded. He wished he had more to offer her in the way of help. Instead, he turned his back, pretending to look out the window, the archive of worry he had for her, her mother, her grandmother too steeped, too well informed for Petal to see.

"Are you here to take me home?" Petal asked.

"If that's what you want," he said, facing her. "I'm here to do whatever you need. I'm here to be useful." Der was speaking his own mantra, meaning it more than ever.

"Where's Rosie?" she asked, suddenly alarmed, as though she were a mother remembering in a dream that soon the baby might need feeding.

"She's in Jerusalem. She doesn't know you're in hospital. She doesn't know I'm here."

"I'm a very bad sister," Petal said. "I was supposed to be taking care of her. I let go of the string."

"No, I let go. It was wrong to expect that of you." Der sighed. "That cannot be your responsibility, Tiggaleh."

"I don't know how to take care of her, but I don't know how not to take care of her."

"You are not your sister's keeper."

But it was an unwritten family fact: Rose's happiness depended upon the buoyancy afforded her by the weight her sister carried on her behalf, and Petal's well-being depended upon Der sharing the load.

"But I am, Der. I have always been," Petal said.

3.

RABBI GLISSERMAN WAS late. Petal thought she had made it clear she would be arriving in Toronto at the island airport. The rabbi was apparently unaware such a thing existed and went to pick her up at Pearson International. By the time they figured out the problem, about thirty minutes after she took the ferry to the terminal building, Petal was ready to take a streetcar up Bathurst Street. Rabbi Glisserman wouldn't hear of it, so she waited.

Petal hadn't been to Toronto since her nephew Avromi Yitzchak's bar mitzvah the previous year. He was Rosie's fourth child and eldest son. After attending the *simcha*, Petal thanked her lucky stars that, of her sister's eight children, only Avromi Yitzchak and the youngest, Simcha Aron, were boys. She would only have to go through that particular ordeal once more and not for another ten years. What she failed to remember was that Orthodox girls are not bat mitzvahed, they marry. As Raizel would say, "God willing, we will dance at many weddings!"

In fact, on the last call they had had some weeks earlier, Rosie had reported that her eldest, Sarah Batya, had been on a successful date with a nice boy from a good Monsey family.

Monsey was a large community of Orthodox Jews in New York. This would have meant very little to Petal except that the author Shalom Auslander hailed from the Orthodox community of Monsey. She had read Shalom Auslander's devastating and hilarious accounts of his struggles to escape and reconcile himself with his ultra-Orthodox upbringing. His writing left her feeling both forlorn and hopeful on her sister's behalf.

Petal found a sunny concrete outcrop of construction debris overlooking Lake Ontario. She planted herself on the sun-warmed slab, careful to avoid the exposed shafts of rebar. Petal positioned her suitcase as a footrest and tried to make herself comfortable. Everything inside her screamed, *Pull your shoulders up to your earlobes, clench your teeth, and squirm with irritation and anxiety.* She fought her default drive with hard-won lessons from years of therapy. So far, she thought she was managing rather well under the circumstances. *Fuck me,* she thought on the heels of her self-congratulation. *I haven't even arrived on Jewish Mars yet.* The spring between her neck and shoulders tightened. She felt it immediately and countered with alternating backward shoulder rolls and frontward head rolls. Deftly, she positioned the tip of her tongue at the front of her palate and whispered, "Nancy" to unclench her jaw.

Petal squinted at her phone in the sunlight. Dr. Farmer had messaged, confirming cancellation of her appointment. He'd suggested they could meet by phone but understood if that wasn't possible. Petal didn't respond. First, she needed to assess the situation at her sister's.

She called Benjamin.

"Hello, my Pet. I wasn't expecting to hear from you quite so soon. Is everything all right?" Benjamin asked.

"The rabbi who's coming to pick me up went to the wrong airport, so I'm waiting for him."

"Take a cab."

"I offered to hop on a streetcar, but he insisted I wait for him. I think he feels bad he didn't know about the island airport. That's my sister's life in a nutshell. Its boundaries are so small, so insular, that this guy doesn't even know there's a downtown airport."

"Even I know that, and I've been to Toronto twice!"

"These people have no reason to venture downtown. Kosher's southernmost border in this city is Beth Tzedek Synagogue three blocks south of Eglinton. I wouldn't be surprised if he didn't even know there was a lake!" Petal took a deep breath. "Let's talk about something else. I need to not spin myself into a frenny before I even get there."

Benjamin knew what she meant.

"I think I should've worn a skirt," Petal said, plucking some lint from her trousers.

"Do you own a skirt?" Benjamin asked.

"Probably not, but maybe if I had worn a skirt it would have been better ... you know, in her home ... with Schmeil."

"You're not staying with her, are you?" Benjamin asked.

"Good God, no! Have you completely lost your mind? I'll stay with Der." Der had always been home base. He was the exception to the rule of blood being thicker than water. Despite the oceans of unlikely interconnection, Der was family.

A horn blast nearly catapulted her into the lake. A filthy sedan pulled up behind her. The windows were so caked with dirt, she couldn't see into the car until he leaned across the front seat to manually roll down the window.

"Mrs. Wolffe?"

"Benjamin, he's here. I'll call you later." Petal pocketed her phone.

Standing, she brushed off her bum and wheeled her small suitcase to the back of the noisily idling car and waited for the trunk to be opened.

Rabbi Glisserman sprang out of the car and to the back, apologizing in his thick Brooklyn accent. "I'm so sorry. My wife drives the newer car. It's bigger for the children to fit. The trunk of this one doesn't really open well. Better to put your suitcase in the back seat in case we can't get it open later," he said, awkwardly leaning down to grab the suitcase.

Rabbi Glisserman placed the suitcase on the back seat on top of a small mound of blankets. In the moment, his back to her, Petal thought, *He's not quite what I was expecting.* She reckoned he was in his early to mid fifties. He wore a dark suit, a white shirt, and a black kippah, his beard was cropped close, and his *peyot* were not long curls hanging down the sides of his face but shortish and discreetly tucked behind his ears instead of trailing behind him. Petal noticed that the strings of his *tzitzit* were tucked into the pockets of his trousers. He was altogether far more put-together-looking than her brother-in-law and most of the men she had observed through the partition at her sister's wedding and her nephew's bar mitzvah. *He looks kind of normal,* she thought.

Opening the front passenger door, Rabbi Glisserman briskly swept refuse from the seat with his hand. "I'm sorry. When the weather gets good, the boys who are struggling start roaming the streets at night. They leave all sorts of garbage in my car."

Petal hesitated. "Should I sit in the front?"

"Of course," he said, moving to open the back door. "Unless you'd rather sit in back."

"No, I'm fine. I just thought, you know, because I'm a woman, you might ..."

"Complete nonsense. The expansion of interpretation of our laws is a big problem in our community. There is no law in *halacha* that forbids you from sitting in the front seat, nor anything that might suggest that sitting beside a male driver is not allowed."

Petal got into the car, brushing a stray soiled tissue to the floor; she noted a stale pungency she identified as eau de morning after the night before and greasy pizza box, with a soupçon of pubertal boy.

"I am Herschel Glisserman, by the way, Mrs. Wolffe. I mean Dr. Wolffe. I'm sorry about the mix-up."

"Please call me Petal, Rabbi. I keep looking over my shoulder for my grandmother when you call me Mrs. Wolffe."

"All right, Petal. Call me Heschy."

"You sure? Isn't that another law of some sort?"

"Petal, rest assured, I will keep track of the laws and traditions that govern my conduct. As I said, don't expect everybody to behave the same way. There are many who don't have the ... let's say confidence in their own ... understanding, and take the letter of the law over-literally. So, you can call me Heschy and sit in my car, and Hashem will not strike either one of us down.

"I'm sorry I kept you waiting. I had no idea there was another airport. I'm a bit embarrassed to admit I've never actually been down here. I knew there was a lake, but this is the first time I've seen it. That must seem strange to you."

"Please tell me about my sister."

"Pardon me for being blunt, but does your sister have any history of mental illness?"

"Are you a social worker? She ... we all ... our mother. There is a long history of mental illness in our family. But Rosie's the best of us. She's a bit crazy, but always good crazy. Up, never down."

"I'm afraid up can be as bad as down if taken far enough, Petal. Raizel, she calls herself Raizel, seems to be in the midst of a complete manic psychosis. It is not good."

"What happened?"

"I promise, I'll make clear everything I can. We should stop for coffee before we go to the house. Talk. A united front will be helpful."

"Whatever you think."

They rode in silence. Petal felt numb. Partial information had that effect on her. It was a defence mechanism she had developed over time to combat her natural instinct to think and believe the worst about everything. Instead, she disconnected. She'd been told it was a type of dissociative behaviour, but she preferred to think of it as "human on hold," like her own personal elevator music, without highs or lows or adagios or crescendos, just background filler. It had taken a long time and a lot of work to make it a choice.

The city rolled by as they drove up Bathurst Street, past the subway station she had known so well as a child, past the synagogues, past the sad, decrepit donut shop in the strip mall at the corner of Eglinton and Bathurst where everybody had bought pot when they were teens, under the bridge where they had stopped to roll their joints, up and down the rolling hills of the city built on ravines, into territory so familiar yet so foreign. Petal had left Toronto a long time ago.

Parked outside the coffee shop in Lawrence Plaza, Heschy broke the silence.

"I'm not a social worker, by the way. Not by training, at least. I'm just a yeshiva-educated *amhaoretz*. Well versed in Torah and Talmud, but not much else. It's another one of our problems. The scope of our education is myopic. But I act as a sort of grassroots community mental health professional. I'm the guy they call when there's a problem. It's nothing official, it's just one of those things that's known in the community."

"How do you become that guy?" Petal asked.

Petal couldn't help noticing the looks she was getting from the Orthodox patrons as she walked to the back of the coffee shop. *I should have worn a skirt*, she thought again. Heschy got coffee and hermetically sealed kosher muffins for both of them. Petal struggled to open hers, quickly losing interest. Heschy returned to the table from washing hands, said a silent blessing, popped a piece of muffin in his mouth, and began chewing and speaking at the same time.

"Technically, a muffin isn't bread, so no washing is required, but after being in my car, a good handwashing is prudent before eating anything, and it always leads to praying." He gave a laugh-snort. "I think if I give you a bit of background on myself, you may be willing to find me credible."

Petal tried not to see Heschy chew like a cow with his open mouth and smacking lips. She was working hard against her own preconceived stereotypes and prejudices, but his barnyard decorum was a powerful reinforcement of all her discrimination receptors.

"Why wouldn't I find you credible? I don't even know you," Petal said.

"Well, you're an educated woman. A doctor. And I'm a *narishkeit*. So I guess I feel the need to give a bit of a resumé before I start telling you about your sister and giving my opinions."

"I'm not that kind of doctor. I'm a PhD. An academic. In fact, I just defended my thesis two days ago."

"Mazel tov. That's a big accomplishment. Your family must be very proud of you."

"Rosie's my only blood family. I'm not sure she even knows what I do. Der is proud of me just for surviving, but my friends are proud of me. I'm proud of me."

"And may I ask your field of study?"

"Education. Literacy and comprehension, specifically."

"We could use you here."

"I thought education was your strong suit?"

"That's a conversation for another time. I'm also a teacher. I was a teacher at the yeshiva. Like the high school for boys."

"Yes. I know what a yeshiva is."

"Sorry, don't want to assume anything," he said, combing his fingers through his beard, brushing the dislodged muffin crumbs onto the floor.

"What you maybe don't know is that at some yeshivas, a rabbi is assigned a class, and he moves up with his class. The same rabbi stays with the same boys for five years. The boys become like children to the rabbi and the rabbi like more than just a teacher. He becomes a mentor and a confidant and a guide into adulthood. That's when it works. It doesn't always work. Sometimes it's just luck or divine intervention or whatever. The relationship gels. Sometimes the rabbi's wife makes all the difference. She welcomes the boys into their home, invites them for Yom Toivim and Shabbes, and cleans them up when they get too drunk on Purim. Sometimes not. Maybe she's too busy or not coping with her own children. Maybe it just doesn't come naturally. I've been blessed. I have a wonderful wife who's put up with many cohorts of boys I've taught. And I've been lucky with most of my boys. Lucky or not, there are always boys who struggle and stray. And like it or not, when you're with these boys day and night, night and day for years, you can't help but get involved.

"Some rabbis, like anybody, have more talent for some aspects of teaching and mentoring than for other aspects. I have a talent with the troubled boys. My wife says it's not a talent but a softness. She says I can't let go of a child who I think is suffering, and I think any child who misbehaves is suffering. She's mostly right. So, sometimes, if another rabbi had a boy who was suffering, I would get involved. Over time, I was getting called to help not only with yeshiva bochers but with all sorts of pain and suffering in the community. So now, I'm the guy they call. But not enough. There are a lot of people who should call who never do until it's too late. These things carry too much stigma in our community. It's another one of our many tragedies."

"So my sister called you?"

"Not your sister. Schmeil called. I don't know how well you know Schmeil, but under his awkward exterior, he's a good man. He means well. In some ways, Hashem has been good to him, and in others he has been burdened by misfortune. I suppose like everyone."

Petal nodded knowingly.

"You know that for Pesach we clean our houses for the holiday. We clean every corner to be sure there is no *chametz*, no leaven anywhere. We change the dishes. We cover the countertops. We throw away or sell off food that is chametz or has been in contact with any food that is leavened. We make sure that at least once a year our homes are spotless and purified from top to bottom. It's a big job, mostly done by women."

Petal rolled her eyes. Rabbi Glisserman saw.

"I know this probably doesn't fit with your worldview, but this is why I thought we should talk first. Before going into a difficult situation, we need to be in agreement about what is and what is not a problem right now. Believe me when I say that Raizel embraces her role as an Orthodox wife and mother. It may not be a choice you would make, but your sister has made the choice, and she is not oppressed by it."

Petal felt she had been softly lulled into believing she could relate to this rational man only to be reminded that they were from different times and places. She made a mental note not to be sucked in. She wasn't in Kansas anymore. This was the Twilight Zone, and anyone who ever let their guard down in the Twilight Zone ended up dead.

"Let's agree to disagree on this one. Go on," she said.

"Schmeil came home two days ago to find all his *seforim*, his religious books, scattered on the basement floor and the bookshelves in pieces. You know a religious text is never supposed to touch the floor. Well, you might not know, but for sure Raizel knows. She was sitting with a pot of boiling water and a pile of Q-tips cleaning every screw from the shelves she had taken apart. She said Hashem told her to do it this way. When Hashem gives explicit instructions, even to Orthodox Jews, well ... even Schmeil recognized this was not normal behaviour. She had burnt her hands. That's when he called me."

"She's manic," Petal said. "She's been manic her whole life. Most of the time, it worked for her. Rosie was always the life of the party. But sometimes, she would fixate. She can't get past stuff. Like religion. She became obsessed with Orthodoxy. And now it sounds as though she's gone completely off the kosher deep end."

"You'll excuse me, Petal, but manic is one thing. This is different. I realize it must seem strange to you to hear me say this, but God spoke to her." He cupped his hands to his beard and shook his head back and forth gently. "We speak to Hashem. At least three times a day, we bare our souls and raise our voices to Adonoi. But his answers are not direct. He doesn't speak to us. Unless your sister is a prophet of some sort, and perhaps she is ... Hashem tends to send prophets during times of crisis. In any case, even to us, even in our world, hearing the voice of the almighty, telling you to bathe each screw for purification ... this is not normal. This is beyond manic.

"Her enthusiasm is remarkable." Heschy slurped his coffee. "She's been a valuable addition in our community. The mothers' committee fundraising event has been very successful because of her and her ability to get other people excited about things."

"She can do that," Petal said.

"But it hasn't been easy for her. Our community is judgmental. There's a competitive side to Orthodoxy. I'm embarrassed by it, but it is very real. Coming from a secular background is thought of as suspect. Like, unless you are born into the ranks of religion, you are not fully kosher."

"You mean she's had to prove that she's religious enough?"

"I guess that's what I mean. People, even religious people, can be cruel. One indiscretion can spoil a reputation and take years to recover from. We're a small community with a weakness for gossip."

"Did Rosie do something?"

"Not really. It was many years ago when they first moved back to Toronto from Yerushalayim. Raizel had the bad luck of miscarrying."

"Twice," Petal said.

"*Kaiyn'nehora*. She was brand-new here. It was known that Schmeil was returning to Canada with his bride, and, of course, it was much talked about that she was an outsider. A girl from an unknown, not Orthodox family. She had the very bad luck of miscarrying a few weeks after arriving. She had the very, very bad luck of hemorrhaging in the supermarket. Right there across the parking lot." He pointed. "She collapsed, and an ambulance was called. She did nothing wrong, but the way people talked, her lack of modesty was her own fault. As though if she had been properly raised, she would have known to stay home and hide her misfortune and disgrace from public view."

"People judged her for that? You are fucking kid … Oh, sorry, shit … my language. It's, sorry, it's just …"

"It's all right, Petal. I've heard it before. And, conveniently, it is only a sin to take Hashem's name in vain. Swearing of other kinds is only a matter of *minhag*, tradition, not *halacha*, law."

"I thought gossiping or judging harshly was forbidden by Jewish law," Petal said.

"Yes, but we have a long tradition of it, and tradition is what we do best," Heschy said with a resigned shrug. "So she had to try harder. We may claim to live to a higher standard, but it's not true. We're flawed like everyone else. People assume that religious and righteous are the same. They're not.

"Raizel worked very hard to be accepted by the women in the community. She's very smart and in some ways more learned than many of our women, but there are subtleties that are hard to grasp from books."

"Like learning a new language," Petal remarked. "It's a cultural thing."

"That was precisely what Raizel struggled with. She tried so hard to fit in, joined every committee, every group, went to every event. But *s'vet gornisht helfen*. It didn't help. She was an outsider and made to feel like one for a very long time."

"Like how?" Petal wanted examples as though she needed more ammunition to feed her resentments, which she decidedly did not.

"It was a long time ago, but if you must know ... Either she didn't notice or didn't care that people spoke behind her back when she dressed too beautifully or colourfully for a community simcha. She ignored the evidence that the kosherness of her kitchen was in question when her cookies went unsold at fundraising bake sales. But when she joined the *shidduch* committee, they couldn't leave well enough alone.

"You know, in the old days, in the shtetl, there were *shadchans*, matchmakers. It's different now a little, but young people still rely on introductions. Women here make it their business to find matches for unmarried youngsters. There was a shidduch committee made up of a group of well-connected women who, because of their seniority and family ties, knew many people in the community. Raizel didn't know what it was other than another thing to join, so she showed up. Rather than letting it be, which is what they should have done, they rudely told her that she wasn't welcome. I believe that she was referred to by a derogatory term for a non-Jewish woman, implying that she was as helpful for matchmaking as a *shiksa*. I had to get involved when Schmeil called and said his wife was being bullied. Some of the women had taken to calling her 'Yenta fa renta.' For Raizel, this was the final humiliation. She told Schmeil she was going back to Yerushalayim. A few women heard about how hurt Raizel was and reached out. Eventually, people forgot. Maybe even she forgot. Maybe not.

"She's not an outsider anymore, but she has a personality that demands attention. It's who she is, and, in our world, where modesty is a virtue, it can be challenging. It hasn't helped that she is very beautiful, like it's her fault that she shines so bright."

"Even in our world, Rosie could be a bit much. I always wondered how that worked for her in this life she's chosen."

"She tries very hard to abide by the letter of the law, to fit in, not stand out, but I think that might have been her undoing. You can't keep the moon in a barrel for long."

Petal sighed deeply. "When can I see her?"

"Soon." Heschy checked his watch. "You need to understand a little bit about our world because we're going to need to cooperate in making some important decisions. But for you to help with the decisions and honour your sister's life choices, you need the right measuring sticks."

"I'm not sure I follow," Petal said.

"You'll excuse me, but have you ever seen a therapist?"

Petal nearly choked on her laugh. "I'm the queen of therapy. I've been hospitalized for severe bouts of depression. I've been suicidal, and I'm happy to say I'm heavily reliant on a wonderful array of psychopharmaceuticals."

"My point exactly," Heschy said.

"If one sister is crazy, the other one must be?" Petal said.

"What I mean is, we just met, and without hesitation you offered an abridged personal psychiatric history. I'm guessing that in your secular New York life, it's not a secret to many people who know you that you have this history or that you see a therapist and take medication."

"Trust me, I'm not the freak. I don't think I know anybody who isn't in therapy."

"Exactly. In your world, it isn't a secret. In our world, mental health issues are deep, dark secrets. It's better than it used to be. At least now people actually get help, but no one can know."

"Now that's crazy!" Petal laughed to indicate that she was teasing. She wasn't at all sure that what seemed like obvious good humour to her would be appropriately interpreted by Heschy as lighthearted. She clicked her heels together under the table.

"Understand that for an Orthodox family, the most important thing is that their children should marry well. You must know that your niece Sarah Batya is looking for a *chossen*, a groom."

"Yes, I hear there's someone in the wings."

"I hear the same, God willing. Schmeil is very worried that if news of Raizel's trouble becomes public, his children will never marry."

"What does one thing have to do with the other?"

"These things run in families. Like intelligence and red hair and diabetes and cancer. Some you want. Some you don't want. Who wants to risk a marriage into a family with mental illness? Do you see what I'm saying?"

"I do. I don't agree, but I understand your concern."

Rabbi Glisserman checked his watch again.

"We should go." He jumped up and raced out of the coffee shop.

Petal was confused by the sudden urgency.

"Did I miss something?" She chased behind him to his car.

"It's the medication. We've been keeping her sedated, and there seems to be a window just before it's time for her next dose when she's relatively lucid and calm. I thought it best you see her then."

"You're managing me?" Petal said. "You're controlling my access to my sister."

"It's not like that, Petal."

"Explain it to me, then. What the hell is she on, and who gave it to her?" Petal's shoulders pressed against her ears. She crossed her arms over her chest and pushed her hands down on each shoulder.

"This is not some kind of conspiracy against your sister. She was out of control. She needed to be medicated. She was hearing voices, and she was suffering."

"It sounds like she needed to be hospitalized, not dosed by a bunch of know-nothings. Who the hell is prescribing?"

Heschy pulled up in front of Rose and Schmeil's crumbalow, as Petal referred to the crumbling bungalow. Before Petal could fling herself out of the car, he caught hold of her sleeve.

Uncomfortably clutching the fabric of her sweater between thumb and forefinger as though the fabric itself might burn him, Heschy said, "If you go in there angry, it will not be helpful. I want to tell you about Hatzolah and about the pharmacist who's been helping. Most of all, I want you to see your sister when she is present enough to know you're there. I want you to give her a hug and reassure her."

"Reassure her of what?"

"I have no idea."

Heschy let go of Petal's sleeve. He followed her up the path to the broken screen door. Heschy knocked. Petal thought she might cry as they listened to the footfalls inside approaching the front door. Looking down at the cracked concrete step covered in children's chalk scribbles, Petal muttered, barely audibly, "Thank you."

Rabbi Glisserman blinked acknowledgement.

Schmeil, even more dishevelled than his usual rumpled, sweaty self, opened the front door, flattening himself against the adjacent wall as though he had advance intel of some highly contagious disease Petal must be harbouring. He mumbled what Petal presumed was a greeting of some sort. To Heschy's "*Vos machts?*" he replied, "*Baruch Hashem*," giving a glance skyward.

Petal thought thanking God at such a time seemed even more preposterous than usual.

Schmeil's back pressed against a grimy wall, smudged with fingerprints and crayon scribbles that ran the length of the short vestibule, stopping about four feet up from the baseboards, except for a lone flourish of purple marker that peeked out from behind his back, curling and snaking its way from the grungy border toward the ceiling as though it had tried in vain to escape the chaos. The entrance was so overrun with shoes and boots and bags that when Petal cleared a spot to stand, she inadvertently upended an open container of Cheerios.

Schmeil motioned Petal down the short, unlit hall toward the back of the house. To the left, Petal saw what was meant to be a living room set up as a bedroom for the two boys, the large windows facing the street covered with a patchwork of safety-pinned sheets and tablecloths. Everything that had ever landed on the floor of that room since the beginning of time was apparently still there in sedimentary layers.

Petal felt embarrassed by the mess, as though in seeing it she was bearing witness to something intensely private. She tried not to look, moving into the small kitchen, the only passage to the rest of the house, chanting a silent mantra to herself.

Don't judge. She's sick. Don't judge, she's sick ... Despite the internal chanting, Petal couldn't help supposing that the state of the house was more par for the course than aberration.

The kitchen had a small counter with a sink in the middle of two distinctly divided sides. The left side of the counter was painted dark blue and the right side fire-engine red, as were the cupboards above and below, the floor, the walls, and the ceiling, which divided the kitchen into two oppressively close halves, the greasy window above the sink notwithstanding. Against the two-toned wall opposite the sink was a Formica table that Petal thought might be pink or peach, but she couldn't tell for sure beneath all the stuff. Every surface was completely covered and cluttered with dishrags, Tupperware containers, clean and dirty plastic plates, endless tinfoil baking pans, and stacks of disposable cups. The air smelled thick and malted. The sink appeared to be the only clear spot in the whole kitchen. Petal noted that there were no chairs around the small table. She shut her eyes, blindly taking the few steps to the bedrooms. Off the small central hall, no bigger than a large cupboard, were three closed doors and one open one. From the dark hallway, a small window in the only bathroom shed an unfortunate light on the equally dismal state of hygiene in there.

Petal had only visited Rosie's Canadian home once, fourteen years ago, when there were only five children and they hadn't yet closed off the cramped dining room or repurposed the living room, turning them into bedrooms. At that time, with kindness and an intentional blind eye, one might have been able to call the house messy. But there was no way to put lipstick on this pig. It was nothing short of a public health disaster.

Petal realized she was holding her breath. She exhaled more forcefully than she had intended.

"Is everything all right?" Rabbi Glisserman asked.

"Fine," Petal said.

"It's a bit crowded," Schmeil said.

"Oh, I'm used to crowded. I live in five hundred square feet. New York. You know." She was trying hard.

"I wanted to make a bedroom in the basement for the boys, but Raizel wouldn't hear of it. It made her nervous. 'In case of fire,' she said. So instead, we closed off the dining room and the living room." Schmeil lifted his hands to the heavens. "What can you do when you are blessed with so many children?"

Petal bit her lips to stop herself saying, *Use a condom, you primitive!* but once the nasty thought made its way through without vocalization, she had a kinder brain wave. This was the most Schmeil had ever said to her. She gave him mental brownie points for that.

Schmeil knocked gently on one of the closed doors then spoke tenderly to the crumpled pile of blankets on the double bed occupying most of the floor space. "Raizeleh, you have a visitor." The pile moved. Petal stepped into the room. Her sister rolled over in bed, adjusting her navy-blue headscarf with a bandaged hand.

Rabbi Glisserman remained in the hall. Schmeil leaned across the bed, opening the curtain a few inches. The floating dust particles danced in the wedge of daylight that bisected the bed.

"Pet?" croaked a voice so tiny and raw that Petal felt the edges of her heart crystalize and shatter.

"Ro," she replied, sitting tentatively on the very edge of the bed.

"Sit, sit," Schmeil encouraged.

Rosie rolled herself close to Petal and, like a puppy, nuzzled her head onto Petal's lap and began to weep. Petal stroked her sister's covered head with one hand and her back with the other. She could feel how thin Rosie was. It was clear to Petal that eating had not been on Rosie's to-do list for some time, and she tried to suppress the rage she suddenly felt. *Has nobody noticed that something is wrong?* Petal thought. *This woman is skeletally thin! Fucking ignorant zealots!* Petal closed her eyes and breathed deeply. Stroking her sister's angular shoulders, running her fingers up and down the xylophone of Rosie's protruding spine, Petal knew she needed to hang on to some of her anger or she would disintegrate into the desperation of tears she felt lurking too close to her own surface. She felt as emotionally thin as a soap bubble. *Don't burst*, she said to herself.

It was some time before anyone spoke.

"I lost, Pet," Rosie said.

"What did you lose, Ro?"

"I lost. I lost."

"Not true, my Rose. The game isn't over. Not nearly."

"We have to go soon," Rabbi Glisserman said, poking his head through the doorway.

"Already?" Petal said.

"Schmeil, *tsi ir hoben genug medesine?*" the rabbi asked.

"*Far itst*," Schmeil said.

"You just asked him if he's going to knock her out again, didn't you?" Petal said. She recognized just enough of her grandparents' secret language to surmise the gist.

"Please, not here." Heschy gestured for Petal to leave the bedroom.

Kissing Rosie's head, she manoeuvred it from her lap onto the bed. "I'll be back soon, Ro. I promise."

"In the morning," Heschy said. "Tonight, she should sleep."

"First thing in the morning, Ro. It'll be a whole new day. We can start from the beginning again." Petal delicately squeezed Rosie's hand and stepped into the hall.

Schmeil stayed with his wife as they showed themselves out.

"You see how fragile your sister is. She was happy to have you there, though."

Petal was glad Heschy didn't start the car right away.

"So now Schmeil is going to knock her out and, what ... just keep it up till she snaps out of it?"

"He'll sedate her. The children will come home. She'll sleep. Tomorrow morning, we'll go back and start to make some decisions."

"What decisions? She needs proper care."

"She needs proper care within the bounds of our community."

"Community! I thought it all had to be kept secret from the community! Where is this caring community in crisis? My sister is completely anorexic! That doesn't happen overnight. Didn't anyone from the community notice that something must be wrong?"

"Your anger isn't helpful. I promise you this isn't the first time I've dealt with this kind of crisis. We will get Raizel professional help. Obviously, medication is only part of the solution. She needs to be overseen by a doctor — one who'll understand the specific pressures and stresses in the life of an Orthodox woman. Someone who will not judge her choices, who will not make assumptions about her situation. At the same time, she needs a professional who'll be discreet. Not an insider, but not an outsider."

"Does such a person exist?"

"There are a few, but it isn't always easy to get an appointment right away." Heschy sighed. "Maybe if we were a better educated community we could look to our own, but our learning is mostly from religious texts. There's little in our study of much use in these situations."

"Little is an understatement," Petal said, not quite under her breath.

"Compassion is a Jewish value, Petal. You shouldn't underestimate it."

"So, why the secrecy? If compassion is held in such high esteem, why can't the community be called upon?"

"Because, like all other humans, we're flawed."

"Where do the drugs come from?"

"We have an organization called Hatzolah. It's like unlicensed paramedics for the Jewish community. They have it all over the world. You've never heard of it?"

"No," Petal said. "Never. Calling 911 is good enough for me."

"They're trained volunteers. They know what to do in emergencies, but they also understand the culture, the laws of our people. For example, a woman in emergency labour might be more comfortable calling Hatzolah, knowing that they'll do their best to protect her modesty. An elderly person might be more comfortable speaking Yiddish in a crisis. They have sensitivity that 911 can't be expected to have. And, you should know, the paramedics and ambulance crews who work for 911 respect and appreciate what they do. Hatzolah isn't just an Orthodox *meshugas*.

"Schmeil called me. I called Hatzolah, and we met at the house. These guys know. I didn't feel comfortable making decisions on my own, so I called them. It was clear to all of us that Raizel was in no shape for a quick visit to the emergency. They would have admitted her."

"No kidding! Because that's what she needs!"

"Well, there is a definite upside to being admitted. When I have a boy who's suicidal or overdosing, I don't hesitate to have him admitted. It gets him the help he needs immediately. No waiting. Baruch Hashem for public medicine!"

"Overdosing? Like a yeshiva boy? On drugs?"

"You'd be surprised what a big problem it is. As I keep saying, we're human. We agreed that the right doctor made more sense than a quick admission that would force a path through a system that can't be controlled."

"Like a cult? Like if you let her out of your world, she might end up back in mine?"

"No one questions her complete commitment to Orthodoxy. No one except you. But for her healing to be successful and her life to resume as seamlessly as possible, we feel a carefully chosen professional is a better idea."

"So, until you find the right doctor, you're just going to knock her out?"

"I know who I want her to see," Heschy said. "He'll have time soon. After *yuntif*. It's a busy time for Jews the week before Pesach. Time is not Raizel's problem, so we need to be patient. In the meantime, there is a sympathetic pharmacist whom I have a very good relationship with, and he, out of a sense of *rachmonos*, compassion, is willing to help. Do you understand?"

Petal was running out of steam. Historically, everything pointed toward her need to act as Rosie's protector, but she could feel another message emerging: *Let us handle it. Don't meddle. You cannot possibly understand. You don't belong.*

"So, why am I here? You seem to have it all under control," Petal said as though she were a helium balloon with a slow leak.

"You're her sister. Her need for you isn't obvious? There's not another woman in the world who could sit on the edge of her bed, her head in your lap, and not have to say a word."

Heschy started the car.

THE NEIGHBOURHOOD, ONCE full of low-rise, postwar apartment buildings like the one where Petal and Rosie had grown up and where Der still lived, had changed. Many of the multi-unit dwellings had been razed and replaced with homes too grand for their lot size and too close to their neighbours, but Meadowbrook Road was still lined with the old cookie-cutter buildings. Their balconies, no longer painted in shades of the ice cream rainbow but an updated geological palette of taupes and greys, were dilapidated and in need of tending. It made her sad. It would have made her bubby sad.

Der stood at the top of the short flight of stairs outside his apartment. The building, like all its cousins on the block, had two central stairwells, one at the front and one at the back, with apartments fanning off the middle on alternate half flights of stairs. Irving and Estie had lived in apartment 2. Der lived in apartment 1A, half a flight down and across the hall from them. Their apartments were mirror images of one another, which always provided the girls with absolute proof that there was, in fact, a parallel universe in which Petal was blond and sunny and Rosie was dark and pensive, a world where their mother Chavie lived with them like all the other mothers, this notion only ever shared between the girls.

Der's apartment was their second home. Like their apartment, it had two bedrooms, but since Der lived alone, the second bedroom was the girls' playroom, much as it had been for their mother when she was a child. Like their mother before them, Rosie and Petal roamed freely between the two homes, taking for granted that Der's door was always unlocked and they were always entirely welcome. He had snacks and treats and toys for them, including a beautiful dollhouse for which he made tiny, ornate furnishings out of champagne cork cages and bits of ribbon, lace, and fur that Irving brought him. It looked like a set designed for an opera or a ballet, and the girls treated it as almost sacred. They called it Havalleh and spent endless hours inventing and exploring their parallel universe.

The girls invented backstories for the dolls that lived in Havalleh. Ironically, the most mundane narratives they could fathom required wellsprings of creative imagining. There was a mother doll they called Ellen, a father doll they called Bob, and two girls named Sue and Nancy. When Der created costumes for the tiny dolls, the girls would insist that they needed to be "less fancy," pointing to pictures in the Sears catalogue as their bastion of aesthetic zenith. "Bob needs a necktie," they said, or "Could you please make an apron for Ellen?"

Bob didn't feature much in their imaginary world because he was generally "at work." His cameo appearances mostly involved him arriving home from work, greeting his family affectionately, and sitting on the sofa, where Ellen and the girls would bring him slippers and magazines and refreshments. Occasionally, Bob would be called upon to discipline Sue or Nancy or both of them for minor infractions, which generally required that they go to their room in the attic of the dollhouse.

Ellen was a maternal invention based on what could only have been an amalgamation of June Cleaver, Carole Brady, and Samantha from *Bewitched*. She was always baking cookies or tending to the first aid or medical needs of Sue and Nancy, of which there seemed to be an endless stream. Since Ellen and Bob had neither a bed nor a bedroom in Havalleh, Ellen was always in either the kitchen or the living room. "Where's Mom?" was not a question ever asked in Havalleh. Dr. Freud was not needed to spell any of it out for Der.

To Petal and Rose, Der was never an age. He was neither young nor old. He was Der. A small, delicate, Jewish-looking man with a round pot belly, a Sigmund Freud goatee, and round tortoiseshell glasses that perched on the end of his Semitic nose. He wore the uniform of an academic: khaki pants, soft sweaters, tweed jackets with patched elbows (or short-sleeved buttoned collared shirts in the warmer months), and expensive loafers. Petal couldn't recall ever seeing Der in shorts, a T-shirt, blue jeans, open shoes, or sneakers. Nor, if pressed to recall, could she have ever remembered seeing him without some reading material in his grasp. He was like one of those moulded plastic toys whose artificial hand is formed to grip an object. In Der's case, the object was a book or a newspaper or magazine, permanently crooked in his grip.

Seeing Der in the fading light that melted through the pebbled glass panes on either side of the entryway, Petal thought, for the first time, that he looked older. Not necessarily old, but older. Older than Der, which was an indeterminate age.

Leaving her suitcase at the bottom of the stairs, Petal leapt up the short flight two steps at a time and threw her arms around his neck.

"Tiggaleh," Der said, returning her embrace, his small volume of Shakespearean sonnets digging into her shoulder blade. "You always stay away too long, my girlie."

"I love that you still call me that," Petal said, descending to retrieve her luggage.

"Miss Tiggy Winkle and Tabitha Twitchet. Tiggaleh and Twitch, my girlies. I don't ever see or hear from her, you know," he said, ushering Petal into the apartment. Pausing momentarily in the doorway, Petal perused the familiar space. Neat, well-appointed in a simple mid-century style — square charcoal-grey sofa, brown leather armchair with well-worn footstool covered in *New Yorker* magazines, oval teak coffee table, Oriental carpets and kilims patchworked throughout, and bookshelves lining every wall except the windowed one that looked onto the balcony overlooking the street — modern academic bachelor circa 1955.

"It's probably better that way." Petal stood in the doorway of her bedroom. "You need her mess in your life like a *loch in kopf*."

Dropping her purse on the floor, abandoning her suitcase in the doorway, Petal glanced at her childhood drawing, still hanging above the light switch.

FOR THEIR EIGHTH birthdays, Der took his girls for an exciting adventure to the Ringling Brothers and Barnum & Bailey three-ring circus! The girls had never been to the circus before. Irving offered to drive, but Der insisted it was his special day with the twins. All dressed up in their new Der-bought birthday dresses, Petal in purple and Rosie in bright green, they took the bus and streetcar down to Exhibition Place, discussing all the way what they might see at the circus.

"Will there be elephants?" Rosie asked.

"It's likely there will be elephants," Der said.

"What about lions?" Petal wanted to know.

"It's quite possible there will be lions."

"And dinosaurs?"

"Rosie, dinosaurs aren't real," Petal said.

"They are so!" Rose insisted.

"You know what else there will be? Clowns and acrobats and trapeze artists!" Der artfully redirected.

The crowded, noisy stadium smelled of popcorn, burnt sugar, and grease. Der bought two voluminous clouds of candy floss, one pastel green and one mauve, and two helium balloons in matching hues, effortlessly bound to the girls' wrists by the balloon man. Petal licked at her skein of floss inefficiently, clutching Der's hand tightly as they waited for the show to begin. Frustrated by her collapsing confection, its increasing stickiness and ephemeral nature, Petal passed the gluey glob to Der.

Rosie twitched with excitement, tearing at her cotton candy with her front teeth like a hungry hyena, lapping it sloppily into her mouth with a green tongue. Petal tried to take hold of her sister's hand, fearing Rosie's exuberance might catapult her in the direction of some distraction or another, but Rose resisted Petal. Petal settled for a pinkie hold on the ribbon of Rosie's balloon.

The clowns were first to appear in the ring. Rosie was instantly on her feet, responding to their antics with a running commentary at full volume, punctuated by whooping, hollering, and exuberant waving of her sticky paper cone. Petal was embarrassed by the attention she supposed Rose was attracting. She climbed onto Der's lap, seeking shelter.

The centre ring filled with a troupe of acrobatic strongmen costumed in faux leopard-skin leotards that crossed over their left shoulders. They threw barbells back and forth to one another, tossing them as though they weighed nothing at all. They were joined in the ring by an equal number of tulle- and sequin-clad women who were switched out for the barbells and tossed into acrobatic somersaults from one man to another, crisscrossing through the air, landing in ever higher, more precarious human towers and pyramids on the shoulders of the men.

Petal was both horrified and mesmerized, holding one hand spread-fingered over her eyes, digging the fingernails of her other tiny hand deeper and deeper into the flesh of Der's forearm. She was too focused on the acrobats to notice the other two circus rings filling with elephants, clowns, horses mounted by standing riders, and a lion in a cage with a top-hatted tamer.

Rosie noticed it all. She pointed and exclaimed as each ring came alive with ever-more-frenetic entertainments, her head spinning to take it all in, her yelps and vocalizations escalating to fever pitch until she was standing on her seat, one foot on the back of the chair in front of her, gummy hand on the head of the stranger sitting there, screaming and crying and trying to climb higher above the crowd.

Petal grabbed her sister by the ankle. Der stood up suddenly to grab her as well, displacing Petal, who fell to the sticky floor, pulling Rosie down on top of her, popping her purple balloon and crushing the awkwardly positioned wrist of Der's outstretched arm.

The stadium medics, each with a Wolffe twin on his shoulders, balloon strings tangled, escorted them to a waiting ambulance.

"An ambulance isn't necessary," Der said, not wanting to add to the drama of the day.

"You need to have that arm taken care of. Fastest way to be seen," the medic said, rolling his eyes up toward the girl on his shoulders.

Irving and Estie met them at the hospital. Irving took the girls home, and Estie stayed with Der while his fractured wrist was immobilized in a cumbersome plaster cast. When they got home, Der came to apologize to the girls. *For what?* Petal thought. *It was Rosie's fault! It's always Rosie's fault!'*

Petal made Der a get-well card. It was a picture of a man with a goatee, glasses, and a Semitic nose, wearing a one-shouldered leopard-skin leotard. On his shoulders stood a girl with dark, wild hair, dressed in a purple tutu. The man held the girl by her calves. On one of his arms was a clumsy cast. Above the girl's head, floating balloon-like by a string tethered to her wrist, was a lithe, fair-haired girl with a lime-green tutu and pink wings. It said "Get Well Soon, Der."

Petal smiled at the ancient, faded drawing, unconsciously cuffing her left wrist with her right hand, as though the phantom ribbon of long ago was still there.

She joined Der in his small kitchen.

"A loch in kopf," he said. "Everyone and his brother make the extra holes in their heads my business. Only you and your sister try to protect me."

"I'm not trying to protect you. It's just …"

"I'm tougher than you think, Tiggaleh. I know I have a reputation as a bit of a sissy, but I also have a reputation as a pretty good social worker."

Der had, in fact, been dean of the Faculty of Social Work at the University of Toronto and still had a small but active private practice. His particular area of expertise had gained notoriety in recent years with a burgeoning interest in post-traumatic stress and intergenerational trauma. In his day, his research focus was on children of Holocaust survivors who presented with common psychopathologies. With each horror in the news of atrocities and wars around the globe, Der was introduced to a new population of sufferers of collective trauma. He knew history by his roster of patients at any given time. Now it was called PTSD and had become part of the vernacular. In the old days, when he was pioneering an early recognition of the phenomenon, he was accused of experimenting, like Dr. Mengele. It took tremendous fortitude for him to pursue his academic work in the field with the type of criticism he endured, but he knew he was on to something. Eventually, his peers' accolades drowned out the voices of his critics, but sometimes — not often, but sometimes — he still had nightmares about some of the letters and phone calls he'd received as a young man.

"Are you hungry? I made soup. You want toast and scrambled eggs? I eat less these days, but I can make you something more substantial." Der puttered at the kitchen counter.

"Soup sounds perfect," Petal said. She hadn't been to town since the bar mitzvah, and the familiar, comfortable smell of the apartment, the nostalgic click of the parquet floor, made her feel bad about her absence. Other than Rosie, Der was her only family, and regardless of his ostensible agelessness, the facts clearly pointed to his accumulation of years. She was forty, which made him ...

"How old are you?" Petal asked.

"I will be eighty at the end of the month. Why do you ask?"

"It just occurred to me that I've never known, exactly. So you and Bubby were the same age?"

"Yes, both born in 1928."

"Huh," Petal said, deflecting a subconscious nod to Der's mortality. "She seemed older than you, but also she always seemed younger than everybody. More childlike, I suppose."

"That was the protective mantle she wore. She was a very strong woman, but no one could bear what she did and face life without a distancing device of enormous magnitude."

"Huh." Petal sat down to eat her soup.

Petal let a spoonful of thick green split pea soup sit in her mouth for a moment longer than would normally be polite.

"Takes me back," Petal said. "Tastes like ... safety."

Der smiled.

Her phone rang. Petal answered on speakerphone.

"Benjamin, I'm just sitting with Der. Can I call you back?"

"I haven't heard from you all day. Is everything okay?" Benjamin said.

"I'm fine. Rosie isn't. I was just going to tell Der."

"When are you coming to visit us again in New York, Der?"

"It's been too long." Der took Petal's hand in his as though he owed her an apology.

"I'm the one who should feel guilty about not checking up on you." Petal squeezed Der's dry hand.

"It's not an equal relationship, Tig."

"Well, by now it should be," Petal scolded.

Petal told her two pillars what she knew and what she didn't know about Rosie's situation. She spoke with an acute awareness of a little rabbi on her shoulder, like the cartoon angel and devil that would appear on Fred Flintstone's shoulders, guiding his internal conflict and decision-making. Her little rabbi kept reminding her to speak with compassion and understanding as opposed to the knee-jerk irritation she was trying to quell.

"So, they need you there why? It sounds as though they have it all planned out," Benjamin said.

"Because she's my sister. Because I'm her sister," Petal said.

"Do you have any siblings, Benjamin?" Der asked.

"No. I was my parents' only disappointment," Benjamin said.

"Benjamin!" Petal scolded.

"It's difficult to understand now how close these girls were as children," Der said. "I have never seen a bond so vital. As though if one were underwater, the other couldn't breathe. True, Petal?"

"I can't leave, Benjamin. I can't leave her in crisis again."

"I miss you already, but I understand," Benjamin said.

"I'll be back soon. Before the food in my fridge rots."

"Don't toy with me, Pet," Benjamin said. "I know there is no food in your fridge. Love you lots. Keep in touch."

Petal put down the phone, returning to the now cool bowl of soup.

"Shall I warm it up?" Der asked.

"Mmn-uh," Petal said, rolling the soup across her tongue.

"Did you see the gift? I left it on your bed." He got up to fetch it.

The small box was a gift in itself, like a delicate, three-inch-cubed ichiban arrangement. Pea-green Japanese wrapping paper with embossed gold waves, crisscrossed with seafoam-blue iridescent organza ribbon, a tiny sprig of green foliage, and a miniature bunch of white pearl grapes, corkscrew vines and all, crowning it.

"Its so beautiful I don't want to unwrap it!" Petal said.

"I can rewrap it after if you like. Open it," he said with an excitement reminiscent of a lifetime of thoughtful treats, doll-house creations, and painstakingly packaged gifts.

Petal unwrapped with care, revealing a silver chain bracelet with three silver charms evenly spaced around the slightly flattened links. The charm in the centre was a flat, silver, slightly concave lozenge engraved with "Doctor Tiggaleh." It felt smooth and cool between her thumb and index finger. Holding it, she looked at the other charms: a Victorian-style house and a tiny hammer. Petal was speechless.

"You don't like it," Der said.

"Put it on me! Forever and for always. I get the medal and the home references, but the hammer?"

"Sometimes we need tools," Der said, shrugging one shoulder.

"Sometimes we need tools," Petal echoed.

4.

FOR A MAN so adept with his fingers, Der was clumsy and ill-equipped for anything requiring tools or heavy lifting. He'd learned this truth during his brief time in Palestine (later Israel) at age nineteen. That it was something he had to learn was testament to the sheltered life of privilege he had led growing up in South Africa. Being white implicitly meant privilege. There was endless domestic help, gardening help, washing, cooking, driving, etc. So much help that it was taken for granted and rendered invisible by its absolute fact. Der never had occasion to either try or fail at any of the most mundane tasks of everyday life.

So, finding himself on kibbutz, it surprised him that he had absolutely no real-life skills and no talent for acquiring them. He was neither strong nor coordinated, and the work needed people of a much more physical nature than his. His feelings of useless-ness were unfamiliar since his experience in life was limited to excelling as a private school boy. Top of the class seemed to dimin-ish the sting of bottom of the rugby heap. Field work, building, digging holes, or even peeling potatoes had simply never come up. When it did, he was astonished by how incompetent he was.

How did a youngster so ill-equipped for the hardships of a pioneering lifestyle ended up in Palestine at the nascence of Jewish statehood? It was not exactly an accident but a coming together of unexpected circumstances — serendipity, of sorts. Perhaps even beshert, if one believed in fate.

Before Der was Der, he was Haimy, the bookish son of Lithu-anian Jewish immigrant parents settled in South Africa. Haimy was in many ways completely unexceptional. He was bad at sports and good at academics, graduating high school at the anticipated top of his class. Since his mother liked to think she was a sophisticated art appreciator, he was allowed to study liter-ature at the University of Cape Town despite his father's complete befuddlement. He wanted his obviously bright son to study at the university, but literature? "*Vos far a prufeshun is dos?*"

"I will be a poet," Haimy told his father.

"From a poet one can eat?" his father asked.

"I will be a great poet," Haimy assured his father.

Ultimately, his mother, who was full of self-derived platitudes about the world and its nature, including a fundamental belief that the suppression of artistic tendencies led inevitably to madness, enabled him to pursue poetry as a *prufeshun*. When he completed his degree and was offered an opportunity to pursue graduate stud-ies in poetry in Cambridge, England, his father acquiesced again. Smart but uneducated himself, Haimy's father was secretly proud that his son was pursuing things that would ensure the only marks on his hands would be from ink, not labour. About madness he knew little and understood less.

Haimy was to begin the fall term of 1948, "reading English" as it was called. He was left with a gap between his South African studies and his Cambridge studies. Again encouraged by mother, his father agreed to let Haimy spend time in London before school, bankrolling the adventure entirely. Haimy would live with his uncle in London before going to Cambridge, so everything was set for a seamless continuation of his life of means, privilege, and intellectual advantage.

All went according to plan for the first month or so. Haimy

loved London. Compared to the provinciality and breathtaking beauty of Cape Town, it seemed both sophisticated and gritty. Within seconds of docking in England and disembarking from the *Winchester Castle*, the military troop ship that had carried him across the ocean in relative luxury, Haimy fell hard for London: grey, soot-covered buildings and majestic, crumbling edifices desperately in need of repair, Europe affected by the war in so many ways that had not touched South Africa. Haimy immediately convinced himself that experiencing this underbelly of reality was the only way to truly wax poetic about beauty and write truly transformational poetry. He needed a foil to the mountains and the oceans of his childhood, and London provided exactly that. The grittiness thrilled him, and he was naive enough to forget that someone else was paying his way to *la vie bohème*, this omission another casualty of the selective lens of youth.

Haimy's dearest friend, Bernie — a new doctor, a few years older and married to Fiona, a new nurse — lived in London. When Bernie and Fiona were not working or at Zionist meetings, they treated Haimy like an adored house pet or court jester. They gave him a key to the rundown flat they rented, greeting him gleefully when they arrived to find him waiting. They cooked him strange meals on their single gas burner from rationed supplies, introducing him to deprivation that seemed to him romantic and avant-garde. Taking him to seedy pubs, getting him drunk, they delighted in his recitations from Shakespeare and Auden and Larkin. They had fun together, and Haimy felt his life was finally beginning.

One afternoon, Haimy arrived at Bernie and Fiona's to find them frantically packing their meagre belongings.

"Where are you off to?" Haimy asked.

"Palestine," Bernie said.

"Now?" Haimy said.

It had always been Bernie's plan to go to Palestine, but at this moment was a shock to Haimy.

"Everyone knows a war is coming," Bernie said. "The passing of the UN resolution seals the deal. They need doctors."

"Just like that, then? You're off?" he said but thought, *What about me?*

He too had been in the Zionist Youth in South Africa, singing the Hebrew songs of the pioneers and dancing the frenzied horas of an independent Jewish homeland. He had participated in endless discussions, impotently passing resolutions about realities over which he had no influence or real understanding. Nonetheless, his friends' departure would certainly put a damper on his remaining months in London.

"Come with us to Paris," Fiona said. "We'll be there for a while before getting the boat from Marseille. It will be fun."

Haimy went to his uncle's to pack a bag for his fortnight in Paris. Twelve neatly pressed dress shirts, ten pairs of underpants, ten pairs of black socks, and a change of trousers were bundled into a brown leather satchel. Wearing his summer wool blazer and a fedora, he tucked a small volume of Keats' sonnets into his breast pocket and went to meet Bernie and Fiona at the railway station. *Such fun! Paris on a whim!* he thought.

They checked into a grubby *pension*, and Bernie and Fiona rushed to the Zionist offices. Haimy tried visiting a friend, but halfway to his destination, the taxi driver explained that he had run out of petrol and rationing meant more would not be forthcoming. Disappointed, Haimy embraced the romantic, film noir lens of his situation and walked the streets of Paris, self-consciously admiring himself in shop windows, fancying himself a brooding poet in Paris: a vision of what he imagined looking like more than what he actually looked like.

Haimy found his friends getting into a taxicab headed for the
railway station again.

"Where are you going?"

"Marseille," Fiona said, unconcerned that they were leaving
him.

"What about Paris?" Haimy asked.

"They need us at the DP camp near Marseille," Bernie said.
"You don't need us to enjoy Paris."

Real Haimy flooded to the surface of the idealized version he
had been trying on like paper doll reflections. Stung and unmoored
by the thought of being alone in a strange place, Haimy said, "I'm
coming with you. I'll grab my bag."

Haimy realized how silly he must seem to his friends. "I can't
very well say goodbye to you without notice. We'll say goodbye
properly in Marseille," he said, embarrassed his cowardice might
show.

Haimy loved the train, but as the young master in South
Africa, a sleeper car was always available for overnight trips to
the countryside. His overnight trip to Marseille was the first he
had spent sitting upright. They arrived in Marseille tired and rumpled, no doubt contributing to Haimy's ill temper and angst.

Bernie and Fiona had a secret address they were to find, but at
the station a man shouted the secret from the platform: "Rue de
Capucines." Whisked away by the emissaries of the Jewish Immigration Aid Services, Haimy was alone again.

He wished he was brave and tough and independent, but he
was none of those. No reflection from a storefront of a well-
dressed young man, fedora perched at a rakish angle, shirt collar
unbuttoned, rebelliously tieless, could mask his overwhelming
sense of vulnerability. Parking his belongings at a hostel near the
railway station in a rough part of town, Haimy ventured out.
The prostitutes, a breed he knew only from books and movies

where they were often granted hearts of gold to go along with their hard-luck lives, called out aggressively, intimidating him with their menacing come-ons. The men on the streets, sailors he presumed, seemed brutish and hostile, making him acutely aware of his own mincing style. "*Coccinelle*," they shouted, recognizing in him something so subliminal he felt faint. There was nothing romantic or fairy-tale-like about any of it. Haimy felt exposed and terrified. He bought himself a baguette and scurried back to his dismal little room, spending the rest of the day and night cowering in his quarters, eating torn morsels of bread and reading Keats poems as though they were a healing balm, alternating between admonishing himself for being a scaredy-cat and patting himself on the back for knowing well enough to not take unnecessary risks. *Coccinelle*, he thought.

In the morning, eager to track down his friends and desperate to leave his dingy room, Haimy found the Zionist offices on Rue de Capucines. His request to visit the displaced persons camp where he was told he might find his friends took no one aback. He was offered a ride on a lorry, brimming with American and Algerian Jews all on their way to help the Zionist cause in Palestine, loud and boisterous, singing and joking with one another, their swagger reeking of pheromone-charged aphrodisiac.

"Choo choo ch'boogie," the Americans sang.

Haimy envied their confidence. He held his hand over his breast pocket, feeling his book of poems pressing against his chest as the truck bumped and swayed toward Le Grande Arenas, the decommissioned army base in Port de Buc that had been repurposed as a DP camp.

Bracing for his disclosure as a fraud, an interloper unentitled to entry, he found instead that no one seemed to care who he was or why he was there. In fact, dressed in a blazer, trousers, a clean pressed shirt, and a fresh shave, he was treated with a degree of reverence.

Plodding around the DP camp, intently focused on finding his friends, Haimy did not see the corrugated metal barracks with strings of laundry hanging at their entrances. He didn't smell the pervasive fermented manure and cow feed from the surrounding farms that helped mask the stench of humans living in close, minimal quarters. Nor did he see the makeshift micro-communities, formed out of necessity for a sense of home regardless of its temporary nature. Haimy was oblivious to the life of the camp, too focused on finding his own lifeline.

The vast camp bustled with throngs of people; nonetheless, he found his friends. With the inadequate medical facilities overwhelmed by the needs of the very sick, Bernie and Fiona were tasked with informal rounds of the camp tending to the uncritically ill as best they could. With almost no drugs or equipment, they had little actual help to offer the ailing, but not incapacitated, population. Escorting them on their rounds gave Haimy a sense of relative comfort. He was with his friends, and they had purpose, so he started seeing and hearing. He listened as Bernie took histories, mostly in Yiddish with smatterings of other languages interspersed, inquiring where they had come from, how long they had been in Marseille, what their primary complaints and symptoms were, and the like.

Haimy's grandparents spoke Yiddish to him, and he replied in English. It was understood that Yiddish was what old Jews spoke. But in the camp, what surprised and moved him unexpectedly was that these people who appeared to be old were in fact closer to his own age than his parents' or grandparents' ages. More profoundly, it was the children speaking Yiddish that untethered him, as though everything he had ever done, wanted, or understood about the world was frivolous and meaningless.

By 1947, the world was aware of the atrocities of the Holocaust, but Haimy had never actually seen or met any survivors
of the concentration camps until his arrival at the DP camp. For
the first time, he saw, both figuratively and literally, people with
numbers tattooed on their forearms.

"*Vos is dos?*" he asked, pointing at the number on the arm of
a man suffering from chronic diarrhea and toothache, ubiquitous
complaints of the previously malnourished.

"*Dos is mine tsifer.* Everybody had a number," the man
answered, resigned to the fact of his permanent branding.

Haimy was overcome. "I'm coming with you!" he said to his
friends.

"Where are you coming?" Fiona asked.

"I'm coming to Palestine," Haimy said.

Retrieving his belongings from the hostel — his new clothes,
bought for him by his mother, laundered by his aunt's house-
keeper — he was suddenly, for the first time in his life, both
conscious and self-conscious of his privilege. He changed into the
creased garments he had worn and scrunched into his satchel the
day before. "Now I am like everyone else waiting for passage to
Palestine." Except he knew he wasn't.

There were all sorts of people going to Palestine who had not
survived the war in any direct Holocaust way, but the real survivors were obvious and visible to everyone. It wasn't just their
tattoos or their accents that set them apart from the American
volunteers or the North African recruits, but a look in their eyes
that testified that they had witnessed things that could never be
unseen and their hearts were broken in ways even they could
scarcely fathom.

In the communal showers, Haimy showered among a group of
universally circumcised men for the first time in his life. In school,

he had been one of the few Jewish boys, and they would cluster together when forced to shower after a gym class or sporting match. Yet here he was, amongst his own and never more poignantly aware of being different. He felt intensely guilty and entirely unsure why. Had he done something wrong? What exactly? For those and other questions he had no answers, nor any vocabulary.

Haimy was assigned to a cool, dank barracks that felt crowded despite the apparent absence of human life. He deposited his satchel on an unclaimed cot.

"Don't leave that there," came a voice in Yiddish.

Squinting into the dimness, Haimy spotted a small, sinewy man sitting on a cot, dressed only in underpants.

"My bag? *Mine zak?*" Haimy asked.

"*Gonoivim*, Thieves." The man lay down on his back, placed one hand behind his head, rubbed his jaw with the other, and turned away from Haimy. "They steal everything."

Taking his collection of sonnets from his satchel, Haimy clutched his book like a shield, slung the bag across his body, and went looking for Bernie and Fiona.

Wandering, he stopped briefly to watch a group of children playing a game of kick the can, shouting at one another in Yiddish. The children were doing exactly what children anywhere in the world might do, but hearing them speak Yiddish struck him as so strange, as though it lit a flashing sign above his head that read, *Here stands a man who knows nothing of the world! Here lives a man with no understanding of the plight of the Jewish people.* Haimy cringed at his own ignorance. So, when he learned through inquiries in his broken Yiddish that Bernie and Fiona had been taken to the port to board a ship, leaving him once again ostensibly orphaned, his thoughts of abandoning his impulsive decision to run away to the war in Palestine were only fleeting.

With nothing to do but wait, Haimy sat down on an over-
turned bucket near the entrance to his barracks, placed his satchel
on the ground, and read his book of poetry in the afternoon sun.

A shadow crossed his page.

"*Vos hobn mir doh?*" A hard-featured, burly man hooked arm
in arm to an equally sour-faced woman with stringy red hair and
no eyebrows or lashes stood over Haimy. Looking up, he blinked
into the sunlight.

"Chaim," he said, holding out his hand in friendly greeting.

His grasp was not returned. The couple circled him like beasts
of prey, he their quarry. Their presence was unmistakably threatening, and Haimy once again had a fleeting moment of regret
about his decision to make his life relevant in the face of history
and the Jews.

"*Der professor is ayn lamdan,*" said the woman.

"*Nein, nein nisht ayn lamdan.* Not a scholar. Not a professor.
Just poems, *poemeh,*" Haimy showed the book he was reading,
instinctively picking up his satchel and clutching it close.

"*Der professor raidst English,*" said the man, continuing to
circle Haimy like a shark.

"Yes, I speak English," Haimy said.

"*Loz ir. Gay avec.*" A thin, neat-looking man appeared, his
long, delicate fingers indicating the direction he wanted the vultures to go.

"*Vos?* We aren't doing any harm," said the man. "We were
just introducing ourselves to Der Professor. He seems all alone,
like he could use a friend or two."

"Der Professor needs someone to take care of him," said the
woman in mock sympathy. She smiled through tightly gritted,
decayed teeth. "This can be a dangerous place."

"Go away, both of you." The man moved closer, revealing
a petite young woman hidden behind him. The young woman,

pretty in a robin's egg way, had striking green eyes that lacked the usual moisture of eyes, rendering them almost velveteen and decidedly un-sparkling. Her hair was thin, short, and the colour of sun-bleached straw. Her skin was so fair and translucent Haimy thought he could almost see the blood moving in her veins. He had never seen anyone so fragile-looking in his life. She mimicked the man's pointing finger with her own.

Scowling like a couple of teenage toughs reprimanded by the police for a misdemeanour, the menacing pair retreated.

"They are harmless. They're nobody's friends, but their bark is worse than their bite. Don't trust them. It won't serve you," the gentleman said. "So, Der Professor, what's your name?" He extended his hand in a courtly gesture.

"Chaim," said Haimy.

"*Nein.* Everybody's Chaim," the woman said. Her childlike voice and naïveté were oddly compelling. "It's too confusing. There is nobody else called Der Professor, so it won't be at all confusing."

"Estie, maybe he doesn't want to be Der Professor." The man spoke so gently, as though the woman was made of powdered sugar that might blow away in even the slightest breeze.

"Don't you think it's a dignified name?" Estie asked Haimy.

"I think they were poking fun at me. Calling me a wimp." Haimy mimed a limp wrist, lest his insufficient Yiddish be mis-understood. "I don't think they meant it as a compliment."

"Yitz, you think he's right?" Estie asked the man as though he were an authority on everything.

"They're not nice people. It is unlikely they were being compli-mentary. Nonetheless, Estie is also right. There are an awful lot of Chaims around, and a name that gives you a new start for a new life … could it be a bad thing?"

Haimy thought for a moment. Introducing himself as Chaim was not due to a premeditated thought that his journey to Palestine presented an opportunity for a name change from the anglicized Haimy to the Hebraized Chaim, it had just come out. Perhaps, stumbling along in his broken Yiddish he presented himself as Chaim, but even his Boba and Zaideh called him Haimy, not Chaim. Perhaps, he thought sheepishly, it smacked of posturing affect. He felt himself blush.

"What are your names?" Haimy asked.

"This is Estie. I am Yitz. From Yitzchak," he said.

"Are there many Haimys? I am usually called Haimy."

"So many Haimys. So many Chaims. Not one Der Professor," Estie said.

"I don't think Der Professor would ever suit me," Haimy said. "It would be like calling oneself *chochem* or smarty-pants, but maybe ..." Haimy paused. There was something about this young woman that made him want to not disappoint her. "Maybe just Der. Like a joke that we share only between the three of us."

"That's wonderful!" Estie cheered as though she had been given a present. "Don't you think it suits him, Yitz? A new name for our new friend Der!"

THEIR BOAT, THE *Negba*, poorly disguised as a leisure vessel with a fresh coat of paint (navy blue on the hull, white on the decks), jounced across the water. The passengers, unaccustomed to the sea and its churning waves, jostled for positions near the railing where they could heave and spew with less public humiliation and mess. Up top on deck was more bearable than the cramped quarters below. Salt air breezes whisked away sweat from brows and bodies. The boisterous, noisy singing of the mostly American crew — "Hey bapa ree bop ..." — drowning out the cacophony of retching that overwhelmed. The lively songs a succour of sorts, an indication of life still being lived to the fullest.

In time, most were blessed with sea legs, which afforded them a modicum of relief from the emetic convulsions of acclimation. Only then did Der realize that he had been clutching his felt fedora so tightly he had destroyed its careful construction, leaving a handprint where his grasp resisted the salt spray of the waves.

The ship stopped to refuel in the Sicilian port of Messina. Unlike many of the passengers, Der had a passport granting him the privilege to disembark. Having shed a thin layer of the naïveté he wore like a soft blanket, he offered a bribe to a less-than-vigilant, probably drunk gangplank guard that allowed his friends to accompany him ashore. The predatory pair he had tried to avoid took advantage and followed close behind.

The passengers were not permitted to leave the grungy, bustling port. Sailors and longshoremen shouted discordantly in the lilting music of Italian dialect amidst vast stacks of blue, grey, and rust-coloured shipping containers and the putrid smells of rotting sea life. The five passengers, relieved to be on solid ground for a few hours, wandered around the dreary enclosure, avoiding pools of oil-streaked sludge. Amidst the dull steel boats and boxes, an incongruous pink-and-white striped awning hung off a bisected shipping container with a hand-painted sign, *Espresso e Cassata*. Behind a moist pink counter stood a plump young girl no more than twelve or thirteen years old, her pink-and-white face framed by a shock of the blackest hair, which was pulled back from her forehead by an Alice band adorned with tiny, naked, plastic babies. The girl sucked on a spoon she intermittently pulled through her rosebud lips and swirled around in a small glass bowl thinly coated in the milky residue of a treat already consumed.

"I will buy you ice cream," Der said, feeling suddenly, acutely that there was still hope in the world and that somehow he bore the burden of confirming that for his friends.

"Oh, ice cream!" exclaimed Estie, her skin as diaphanous and pale as an embryonic sack. "I can't even remember ice cream."

Squeezing her delicate hand with his spindly fingers, Yitzchak choked back the emotion that welled up so strong and sudden inside him. "I remember ice cream," he said.

"I remember ice cream too," said the rough man.

"Will our little professor buy us ice cream?" The other woman batted her nonexistent eyelashes.

Der didn't want to buy ice cream for everybody. He wanted to treat his friends, but he was afraid of the toughs. They were brutes, and he knew it was better to appease them than to cross them.

Standing in the misty drizzle of a Mediterranean winter, the five unlikely companions ate ice cream. It was sweet and salty and creamy, made from what could only be real milk and cream and sugar: real ice cream, potent enough to evoke memories of past lives.

Two shoeless, dirty, threadbare children appeared; they drew their right fingers close, claw-like, to closed lips while their other hands circled their concave bellies.

Handing over his ice cream, Der said, "I would buy them ice cream if I had more money."

"You're an idiot," the nasty man scoffed.

"They are hungry." Der checked his pockets for coins.

"And you think that your ice cream will make them not hungry," said the soulless woman. "Tomorrow they will be hungry again. You change nothing."

Der shrugged.

"Shh," said Yitzchak, watching Estie eat her ice cream, eyes closed, a faint tune humming through her cold lips.

Yitzchak was not a man of many words. He said what needed to be said and little else. That was not a problem because when she felt at ease, Estie talked enough for at least two people. Estie and Der spoke from Messina to Palestine. The seasickness now more or less abated left many idle hours on board. As though the ice cream had had a Proustian effect on Estie, memories and recollections of things past and entombed were unleashed. She spoke of things she had never given voice to before and would never in her life speak of again. Yitz contributed parts of his own undisclosed narrative, also never divulged, now carried from his tongue far out to sea. Der listened and learned, asking questions about the war, the camps, the atrocities, the loss, the heartache, the things too unbelievable for reason or understanding applied from anything he knew or, in fact, the lexicon of humanity in general.

The ship dropped anchor three miles off the coast of Palestine in the Mediterranean Sea, and with the dropping of that anchor, Estie and Yitz took a private oath that they would start their new life, that they would not revisit the horrors of the past, and that they would never leave one another. Locking their promise up, they dropped the key overboard. It was the only way they knew to move forward.

Because of the British blockade and the numerous ships of refugees that had already been stopped and turned back around to Cyprus and Italy and other ports whence they came, the passengers from the *Negba* were disembarked into small fishing boats and ferried clandestinely past the military patrol boats under cover of night into the port at Netanyah. Der, prone to imaginings of literary proportions, was titillated by his foray into the undercover mission — more so than the other passengers, whose experiences left them significantly more apprehensive.

In truth, by the time the *Negba* had arrived on the shores of Palestine, with the United Nations plan signed, the British already had one foot out the proverbial door. The stealth operation was successful not because of the skill with which it was carried out compared to previous vessels that had been caught and denied entry, like the *Exodus* and many others, but rather because by then no one was watching too closely. They made land in darkness while the Brits turned away.

The jubilation, silently experienced, sparked an electric current that ran from the land through each passenger, completing a circuit so vital it restarted hearts long stopped, lit eyes that had been dark since before hopeful memory served, circulated blood congealed in veins. The juxtaposition of trust, belief, and hope against pain, anguish, and bereavement too vast to be defined hung heavily on the damp salt air that night in late 1947.

Estie, Yitz, Der, and the rest of the passengers were piled into trucks and whisked to an encampment of large tents: Beit Lid Absorption Centre. Passports were seized, and passengers invented their own names, declared their self-ordained marital statuses, passing themselves off as teachers who had never taught, farmers who had never dug in the soil, or tailors who didn't know how to sew. Possibility was the only defining parameter.

"Yitzchak Wolffe *un* Esther Wolffe," Yitz said to the young woman completing identity documents.

"Haimy Der Levy," Der chose.

Der was up with the sun and an unsettled tummy after a night on an auditorium stage. Yitzchak and Estie, for the first time in their remembered lives, slept the kind of sleep only the worriless sleep.

Wearing his blazer, a crumpled shirt, and his salt-stained fedora, Der went walking. Had he been wearing an African tribal costume, he could not have looked more out of place.

In a small, sandy garden, humming Zionist tunes, *shiray sochnut*, a young woman planted tiny purple flowers. Der, always up for a good romantic cliché, slowed to listen and watch the young pioneer working the land. He thought he recognized the girl but knew this phenomenon of seeming to recognize familiar faces when one is far from home. In London, he thought he saw his parents and grandparents repeatedly in the faces of strangers at a distance. Approaching, as though he had not crossed continents and oceans and seas arriving in a brand-new place, neither apparition nor mistaken identity were the culprits. It was his old friend Naomi. Der felt a surge of joy known well by newcomers in strange lands: the elation of the familiar, a *landsman*, a gateway to belonging.

Though Naomi had been among the first of his peers to go to Palestine, Der didn't trust his own eyes. "Naomi?"

"Haimy! What in God's name are you wearing? The heat will be here soon, and you look like you are off to a lecture."

"I've just gotten off the boat," he explained.

"Never mind that. We need to dress you for the world you are in now."

Having left the encampment dressed as the young scholar he was meant to be, Der returned to Beit Lid in a navy-blue kibbutz work shirt, khaki pants, and a *kova tembel*, the iconic bucket-shaped sun hat popular in the early years of Jewish settlement.

"So fast a pioneer you've become, *mine Der*," Estie said, seeing her friend.

Nothing was more and less true. Der was quite a useless pioneer, but he remained Estie's "*mine Der*" for the rest of their interwoven lives.

BEIT LID ABSORPTION camp was, despite its hardships, a happy place. Barely edible but adequate and plentiful meals were served in a defunct military dining hall, and no one went hungry. There were olives aplenty, margarine, rough bread, and sometimes fried fish that was everybody's favourite. Shower and bathroom facilities were crude and communal, but there was clean running water, which was sometimes warm. The accommodations were primitive and crowded with people assigned to family tents, sometimes with members of their actual families and sometimes not. Yitzchak and Esther shared a tent with another young couple with a small baby born in Marseille only weeks before the *Negba* sailed. They strung a blanket between the two halves of the tent for the pretence of privacy. Nonetheless, most people expressed few grievances. Most of the temporary residents of the camp felt Zionistically optimistic, and that often, though not always, translated to happy.

A stream of visitors came to Beit Lid, people who had immigrated to Palestine from Europe before the war, in search of family and friends they prayed had survived the genocide. More often than not, they were disappointed.

"*Haut ver es iz phoon Saposkin aungekumen?*" they asked, the names of shtetls or towns from which they wondered if anybody had arrived interchangeable. A mother from Bialystok, a brother from Minsk, a cousin, a sister, an aunt from Motol or Babtai or Przytyk, who by some miracle had arrived on the shores of Palestine perhaps? Or if perchance anyone knew, had information of any sort, this too was more than could be hoped for. On rarer occasions, when a connection, however tenuous, was made — someone who had seen a common relative at some point still alive during the war, maybe a rumour about a shtetl where people had been hidden by sympathetic neighbours, or, the ultimate jackpot, an actual reunification with loved ones — the rejoicing was epic. Likewise, confirmation of annihilation elicited monumental, inconsolable grief. Differentiating between the emoting of either outcome from any distance was impossible.

Whatever help could be offered was forthcoming. The luckiest, the ones whose family, friends, or townsfolk found them, were offered housing outside the camp, introductions toward employment, opportunity to start over, optimism. But no one came looking for Yitzchak or Esther, and they knew no one would.

Even with the disappointments of watching others leave Beit Lid to begin their new lives, life in the camp in all its squalor was not without celebrations. Boys who had missed out on bar mitzvahs and circumcisions during the war were welcomed into Jewish ritual with singing and dancing and tears enough to fill oceans. But the event that generated the greatest excitement in the camp was a wedding! The first wedding in Zion! Hallelujah had never been so true.

The young couple, she sixteen, he minutes past seventeen and barely old enough to marry, had, like Yitzchak and Esther and many others, no one but each other and demanded they be allowed to wed, despite the girl being underage. The rabbinate in Netanya made exception to the minimum age of seventeen but refused to provide a ketubah, the traditional Jewish marriage contract.

Preparations ensued, and in the face of nothing, everything seemed luxurious. In lieu of a wedding feast, youngsters from a nearby kibbutz working in the camp as provisional settlement workers brought sweet fizzy drinks, wafers filled with sugary frosting, and oranges for the bride and groom. Someone rummaged through bundles of second-hand clothes sent by the Joint Distribution Committee in America and found a white dress that Yitzchak transformed into a beautiful wedding dress. The groom wore a white blouse, a *chultza Russit* — a Russian shirt — that laced in a series of crisscrosses between the neckline and the left shoulder with a blue string. The bride wore a wreath of purple flowers in her hair. A garbage truck, aggressively scoured and decorated with shrubbery by excited well-wishers, was transformed, as effectively as Cinderella's pumpkin, into a wedding chariot that carried the young couple to the rabbinate in Netanya.

Revellers sang and danced the hora around the truck before it left Beit Lid. The newlyweds were given a wedding gift by the Jewish Agency of two nights in a hotel in Netanya. After their honeymoon, they returned to Beit Lid to a small, two-person pup tent, their new marital home. The Jewish Agency gave them a bed and a pair of austere candlesticks. Scrounged packing crates that smelled vaguely of the fish they had transported were repurposed as makeshift furniture in their private tent.

Esther was jealous. Not that she wasn't delighted for their happiness, but she too wanted a private tent, a pretty dress to wear even if only for a few days, a hotel holiday, a wedding, but most of all, she wanted her own candlesticks.

"Let's get married, Yitzchak," she said, never disclosing her covetousness. It would have been unseemly to confess her material desires in a place, at a time, when no one had anything and every-one else seemed entirely content with their nothing. Esther was embarrassed by her avarice, but she begged, "Please, Yitzchak, let's have a wedding."

Yitzchak, who from the moment they had met did whatever he could to care for, to protect, and to please Esther, refused. "I don't need any fanatical rabbi or any undependable God to sanction my love for you, Esther."

In March, when life in Beit Lid was wearing on Esther's nerves, a saviour appeared in the form of Mr. Eliezer Boim, an immigrant to the Levant from Latvia just before the European borders closed in 1939. He and his wife had escaped because being childless made running easier.

Like the others, Mr. Boim came hoping erroneously that the angel of death had by some miracle passed over their families' houses. Beit Lid was not the first camp he had visited. He was already fairly certain his family would never appear.

Stopping a towheaded young woman, he asked, "*Bist ir durkh gelegnhayt Letland?* Are you by chance Latvian?"

"Yes," Esther replied to the squat, square man with thick, hairy ears, a meaty nose, and sausage fingers.

"*Riebini?*" Mr. Boim specified.

"*Nein, Viski.*" Esther deflated.

Mr. Boim threw his arms around Esther's neck and began to weep, because Viski was the closest he had gotten to Riebini.

Esther joined him in his anguish. They stood forehead to forehead, surrendering to the grief they resisted most of the time, because only thus could they continue to live. At this precise moment, Mr. Boim admitted to himself that his family were never coming. His modest assistance need not be saved greedily for ghosts.

They cried together until their wells ran dry. Mr. Boim blew his considerable nose indelicately into a white cotton handkerchief, which he then folded neatly and returned to his trouser pocket.

"Are you alone here?" he asked Esther.

"Yes, just me and my Yitzchak, my husband," she said, embarrassed by the word *husband* on her lips.

"No family?"

Esther looked at the ground, shuffled her feet in the dirt, and shook her head in a barely perceptible "no." More than that would have been too painful.

"Can you take me to your husband?" Mr. Boim asked.

Yitzchak sat on a wooden crate, sewing a button on a woman's skirt. He looked up. "For the young mother. Her clothes are falling off of her."

"You can sew?" Mr. Boim asked.

Yitzchak nodded, suspicious of exploitation.

"You can use also a sewing machine, maybe?"

Yitzchak nodded again.

"Excellent!" Mr. Boim said.

"And who are you that my capacity to sew is of interest?" Yitzchak asked.

Esther introduced Yitzchak and Mr. Boim and explained where he was from and when he had left. Yitzchak understood his presence in the camp.

"I think perhaps I can be of help to you." Mr. Boim sighed deeply.

Mr. and Mrs. Boim had a two-and-a-half-room storefront flat that shared a kitchen and bathroom with the three other flats in the building at number thirty Shenkin Street in Tel Aviv. Had it been up to Mr. Boim, he would simply have given the front room to Yitzchak and Esther, but Mrs. Boim was not as generous. Probably no more than thirty-eight or thirty-nine years old, she looked like an old witch with sprouting moles on her chin and nose — the undiagnosed hormone imbalance that no doubt caused her barrenness also responsible for her unfortunately manly features and follicles. Her sour nature could not be so easily explained.

"Are they going to spend their whole lives as victims?" Mrs. Boim said. "We should pay because we had the sense to leave?"

"From what would you like them to pay?" Mr. Boim asked his wife.

"You said he can sew! So let him sew!" said the witch.

In the large plate glass window that faced the street, Mr. Boim put a small wooden table and a Pfaff 130 sewing machine that he and his wife had brought with them from Europe, though neither one of them could sew. He took Yitzchak to the fabric merchants on Nahalat Binyamin to purchase a piece of cloth, for which Mr. Boim paid, swearing Yitzchak to secrecy, lest the miserly Mrs. Boim catch wind of her husband's generosity. Yitzchak sewed two curtains from the green gingham with yellow flowers; one he hung

in the window and kept open during business hours. The second
he hung behind the sewing machine, hiding their Jewish Agency
standard-issue bed from the storefront.

During the day, Yitzchak mended whatever he could — zippers,
hems, buttonholes, let this out, take this in — whatever people in
a time of rampant pauperism were willing to pay a few *grushim*
for. Before the war, Yitzchak's family had been prosperous fur-
riers, making coats and sundry for the most exclusive clientele
in Europe. Trained at the school for fashion design in Warsaw,
Yitzchak developed a small reputation in Tel Aviv as a skilled and
conscientious tailor. Women's fashion was his speciality.

Mr. Boim took an immediate paternal liking to Esther, taking
her under his wing and teaching her bookkeeping. Esther's school-
ing had abruptly ended before she was nine, but she demonstrated
a facility with numbers and was extremely organized. Eliezer Boim
took Esther with him up and down Shenkin Street, along Allenby,
and even in the fancier Ben Yehuda Street shops he kept books for,
standing over her as she tallied numbers with a fountain pen in
neat ledgers, cheering and encouraging her flawless penmanship,
her accurate sums, and her rigorous review of all her accounting.

"Always ink!" Mr. Boim instructed. "Should anyone ask that
you keep two sets of books, you tell me!"

With Esther in tow, Mr. Boim's clientele grew. She was pretty,
delicate, and completely oblivious to the attention she attracted.
Mr. Boim was not. When he started sending Esther out on her
own, he chose carefully, sending her only where he trusted she
would be treated gently.

After Mrs. Boim collected her rent, Yitzchak bought fabrics
with what was left, one piece at a time, sewing fashionable dresses
for Esther. He wanted her to feel confident and hoped his dresses
would provide a protective layer. He hoped she might feel as
beautiful as she objectively was.

UNLIKE YITZCHAK AND Esther, who arrived as immigrants, Der found himself a bit lost in the tumult of the historic gap between the British Mandate and a Jewish State. Having relinquished his passport upon arrival, he had no official status nor confirmed identity. It seemed as good a choice as any he had made since his departure from London to attach himself to a group of not quite friends but more than acquaintances from Cape Town going to the Lower Galilee to Beit Keshet, a kibbutz established in 1944 by Youth Movement members from abroad on land purchased by the Jewish National Fund.

Though indisputably formative, Der's year on the kibbutz bore no resemblance to the pioneering he'd envisaged from the Zionist posters of his youth: muscular boys, olive-skinned girls, all sporting de rigueur *kova tembels*, happily working the land and making the desert bloom. What he'd imagined was himself seamlessly inserted among them, but the reality of Der's kibbutz experience was significantly less romantic and decidedly less pretty both personally and collectively. While it was a time of great excitement and optimism in the country, it was also a time of harsh and brutal realities. The kibbutz had nothing except for mud when it rained and dust when it was blisteringly hot. From the moment the United Nations signed the Partition Plan, Arabs began killing Jews and Jews began retaliating against Arabs. It was the Wild West Mideast style and a jarring reality kick in the pants for a starry-eyed poet.

Beit Keshet had a population of about one hundred permanent members and two dozen transient volunteers. Each day before dawn, the volunteers gathered in the communal dining room for work assignments. "*Mishka, lool. Nina, sadeh. Yaki, sadeh. Ruti, machbesah. Leonora, mitbach.*" Each day, Der waited anxiously. He wanted to toil in the chicken coops and the fields with the burly *chalutzim*, working the land and fulfilling the Zionist dream. For a brief time, that was in fact what happened.

On the sixteenth of March, 1948, an ambush of armed assailants emerged Trojan horse–like from a herd of Bedouin sheep in the fields. In an attempt by Lebanese and Syrian troops to capture Sereja, a neighbouring village, and Beit Keshet. Seven members of the kibbutz were killed in a fierce battle that took place in the very fields where Der so desperately wanted to till the soil, sing Zionist songs, and dance the hora. After that, nobody wanted to sing or dance.

Collective tolerance grew thin, and paranoia about their neighbours in the surrounding Arab villages coloured the community in suspicious fear. Arriving for dinner one night, Der, the other volunteers, and some of the members were barred from entering the communal hall, watching and listening through the windows for hours as a group of *kibbutznikim* surrounded an Arab youth from a neighbouring village.

"Spy! Murderer! What were you doing in our fields? Who sent you?" They hurled epithets and threats at the terrified boy of no more than eighteen or nineteen years old.

Contrapuntally, a minority group of members voiced an alternate sentiment. "Leave him be! He's just a boy who wandered into our field accidentally. This mistrust will be our undoing!"

The stress of a war that was literally in their backyard, combined with Der's fundamental ineptitude, became a catalyst for short tempers and less-than-good-natured razzing. The kibbutznikim began calling Der *"Geveret Der Ha'chofer"* — Mrs. Der the digger. Unable to keep up with most of the backbreaking tasks, he was handed a shovel to dig rows from the hard-baked dirt of the fields, where his pace didn't hold anyone else up. In the poultry coop, he dug a hole for composting the putrid chicken guano that accumulated at rates disproportional to the meagre number of chickens, to which he contributed vomit retched up from the overpowering stench.

Der was clumsy and weak and, despite his African upbringing, completely heat intolerant. He passed out in the fields, the orchards, and the gardens before being relegated to indoor tasks. Reality didn't afford the kibbutznikim any extra patience for a bourgeois milksop.

He was not much better in the kitchen or laundry than at digging. He was overwhelmed by the steam of industrial kettles used for both washing clothes and cooking. They put him on a stool in the furthest corner of the kitchen, peeling vegetables, when they had any, which he detested. He didn't mind folding socks and underwear in the laundry, where he got to work with Shula, a girl from Cape Town. She was good company and amused Der with her lack of filter, capacity for inventive conversation, and kindness.

"Imagine you are stranded on a deserted island; which three books would you take and why?" she asked, always answering her own questions thoughtfully in turn. "If you could only choose three historical characters to help you, who would you choose to build a ship with? I'll go first! Noah and Jesus. Noah has experience, and Jesus is a carpenter. I'm sure you'll think of someone much cleverer, but I think my choices are sound."

Shula had a unique capacity to find the good in people, particularly when they were not at their best. Der quite happily, if a bit slowly, folded community socks owned by no one and underwear marked with secret codes ostensibly identifiable only by their wearers and talked with Shula without feeling like less of a person.

At twenty-three, Shula was possessed of a maturity that made Der forget they were practically the same age. "You must eat even

in the heat. Take a break and drink water! Go fold away from the
heat. I need you falling down like a *loch in kopf!*"

Despite Shula, Der's work apart from the community was iso-
lating. When loneliness defeated him, he left for a few days.

"I need to track down my passport," Der would say, but he
was aware his contribution to the collective was so minimal that
his absence was immaterial.

Hitching a ride, sharing space with bleating sheep or bales of
hay, always got him to Tel Aviv, where he knew only two people.
Frequently, Der arrived at Yitzchak and Esther's modest home in
his khaki work shorts (rolled up with the white pockets sticking
out the bottom), a blue work shirt, standard-issue sandals, and
kova tembel.

"*Oy, mine Der! Du bist a chalutz gevoren!*" Esther greeted
him, so happy to see her Der. He filled with false pride and embarrassment. He knew he was so far from being a pioneer that his
clothes were akin to a child's dress-up version of a king with a
cardboard crown.

Yitzchak and Esther, like everybody at the time, had next to
nothing to offer a guest but were always happy to see him. Food
was scarce. There were eggs and olives, something red and sticky
that resembled jam, dense greyish bread to spread it on, and never
any question that there was enough to share, even though there
was not.

Der would spend a few days with his friends, sleeping on the
floor of the small corridor outside their rented room. Those days
in Tel Aviv were some of the happiest of Der's life. Despite the
infancy of the country, the war that raged, and the abject poverty,
Tel Aviv was, bizarrely, a place of culture, art, theatre, and even
opera! There were several movie houses, numerous theatres with
performances in Yiddish, German, and Hebrew, and an opera
house in Herbert Samuel Square. There were fashionable beauty

salons and cafés full of people. Elegant women with hats and gloves in the heat of summer sat at Café Piltz on the beachfront as though they had not a care in the world.

While Yitzchak and Esther worked, Der wandered the white Bauhaus neighbourhoods of the city, gleefully discovering the Tel Aviv Museum and its ever-changing collection of great European paintings and artwork housed in the basement of Beit Dizengoff on Rothschild Boulevard. Standing guard was a homely and obviously lonely woman with a Polish accent.

"What do these signs next to the paintings mean? The ones that say 'From the Private Collection of So-and-So'?" Der asked her.

Licking her dry, chalky lips as though lubricating a stagnant machine, she replied. "Before the war, many European Jews, in anticipation of the impending conflict, and encouraged by Marc Chagal himself, sent their valuable artworks to Tel Aviv to wait out the war in a secure place. Funny that this was considered a safe place. The additional irony is that the artwork remained safe, but many of its owners did not. Until somebody comes to lay legitimate claim to any of what we have here, we display it on a rotating basis as from the private collection of the owners. We have such a vast collection that I was hired to curate the revolving exhibits. Our city cannot afford its own collection of artwork, and yet we are the keepers of some of the greatest masterpieces of Europe."

"Fascinating," said Der, who was only just beginning to comprehend the impact the war had had on the Jews of Europe.

In the evenings, the green gingham curtain drawn across the storefront window, Der recited poetry for Yitz and Esther, because they had no music, and he couldn't sing. Even though she understood nary a word of what Der spoke, it was music to Esther's ears. Yitzchak and Esther danced, their feet not touching the ground, like the images in the paintings of Chagal; the silt-like dust that collected on every surface, despite Esther's perpetual efforts, swirled on the cool tiled floor. At sunset, the three friends walked down to the beach, shedding their shoes to stroll by the seashore.

Esther loved watching Der build sand sculptures of nudes and mermaids.

"Why can my hands make things that are beautiful and not do anything that is useful?" Der said.

"Because you have a beautiful brain and a gentle heart, mine Der," Esther said, soothing Der's existential kibbutz life bruises.

He was honest with Yitz and Esther about his shortcomings and failures as a *kibbutznik*. Yitz sympathized with Der's feelings of inadequacy. His skill crafting pelts into finery was neither needed nor wanted in the climate of their new homeland.

"It's the heat that's getting to both of us. We should all move to Canada," Yitzchak joked, as though moving to Canada, a place so remote, was preposterous and hilarious.

Despite Der's impulsive relocation and abandonment of his studies, his father was still not only funding his son's adventures but declaiming with Zionist pride his boy's whereabouts. Der treated Yitzchak and Esther to ice cream and movies and arcade games at the seashore. They could see a double bill at the Mograbi Cinema for one lira and twenty agurot. They bought corn on the cob on the beach from an Arab vendor who fished the ears from the milky water. Yitz doused his in so much salt, Der and Esther teased that he should swim in the sea while eating his corn.

Der loved the shooting gallery at the arcade, where he discovered he was quite a keen marksman. Hitting the target with the pellet gun, he won a square of chocolate the three of them nibbled like mice as it melted between their fingers.

Yitzchak was shy about Der's generosity. "Let's go for a walk on the beach," he said when Der suggested movies or cafés.

"That too," Der said, as though a walk on the beach cost the same as a luxury item.

Yitz always reached for his billfold, but Der said, "You'll get it next time" or "Take it off my bill."

When Der suggested a trip to Whitman's ice cream shop on Allenby Street, Esther glowed, her fair skin and flaxen hair shining as though a light had been turned on inside her. Yitzchak couldn't bear to be the naysayer who might turn off her light.

People came to the city from around the country for the explicit purpose of visiting Whitman's. It was the only real ice cream parlour in the whole country, and people spoke about going as though it were a religious pilgrimage. When the horse-drawn cart that delivered the large blocks of ice clip-clopped along Allenby Street, children ran behind it like the circus was in town. Watching the heavy blocks of ice carried in giant wrought iron calipers from the wagon, they applauded the iceman, chasing behind the horse-drawn cart when he left.

There was an icebox with a glass front containing tubs of ice cream one could see and point at when choosing. They sold milkshakes and fizzy drinks — things no one needed but that represented a fundamental freedom that had so recently been unimaginable to most of the customers. The extravagance of ice cream laughed in the face of the war outside their windows like whistling in the dark. Mr. Whitman, a red-headed man, sat by his cash register all day counting his money. Children who dreamed out loud about their future riches said, "I'm going to be as rich as Whitman!"

When Esther ate ice cream or sipped a thick, creamy milkshake, she lowered her paper-thin eyelids over her velvet eyes and hummed quietly to herself.

Der didn't know how to explain the joy he got from Esther's delight when she laughed at a funny film or lost at an arcade game or, most especially, when she ate ice cream. Nor could he give voice to how much at home he felt with the two of them. He only knew that with them, he felt he belonged in a way that he didn't anywhere else. They were family.

One spring evening, when Der was visiting his friends, Mr. Boim shouted to Yitzchak and Esther from the back rooms of the flat where he and his *machasheyfeh* wife lived. "Come quickly and witness history!"

Yitzchak and Esther, unaccustomed to being invited into their landlords' home for any reason, let alone to listen to their radio, hesitated. Der hung back.

"Ben Gurion is announcing the declaration of the state! Come! We must all hear it! It must be real to us all, that no one should ever be able to say it didn't happen," Mr. Boim encouraged.

Yitzchak and Esther joined their neighbours in their one and a half rooms. "Bring your friend as well! Everybody must bear witness." Mr. Boim ushered Der into the cramped bedroom. Five of them perched on the edge of the bed while David Ben Gurion made his historic announcement over the wireless waves. They all wept tears of joy and disbelief. They embraced one another and kissed — even Mrs. Boim. Then, as though it had been planned, they drifted outside along with every other resident of Shenkin Street and every other street from the southernmost point of the country to the northern tip of the Jewish State. Jubilation and celebration, an impromptu flow from side streets to main thoroughfares, resulting in an independence parade, with singing and dancing and kissing and hugging and a resulting baby boom in February 1949 that the infant state was ill-equipped for.

The bloodshed that had begun in an unofficial, haphazard manner with the signing of the United Nations Partition Plan in

November 1947 escalated on May 15, 1948, into full-scale war, with the newly declared State of Israel coming under attack from all sides by its surrounding Arab neighbours. The war, which raged through the hot summer months, shook the country and crept beneath Esther's finely cracked veneer, opening painful wounds and old sadness. Esther's life was made up of broken bits of thread tied together between unfathomable losses. She managed, for the most part, to live behind her cobbled-together facade of innocence and naïveté, but beneath the brittle surface lurked pain so unbearable that sometimes her carapace could not withstand it and she retreated to the safety of her bed, sometimes for weeks. There she would stay until she could get up and face the world again. The word *depression* was never used.

A visit from Der was always a balm to her wounded spirit.

Der made a special trip to Tel Aviv just over a year after their landing at Beit Lid to tell Yitz and Esther he was returning to South Africa to pursue his studies. He would have left Israel earlier, but tracking down his documents had been complicated in the burgeoning bureaucracy.

Yitzchak and Esther had news of their own, which Esther, slight as she was and reluctant to beg the evil eye, had kept secret as long as she possibly could. The three friends shared an almost undrinkable bottle of sacramental wine to toast Der's departure, the new baby's impending arrival, and a promise to remain friends.

5.

PETAL SLEPT POORLY. At 6:00 a.m., she followed the sound of Der's slippers to the kitchen.

"Coffee, Tiggaleh?" he asked.

"Yes, please. I barely slept."

"Not surprising. You have a lot on your mind."

"Obviously, I'm super worried about Rosie, but it's out of my hands," Petal said, plunking herself down in one of the white tulip chairs at Der's white pedestal table.

"That's one of life's great conundrums. One's capacity to influence a situation has little to do with one's magnitude of worry about said situation. I can offer nothing more than a sleeping pill if you want one tonight," Der said, putting a cup of black coffee on the table in front of Petal. "Black, yes? And nothing to eat until your coffee is done."

"Der, what you have given me yesterday, today, and my whole life are so much more than a sleeping pill." She stroked the back of his liver-spotted hand as he put the mug down.

Der stood behind Petal's chair with his hands on her shoulders; bending forward, he kissed the top of her head. Der's head kisses were deeply embedded in Petal's muscle memory of comfort. When Chavie would take off on yet another manic adventure, when Estie would climb into bed — a conspicuous correlation between those two repeated occurrences — Petal would take refuge in apartment 1A, where Der kissed the top of her head, fed her pea soup, and assured her that everybody was doing the best they could.

"If it weren't for all of you, I would have had a much lonelier life. Your bubby and zaideh took me in when I needed taking in. I am forever grateful. And because of them, I got to have you." Der planted another kiss on her crown.

By eight o'clock, after two cups of black coffee, half a bagel with orange marmalade, and a catch-up with Der, Petal had dialled Heschy Glisserman's number half a dozen times, reaching a voicemail box too full to leave a message.

"Maybe I'll just walk over to Rosie's place," Petal said, scrunching gobs of cream into her showered curls. "I don't need the rabbi's permission to go to my sister's house."

Through all her years of therapy and self-exploration, the one existential wound with which Petal had never reconciled was how she became the outsider in Rosie's life. The blood between them seemed to run thinner than air, let alone water. This psychic gash, which she avoided as though venturing in were akin to diving headfirst into the fiery opening of an active volcano, was too raw, too painful to address.

Petal called Benjamin.

"Hello, Pet!" he said, falsely upbeat for the early hour. "It's only five past. A bit early for our daily dose."

"I can't get hold of Rabbi Glisserman," Petal said. "I think I should just go over to their house."

"Why not?"

"Good question."

But that was exactly the problem. Petal wasn't on terra firma. She didn't know the rules. She was barely clear what the game was.

"She's my sister. I'm going to go to her house and ... and ... Oh, fuck! Benjamin, what the fuck am I doing?"

"I don't have anything clever to say, Pet, but I know you'll figure it out. You're good at that. At least when the conundrums are mine."

Petal hadn't walked more than a couple of blocks when the dirty sedan pulled up on the other side of the road.

"Get in," Heschy said, rolling down the window.

"I've been trying to reach you for ages!" she said, getting into the car.

"*Davening*," he said.

"I forgot morning prayers were a thing. We're going to Rosie's house, I hope?" They were driving in the opposite direction.

"Have to make a stop on the way. Hashem has answered our prayers."

Petal waited for him to continue. He didn't.

"I'm hungry. I can't talk when I'm hungry." Heschy reached into his breast pocket, pulled out three bananas, and ate one after the other in quick succession, peeling them from the back end with his teeth, like a monkey.

Petal watched.

"Can I talk? Is there a prayer now or something?" she said when he finished chewing the last morsel of banana.

"Speak."

"Where are we going?"

"I was going to go pick up Dr. Gold. He's the psychiatrist. Brilliant, Orthodox, not ultra-Orthodox, but he understands the complexities."

Heschy stopped, got out of the car, and went to the door. Dr. Gold was a big, round, shiny mountain of a man. He dwarfed Rabbi Glisserman so much that Petal half expected the doctor to take hold of Heschy's hand like a child who needed to be escorted to the waiting car. Dr. Gold wore a knit kippah on his head (indicating a more moderate, modern Orthodox affiliation), an unseasonably warm parka, and shoes so big Petal mentally questioned whether his feet could possibly be big enough to fill his own shoes.

The metaphor was not lost on her. Walking toward her was Rosie's saviour. At least, she hoped he was.

"Dr. Gold, this is Dr. Wolffe, Mrs. Hirsch's sister," Heschy said.

Petal nodded, avoiding the issue of handshaking. Moving to the back seat, she pushed the grimy fleece blanket in her way along the length of the bench like a broom, sweeping away the accumulated garbage in its path.

The men *kibbitzed* — bantered, as though they knew one another well — about kids, community, the rabbi's *drosh* from last Shabbes.

Petal couldn't believe the crumbalow was more chaotic than the previous day, but the mess appeared to have doubled, been looted by alien invaders, and then been caught in a terrorist attack!

Rabbi Glisserman introduced Dr. Gold to Schmeil in the cramped kitchen.

"What can you do? I have to take my kids to my mother and sister for yuntif. I'm not used to getting it all organized without my Raizel," Schmeil said apologetically, as though that was both the reason for and the explanation of the crumbalow's state of disarray bordering on hoarder crazy.

Petal tuned in. "You're leaving Rosie alone?"

"Of course not," Schmeil said turning his attention to the ringing telephone. "*Vos machts, Rebbe?... Yoh, mine froi un eiyr shvester ... Auber der chametz? Vos far der chametz?*"

Schmeil continued on the phone, progressively more agitated.

Eager to see her sister and, more importantly, have Dr. Gold see her sister, Petal gave Rabbi Glisserman a "what the hell is going on" raised eyebrow and dagger stare.

"He's worried about selling his leaven before the holiday," Rabbi Glisserman explained as though it was a completely rational concern while his wife lay in drugged unconsciousness in the next room.

Petal inadvertently let out a "pffft."

Heschy took hold of Schmeil by the elbow. "Schmeilkeh, it's not important now."

Schmeil pulled away, continuing his conversation.

"What's going on?" Petal asked.

"His house, which would normally be sterilized for the holiday — cleaned of any bread or crumbs and completely kosher for Passover — isn't. No big deal, people go away for the holiday all the time and don't bother to clean away the chametz. Instead, they 'sell' their property to a non-Jew." He made air quotes with his fingers.

"They sell their house?" Petal asked. "I thought I'd heard everything, but ..."

"Well, technically they sell their chametz. Instead of throwing away perfectly good food and things, the rabbi arranges for it to be sold to a non-Jew for the duration of the holiday. The money that changes hands, nominal sums, becomes a way for the congregants to give the rabbi a little gift for the holiday. At the end of Pesach, the rabbi buys back the major property, not the food, and returns it to the owners. It's a loophole, but to some people, it's important that they don't own anything leavened during the forbidden period. The only problem is, his rabbi is giving him a hard time because Raizel will still be in the house, so technically the arrangement isn't strictly kosher."

"You're kidding me, right?" Petal said.

"Not kidding. But, if you'll pardon me saying so, his rabbi is being ridiculous. Schmeil is so devoted to his rabbi, he won't proceed without a *hechsher*. You know what a hechsher is? A seal of kosher approval. I'll talk to them." Heschy motioned Dr. Gold toward the bedroom.

Petal climbed onto the bed over the motionless mound and tugged at the drapes to let a little light into the room.

"Rosie," she whispered. "Rosie, can you wake up, sweetie?"

The blankets shifted.

"Rosie, I promised I'd come back," Petal said, her fingers fumbling to find the edge of the blankets, lowering them to reveal the top of Raizel's headscarf, the tips of bandaged fingers clutching the frayed border of the bedsheet, pushing it down and exposing Rosie's gaunt face, her eyes squinting against the dim light.

"Pet?"

"Yes, it's me. I've brought some company, someone who wants to see how you are."

Raizel's hand shot up to her head and tugged at the scarf.

Heschy and Dr. Gold pushed into the room. The doctor's size and the close confines necessitated an unsteady perch on the end of the bed.

"If it's all right with you," Dr. Gold said, looking at Raizel for permission.

She nodded.

"I'm Dr. Gold. I'm a psychiatrist," he said.

"Do you want us to go?" Heschy asked.

"No, I don't think that's necessary. We're just gong to talk a bit. Is that all right with you, Mrs. Hirsch?" Dr. Gold spoke to Raizel with respect and deference, presuming, despite her current condition, she was a competent, intelligent woman. Raizel and Petal were quickly disarmed.

"I hear you've been having a difficult time."

Rosie nodded.

"Let's see if we can help make things easier. How's your appetite?" he asked.

Schmeil, now wedged in the doorway next to Rabbi Glisserman, began answering. Without taking his eyes off Rosie, Dr. Gold raised his hand in Schmeil's direction in a firm but not hostile gesture.

"Let's hear what Mrs. Hirsch has to say. We can talk with the others after, if that's okay with her. Is that all right with you, Mrs. Hirsch?"

Rosie nodded, eyes on Dr. Gold. They were a committee of two.

"So, how's your appetite been?"

"I'm not hungry," Rosie rasped.

"What was the last thing you ate?"

"I don't know."

"Do you know that you're taking some very strong pills?"

"I know."

"Do you know why you're taking the pills?"

"To help me sleep," she said, stopping short as though she had more to say but not saying more.

"Anything else?"

"The women," she said, shifting her gaze downward.

"What women?"

"The ones that shout at me."

"What do they say to you?"

"They tell the truth."

"What's the truth?"

"That I'm unclean. That my soul is not pure." Rosie started crying.

"Do you think they're right?"

"Hashem is always right."

"So, it's Hashem who speaks to you?"

"Sometimes. Sometimes just the women. They're mean," she said, choking the words through her sobs. "They say horrible, hateful things. But Hashem teaches me how to be clean. All things are cleansed with blood, and without shedding of blood there is no forgiveness. Hashem told me." Her agitation was escalating. "'KA! ... KA KA!' they shout at me. Like an axe. But not. No, no. A voice. 'KA! KA!' Two voices. Two women's voices. And in between, sometimes — like a drum — 'KAKAKAKAKA,' sometimes — like electric shocks — 'KA!' or 'SLUT!' I know exactly when they started — a week and a half — but with so much to do, I really couldn't ... didn't have time for 'KAKAKAKAKASLUT!' I tried to get away, but they followed me from room to room. I closed the curtains and shut the doors so they couldn't see my sins," she sobbed.

Petal inhaled deeply, as though willing her sister to breathe.

It was impossible to tell if Rosie was reporting or repeating the voices inside her head. Her distress was overwhelming, and Dr. Gold let her flail. It was difficult to watch, but it was clear that the doctor was paying close attention. He didn't interrupt. He was still listening. Petal resisted her urge to touch her sister.

Suddenly calm, Rose continued. "Every year, I try to break up the job. I work backwards from the kitchen, which has to be the last room purified of leaven, so it makes sense to end there. I go backward through the children's bedrooms, the closets, and finally or firstly the basement. Some women say they tape doors closed for the holiday, but I don't have the authority to do that. KA!" she shouted as though the voices in her head were escaping painfully through her skull. "And usually, normally, KAKAKAKAKA, don't you hear it? Not that it isn't always a big job, but SLUT! You hear that? With Hashem's help, I get it done. So I put cotton balls in my ears. I taped them down with Band-Aids. I covered them in tinfoil. KAKAKAKA! If only they would stop ... I could ... begin. But each time I tried to start, they started, and I'd have to leave the house or hide. When I was alone, I tried singing to drown them out, but it isn't modest. SLUT! WHORE, shameless, shamelass, shamlass, shamlitan, charlatan," Rosie shouted, echoing her internal torment. "KA KA!" She jolted as though being zapped with electricity. Hyperventilating.

Dr. Gold waited.

Eventually calmer. "My prayers were answered, and he led me down the stairs, and he gave me the tools and he spoke to me. Hashem said, 'Be nOT ashAmed oF yOur sIns. Purify whaT is saCRed and you shalL bE cleansed.'" Her speech was halting, as though God was actually caught in her throat. "And I took the books from the shelves, and with each book the women shouted less. 'Ka. KA.' And as the pounding of my eardrums, keeping time with my heart, slowed, Hashem spoke so gently, 'Your righTeousness sHalL noT DeliVer you froM your traNSgressionS onLy your puRification shAll RiGht. Boil. BoIL. Toil. BoiL.' 'Kakaka.'" She squeezed out her words as though snaking a particularly clogged drain.

Rosie inhaled deeply and let her breath out slowly like a balloon with a small, slow leak.

Dr. Gold waited before speaking. "I think you are a righteous woman, Mrs. Hirsch. I believe you want to do what is right and just. You have a good heart."

"I try, but sometimes ..." Rosie again disintegrated. Dr. Gold indicated with his eyes for Petal to embrace her sister.

"Your sister loves you. Your husband loves you, your children love you, and by all accounts, Mrs. Hirsch, you are an *eshes chayil*. We will help you remember what we know you know to be true." Pushing himself off the end of the bed, Dr. Gold shooed the men back into the kitchen, motioning Petal to follow.

Petal slithered off the foot of Rosie's bed. "Can I make you a cup of tea, Ro?"

Rosie nodded tentatively. Petal joined the men.

Dr. Gold prompted them to switch from Yiddish to English. "Schmeil was saying what a blessing it is that you're here."

Schmeil shoved his hands deep into the baggy pockets of his shiny black trousers and looked down at the floor. Petal decided to interpret the slight Talmudic rocking of his head as concurrence.

Petal shook her head back and forth. "That was intense! Is this how she's been without the drugs?"

"Worse," Schmeil said.

"The timing of all this complicates matters, with the holiday." Dr. Gold reached a finger up and tucked an escaped lock of hair back behind his ear, reminding Petal he was one of them. "It's a big relief to Schmeil you can be here with your sister while he goes for the holiday with the children."

Schmeil rocked gently back and forth on his heels, dragging the back of his hand across his moist eyes and nose.

"Has it occurred to anyone that I might need to be asked? Obviously, I would do anything for my sister, but what exactly are we talking about? I'm trying really hard not to make presumptions about you, but it feels as though you're not affording me the same courtesy. What makes you think I can handle that?" She flung her arm toward the bedroom.

As soon as it was out of her mouth, Petal felt bad. There was no question in her mind she would stay with Rosie. In fact, if she were inclined to let herself feel her own feelings, she might have realized a part of her was overjoyed to be invited back into Rosie's life, despite the circumstances. Why did she need to assert her will? Had her life been so inextricably formed by Rosie's "possibilities" that she needed to give voice to something irrelevant in the moment? Was the hurt she harboured so chronic as to make her mean? She too took interest in the grimy vinyl floor tiles.

Heschy broke the awkward pause, rattling off the logistics in such rapid-fire staccato it took Petal a moment to realize he hadn't begun to pray.

"Tomorrow is Shabbes. Then, right away, Pesach. Much to do, and not a lot of time for good manners. Apologies to everyone. Schmeil's taking the kids to stay with his mother and sister. It's not an ideal solution, but the best there is for now. They live north of Steeles in Chabad Gate. It's too far to walk between here and there, and with no driving on yuntif and this house not properly kosher for Passover, it's best for them to stay with his family. We assumed — and again, I am sorry for assuming — you wouldn't mind staying where it isn't strictly kosher for the holiday and you would move in with your sister for a few days?" Heschy raised his intonation to interrogative.

"How many days exactly?" Petal said, inadvertently curling her upper lip at the surrounding chaos in autonomic disgust. Judgment provided sanctuary from the complex cacophony of issues she was suppressing, none of which had anything to do with the measure of strict kosherness of the home.

The men made mental calculations and consulted in Yiddish, using their fingers to count the days.

"*Frytick, Shabbos, auber pesach, Zuntik, Muntic es bin yuntif. Dinstik, Mitvoch, unt Donerschtik er ken cumen un bazuchen. Demolt vider zaiyn Shabbos unt yuntif.*"

While they figured, Petal found a kettle. She rinsed it and put it to boil.

"Ten days," Heschy said. "Not ten whole days. Ten days total."

"What does that mean?" Petal asked.

"Tomorrow's Friday. Schmeil's taking the kids until the end of Pesach. Between Shabbes and the holiday, it'll be ten days. Most are days he can't travel. On the days he can travel; Tuesday, Wednesday, and Thursday, he can come visit Raizel, and you can have a break. In the meantime, he can rest easy, knowing she's in good hands."

Petal felt the addition of gratitude and trust was disingenuous ass-kissing. She restrained herself from saying something snarky.

"And what do I do during that time?" she said, turning to Dr. Gold. "Just continue to sedate her? What about treatment?"

"A very important question, Dr. Wolffe. I believe, given her history of hypomanic episodes, your sister is in the midst of a manic psychosis. There's no reason to think that, with the proper medication, we can't set her right again. But it isn't immediate. Given her obvious agitation, some degree of sedation we can taper off as the other medications take effect is prudent. Do you know if your sister's ever been prescribed any psychotropic medication?"

"Not on my watch, but I've been a bit out of the loop since ... Schmeil?" Petal hated deferring to Schmeil, but for twenty years she hadn't been the gatekeeper.

Schmeil shook his head. "Raizel's always been happy and energetic. I had no idea she had a history of ..."

It bothered Petal that he didn't finish the sentence. *More fucking mentors*, she thought.

"Mental illness," she said. "We come from a long line of mental illness. But Rosie got the best kind. She got the ying. I got the yang."

The men stared blankly.

"Never mind," Petal said.

"No, it's important to know. Have any members of the family taken lithium?" Dr. Gold asked.

Petal shrugged her shoulders. "Other than my own medical history, the rest is shrouded in silence and mystery. Lots of *mentor nischt zogen* in our family," she said to alert the men that she wasn't a completely lapsed Jew. She pulled her phone from her pocket. "Maybe Der knows."

Der hesitated. Part of him believed that no good could come of adding to the immediate crisis with history that had never been disclosed. But he knew information was power, and if nothing else, he had tried to do his best to empower Petal. He knew better than anyone that the cards were stacked against his girls. His job, as he saw it, was to give them the best possibilities under limited circumstances, so he hesitated.

"Your mother was prescribed lithium on a number of occasions, but I don't believe she ever actually took it compliantly. Things might have turned out differently if she had. I think lithium is a good place to start."

Petal delivered only the "need to know" answer. "No one has taken lithium, but he thinks it's a good call."

THE DISTANCE BY foot between Rosie's world at the corner of Ledbury Street and Stormont Avenue and Der's world at 19 Meadowbrook Road took twenty-one minutes to walk at an "I'm not in a rush" pace, which translated to an eighteen-minute New York clip.

Less than a block away from Rosie's house, Petal called Benjamin.

"Hello, sweet Pet," he said.

"*Fuuuck!* This is such a fucking shit show!"

"I'm sorry you're stuck in it. Tell me what's going on."

"Nothing. I don't think there's anything either of us can actually do. I'm moving in with my sister for the next ten days."

"With the penguin and all the baby penguins too?" Benjamin had adopted Petal's pejorative references.

"They're going to his family for the holidays so they don't come into contact with anything unholy, like God forbid a slice of bread or a cracker that hasn't been farted on by a team of rabbis!"

"I sense some hostility, Dr. Wolffe," Benjamin said.

"You have no idea. I'm trapped in a parallel universe. I need sympathy, not judgment!"

"I'll stop."

"No, don't stop. Just let me thrash a bit. The shrink wants to start her on lithium and slowly take her off the sedatives."

"And you're supposed to be monitoring all of this? Not okay, Pet. Too heavy to carry. Not cool."

"I kind of agree, but that's always been the way. Responsible Petal looking out for flighty Rose. I resent it, but it makes sense. It always did. Well, except when it didn't; except when I was the untethered one. She's my sister. I love her. In a way I could never explain, I need her as much as she needs me. Benjamin, they're letting me into their very insular world. It's kind of an honour."

"You sure that's not just something you're telling yourself to prevent fratricide?"

"She's like my left arm. I rarely use it, but I'm not sure I could manage without it. I hate that I'm here and that this is happening, but there's nowhere else I could imagine being right now."

"As long as it's you helping her float and not her making you drown, I support your decision. So, how can I help?"

"This: Be there to talk. I'm going to have a lot of down time while she sleeps her sedated sleep."

"You know you have that anyhow."

"'I wish you'd say where you are going and what you are doing; how are the plays and after the plays what other pleasures you're pursuing,'" Petal recited.

Benjamin laughed. "Got it! I'll Elizabeth Bishop you back to New York with regular updates. Where are you now, Pet?"

Petal looked around her. "I'm about halfway between Jerusalem and Tel Aviv."

"Where?"

"I'm walking back to Der's place from the crumbalow."

"What does that have to do with Jerusalem and Tel Aviv?"

"Remember I told you I used to need to escape from Jerusalem? I'd get on the bus and, forty-five minutes later, I'd be on a different planet?"

"I take it the crumbalow is the metaphor for Jerusalem in your construct?"

"It's not like Der's neighbourhood hasn't been annexed by ultra-Orthodox also, but ... at least at his place I have some sense of what to expect.

"You know that scene in Nabokov's novel *Pnin*. The can't-get-anything-right, complete-fuck-up, bad-luck professor ... he's standing at the sink washing dishes after a party, and there's this beautiful bowl. The author has made it clear the bowl is special. Pnin fills the sink with soapy water, and it's all frothy and opaque, and he puts in all the stuff from the party — the dishes, the silverware, the glasses, and the beautiful bowl. As the reader, you just know that the bowl is destined for disaster because that's how the author has set up the novel. And Pnin carefully washes all the silverware to get it out of the sink because even he knows it's an accident waiting to happen ... we're all functioning within the same accepted parameters. But then he finishes washing the cutlery, and the bowl and glasses are still in the soapy water, and he accidentally drops a nutcracker back into the sink. *Crack!* You just know the bowl is broken ..." Petal paused. "He sticks his hand in to feel for the bowl ... but having set the reader up, Nabokov doesn't do it. He breaks one of the wine glasses instead. He spends all this time preparing us for the expected outcome and then does a bait and switch. Then we don't know what to expect

anymore. You know what I mean? There are things we count on
to help us navigate the unexpected, but ... in Rosie's world ... all
the expectations are completely unknown to me. Like the whole
of it is a sink full of bubbles, and I can't see any of what is under
the surface. I assume since it's a sink and there's soapy water there
are dirty dishes, but in her world, nope! No dirty dishes, ironically, given the vast quantity of dirty dishes ... but in the proverbial
sink that is her world, I could just as easily find a fish composing
a fucking opera under that water. I haven't got a clue how to
anticipate anything."

"I guess you need to try let go of anticipation. Release expect-
ation. Channel your inner Zen."

"You mean play to my strengths" Petal smiled.

"That's my cynical girl!" Benjamin said. "It doesn't sound like
anyone expects you to control the outcomes."

"They don't, but I'm not good at letting go. I can't help feeling
a bit like the inmates are running the asylum. I have to take such
a huge leap of faith that this doctor isn't just some voodoo witch
doctor."

"What did you say his name was?"

"Gold."

"First name?" Petal could hear Benjamin's fingers clickity-
clacking on his computer keyboard. "Psychiatrist, right? First
name?"

"Not a clue."

"Could it be Morton?"

"Could be."

"I'm on this 'rate my doctor' site, and this guy Morton Gold,
Toronto shrink ... looks like Danny DeVito?"

Petal chuckled. "I suppose in a tiny picture on a tiny screen
he might."

"Balding with kind of stringy, too-long-in-the-back curls. Friendly round face ... Danny DeVito ..."

"Except the guy is like seven feet tall, and he weighs about three hundred pounds."

"On my computer, he's about an inch and a half tall. If he's the guy, people say, 'a gem of a human being.' Another one says, 'wise beyond is an understatement.' They kind of go on in that vein. 'He saved my life,' which is always good. Here's one that says 'he unplugged all the holes in the closet and let Jesus Christ right back in after I had spent months sealing the whole thing off.' I don't think I would take that one to heart. Generally, he seems well regarded, if that helps."

"Good to know," Petal said.

"I have to run, Pet. I'm doing a reading at Symphony Space tonight, and I have to go do a sound check. I wish you were here. I get nervous without you."

"Sorry, I forgot," Petal said. "I'm a bit myopic at the moment. You will be as brilliant as always. You don't need me to be your magic feather, Dumbo. You can fly all on your own."

"But I like when you're my magic feather. And I have to do the fucking crosstown schlep to the Upper West Side alone!"

"Who's coming to cheer you on?" Petal asked.

"Oh, the usual suspects. We'll all miss you! After tonight, I'm kind of freed up of commitments for a bit. Whatever you need from me. I can even come up there if you want."

"I love you, Benjamin Vessel!" Petal said. "I miss you."

"Oh, you poor deluded girl," he said.

Petal crossed from the east to the west side of Bathurst and wound her way to Der's apartment through streets once so familiar.

She fished in her purse for the key she had carried since she was old enough to have keys. Nine times out of ten, Der's door was unlocked or he would hear the jangling and open the door, as he did this time, a book clutched in his left hand, glasses sitting slightly askew on his face as though he had dozed off while reading.

"I didn't mean to disturb you," Petal said.

"How's Rosie today?" Der sat down in the well-worn leather armchair and put his book down on the matching footstool. Petal collapsed onto the soft wool of the couch she'd lain on as a teenager when she would lament repeatedly that Bubby and Zaideh didn't understand her. She ran her hand along the smooth wooden arm of the couch, finding comfort in the remembrance of the motion.

"Der, I saw her wig out! It was scary. She was screaming at the voices in her head, and I could feel her pain."

"Oy, Tiggaleh! I'm so sorry. How can I help?"

"I don't suppose there is much anyone can do," Petal said. "They're still zonking her out of her mind. But at least the doctor came and saw her."

"Who?"

"A guy named Gold. Maybe Morton Gold?"

"Mort Gold," Der said, smiling. "A mensch and a half! A decent fellow and an effective practitioner. Good, I'm glad to hear."

"Me too," said Petal. "We picked him up, and he came to the house."

"House calls, no less! There aren't many psychiatrists who do house calls. I'm telling you, a mensch. He thinks she's bipolar?"

"He believes she's in a manic psychosis," Petal said. "He's probably right. You should've seen her! What do I know? He's going to try her on lithium and ease her off the sedatives." She shifted to horizontal and fumbled for the small cushion, shoving it behind her head. Muscle memory.

"It can be a rough road. Will they admit her somewhere?"

"Admit her! That would make too much sense. I'm going to be her psych ward. Schmeil and the kids are moving out, and I'm moving in."

"Are you comfortable with that?"

"Do I have a choice?"

"You always have a choice," Der said sternly.

"It wasn't my plan ... but it's less than two weeks. Then I'll go back to my life. She'll go back to her life."

"If you're sure you can manage it ..." Der measured his words.

"Der, I'm better than I've ever been. I'm medicated and therapized and supported by wonderful friends and colleagues, and I'm okay in my own skin. I have a great life. Don't worry," Petal said, moving to sit on the footstool, facing Der.

"But I do worry, Tiggaleh. All the time."

"I know," she said, taking his hand in both of hers, trying through osmosis to set his mind at rest on her behalf. "It might be fun. It's been twenty-two years since we lived under the same roof. Maybe it'll be good?"

"Can I come see you there?"

"You better come or I might just go crazy."

"Crazy is not something to make light of, even in jest."

"I'm going to start getting my things organized," Petal said.

"I'll make us a light lunch. Dinner — I'm taking you out to celebrate. No arguments."

"What exactly are we celebrating?" Petal asked.

"So soon you forget, *Doctor* Wolffe!"

Petal's shoulders sprung toward her ears. She had allowed her sister's chaos to overshadow her accomplishment. Closing her eyes, she pulled her shoulder blades together to release the tension, took a deep breath, and let it out slowly.

"Thank you, Der," Petal said, acutely aware, not for the first time, how grateful she was that he had stuck.

6.

AT THE END of 1948, Der returned to Cape Town, once again Haimy. Family and friends gathered at the airport, as much to watch the plane land as to greet the returning hero, the paragon of Zionist dream fulfillment. He had tilled the soil as a pioneer, made the proverbial desert bloom, and been present for the declaration of the Jewish State.

Haimy hid his shame. Had the words been available at that time, he would have acknowledged that he had no self-esteem. He had borne witness to war, its aftermath, human suffering, and the cruelty of man's inhumanity to man, which eclipsed any romantic notions of poetry or poets. He ached with the knowledge of how little he could actually do and yearned to be existentially useful. What that looked like was a mystery.

Haimy found unfulfilling work supply teaching in a working-class neighbourhood, where the boys taunted him as a poofter. *What use could these roughs have for literature?* he thought, preparing lessons and assignments he knew would be ignored.

"My father says we doesn't do any work after hours in our house, sir. If I brings any homework, he's gonna come after hours to your house, sir, and beat the crap outta you." *Sir* — a jeer, not a reverence, mocking his ineffectual nature. He silently agreed.

On weekends, he helped his father and grandfather in their dry goods shop, ashamed of his boredom and loathing of the honest, necessary work. His father and grandfather slaved day in, day out, so he was afforded the privilege of education, travel, selfishness, and the frivolity of being a poet. The word itself acquired a metallic, off-putting taste on his tongue. *Poet.*

Yet he couldn't think of an alternative. What was he any good for?

For two years, Haimy lived in an aimless fog of self-flagellation. He knew he could not abide the politics of South Africa. He knew he was not strong enough to fight against it. He knew he could not stay and silently bear witness. He knew that he must make something of himself.

IN FEBRUARY 1949, Yitzchak and Esther became the overprotective, entirely consumed, anxious, and loving parents to baby Chava. They agreed to speak only Hebrew to their daughter — another attempt to erase the past.

Esther blossomed into a head-turning beauty with pregnancy, mothering naturally, as though all that had been missing in her life was a baby. Esther took Chavie everywhere, showing her off to her clients. Chavie was remarkably beautiful and content. Things seemed blissfully easy for the first year.

The winter of 1950 was harsh, and the young state couldn't cope with the massive influx of immigrants streaming in from Yemen, Libya, Iraq, and North Africa so close on the heels of the postwar European refugees. Across the country, there were storms and shortages. Stories from the absorption camps, which housed tens of thousands of new arrivals, were told in the cities like mythology.

"I heard the wind blew so hard not a single tent remained standing. Women clutched so fiercely at their tent poles their arms were pulled off."

"I heard it rained so hard a river washed the whole camp out to sea!"

"I heard it snowed, and neighbours frozen into blocks of ice needed to be brought back to life on gas burners!"

The spurious tales helped distract from the hunger and deprivation to which no one was immune. Food stamps and rationing presented fine fodder for a litany of folk songs and jokes about chickens that only knew how to lay half eggs and boys too hungry to even notice the pretty girls that chased them. *Ain li lechem, Ain li mayim, Ain li shum davar.* "I have no bread, I have no water, I have nothing." *Od lo achalnu shum davar, v'shum davar od lo shatinu! Im ain champagne v'ain caviar, tnu lanu lechem ve'zaytim.* "We haven't yet eaten. We haven't yet drunk. If there is no champagne and no caviar, give us bread and olives."

Stale bread crusts in brown paper packets were sometimes stuffed into nooks and crannies around the city, a tithe for the less fortunate, an inability to let anything go waste.

Esther fought fierce internal battles to tamp down the anxieties triggered by these hardships. Her ingenuity kept them from real hunger, the kind she could never forget, but even when they had enough, she squirrelled away more. She acquired consumables greedily, hiding her pathological need to stock her pantry.

Occasionally, Esther brought home packets of scavenged bread she grated and mixed into dumplings boiled in a sauce of crushed tomatoes.

"Where did you learn to cook like a wizard, my darling?" Yitzchak asked his wife. "No one has anything, and we eat like kings."

Esther blushed crimson, ashamed of her greed but surreptitiously proud of her resourcefulness. She learned that the Arab merchants sometimes had things, smuggled in from Lebanon and Jordan, that the Jewish vendors did not. She knew that on Mondays the egg man would pass by with his baby carriage full of eggs, and if he had slightly cracked eggs, she could buy them at a discount without wasting food stamps. The milkman, who notoriously watered down his milk, put aside the creamiest portions for Esther, who always offered him a glass of water when he delivered her order. She learned of a peddler from Jaffa who sold olives, oil, and apricot preserves that she purchased for grushim and an alluring smile. If one knew where and when to go, underpants, undershirts, trousers, shirts, and simple dresses could be bought at bargain prices from the seller of clothes who carried his wares in a big bundle on his back. He would open up his "shop" on the dirt patches of the boulevards and rummage through to find what his customers needed. Esther was an expert at gleaning something from nothing and felt proud of her survival instincts, mostly oblivious to the preferential treatment her looks afforded her.

Der, her guardian angel, sent packages from his father's shop of delicacies unthinkable in those days; tins of cling peaches, canned fish, sausages, chicken and sometimes even coffee and sugar, always including letters and gifts for Chavie of ribbons too silky for her fine hair and dresses she needed time to grow into.

When she felt good, Esther was a capable, competent, energetic wife and mother. But sometimes, it was all too much — the weather too cold or too hot, the baby too fussy, work too demanding, cramped living too stressful. And then she would crumble and take to her bed.

In March of 1950, when the tempests of the legendary winter had subsided and things were relatively calm in the country, Esther fell down a very deep rabbit hole. On a day like any other day, she was out and about visiting clients with Chavie. Chavie charmed the shopkeepers with her sparkling eyes and her cherubic lips while Esther reviewed the monthly accounts. On their way home, they stopped by the market to pick up salted herring for Yitzchak and whatever else there might be to add to the stock-pile beneath their bed. Suddenly, a woman shrieked as though she had been shot or stabbed, her cries so bloodcurdling everybody up and down the crowded market stopped to look and see what horror had befallen her.

"Libe, Libe, Libe, Libe ..." she screeched.

"What happened? What's wrong?" passersby asked, the woman too distraught to answer.

"Libe, Libe, Libe, Libe!" she continued, immune to the attempted consoling of onlookers.

Through the crowd that encircled the panic-stricken woman pushed a little girl, no older than five or six years, with blond pigtails and a blue romper. "Eemma," she said, gently tugging at her mother's skirt. The woman collapsed, taking the child down with her, her sobbing so breathless a medic was summoned. Estie stood in the throngs of people, feeling every ounce of the woman's hysteria inside herself, hearing whispers in the crowd.

"Poor woman, she was there."

"They should just try and forget."

"You see the tattoo? They aren't the same after what happened to them."

"Some of them are so afraid of the police they run when they see them."

"This isn't what our new citizens should be."

"This kind of frailty is what led them like lambs to the slaughter in Europe."

"Don't they know there's no place for weakness in Am Yisrael?"

"They should keep these things to themselves."

Barely breathing, running, Esther pushed onto a side street. Chavie's stroller bumped along the uneven cobblestones, jostling the baby to tears. Though it was a part of town she knew well, when she arrived at the junction at Nahalat Binyamin, only a short block from the market, Esther lost her bearings and froze, paralyzed, uncertain which way to turn to get home while Chavie wailed. The owners of the fabric stores lining the street knew Yitzchak and recognized his attractive wife and daughter. Somehow, they managed to point Esther in the right direction. When she got home, she left Chavie in her stroller with Yitzchak at the front of the room and crawled into bed behind the happy green gingham curtain.

It was days before Yitzchak could get Esther to talk about what had happened. "There is no place in this new land for the history we keep inside of us. We're not welcome here."

"How can you expect anyone to understand? So, we don't speak of it. We decided together. They didn't decide. The baby, she will be the new Israeli. She will be strong and unscarred by our past. Shh, Estelleh, shh."

"I won't ever leave this flat with my arms out," she said. "I don't need their pity."

"Shh," Yitzchak said. "We will make it so."

With Chavie in her stroller, Yitzchak walked to the fabric shops on Nahalat Binyamin to look for something special. He wasn't sure exactly what, but was sure he would know it when he saw it. He went in and out of several shops before he noticed exactly the colour and texture he was looking for. He purchased three and a half metres of green polished cotton poplin and a spool of cherry-red thread.

While his wife and daughter slept, Yitzchak worked through the night, drawing, measuring, cutting, and sewing, until, with the rising of the sun, he had finished the dress. He hung it from the curtain rod separating the storefront from their bedroom so it faced Esther as she slept. Then, he lay down beside his wife and baby girl and went to sleep.

When Esther opened her eyes in the morning, she saw the beautiful emerald-green dress — full-circle skirt, fitted bodice with a collar and three buttons down the front, cherry-red stitching, a matching red belt with a big buckle, and three-quarter-length sleeves exactly long enough to cover her number and expose her delicate wrists — just like in the movie posters they saw outside the Mograbi Cinema. She rolled over, leaned across her baby, kissed the back of her husband's neck, got out of bed, and cooked up a pot of kasha and bow ties on the hotplate in their shared kitchen.

WHEN ESTHER WORE the green-and-red dress, which brought out the colour in her fair eyes and brought in the enviable curve of her tiny waist, accentuating her maternally acquired bosom, she was a vision of Hollywood proportions. There was not a man, woman, or child in the streets of Tel Aviv who didn't turn to take a second look at the goddess in green when she passed.

"If I had the money, I would buy you red shoes," Yitzchak lamented. "You could sit like the fancy ladies in Café Piltz and drink coffee and eat crème schnitte."

Esther blushed. "Yitzchak, I already have the most stylish dress in all of Tel Aviv. People will think we are misers, living like paupers but wealthy enough to afford a dress like this. Better I shouldn't look too good, or people will talk."

But talk people did. Esther worked in the prosperous neighbourhood of German Jews who had arrived in Palestine in the thirties at a time when they could leave Europe with assets and money unfathomable to the newer refugees. It was only a matter of time before someone asked about her elegant clothing.

"My husband made it for me," Esther said. "He's a wonderful tailor. He can do anything with his sewing machine."

Esther was unaware of the powerful advertisement she was. And soon the orders began flowing from the fanciest ladies in Tel Aviv, all of whom wanted "the dress." Yitzchak made excuses about not being able to find the exact same fabric, but offered alternatives. Only his Esther should have the green dress with the cherry-red sash. Only his Esther got dresses with superpowers. He recreated that same dress in sapphire blue with orange stitching, amethyst purple with red stitching, and ruby red with orange stitching. Soon, the women began asking for changes. "Make it for me, but different than you did for her," they said, hoping to outshine their friends and neighbours. Yitz made dresses with buttons in the front or down the back, with a boatneck instead of a lapel, going to the movies to get inspiration, creating patterns from old newspapers, sewing day and night to keep up with the orders. When he had a spare moment, he would sew a new dress for Esther — this time with a pencil skirt that hugged her shapely thighs and bottom, next time with an open neckline that showed off her beautiful collarbones — each time attracting more clientele to his tiny shop on Shenkin Street.

With business thriving, Yitzchak saved enough money for a three-room, fourth-floor walk-up flat in a square, white Bauhaus building at number 14 Rupin Street, right at the top of Shalag Street. The flat had a balcony that ran along the western front with a cool breeze so rare in the humid city and a clear view straight down the palm-lined street to the sea. He paid the landlord an untold fortune in key money, and the Wolffe family moved into their new home in the fall of 1952.

Mrs. Boim agreed to let Yitzchak continue to rent the storefront on Shenkin Street in exchange for not just money but also dresses. He sewed for her what he called "one of a kind," which met with her approval and saved him from having his brand sullied by her unfortunate homeliness. There was never any concern that someone might ask from where her clothing came.

Life was good for the Wolffe family. Chavie was growing into a beautiful, smart, willful little girl with energy to burn. Esther loved domesticity and her beautiful new home: a kitchen of her own with not one but two gas burners, a bathroom she didn't need to share, a private bedroom with a door that closed, a picture of the sea from her window laid out in horizontal stripes of blues, greens, and golds, a table with a tablecloth and fresh flowers for Shabbat. Happiness was hers. Yitzchak revelled in her satisfactions. If his Esther was content, he was delighted.

Esther believed Yitzchak was unaware of the bounty that had reached them from South Africa courtesy of their friend, but Yitzchak was only too keenly aware of it. He was grateful to Der for sharing his own family's prosperity, but their need embarrassed him. He wrote a letter: *Business is good. I have now two employees and a reputation as the "Dior of the Desert." We have been grateful for your gifts for these years of scarcity, but as you can understand, we are now in a period of relative affluence and no longer in need.* Esther was happy she had secretly saved some of the tinned delicacies that Der had sent.

Der understood but was sorry to lose one of the few things that made him feel somewhat useful in the world where he remained Haimy. From then on, he sent only gifts for Chavie.

ONE SUNDAY, FEELING particularly disheartened and lost, Haimy went for a stroll on the beach in Muizenberg. The rhythmic crash of the waves against the shore blocked out the cacophony of self-doubt he heard almost constantly. The chalky grey sand, the deep

green-blue of the sea, the primary paintbox hues of the rented
beach huts along the shoreline, all illuminated by the blazing African sun, awakened in him a sense of possibility. There was no
doubt that this was the most beautiful place on earth.

On that impossibly glorious Sunday, Haimy ran into an
acquaintance from his Zionist Youth days. He was a few years
older, and Haimy remembered him as popular, charismatic, and
cartoonishly handsome. He had such a white, toothy smile it practically pinged and glinted when his lips parted above his square,
cleft chin. Haimy was embarrassed by his attraction to the young
man, but therein lay yet another thing for which his world had no
space, no words nor feelings that might be said out loud or felt
with comfort or pride.

The wind on the beach, in typical Muizenberg fashion, blew
hard, stealing away the words of conversation and whisking them
out to sea. "What?" they shouted back and forth at one another,
hands cupped acoustically around ears, to no actual avail. The
beautiful young man hooked his arm into Haimy's and pulled him
away from the beach into a small café.

"I hear you were there," he said.

"Where? Oh, Israel. It was a couple of years ago already,"
Haimy said.

"I wanted to go, but I didn't have the guts."

"Guts? It didn't take guts. I went, but I didn't stay. Staying is
what takes guts," Haimy said, the metallic taste of humiliation
filling his mouth.

"You tried. I stayed here. Even as the politics became worse
and worse, I just stayed. I want to change things. That's why I'm
studying to be a social worker."

"That sounds like a good idea," Haimy said, not yet understanding sublimation or transference and instead believing that

fortuitously the seed he had been looking for was found and planted.

Haimy enrolled in a Masters of Social Work program at the University of Cape Town, where he excelled in his studies. His clinical placements took him to parts of the cape he had never been to and exposed him to situations that reminded him of the DP camp. He was skilled at speaking with people in need, commanding their trust, and had a talent for finding workable solutions to very real problems. Haimy felt he was actually helping. At the same time, he recognized that his privilege as a white South African required he either take a political stand or get out. He saw what was happening to people who opposed the government and knew he was not brave enough for violent protests or incarceration. Before he began his final term, Haimy applied to doctoral programs around the world under the name H. Der Levy.

In July 1954, H. Der Levy set off to Canada as a doctoral candidate in social work at the University of Toronto. He never returned to South Africa.

When Der arrived in Canada, he sent Chavie a gift — the latest craze from America, a pair of roller skates — along with a note for her parents: *My dear friends, I am in the furthest place on earth but remain close to you always. Please give the girly a big kiss from her Uncle Der.*

"Oy vey!" Esther said to Yitzchak when the package arrived just before Chavie's sixth birthday. "A *geferlecher* present! Such danger no one should know! We'll tell Chavie they broke and buy her something safer."

"Shh," Yitzchak said. "She'll be fine."

They were better than fine. They had time and money for leisure and occasional luxury. Both Chavie and Esther loved the cinema and took particular delight in attending screenings of films from around the world at the Esther Cinema on Zina Dizengoff Circus in the middle of town.

"We are going to Eema's *kolnoah?*" Chavie thrilled in her belief that her mother had her own movie house, rushing ahead of her parents on her roller skates, the envy of every passing child along Dizengoff Street.

One night, on the way to the cinema, fuelled by Chavie's contagious exuberance, Yitzchak went into one of the shops along the way and bought Esther a pair of tall silver candlesticks with swollen bulbs of corrugated silver, splayed brims, and embossed grapevines.

"Suddenly we are so rich!" Esther said, trying to smother the complex emotions battling inside her, threatening to break through and steal the happiness of that moment.

"I am rich with happiness," Yitzchak said.

"Candlesticks," she said, choking on the word because, for a Jewish woman, candlesticks represent the mandrel upon which the broken axis of the world might be mended.

"Shh," Yitzchak said, holding her tight.

After every movie at the Esther Cinema, Yitzchak and Esther climbed the spiral marble staircase to the fourth floor and snuck out onto the curved balcony along the front of the white Bauhaus building overlooking the rooftops of Tel Aviv. Even in the heat of summer, there was a cool breeze that blew softly. Yitzchak hoisted Chavie into his arms so she too could see all the way to the Mediterranean Sea.

"You are my most precious princess," Yitzchak whispered softly into his daughter's ear.

At the end of October 1956, after two years of escalating hostilities, Israel invaded Egypt through the Sinai desert. Any happiness derived from Esther's full, comfortable life was eclipsed by the war. Esther Wolffe got into bed. She took her seven-year-old daughter with her, refusing to let her leave their flat.

"Estelleh, be reasonable. The war is far away. She's a child. She needs to go on with her life," Yitzchak pleaded with Esther.

"That's what we said last time," Esther said, pulling the waffle-weave blankets over her head.

The war did not last long, but when a ceasefire was called and Israel had taken over all of the Gaza Strip and the whole of the Sinai Peninsula, Esther got out of bed, cooked her obligatory pot of kasha and bow ties, and began packing their belongings.

"What are you doing, Esther? Where are you going?" Yitzchak asked, grateful that she had found the wherewithal to get out of bed but a little frightened by her sudden Herculean energy.

"We're leaving," she said.

"Who is leaving?" Yitzchak asked.

"We. Chavaleh and me and you. The trouble will never end. We cannot live here."

Yitzchak, used to being the voice of reason, ran his hands from her shoulders down her arms to soothe her. "Don't worry, mine Estelleh. It's over now," he consoled.

"It will never be over," she said, slapping away his caresses and continuing to pack. "We've taken another's land. We will never have peace. Once taken, it cannot be untaken. We have secured a place of ongoing war in the history of our people. We must make a life for our daughter where she can be safe."

And Yitzchak could not argue. He had no words for depression or anxiety to explain his wife's fragility. He had no tools or medication to call upon to help. He couldn't deny that Esther spoke some truth, and his own scars, which he chose not to feel, ached with an intensity he could not ignore. He must keep his beautiful Chava safe. He had no way of predicting the ten years of relative calm the country would experience, nor anything else. "But where will we go?" Yitzchak asked.

Esther, having sworn she would never return to Europe under any circumstances and having nothing and no one tying her anywhere else in the world, said, "We will go to Der."

Yitzchak, who had no better ideas, nodded agreement.

By the time the details of their immigration had been sorted, Der had already been in Toronto for three years. "Arrange to arrive between May and August. You will find it easier," he wrote in one of the many letters exchanged in the months leading up to the Wolffe family's arrival in Canada. Neither Yitzchak nor Esther questioned his reasoning, choosing to forget that, before Israel, they had had experience of winter.

As luck would have it, just weeks before Yitz and Esther's arrival in Toronto in July 1957, the tenants in the apartment across the hall from Der came to tell him they were moving at the end of the summer. "Good news," he wrote to his friends. "I have found you a flat in the same building where I live. Until it is ready, I insist you stay with me. I am so looking forward to having you all back in my life. I can't wait to get to know my beautiful Chava."

Yitzchak and Esther left Israel for what they hoped would be a safer, more secure future and arrived in Toronto, Canada, on July 20, 1957, almost as penniless as they had arrived in Palestine almost ten years prior. Their Israeli-German landlord, who was by law required to refund them two-thirds of their original key money, was nowhere to be found.

"Never again!" Yitzchak shouted. "One month at a time is the only way I'll ever live ever again! Bastard! Pig!" Chavie and Esther were frightened by his out-of-character anger and swearing. It was not the first time he had been swindled of property.

They entered Canada as Irving, Estelle, and Heather Wolffe. They believed these names would help them blend into their new lives. They believed blending in would protect them.

Chava, or Heather, as she was only ever called in school, was, objectively, a particularly beautiful eight-year-old. Golden, honey-coloured skin, strawberry-blond hair, deep-green eyes, and features so exquisite that they seemed to have been painted on by a skilled dollmaker with the finest paintbrush imaginable. She was precocious, bright, sunny, and delightful with her mongrelized mix of Yiddish, Hebrew, and English. But she could be moody.

They doted upon their daughter as though she were royalty and they her servants, and she behaved accordingly. Chavie called the shots. She was not unpleasant or unkind, but of the three of them, she had the strongest opinions. She made the decisions about where they should go on weekends, what they should eat for dinner, what they should listen to on the radio, who would be allowed to help her with games and puzzles and homework, and generally what the pace and timbre of their household might be on any given day.

Der was completely besotted with his little Chavaleh but refused to be bullied by her. In response, she fell madly in love with her Der, whom she called "Derroosh" with a long, guttural roll of the "rrrrr" in her Israeli accent, which didn't last otherwise. If Der was around, she always deferred to his desires. "Do you want Eema to make spaghetti or fish, Derroosh? Which puzzle should we do tonight, Derroosh?"

And Der, who observed the dynamic between the girl and her parents, made sure to always have an opinion and never defer. "She has too much power," he would suggest gently to Irving and Estie. "It's too heavy for one so young to carry so much responsibility," hoping they might interpret his interventions as concern, which they most definitely were, and not admonition, which they were not entirely.

Irving smiled. "Too much power is a bad thing? About this we shouldn't worry."

The complex and unique nature of the relationships between parents and children in Holocaust survivor families was, through his work, beginning to emerge as a recurring theme in Der's life. With the arrival of the Wolffes, it took up residence in his home. After five and a half weeks in Canada, the Wolffes moved across the hall. Der stood in the hallway between the two apartments with Chavie and had a very serious conversation.

"You are a very lucky girl, Chavaleh! You have not one but two homes — one on each side of the hall," he said, pointing to each of the units in turn. "In apartment 1A, the door is always open, you are always welcome, and I am the boss. In apartment 2, your Eema and Abba are in charge. That way, you get to be the little girl. If you are the boss, you have to be the Eema, the Abba, or the Derroosh."

"I want to be the little girl," Chavie said, because he was her love, her Derroosh, and she was his Chavaleh. She jumped up, wrapped her arms around his neck and her legs around his waist, and he carried her over the threshold of her new home.

For her ninth birthday, Der bought Chavie a beautiful doll-house. It had two floors and an attic, a removable bifold roof, and two louvred doors at the front of the house that opened to reveal all of the rooms. It came with a family of five dolls — a man, a woman, two girls, and a boy. Chavie was over the moon with her birthday gift.

"Derroosh! A house where I am the boss!" Chavie said.

Der wasn't sure if he should be happy that she remembered their long-ago conversation or concerned about her need to control.

Chavie spent endless hours at Der's apartment playing with

her dollhouse, much of which consisted of her giving Der orders for retrofits of furniture, costumes, and even dolls.

"Make the boy a man with a beard," she commanded. "No, not that kind of beard. Like you have." Der drew a small goatee onto the doll with Magic Marker.

Der encouraged Chavie to play by herself, but she liked giving orders.

At twelve, Chavie was becoming increasingly difficult. "Write numbers on their arms for the mother and father," she demanded.

"I won't," he said.

"You have to," she said. "It's my house, and I'm the boss. I want my house to have a mother and father with numbers."

"Chavie, those numbers your parents have are not something they chose." Der wasn't sure how much to say. He knew it was never discussed. "It will upset them."

"It's my house! I'm the boss!" Chavie said, kicking the doll-house, taking out one of its supporting walls.

The ensuing rage and wreckage came so quickly, Der was paralyzed by shock. Chavie's mixture of postapocalyptic remorse and fury left him terrified and the dollhouse in ruins. Overcome with the exhaustion of her own tempest, she collapsed on the floor next to the broken pieces of her beloved toy and fell into a deep sleep.

Der tried to repair the damage but gave up, reluctantly admitting that it was just too broken.

Der and Chavie shared a special bond, but by the time she was fourteen, it was clear she was a very troubled girl and, despite the best intentions of all the adults in her life, hers would be a challenging path. Like most adolescents, she ran hot and cold. Her moods changed on a dime from almost hysterical enthusiasm to glum at best and uncontrolled rage at worst. Irving and Estie walked on eggshells, never knowing which way the wind was blowing and when it might shift.

"This is normal?" Estie asked Der.

"Shh," Yitz said, unwilling to even open the door to the possibility that it might not be.

Then Chavie disappeared for the first time. Irving dropped her at a friend's house for a sleepover one Friday night. He didn't notice that Chavie left her sleeping bag and empty overnight case on the back seat. He didn't wait to watch Chavie go into the house. In fact, none of that registered as significant until Saturday evening, when Chavie was still not home.

"Don't worry, Estie," Irving said. "They've probably taken the girls somewhere and just haven't come back yet."

"Don't tell me don't worry. I'll worry if I want," Estie said, growing irritable as the sky darkened. When unreasonable worry began to feel reasonable, Estie got angry with Irving, because getting angry was easier than feeling fear. "Go find my Chavaleh."

Irving drove around and around their neighbourhood while Estie frantically called all of Chavie's classmates, friends, and acquaintances.

One after another, the sympathetic voices had no idea where Heather might be or whom she might be with.

By Sunday morning, the police were notified. Estie was unravelling. Irving and Der were used to Estie retreating when she couldn't cope, but this was different. She wailed and screamed and tore at her clothing and scratched at her own flesh.

"My baby is gone! My Chavaleh is gone! Kill me too that I shouldn't feel the pain of losing again!" Estie was inconsolable.

Der recognized that a threshold had been crossed and coaxed her to the emergency room at Toronto Western Hospital. They had little to offer her in the way of medicine but suggested that she try to "get into her housework" as a way of taking her mind off her missing child. "Teenagers misbehave," they said. "It's normal," they reassured.

"With all due respect, you have no idea. You cannot possibly understand," Irving told the condescending doctor.

Chavie returned late Sunday night as though nothing was untoward. Other than being tired and wanting to go to bed, the girl appeared unharmed nor any worse for wear. Der thought some discussion regarding her disappearance, her whereabouts, something was in order, but Irving said, "Shh" as they watched Estie climb into bed with their daughter. "Now she is back. Now we close that door."

As Chavie's disappearances became more frequent and of longer duration, Estie learned to accept them as part of who her free-spirited child was. And because Chavie always came back, Estie was able to build herself a fairy tale to step inside of when Chavie went away. Her construct conjured up a world so safe and forgiving, so outside the realm of her own horrifying experiences, that a girl like Chavie, made of silk and candy floss, was free to go out into it and experience all the wonders it had to offer.

Estie was not a stupid woman; quite the opposite, in fact. It was her intelligence that both plagued her and saved her from reality. She knew her only way to continue living after everyone else had perished was to wear a mantle of guilelessness. Sometimes, despite her best efforts, the mantle slipped or was violently yanked off, and she retreated to the safety of her bed.

When Chavie gave birth, instead of lamenting the plight of the unwed teenage parent, Irving, Estie, and Der gave silent, sacred thanks that they had been granted another chance to witness their children grow into healthy, happy adulthood.

They never discussed the reality that declared itself as the girls' first birthdays approached: Chavie was an unreliable mother, and the responsibility of raising the children was theirs. Chavie had been energetically planning a much too elaborate birthday party for Petal and Rose when, days before the event, she disappeared

in the middle of the night for the first time since before she was
pregnant.

"She'll be back," Estie assured herself more than anyone.

"Of course, she'll be back," Irving echoed.

But Der was not as certain. He knew bipolar was a difficult
and dangerous diagnosis, and Estie and Irving's refusal to discuss
it was not an effective safeguard against worst-case scenarios.

Chavie's patterns were both unpredictable and completely pre-
dictable. There were two repeated scenarios that played out.

One, she would return home as she bottomed out and crashed
into despondency, taking to the bed she shared with her daugh-
ters, who piled on her like puppies who had been ignored by their
mother and now wedged themselves into her crevices, searching
for affection. When the wind shifted or the tides turned or chak-
ras were aligned or who the hell knew why, Chavie would cycle
from depression to mania. No matter how many times she came
and went from the apartments on Meadowbrook Road, no one
was prepared for her ascent. Sometimes it took days between
Chavie emerging from her chrysalis and her climb to a pinnacle of
exuberance, sometimes only hours. Usually she mobilized around
an event, activity, or celebration, catching bystanders in her tor-
nado of frenetic activity. She had a remarkable capacity to siphon
others into her funnel cloud, building up to a crescendo she inevitably abandoned before the climax, disappearing and leaving her
disciples in forlorn freefall, repeatedly surprised.

The less common scenario was when Chavie showed up
looking for money and had to be chased away by her desperate
father. Those were the worst times. Those were the times the girls
were ushered away to the safety of Der's apartment for soup and
crafts and stories of attempted distraction. But Petal was never
distracted enough. She retained neuropathic pain she couldn't
entirely understand. Dr. Farmer was the first to utter the word

trauma. Up until then, it was something she thought happened to other people.

Once, the police brought Chavie home. Petal never knew why, but it was another thing she knew not to ask about.

7.

PETAL SPENT THREE weeks in the in-patient ward of the Shalvata Hospital in Hod Ha'Sharon. Dr. Boded and Der discussed at length the pros and cons of medicating her, and each in their own way helped her understand the benefits and risks.

"We believe, given your family predispositions and your own accounts of how you have been feeling and behaving, you could likely benefit from antidepressant medication," Der said to Petal with a clinical disengagement he didn't feel. Petal chewed her fingernails down to nubs behind her wild mass of uncombed hair. Of the two sisters, Petal looked entirely unlike her mother, but Der recognized the red, swollen cuticles and ragged nails that resembled Chavie at her most vulnerable.

Der tried to get Petal up for a walk outside her room daily. He negotiated the privilege of clothing on her behalf, insisting she get dressed. Despite the odds stacked against her, Der was determined to help Petal have an emotionally regulated life. He had borne witness to three generations of psychopathology in this family. But more than that, Der was haunted by self-judgment that his capacity for usefulness was at best limited and his failures historically deadly. Der wanted the best chance for Petal's survival and happiness — not the best chance given the circumstances. Where Petal was concerned, he clung to a romantic notion that with enough, she would be fine. Enough what remained unclear.

"I'm afraid, Der," Petal said.

"That's understandable, Tig. Can you tell me what you are afraid of?" Der asked, silently enumerating his own plethora of fears.

"I'm afraid to not be me," she said. "For good and for bad, this is who I am. I'm afraid to take a pill that will change my personality."

"That's not how it works," Der said.

"I don't want to be in the black hole, but maybe that's where I'm supposed to be. It's what I'm used to. Sometimes the hole gets so deep and tight it squeezes my ribs and chest into my throat, choking the air out of me. That's when I don't want to feel that feeling of not being able to breathe. But other times, it's just like a little puddle that I need to step in. I need to get my feet wet. I can't ignore the puddle. Maybe I'm just supposed to be that person. I'm not Rosie. I don't see everything as sunny and bright. I never have. What if I take the pills and I don't recognize myself? Or worse, what if I take the pills and stop being me? I'm afraid to disappear, Der."

"Antidepressants don't alter your personality."

"Then maybe they won't work on me, because maybe I just have a depressive personality."

"I'm not sure I can explain what you might feel because really, when they work well, it's much subtler than altered personality. I suppose it might be described best as what you don't feel, rather than —"

"That's the trouble, Der! I need to feel! The problems start when I try not to feel!"

"I'm not explaining well. It is not absence of feeling, but rather absence of or diminished bad feeling. You'll still be able to see the puddles and the holes. You'll probably still be able to get your feet wet and even climb into the holes, take a look around, touch the edges, and feel them press up against your ribs, but you'll be able to climb out of the hole or walk around the puddle if you choose to. And, with luck, you will choose to before you feel the need to hurt yourself."

Dr. Boded's approach was less esoteric, more Israeli. "Amitriptyline is a very good drug when it works. When it doesn't work, it can be bad. Because you are an adolescent, it's less likely to work. There's increased risk of psychosis, suicidal ideation. For this reason, we keep you in hospital for maybe a few weeks until you become used to it. Then, if you stay in Israel, we follow you." His face crinkled and folded like it was made of thick velvet.

"So you think I should take medication because of what you say is high-risk behaviour, but the medication you want me to take might lead to higher risk shit?"

"Trust me, you don't have to feel the way you've been feeling. I have been doing this work long time, enough to see miracles happen many times. Give me a few weeks, let me prove to you."

"Then what?"

"Then we see. If you feel better, more stable, you continue doing whatever you were doing. If not, then we try something else or you go back to Canada and try there."

"Okay. Let's try."

The first week was rough. Petal had trouble sleeping, her stomach was upset, her mouth was dry, she had a low-grade, unrelenting headache. She was angry and uncommunicative.

A nurse came to draw blood. "We need to test for HIV. You had unprotected sex with multiple partners."

"I should have done this the easy way and just killed myself," Petal said. They put her on suicide watch.

"I'm not actually going to kill myself! I didn't mean it," she repeated to the silent young man stationed at the door of her room.

Her clothes were taken away, and she couldn't go outside. She ate in her room on paper plates with plastic spoons, or with her hands like an animal. The bathroom door stayed open.

"I can't shit if I'm being watched," she screamed, her belly cramping from the new meds. "Get me the fuck out of this place," she begged Der. "I have no control!"

Der gave her some space. He spent a few distracted days wandering his old haunts in Tel Aviv and Jaffa, marvelling at the changes and evolution. Israel, less than forty years old, was a remarkable place. *If only its history and politics didn't weigh so heavily against achievements and success*, Der ruminated, aware it applied both to country and child.

When he felt Petal had settled a bit, he made the short bus trip between Tel Aviv and Jerusalem to visit Rosie.

He took a chance the message he'd left at Bais Bonos had reached Rosie and hoped she would show up at the entrance to Machaneh Yehuda.

Rose emerged through the thick mist of a foggy Jerusalem day, conspicuously avoiding the embrace Der offered. Instead, she rambled effusively as though harnessing the energy of her repressed affection into frothy babbling.

"My Der! What are you doing here! I can't believe we are here together in Yerushalayim!" Instead of grabbing him by the arm and pulling him in the direction she wanted him to go, as had been her lifelong pattern, Rosie raced ahead into the throngs of the marketplace, talking backwards at Der through the crowds.

"Twitch! You look wonderful!"

"I am wonderful, Der! I am the happiest I have ever been, and I've always been happy!" She laughed. "Why didn't you tell me you were coming? How long are you staying? You have to come to the Old City! It's beyond magical! It is truly a blessed and holy place, Der. My heart and soul have never been so full! You have to stay for Shabbes. Der, you've never felt anything like Yerusha-layim getting ready for Shabbes. The hustle and bustle and business and excitement every week as though each week is the first. And then, calm and quiet and peace settles in with the setting of the sun. There's nothing like it in Toronto. There's nothing like it any-where else in the world. Everyone stops, and for a full twenty-four hours, instead of doing, we are focused on being."

Der followed two paces behind, past the stalls selling kitchen-ware, legumes, dried fruits and nuts, aromatic spices that evoked memories, halva, bourekas, fruits and vegetables smelling like the earth and the sun and rose petals.

Suddenly, Der was awash in the feeling that lay dormant beneath his skin, awakening each time he returned to Israel — pleasant but not comfortable, like a drug he knew too well, loved too much, but recognized as less than safe. Funny he should feel it here, in Jerusalem, a city he believed he was mostly indifferent to. After all, Jerusalem was not a place to visit in the early days unless one was religious or Arab. Nonetheless, Der had never fully come to terms with his aborted mission to Israel, his powerful connection to the place, and his lack of place within this powerful pull. It, the country, required thicker skin than he had. Instead, he had a hole in his heart that filled when he visited and needed to be ignored when he was away.

Rosie stopped abruptly.

"We're here!" she said, standing in front of a restaurant on Agripas Street. It seemed vaguely familiar to Der. The sign in the window read *Hatzot*.

"This place has the best meurav Yerushalmi in the city! It's a dish they make only in Jerusalem. They grill all sorts of different meats and spice them with a secret mixture. You've never tasted anything like it!"

Der had eaten it many times. "I'm looking forward to trying it."

"It was invented by a Jew and an Arab to feed a visiting Christian high priest. That's why it's called Jerusalem mixed grill. A lot of people think it's because they mix a bunch of different meats together, but it's like an inside joke. It's really about the mix of people who claim Jerusalem as their own."

"Twitch, I need to tell you something," he said.

"I'm so excited I haven't shut up for a second."

"It's about Tiggaleh."

"I just saw her! I stayed at her dorm."

"She's not in a good way."

"Because we argued? It was just a stupid fight!"

"No, Twitch, she's in hospital. She's clinically depressed. It has nothing to do with you."

Rosie jumped to her feet. "What are we doing eating in a restaurant when she's in hospital? Let's go!"

"Please sit down. I need ... Tig needs you to be level-headed. This is a marathon, not a sprint," Der said, donning his therapist hat.

"Which hospital?"

"A mental health facility in Hod Ha'Sharon, near Tel Aviv. There is a doctor there I trust. It's the right place."

"All the way in Tel Aviv?"

"Have you been to Tel Aviv?"

"No."

"I don't believe she'll return to Jerusalem."

"Are you taking her home? Are you here to take me home?"

"I'm not here for any of those reasons. I'm here to help. I don't know what she'll decide to do, I just know that she was very unhappy here."

"How could anyone be unhappy here? Hashem is everywhere!"

Der sighed deeply. Rose had always drained him, and with his energy stores depleted, he found her challenging.

"She's having a difficult time, and I don't believe she wants visitors just yet."

"Not even me, Der?"

"Especially not you. You know how much she worries about you, how responsible she feels for you. She feels she has failed you."

"That's ridiculous!"

"A lot of things are ridiculous, but trying to convince someone their ridiculous thinking is ridiculous is useless. People must travel their own paths and come to their own enlightenments."

"Yes, I agree. Now that I have found Hashem, I truly believe that."

WHEN PETAL WAS released, the almond trees were bursting with pink blossoms. It was spectacularly beautiful, and Petal felt optimistic. Der felt momentarily relieved. Both conjured positive thinking as a conscious countermeasure.

They sat on the patio of a pub on Hayarkon Street with a view of the sea, eating greasy french fries slathered in ketchup and vinegar from a basket lined with waxed paper.

"Tell me about my mother," Petal said, licking her index finger. Der hesitated.

"Because no one ever spoke about her after she left, and I need to know if I'm crazy because she was crazy!"

"You are not crazy. I won't have you speaking that way."

"I'm pretty sure three and a half weeks in the loony bin gives me membership in the crazy club," Petal said.

"You were suffering," Der said. "You needed relief. You're not crazy. In any case, neither I nor anyone else has any way to determine if your mental health is the result of history, genetics, circumstance, or a combination of these and other factors."

"You're avoiding my question, Der. Why is everything in our family a secret? Other kids know about their family history, about their parents' childhoods, about where their families come from ... I know almost nothing. I'm not even sure if the memories I have are real or invented. Did it happen to me or Rosie, or did we make it up? We weren't allowed to ask. There aren't even any family photographs. All I have is this feeling that I'm being dragged down by some mythological creature, and I'm constantly trying not to drown. *Mentor nischt zogen!* That was our family mantra. Please, Der, show me the monster so at least I can have a chance to escape its grasp."

Taking Petal's hand, Der looked out at the sea where history was discarded. "I loved your mother like she was my own child. When she died, we all lost pieces of our souls. Yitzchak and Esther had already lost so much. Their only way to cope was to suppress their pain, to never speak of their unfathomable losses. I couldn't pour salt in their open wounds, so I kept the silence. Even now, I feel I'm somehow betraying a sacred trust of ineffability."

"What the fuck is ineffability? Stop tiptoeing around me, Der. How do I know if I can handle the truth if I never know it?" Petal said.

"It means unmentionable. I suppose it is another way of saying *mentor nischt zogen.*"

Der stopped talking and took hold of Petal's wrist as she reached for the french fries. He looked at her intently, as though by feeling her pulse and searching her eyes he might know what to say next.

"We all had to soldier on, for your sake, for your sister's sake. We weren't young, but we recognized that your mother was never going to be a reliable parent, so we stepped up."

"That's the part I know, Der. Tell me what she was like. Tell

me when things fell apart. Tell me how she died. Tell me how you
knew. All I remember is that one day we knew she wasn't coming
home again."

"I've also gotten used to locking away the pain," Der said,
willing himself to be brave. "I feel like I knew her from the time
she was born, but really, I didn't meet her till she was about eight.
She looked a lot like Twitch. She had an unpredictable temper-
ament: sweet as honey one minute and tropical storm the next
and then back to delightful as though nothing had happened.
Now we know that she had bipolar disorder, but we didn't at the
time. It's difficult to diagnose in adults, let alone in children who
swing wide at the best of times. By now you also know that your
bubby suffers from depression. Even though no one calls it that, I
don't have to tell you what 'getting into bed' means."

Petal rolled her eyes.

"It was a different time, Tig. We didn't speak about mental
health, let alone mental illness. Not just us, everyone. We lived
in a time of taboos. When we got to Palestine, no one wanted
to hear what they had been through. Even if they had wanted to
talk about it, there was no place for it. The subliminal message
that came through loud and clear was, 'Those scars only weaken
the fabric of our precarious little state. Keep them to yourselves.'
There was no room to express sadness or grief or brokenness. The
new Jewish people were strong pioneers and fierce warriors. So,
everything stayed bottled up.

"Anyhow, that's how Estie coped. And when she couldn't
cope, she got into bed, and we didn't talk about it. I helped in
the only way I could. I made a second home for Chavie. But I
failed them. I should have known better about Estie. I should have
known better about Chavie. I should have done more. I should
have found the vocabulary for so many things, but I didn't."

Der looked around for the waitress. "I'm going to order a beer. Do you want a soft drink or something?"

"Can I have a beer?"

"It's not a good idea with your medication, but I won't stop you."

Petal ordered a cola and a plate of hummus.

"Go on," she said.

"Round about the time puberty and hormones hit, things got more difficult with Chavie. She would disappear for days, then weeks, then months, which, as you can imagine, weighed heavily on your grandparents. An out-of-control adolescent is always concerning, but add in the extenuating circumstances of their lives and we were all just barely keeping it together. We hid behind words like *flower child* and *hippie*, but they were at best excuses. Then Chavie showed up pregnant. Before you were even born, I claimed you. I made a pact with myself that you would be my responsibility, and I was determined to do better by you.

"A few weeks after you, Twitch came along, and there was more than enough responsibility to go around. In the end, I couldn't do anything. Chavie fell through the cracks. She was feral. We were up to our eyeballs with the two of you. She was cycling between manic and depressive episodes so rapidly. Eventually, we managed to get her admitted to hospital. We thought she was in a safe place, but she left. It was never clear how, despite an inquiry. I'm fairly certain her good looks and hypersexualized mania played a part. Who knows how she ended up across the country, but pretty girls who are eager to party have no need for money or cars or anything else. That was your mother. I blamed myself. I blamed the porous system that failed her.

"She hadn't been gone long when the call came from the police. I flew west to identify the body." Der took a long sip of his beer.

"And?" Petal prompted.

"And the rest is obvious, I suppose. She died." Der wiped at the condensation on the side of his glass with his index finger.

"How?"

"Drug overdose ... in Vancouver. Estie unravelled, and, given the situation, she had no faith left in hospitals or doctors. She got into bed. Yitz held on by a thread because of you and your sister. After Estie had been in bed for three months, the longest she had ever stopped functioning, I spoke to her for the one and only time about grief and about depression. We managed to get her on clomipramine, an early-generation, moderately effective antidepressant. We didn't have the options of today."

Der and Petal sat silently for a while.

"You did your best, Der," Petal said. "You didn't fail them. You're here. You came to save me. And you did. I'm better. Now I can get on with my life."

"What do you suppose that looks like?" Der asked.

"I'm going to rent an apartment in Tel Aviv, get a job as a waitress, and stick around to keep tabs on Rosie."

Der had been sure Petal, fundamentally reasonable Petal, would be heading back to Toronto with him. He had been so sure of it that he had all but promised Estie that he would bring her back.

"Out of the question!" he said and immediately regretted it.

"You tell me not to let Rosie control my decisions, but it's okay for you to control my decisions!" Petal was as surprised as Der was by his reaction.

"I shouldn't have said that. It just took me by surprise that you would want to stay. You're not responsible for Rosie. You mustn't let her decisions control your actions. I'm not trying to control you; I'm just trying to keep you safe. You must understand my worry."

"I'm not my mother!" Petal said, stabbing Der more deeply than she could know. "Rosie got me into this mess, and unless you want me to resent her forever for highjacking what was supposed to be *my* freshman year of university, *my* future, I need to make something of my time here. It can't forever be remembered as 'the time Petal ended up in the nuthouse.'"

Eventually, Der admitted to himself that nothing he said or did, short of bashing Petal over the head, tying her up, stuffing her in a suitcase, and throwing her in the baggage hold of the plane, was going to have any effect on her next step.

Der couldn't disagree entirely with Petal's arguments.

"You want your bubby to get into bed? She's already worried sick about you. You stay and do and make something of the rest of this year, but you do it somewhere with a little bit of a safety net. It will still be an adventure. It will still be something new. Most importantly, it will be somewhere you cannot take responsibility for Rosie."

Before Der boarded his return flight and after much negotiation, he made sure Petal was settled in on kibbutz Beit Keshet in the Jezreel Valley where he knew his old friends would keep an eye on her.

SHUKI, AN ISRAELI poet of some renown, had been one of the early settlers of kibbutz Beit Keshet, where he met and married his wife, Shula. Der had been there when they'd met and, given the chaos of the times and Der's gift with words, he had been the unsanctioned officiant at their wedding. It was a celebration at a time when the community was desperately in need of something to celebrate. In hindsight, it had been perhaps the most meaningful, legally meaningless contribution Der had made during his time on the kibbutz.

Shuki and Shula were salt of the earth, die-hard kibbutznikim. Their original chosen home had not recovered well from the loss of seven members during the battle of Beit Keshet. The small collective was left with a chasm of grief, further inflamed by the catastrophic difference of opinions regarding the Arab youth who had happened — either by accident or by design, depending upon one's perspective — into their fields. The more moderate voices, amongst them both Shuki's and Shula's, lost out to the more enraged, frightened sentiments held by those who took the young man out to a field and shot him as an example to others who might think stumbling onto kibbutz land was all right under any circumstances. It was a wound that could never heal. Shuki and Shula left Beit Keshet and the more radical Kibbutz Artzi movement and moved to kibbutz Ein Harod in the Jezreel Valley, a kibbutz affiliated with a more moderate political alignment. Leaving almost broke their hearts. Finding a new home helped mend them.

Over the years, Der had visited his friends many times. He knew Petal would not be the first adolescent in need of supervision who had crossed their threshold. They were remarkable parents to their own now-grown children and to many other people's children. Der knew they would look out for Petal, and he hoped that she might join the other adoptees who considered Shuki and Shula surrogate parents. They were the kind of folk Petal could use on her team.

In a top-down sports car, Der drove Petal to the caring protectorate of his old and dear friends. She was quiet on the drive up from Tel Aviv to Ein Harod, the gusting wind a good excuse for silence. They took the coastal road until the Caesaria interchange, where they turned inland and headed east toward the kibbutz. Petal refused to admit she felt some excitement about this new chapter. She had enjoyed her brief stint on a kibbutz during the summer. For some reason, she needed Der to believe she was resistant. Perhaps claiming it as her own felt like too much responsibility for success.

Past the entry gate and up a ficus-tree-lined hill, Petal turned to look across the back of the car. In the distance, across the

Mondrian patchwork of green and yellow fields, she could see what she did not know at the time was Mount Gilboa. What she believed she saw was the hill she had climbed to leave trouble on the far side.

They stopped in front of a small, two-storey fourplex, each unit adorned with the personalities of its residents in the form of children's wood and ceramic creations. The exterior tiled stair-cases leading to the upper apartments were lined from top to bottom with plant-filled, mismatched pots, cracked and chipped over time by the many footfalls on the stairs. From the banister posts hung tarnished brass bells and blown glass spheres of cobalt blue and emerald green. It looked dishevelled and inviting. Petal liked the imperfection of it. *A fractured person in an imperfect place. Maybe I can fit*, she thought.

Der honked the horn, announcing their arrival. Two androgyn-ous people, a bit older-looking than Der, came down the left-hand staircase. They both wore Birkenstock clogs, baggy blue jeans on skinny bird legs, and plaid shirts on round, poultry-like chests. They wore their hair in identical, short, mostly white, coxcomb disarray. Not until they had traversed the patch of lawn in front of the house did Petal see that the woman wore long, dangling earrings that reached almost to her shoulders and a silver cuff with two rams' heads on her wrist.

The three threw arms around necks and waists, hugging and greeting with the adoration of long-lost love. "You and your con-vertibles!" the man good-naturedly chastised Der. "You always were the bourgeoisie among us."

Petal felt jealous. Her lifelong presumption that Der belonged to her was being challenged.

"Shula, Shuki, I want you to meet the daughter I never had," Der said. "This is Petal Wolffe, my most precious treasure. You know I wouldn't bring her anywhere but here."

Shula reached out a hand as though to shake, but when Petal responded in kind, she was pulled into an enthusiastic hug. "Family is family," Shula said in her high-pitched, South African-inflected shrill.

"What a glorious day! Isn't it perfect, Shuki? We'll have coffee outside!" Shula decreed, proceeding to produce blankets and lawn chairs and cushions from a small, dilapidated shed. Shuki disappeared upstairs, reappearing shortly with a tray of coffee and baked goods, fruit, nuts, and seeds.

They had barely had time to catch their breath and have a sip of coffee when Shula spoke her mind.

"Der tells us you have just come from a few weeks in Shalvata. It's a good hospital. But the proof of the pudding, so to speak, is not in how well you do on the inside but how well you manage on the outside. The kibbutz will be your testing ground, and you can consider us your security blanket."

Petal looked uncertainly at Der.

"You wanted no secrets," Der said. "Shula has no sacred cows. Everything is on the table and open for discussion. You'll get used to it."

"Absolutely!" Shula said. "*Nachon*, Shuki? No secrets. Lots of conversation."

"Forthright. Isn't this how you called her, Der?" Shuki said.

"Entirely! I think it will be good for you, Tig."

"Thank you for everything and for always," Petal said to Der before he left.

"Tiggaleh, you are not your sister's keeper. When you are compelled to tether Rosie, please try to remember that you never have to do it alone. I am always around to help. Forever and for always."

Der crossed his fingers, hoped for the best, and returned to Canada with enough faith to reassure Estie and Irving that Petal was in good hands. Between his friends Roie Boded, Shuki, and Shula, Der had surrounded Petal with a force field he trusted. The rest would be up to her.

Mornings, Petal studied Hebrew in the Ulpan, where enthusiastic, sincere, and remarkably demanding Shula was her teacher. After lunch, Petal worked in the kindergarten, where she got her real Hebrew lessons. The precociously self-assured children demanded she communicate their way. She loved her work with the children, and they loved her. They called her Mitz Petel, the Israeli equivalent of Kool-Aid, and she let them climb her like a tree and braid small plastic toys into her wild hair.

Given her recent history, Petal was more reticent than usual of socializing. With the other volunteers she was friendly but not friends, avoiding the nighttime parties and flirtations. She didn't trust her instincts. So, it was convenient that she had a standing invitation every evening at the home of Shuki and Shula.

Like most homes on the kibbutz, Shuki and Shula's was small and crowded, but that didn't stop them from welcoming a constant stream of visitors. When their flat grew too full or too hot, they would spread blankets on the lawn at the front and move outdoors. If more guests arrived, more blankets would be spread. And if the weather grew too cool, shawls and sweaters were provided. There was always more space, more coffee, and enough cake, fruit, nuts, and sunflower seeds to go around. Another trip up or down the staircase was never begrudged. There were musicians and artists and teachers and interesting, frank conversation. The guests spoke passionately about politics and history and philosophy. They shouted at one another when they disagreed and laughed robustly when something funny was said. There was music, singing, young people, and old people, and Petal thought it was wonderful! Petal was happy.

In fact, Petal was more than happy. She was content.

Every month, to uphold the bargain she had struck with Der, she would reluctantly leave the kibbutz to check in with Dr. Boded at his clinic in Tel Aviv and visit with Rosie, who would come from Jerusalem to meet her. Leaving the cloistered world of the kibbutz caused no small amount of anxiety leading up to each excursion. Shula, cautious of allowing her to treat the kibbutz as a sanctuary from the real world, escorted her to the bus stop and waited with her until she boarded. No matter how late, Shula was always there to greet her upon her return.

Eema Shula, a nickname used as often as a compliment as it was an admonishment by many on the kibbutz, had a reputation for taking on the most burdensome, lost, needy souls and giving them a place to call home. This meant that sometimes the kibbutz was forced to take in people who were less equal in their capacity to contribute. They called her Mother Shula when being kind and Mother Teresa facetiously when the undertone of disapproval was one of running a convent for wayward teens. Her reputation among some for being a do-gooder elicited an equal and opposite not-in-my-backyard resentment from others less accepting of her compassionate nature. To be sure, Shula was a bit loopy, but in the kindest, most benign way.

For Petal, Shula became more of a mother than any she had ever had, because her bubby loved her, cared for her, and raised her, but she never challenged her or questioned her or forced her to examine herself or told her the truth. Shula was not nearly as much of a pushover or bleeding heart as some liked to believe. Acceptance, not absolution, was her MO. Her door, her ears, and her heart were always open, and Petal let herself be let in.

The months passed, summer came and went, and neither Petal nor Rosie was ready to leave Israel or the new lives they had found and the new families they had made.

8.

PETAL HAD BEEN up for hours anticipating her move to Rosie's world. She and Der had had such a lovely time at dinner the night before, but she hadn't slept well. It was going to be a long ten days.

"Hashem this and Hashem that and fucking with the help of God!" Petal ranted from the bedroom. "If only they would stop with the religious prattle."

"Tiggaleh," Der said, "I understand your exasperation, but it's hardly the salient point in this moment. Keep in mind that, in their world, they rely on God. Faith is powerful and sometimes enviable. A belief in God offers an option that doesn't require one to hang on so tightly to control. The chips fall where they may. Perhaps you shouldn't be quite so dismissive."

Petal dug her vibrating phone from her pocket and answered it.

"I'm here. Are you ready?" Heschy said.

"You're early. No davening this morning?" Petal asked, pulling her suitcase toward the door.

"Yuntif. Early prayers this morning because of the holy days. You need more time?"

"I'll be right down," she said. "Der," she shouted toward the kitchen, "I'm going. Rabbi Glisserman is here to get me."

"Tiggaleh," he said, coming through the swinging kitchen door, "she's your sister, but it's a heavy load to carry alone. You must lean on me. Call me when it's a good time, and I'll come see you two. For everything and for always, huh."

"For everything and for always, Der, especially in all matters Rosie."

Petal approached Heschy's waiting crumbalow-on-wheels. She walked around to the passenger side, but someone was in the front seat. Petal got in the back.

"*Gut Shabbes. Gut yuntif,*" Heschy said as Petal brushed fast food refuse from the seat onto the floor. "Ari, Dr. Wolffe. Dr. Wolffe, Arieh."

Heschy motioned to a barely visible adolescent boy hooded and wrapped in a blanket Petal recognized from the floor of Heschy's car.

"He needs to be watched," Heschy said as explanation for the boy's presence.

"It's not kosher," Petal said.

"What's not kosher?"

"McDonald's ... the wrappers on the seat," she said, stirring the contents of the floor well with her foot. "Orthodox kids eat all this crap?"

"Unkosher crap is the least of the problems for the kids who ride in my car," Heschy said, tilting his head subtly toward the boy. "You, on the other hand, don't need to worry. For you, we have arranged kosher." He smiled into the rear-view mirror.

Petal smiled back.

"My wife has arranged a roster of people to bring you and your sister meals through to the end of yuntif. Not just kosher! Kosher for Passover!"

"That's completely unnecessary. I know how to cook."

"Actually, cooking isn't the point. You remember Schmeil was worried about the house not being kosher for the holiday? He sold the kitchen for the duration of the holiday. It's unrealistic to expect you to stay out of the kitchen, but he'd like you to treat it as though it doesn't belong to you. *Farshteist?*"

"Can I pretend that I'm the maid and clean the kitchen at least?"

"I don't suppose there would be any objection to cleaning. It could use it," Heschy said.

"Can I ask you a question?"

"Anything."

"I don't mean any disrespect, so I hope you don't take it the wrong way, but ... do other families in your community live like they do?"

"Like I told you, some manage better than others. Children are a blessing, but not an easy blessing. There are issues of time and money and personal capacity. Not everyone manages, and some people are only able to manage by letting go of certain expectations: cleanliness, discipline, homework. Everybody finds their own threshold of tolerable. There are likely many households in our community where the level of disarray and chaos might seem unfamiliar to you but is not uncommon to us."

Heschy pulled up in front of the crumbalow. "I'll drop Ari off and come back. Dr. Gold will be by at some point. Good luck."

Despite audible activity inside the house, no one answered Petal's knock. She let herself into the cacophonous three-ring circus.

It looked as though the alien invaders from the previous day had celebrated their annexation of the crumbalow by churning the sedimentary layers of clothes and crud on the floors, throwing it all up in the air, and letting it land like confetti, leaving behind a gaggle of screechy girls in long skirts, opaque tights, and sweater sets and one adolescent boy with crumpled clothing and ear locks to contend with the aftermath of the alien victory celebration.

"Hello," Petal said to no one in particular.

A skinny, pimply boy of about fourteen stood by the bed in the front room peering into an empty suitcase. Avromi Yitzchak had grown significantly since his bar mitzvah. Petal would not have been able to identify her nephew out of context.

Under the bed, a child about three years old was playing with a yellow bulldozer. *Simcha Aron*, Petal noted. *The girls are harder to pick out of a lineup.* Through the kitchen, Petal could see Schmeil on the edge of his bed, doubled over, head in hands.

A small girl — plaid kilt, navy-blue tights with holes in the toes — marched into the front room, crouched down, and wrestled the little boy out from under the bed by his ankles. "Simcha Aron, *mine zeiskeit!* Let's get you packed," she said, hoisting the reluctant child onto her nonexistent hip in a disconcertingly maternal gesture only to be intercepted by a slightly larger version of herself — plaid skirt, holey stockings — limbs flailing and high-pitched, grating, singsong voice running full volume. "Estie! Put him down! You also need to pack! Simcha Aron, go to Sarah Batya, *gei!*" The boy child scurried through, past Raizel and Schmeil's room into the next room, slamming the door. Girls continued to wail at one another.

"Chava Malka, just because Mameh is sick doesn't make you the boss of me," the one called Estie said.

"Estie, just because Mameh is sick doesn't make you Simcha Aron's mother."

"*Genug!*" An older girl appeared in the boys' room. Petal was losing track. This one looked like all the girls Rosie had met in Yerushalayim. "Stop arguing and pack!" She poked her brother, who was still staring into the suitcase. She started picking through the clothes on the floor, tossing them toward the open suitcase.

"Stop it!" Avromi Yitzchak said.

"Well then, do it yourself! Mameh isn't going to do it for you!"

"Are you going to pack for Simcha Aron also?"

"Leah Rochel!" A small girl raced past Petal, through the kitchen, into another room. "Leah Rochel, come help the boys! They can't do anything!"

"Gittie Freidle, I'll come when I'm ready!"

Petal watched the entrances and exits through doors and passageways in seemingly endless loops around the small, square house, each room leading into the next, as though an old farce was playing and she was the invisible audience.

"Schmeil? Rosie?" she said, pushing on the door to their room.

Schmeil stood up. "Sorry. Things are a bit hectic. My Raizeleh usually organizes," he said, gazing at the dishevelled heap of bedding.

"Is there anything I can do to help?"

"The girls will manage, Baruch Hashem."

"Schmeilkeh?" the bedding croaked.

"Raizeleh, your sister is here." Schmeil patted the bedclothes. "Pet?"

"Hi, Ro. How are you, sweetie?" Petal asked.

"Lie down with me, Pet." Rosie pushed her head through the blankets.

Petal looked at Schmeil for a sign of approval. "Of course," he said, awkwardly squeezing into the hallway.

Petal lay down next to her sister, breathing in the stale odour. She put her hand on Rosie's cheek. "We haven't lain in bed together for so long, Ro. I'm glad to be here."

Reaching her blistered hand up from under the covers, Rose covered Petal's hand, blinking agreement.

PETAL WOKE, DISORIENTED, in her sister's embrace to her vibrating pocket.

"Hey," she whispered into her phone.

"Am I waking you, Pet?" Benjamin asked. "Sorry. Go back to sleep. We'll talk later."

"Hold on a sec." Petal climbed off the bed gingerly. Stepping into the bathroom, she closed the door. "I'm at Rosie's. I can't believe I fell asleep with all the chaos. What time is it?"

"Eight forty-five, natch. Did you stay there last night?" Benjamin asked.

"No, I just came this morning. Total mayhem here with everyone packing to go up to Schmeil's family. I just lay down with Ro and fell asleep."

"You've seen the kids? How do they seem?"

"I'm invisible to them. It's weird." Petal scanned the bathroom. Clumps of blue-green toothpaste splotched the sink, tangled lumps of hair collected in the corners of the darkly ringed tub — cracked, grimy remnants of soap on the ledges of both sink and tub — and a toilet that demanded the lid be closed or her gaze averted. Lowering the lid, she flushed and sat with a sigh of surrender.

"How do you feel about that?" Benjamin asked, interrupting her critical assessment.

"I guess I'm just not thinking about it. I gave up on being part of their lives a long time ago. You're my family. They are my relatives."

"That must be hard."

"Tell me about last night," Petal deflected. "Was it in the big theatre or the little one?"

"The big one. It was totally packed, but not for me."

"If not for you, for whom?"

"David Rakoff was reading. He was the main course. I was the appetizer."

"Cut it out, Benjamin! It's not true."

"I'm not being falsely modest. I did all right, but he's a total pro. I chatted with him before we read. I was a total goofy fanboy trying desperately to be cool. He said he'd enjoyed my work, and I think I started drooling. Very cool, huh? To add to my asinine bumbling, I asked him for 'any tips from a successful author?' I'm such an idiot."

"You wouldn't let me talk about myself that way. I'm sure he was flattered. He probably thought you were hitting on him."

"I might have been. I certainly wouldn't have said no. But, alas, deep sigh ..."

"Now you're being goofy. Did he have any tips?"

"He said, 'Hate yourself just enough to be sure everyone else will. Love yourself just enough to test your theory and put yourself out there.' Then he kind of smirked adorably with just the left side of his mouth and said, 'It's a crapshoot. Do the work. See what happens. Hating yourself is just a side effect.'"

"I never realized you found self-loathing so adorable. That explains a lot about our attachment."

"Verily, my Pet. After, people waited for ages in line. He must have been signing books long after I left."

"I have no doubt you were as brilliant as always and that even David Rakoff thought so."

"How am I supposed to hate myself and be a successful writer if you're always telling me supportive lies?"

"You're impossible!"

"I'm not saying I have no talent, but there's a whole other stratosphere of talent out there that I can only catch a whiff of through my own stench of desperation. When I see that, I can't help wondering what the point of trying is. Then I double back and wonder if the point is to try and find inspiration from the kind of creativity I can't even hope to achieve."

"And what about us mere mortals who don't even try? You know I think you're talented, but your track record doesn't need my seal of approval. You already belong to an elite group of artists that exist in an echelon of accomplishment beyond the norm. And rest assured, you already have the self-loathing in the bag."

"It takes one to know one."

"Very mature, Benjamin. If only you could see yourself the way I see you!" Petal felt relieved talking about something other than her sister.

"That's the trick, the challenge of life. Or half of it at least; to see yourself as others see you and to see others as they believe themselves to be ..." Benjamin paused.

"I'm trying hard to see my sister as she believes herself to be."

"I know you are, Pet. I can only imagine how complicated it must be. Our city is glorious today. I wish you were here to play hooky with me."

"I wish I was too. I miss you, and New York. What will you do to share it with me?" Petal said.

"I'll pretend to work for a bit and then I'll reward my good intentions with a stroll. I need to pop into the library, then I'll call you, and we can have a virtual drink together in Bryant Park."

"Deal. Things should settle down around here by then. I need you to remind me of my life." Petal rose from her ignoble seat.

The house was significantly quieter. The bedroom doors were closed, the kitchen empty. She poked her head into the boys' room. On each of the two beds sat one boy and three girls, all stiffly pointing to a row of small suitcases. Schmeil faced the children, one finger to his lips, while he listed the packing requirements. "Toothbrushes?" he said, holding up his thumb.

The children nodded, except the youngest boy, who pulled at the sleeve of his eldest sister, who nodded silently back at him.

"Pajamas? Yuntif clothes? Yuntif shoes? Regular clothes? Regular shoes? Socks? Gatkes?" Schmeil said, raising fingers with each item, beginning again from the thumb when he ran out of digits. "Sarah Batya, what am I forgetting?" He looked to his eldest daughter, who in turn looked at her sisters.

"Leah Rochel and Miriam Ruthie were helping the girls, and I was helping the boys. I think we're all set," she said.

"Baruch Hashem!" Schmeil held his hand up to his restless children. "One more thing," he said. He noticed Petal, who ducked into the kitchen, "Two more things. Petal?" he called, addressing his sister-in-law directly and by name for the very first time. "Can you come?"

Petal stood in the doorway.

"This is your Tante Petal; Mameh's sister from New York. You remember her?" The children stared as though she was from somewhere much more alien than New York. "She, b'ezrat Hashem, will take care of Mameh while we're away. Petal, these are our blessings." Schmeil pointed at each of the children in birth order, as though he could only recall their names in a particular sequence, though Petal realized he was probably doing that for her benefit. "Sarah Batya, our eldest, Leah Rochel, Miriam Ruthie, Avromi Yitzchak, Chava Malka, Gittie Freidle, Estie, and our baby, Simcha Aron."

"I'm not a baby!" Simcha Aron chimed indignantly.

"But you're Mameh and Tateh's baby," Estie said, patting him on the head with a stiff-handed bounce.

The children stared silently.

"They're not used to strangers," Schmeil apologized awkwardly.

"Is she a woman?" Gittie Freidle asked. Chava Malka gave her a sharp elbow to the ribs. "What? She's wearing pants like a man." Gittie Freidle was rewarded with another nudge from Avromi Yitzchak.

"What's the second thing?" Chava Malka asked, blushing crimson on her sister's behalf.

"The second thing?" Schmeil said.

"You said two more things," the children all said in unison and giggles, evoking a decidedly Von Trappian flashback for Petal.

"Of course! We must say goodbye, *gut Shabbes*, and *gut yuntif* to Mameleh. Two at a time. Oldest takes youngest — and next and next. Like you know," he said, looking proudly from his children to Petal and back to his children. "My *neshoma!* My whole soul, Baruch Hashem! And my hands," he said, indicating the older girls.

Two by two, the children went into their mother's room, kissed her, stroked her face, wished her well, told her they loved her and they would miss her, kissed her some more, and stroked her hands, and it was obvious to Petal that her sister was a good mother and her children were good children, and at that moment she believed she saw Rose as Raizel, a woman of valour.

"Everybody take their own suitcase. Avromi Yitzchak, you take for Simcha Aron and yourself. You are in charge of getting everything and everyone into the car. I will be out in just a few minutes, and I expect you all to be ready and waiting," Schmeil said, fishing into his trouser pocket, handing the car key to the pimply adolescent. Petal had not thought him capable of such leadership. *Wrong again*, she thought, ashamed of her presumptions.

The boy plucked the keys from his father's hand, lifted a black fedora from a hook on the wall, flipped it onto his head, picked up two of the small suitcases, and strode out of the house in as manly a way as his skinny frame could muster. The rest of the children filed out behind him, like ducklings with luggage.

"I don't know what to say," Schmeil said, awkward again.

"No need to say anything."

"I know Raizel is in good hands with you and Hashem ..." His eyes welled with tears.

"We'll be fine. You go and enjoy with your family ..." Petal thought about saying *don't worry* but realized it was a stupid thing to say.

"Heschy and Dr. Gold will tell you what to do. They know much more than a *narishkeit* know-nothing like me."

Petal suppressed her instinct to place a hand on her brother-in-law's shoulder. "We'll be fine." She inched toward the door to dislodge Schmeil from his reluctance to leave.

Petal watched Schmeil trudge to the van that was bursting full of his children and their belongings. *Jews with baggage*, she thought. *History repeating itself.*

Peeking in on Rosie, safe in her bedding cocoon, Petal heard pounding on the front door. "One of the children must have forgotten something," she said to no one. Petal opened the door.

"*Vos machts?*" said Heschy Glisserman from behind a stack of foil containers. He was flanked by an extraordinarily small wigged woman in generic Orthodox garb — dark stockings, long skirt, flat shoes, oversized coat — and the monolithic Dr. Gold; the pair were also overloaded with packages.

"My apologies! I didn't have a free hand. I just kicked the door." Heschy fumbled.

Stepping aside, Petal ushered them into the kitchen. Holding their packages, they gazed around. With no obvious place to rest their loads, the men looked to the small woman for guidance. Petal followed suit.

"*Gevalt!*" said the woman. "A complete *hegdish!* Such a state!"

"Simmaleh," Heschy said, cutting her off, "this is Dr. Wolffe, Mrs. Hirsch's sister. Dr. Wolffe, this is my wonderful wife, Simcha."

"Call me Petal, please," she said. "Can I take some of these things off your hands?" She moved to relieve the woman of her packages.

"Don't touch!" Simcha flinched. "It has to be right!"

Petal stepped back, realizing she was in unknown territory again. The men did the same.

"Drop the two bags in your left hand into the sink. I'll sort them out later," she ordered the doctor, moving as fast as she barked. "Call me Simmy," she said to Petal. "With yuntif coming on the heels of Shabbes, there's so much to do, and it can get complicated. If I pretend I'm a general, they behave like soldiers and take orders." She smiled, looked lovingly at her husband, and blushed a little.

"Now, the problem of where to put the Pesachdik food. Technically, it's all Pesachdik.But for Shabbes we need challah, so the Shabbes food is in the sink for now." It was as though she was singsonging her way through a Talmudic treatise, either for Petal's sake or to gather her thoughts — or both.

"This is all food for the two of us? Did you make all this?" Petal said.

"We have big families. We don't know how to make small amounts, so I made a little extra. It was easier than trying to arrange a roster on such short notice and before Shabbes yuntif. Next week, you'll have other people's cooking. Until then, you're stuck with mine."

"She's just joking," Heschy said. "My wife is an extraordinary cook. But, Simmaleh, I can't hold all this stuff much longer."

Simmy looked around the unkempt kitchen, spinning three hundred and sixty degrees on her ballet shoes. "Hold this for a minute," she said, shoving her packages at Petal. Slipping her coat off and flinging it away, she revealed a crud-splattered black sweater set that hugged a torso no bigger than a twelve-year-old girl on the cusp of puberty; the juxtaposition of fierce military commander in a child's body was disconcerting. Petal tried to remember how many children had been borne by this minute woman. Simmy crouched down to the cupboard underneath the sink and pulled out three large green garbage bags and a fresh J Cloth. She tucked the cloth into the waistband of her skirt, pushed the others aside, and spread two of the garbage bags on the floor in quick, fluid motions. "Put!" she commanded with two tiny index fingers crooked downward, indicating the makeshift clean space on the floor. The third garbage bag she snapped open at the edge of the cluttered table. Leaning her entire body across the table, both arms fully outstretched, she gathered all the debris and pulled it into the open bag in one smooth, efficient movement. Without skipping a beat, she pulled the red plastic drawstring at the top closed and swung the whole thing out toward the front door.

Next, Simmy rummaged through drawers. Finding an industrial-sized box of aluminum foil, she hoisted it onto her hip, a gesture that reminded Petal of her tiny niece. *They start training young*, she thought. Holding the box of foil with one hand, Simmy used the other hand to dampen her J Cloth, gave the table a serious scrub, and put the foil down. Petal was impressed.

As though reading Petal's mind, Heschy said, "Simcha says that the definition of a real eshes chayil, a true woman of valour, is someone who can find their way around another woman's kitchen."

Dr. Gold shuffled around the garbage bags, nudging Heschy to the bedrooms. "We'll go check on Mrs. Hirsch."

"Shall I come with you?" Petal asked.

"You stay with Mrs. Glisserman," Dr. Gold said. "We'll talk after she explains the meals to you. I'll have a word with Mrs. Hirsch first."

Simmy rolled out sheets of foil on the Formica table. "See if there's some tape in one of the cupboards or drawers," she said to Petal.

Simmy taped together the sheets of foil, tucking the edges under the table, hermetically sealing in the leaven of daily use from the kosher of Passover. She did the same to the counter. "That'll have to do," she said. "Everything is labelled. In the sink, we have Shabbes food. Put it all in the oven this afternoon, even the cholent. It's supposed to cook all night on a low heat. Set the oven at 275 degrees and leave it on until after yuntif ends on Monday night. That way, you aren't breaking any commandments about creating fire or doing work on holy days.

"The difference between the Shabbes food and the rest of the food is the kezayis. You know what a kezayis is?"

Petal shook her head.

"It's the amount of bread you must eat for the blessing over bread to be kosher. When Pesach falls immediately on the heels of Shabbes and our houses have already been cleaned for the holiday — *vey iz mir!* Believe me when I say you don't want to get crumbs in an Orthodox woman's home after she has scoured it top to bottom for Pesach — so we don't want crumbs or leftovers, just enough for a kosher blessing. The baker makes tiny challahs called kezayis."

"Like the Hebrew *k'zayit?* As in the size of an olive?"

"Exactly," Simmy said, "depending on who you ask. Our rabbis like a good argument about the finer details of the law. An olive, an egg, a fraction of either … who knows? I buy what the baker sells me. You, you eat it over the sink!"

Sorting containers from the floor to the silver table in neat stacks, Simmy instructed, "Don't forget to take the plastic under the foil off before you heat it up."

Nodding, Petal wished she owned shares in aluminum foil.

"That's a lot of containers for two small women," Petal said.

"The containers are big but not full."

"Cholent was the only thing our zaideh cooked. When Bubby

would get ... sick." Petal thought better about revealing their bubby's history to this virtual stranger. "Zaideh made cholent, and we ate it for days. Sometimes he would add dried tangerine peels to the stewed meat and beans, and the whole apartment would smell like orange blossoms. My first autumn in Israel, when the citrus trees bloomed, I thought the whole country smelled like Zaideh's cholent."

"What a beautiful memory. I'll have to try that sometime. This time you just have regular meat and potatoes without the beans cholent."

"There's nothing regular about any of this. I don't know how to express my gratitude." Petal raised a hand to her mouth, feeling for words that might express her sentiments more profoundly.

"You're here to take care of your sister. Cooking's not important — necessary, but not important. This," Simmy gestured toward the labelled containers, "this is just pragmatism."

"A pragmatic mitzvah," Petal said.

She watched Simmy organize food into heat and don't heat, Shabbes or Pesach, emptying things from the stuffed refrigerator, making executive decisions, throwing things away, rearranging, covering shelves with sheets of foil, creating order from chaos, and stopping along the way to point out what was what. "These two are salad," Simmy said, pointing to the foil containers labelled *salad*. "Don't put these in the oven by mistake."

Witnessing this soldiering through the quagmire with such competence, as though the task were one repeated regularly with precision timing and unwavering speed, was awe-inspiring. She'd assumed that because her sister's world was a mess, because her sister could barely cope with all her children, that it was the norm in the Orthodox community. But here was this woman, so obviously a horse of such a different colour — a workhorse whom Petal had painted with the same brush she had used for all of her

Orthodox presumptions. *I'm the small-minded one*, she thought, tasting her own prejudice.

Dabbing her neck and brow, Simmy looked at Petal with palpable discomfort. "My husband asked me to speak with you about something a bit personal.

Apparently, it's been a while since your sister, *kaiyn'nehora*, has bathed. It's forbidden to use hot water through Shabbes and yuntif, so it'll be Monday night before she has another opportunity to wash. It would be good if you could encourage her to have a shower or a bath before sundown."

Petal smiled.

"What's so funny?" Simmy asked.

"I just didn't know what to expect when you said something personal. I thought you were going to ask me something about myself or secular life."

Simmy smiled back at Petal. "We live very private lives. It may seem foolish to you, but for me to come and speak with you, a stranger, about another woman's personal hygiene, it's not normal."

"I'll do my best," Petal said, releasing this good woman from her discomfort.

"Tuesday morning, someone will bring more food. Not me. We're leaving town Monday night till after end of yuntif. Again, someone will bring food before next Shabbes. By then, you'll get the hang of it."

Simmy shouted toward the bedroom, "*Ich gayst, Heschy. Ich hoben a platz tsu ton. Gut yuntif*, Dr. Gold. *Zei gezunt.*"

She turned to Petal. "B'ezrat Hashem your sister will turn a corner quickly. Have a good yuntif. I'm running. I have a lot to do." She gathered her coat from the floor, grabbed the garbage bag, and left with it.

For the first time, Petal didn't recoil at the mention of God's help as the definitive answer to her sister's recovery. With a deep breath, she silently confessed that a little divine intervention couldn't hurt.

Dr. Gold joined Petal in the significantly less chaotic kitchen.

Rabbi Glisserman ran down to the basement, returning moments later with three folding chairs he placed around the foil-covered table.

"I was wondering about chairs," Petal said.

"We live tight," Heschy said. "You'll find a lotta stuff tucked away in the basement."

Dr. Gold sat down on a chair suspiciously unequal to his weight and placed two plastic boxes half the size of school binders on the table, one pink and one blue. Each box was divided into twenty-one compartments, laid out in seven rows of three and marked with the days of the week and the words *morning, noon,* and *night.* In each compartment were pills. The pink box was fuller than the blue box.

"This is week one," Dr. Gold said, indicating the pink box. "I've divided her medication to make it easy for you. We started her on a very low dose of lithium last night. We'll have to gauge whether or not we should increase the dose. We'll know fairly quickly if it is or isn't the right approach, but not quickly enough that we can risk taking her off the anti-anxiety meds and the sedatives too abruptly."

He picked up the blue box and shook it a little bit. "You see here that there are fewer sedatives as the days go on. By the time yuntif is over, we're hoping only a little nighttime help might be necessary, though it may take longer."

Petal nodded understanding, which she hoped would not be misinterpreted as agreement. To be sure, she spoke her mind, trying not to sound belligerent. "You think after seeing her twice you know what's right?"

"A fair question. I'm fairly confident medication is necessary. What I am less confident about is whether lithium will be the right drug for her. That must be tested on a trial-and-error basis. We're limited in the field of mental health. We have no tests we can run to provide conclusive evidence, so we have to trust our experience, our training, and our faith. Lithium, after all these years, remains the overall best option for bipolar or manic disorders, but as with all these things, it doesn't always work. Let's try and think of it as a first choice and remain optimistic that it will be our best option."

"So I give it to her at night?"

"Yes. The lithium is the pink-and-white capsule. We'll start her with one capsule at bedtime and increase if necessary. Before bed, she can also have the red capsule, which is Seconal, if she's having trouble sleeping. The small white tablets are lorazepam, for anxiety and a less aggressive type of sedation. It will make her drowsy, but it won't necessarily knock her out. I've kept the dose as low as I think is safe and have, as you can see, broken the doses in half and skipped doses as the days go on to try and wean her off the sedatives in a safe way. Believe me, Dr. Wolffe, we want your sister functional as soon as possible. We have no interest in keeping her sedated."

"I have one more question," Petal said. "Given the circumstances, with the family away, et cetera, wouldn't it be better if she were in hospital?"

"Not necessarily, but it's moot. I looked into an inpatient bed as an alternative, but the wait is long. We could get her a crisis admission somewhere, but in seventy-two hours we would likely be back at the same conclusions. You can do for her what no one would do in hospital."

"What's that?"

"Talk to her. Bring her into the real world. Get her up. Take her for a walk. Encourage her to be present."

"I guess this is a go. Should I know about any side effects or anything?" Petal asked.

"It sometimes takes time to get the doses just right, but we can tweak that once we establish a baseline. In the beginning, people often experience the usual side effects of any new drug — nausea, vomiting, dizziness, irritability. They generally pass within a few days or a week," Dr. Gold assured.

"And what's my abort button?" Petal asked.

"I'm sorry? Your abort button?" said Rabbi Glisserman, who had been listening quietly.

"I mean, if anything goes wrong?"

"Baruch Hashem all will be all right," Heschy said.

"No disrespect, but as much faith as you are willing to put in God, I need to know what my tangible backup plan is."

"I'll be out of town, but you can reach me by phone from Tuesday through Thursday. Don't hesitate," Dr. Gold assured.

Heschy shrugged. "I'm walking distance away until I leave for Brooklyn on Monday night. I'll come by after shul on Shabbes."

Before leaving, Dr. Gold handed her three pill bottles with additional medication. Heschy promised to say a *meshebairach* in his prayers.

Petal took the bottles and boxes of pills to the bathroom. "Gross!" she said, unable to find a surface to put them on. She took them back to the kitchen.

She went to the basement in search of cleaning supplies. The basement, like the house, was a small square with one open big room and two small closed rooms. Petal flicked the light switches at the bottom of the stairs. A series of fluorescent tubes in the dropped ceiling revealed a shambles of toys, clothes, and furniture. Petal approached the bog, then thought better of it. She couldn't imagine there was anything in the mess that she needed immediately.

She opened the door of the room closest to the stairs and flicked on another fluorescent tube of cold, blue light. On an old, rickety wooden table were piles of religious books, which spread beyond the table onto a yellowed plastic-covered sofa. On the wall above the sofa, there was a terrible portrait of an elderly rabbi by an artist who should have his hands cut off. On the floor lay what appeared to be the pieces of the dismantled bookshelf. Petal stepped into the room and wondered if it was forbidden for her to touch the books. *Suddenly I'm concerned about what might be forbidden!* she thought. She pushed aside the books on the couch and sat down. Immediately, she recognized the feeling of her bubby's couch. Unmistakable and like a memory serum, the familiar, long-ago crackling of plastic surrounding foam and fabric unleashed a torrent of sadness in her. Sadness for her sister, sadness about life, and sadness for her bubby's sofa — the one Estie had treasured as a symbol of her new, safe, secure life, the life she was meant to live without complexity or burden. The couch that she had encased so carefully in plastic that it would last forever in pristine condition was the only thing that had actually survived, without a doubt worse for wear but more or less unscathed. For the first time since she'd received the call in Washington Square Park, Petal wept.

She wiped her face on her sleeve, got up, turned off the light, and tried the next room. A furnace, old boots, ice skates, baby clothes, stacks of foil containers, paper plates, disposable cups, a hot water tank, folding banquet tables and chairs, and other miscellaneous junk, but nothing resembling cleaning supplies. She headed back upstairs.

Armed with the J Cloths and dishwashing soap from the kitchen, a less than adequate arsenal, Petal tackled the bathroom.

"Yuck!" She looked around, trying to decide which toxic surface to attack first, and there, above the medicine cabinet, her eye caught hold of a treasure trove she had missed before: gallons of Windex, Comet, bleach, and, Baruch Hashem, a toilet brush. "Amen!" Petal said.

After scrubbing the bathroom from stem to stern, proclaiming it not just kosher but kosher for Passover, she went to check on Rosie. Looking at the barely-there outline of her sister, Petal couldn't help playing her lifelong internal dialogue; it had evolved and become more sophisticated as she had, but the fundamentals were like a reoccurring anxiety dream. *I wonder to what extent genetics and to what extent history and circumstance are responsible for the myriad of mental health issues that run so deep in the Wolffe family. I know it's impossible to know. Who can measure if the untold horrors that Bubby and Zaideh experienced were responsible for our mother's problems. Were Irving and Estie depressive by nature, or were they damaged by life? And us? Did having a crazy mother mean we have crazy genes or did it mean we too suffered and reacted? And, since our mother disappeared when we were seven years old and we were raised by our survivor grandparents, are we not in fact children of survivors? Or maybe if we had heard the stories, if it hadn't been taboo, if we had had that to process … God knows.*

She knew this type of thinking wasn't helpful.

"RO? YOU AWAKE?" Petal said, sitting at the edge of Rosie's bed. "Ro, maybe you want to have a shower before Shabbat?" she asked.

"What time is it?" came the small voice from under the covers.

Petal pulled her phone from her pocket. "Three o'clock. Ro, I could wash your sheets before Shabbat if you get up for a bit," she said, trying to engage Rosie in real-world mundanities.

"I'm too tired, Pet."

Petal pulled back the covers, and Rosie curled up like a potato bug. "Come on, Ro. How 'bout you go lie down in one of the kids' beds while I do a bit of laundry. Then you can have a shower. Or we can have a bath together. Like when we were kids. Remember, Ro?"

"'Hydroterapies,'" Rosie said with her bubby's thick Yiddish accent.

"Yeah, we can have some hydroterapies." Petal smiled. Petal had been quite old before she'd realized that Estie's regular encouragement that the girls take a bath had less to do with hygiene and more to do with calming her sister's perpetual exuberance. Estie would run a bath and bring the girls kitchen mixers and beaters and bowls, which they would fill with bathwater mixed with creams and lotions, pretending to be chefs or scientists or witches concocting potions, until the water turned too cold to sit in and they would get out of the tub more sedate than they had gone in, the "frenny" of the moment forestalled.

Petal pulled Rosie toward the edge of the bed, pushed her legs over the side, and pulled her ragdoll-like to a sitting position.

"No, no, Pet. Please," Rosie said, trying to lie back down. "I'm dizzy, Pet. I need to lie down. If you pull me up, the voices can escape."

"I know, Ro. Take it slow. We have lots of time. No rush," she said, wedging herself behind Rosie to keep her upright. "The voices are just voices, Ro. I know you hear them. I know they scare you, but ..." Petal stopped talking. She wasn't sure if she should force the issue of reality versus hallucination.

Petal pulled Rosie up, walked her to the next room, and let her lie back down on one of the children's beds. She returned to Rosie's bedroom. Willing herself to reserve judgment, she stripped the bed, gathered up the scattered clothing from the floor, and took it down to the basement.

Petal's phone rang. "Hey, Benjamin, where are you?"

"Just leaving the library. I ran out of self-deception and admitted I was accomplishing nothing of value," Benjamin said, the noise of the street audible in the background. "What's going on there?"

"I dunno," Petal said. "I feel like a judgmental ass. You should have seen the woman who was here. She brought food and tackled the chaos in the middle of her own holiday preparation, not to mention her seven or eight kids. It was kind of something! I assumed that being *frum* and being overwhelmed or incompetent went hand in hand — like they aren't individuals with differing capacities."

"Interesting — a bit of a forest versus trees paradigm," Benjamin said. "I suppose generalizations are to blame for a good deal of prejudice."

"So, I'm not just a bigot, I'm also unoriginal! Where are you going now?"

"Shall we have a drink in the park? Then I can be an unoriginal stereotype as well — afternoon-drinking, washed-up writer. If I pretend you are with me, then I don't have to add drinking alone to the stale old chestnut."

"It's after five," Petal said. "You're too late for afternoon self-contempt. You would just be getting a jump on weekend merriment."

"Ah, there she is! My girl in the rose-coloured specs."

"Yup, that's me all over. I think I'm going to have to leave you to your own tawdry demise. I'm trying to get some stuff done before sundown. Trying to make myself useful and all."

"No worries, Pet. Talk later, honey. I love you and miss you."

"Love you and miss you too."

With the washing machine done, the dryer doing its duty, and just a couple of hours before sunset, it was time to get Rosie to bathe.

"Rosie," she said, pulling back the bedding less gently than before. "Time for hydroterapies! You want to be clean for Shabbes, don't you?" Petal tried appealing to Rosie's religious fervour.

"Shabbes already?" Rosie said, stretching the words like taffy.

Petal pulled her from the bed, stood behind her, and, wrapping her arms under Rosie's armpits and around her chest, inelegantly guided her to the bathroom. Petal sat her limp sister on the edge of the tub and filled the bath with warm water.

Petal tried pulling her nightgown over her head, but Rosie resisted.

"Come on, Ro. It'll feel good to have a bath. You can't have a bath with your clothes on."

"It's not *tsnius*, Pet."

"It's not what?"

"Modest. It's not modest to undress in front of someone."

"Ro, it's just me … Do you want me to leave?" Petal asked.

"No," Rosie said, her eyes darting about the bathroom as though checking for intruders.

Petal eased Rosie into the warm water, like the opposite of birth, gently back into the safety of warm, enveloping fluid. Pulling the scarf from Rosie's head, Petal released the clips holding the matted hair hostage. She pulled the showerhead from its mooring and leaned Rosie's head back against the wall, running the water over her rose gold locks, down onto her skeletal shoulders. Rosie closed her eyes and relaxed into Petal's hands. Petal supported the weight, massaging lavender-scented shampoo into her sister's scalp, along the shaft of hair that reached almost to her navel, past her sunken chest with its deflated, small breasts that had fed so many babies, across her emaciated ribcage, sending rivulets of lather into the pool of still, clear water.

Petal wrapped Rosie in the cleanest towel she could find on the back of the bathroom door. Sitting on the edge of the tub, she pulled her sister, infantilized by circumstance, onto her lap and into her embrace.

Dressed in a clean nightgown Petal had found in the bedroom dresser, Rosie sat in the kitchen and shivered while Petal combed through the nests in her silken hair the colour of Jerusalem at sunset.

"Take my sweater, Ro," she said. She put her hoodie around her sister's shoulders, which didn't help at all to quell the Parkinsonian quaking. Petal knew withdrawal when she saw it. Was she being cruel trying to stretch the time between Rosie's doses? "You okay, Ro?"

Rosie nodded and shook, teeth chattering like automated machinery. "I have a headache. They're trying to get into my head and control my thoughts, you know."

"Just sit here while I put clean sheets on your bed," Petal said, running down and back up the stairs as quickly as she could, afraid to leave her sister alone. "You okay, Ro?" she shouted from the bedroom as she tucked the blankets underneath the mattress.

Petal tucked her quivering sister into her fresh bed and gave her half a lorazepam.

"Don't you feel better washed and clean, Ro?" she said rhetorically, tucking the covers under her sister's chin like their bubby used to do, as though safety through the night depended upon full and complete coverage. "I'll be back when dinner is ready, Ro."

Rosie pulled the blankets over her head and rolled onto her side.

Petal went to the kitchen, turned the oven to 275 degrees, stripped the outer layer of cellophane from the foil containers labelled *Shabbes*, and pushed them into the oven.

Given the ambiguity of their grandmother's relationship with organized religion, her refusal to set foot in a synagogue, and their grandfather's scorn for theological belief altogether, it was ironic that the most consistent thing in their family had been lighting the candles and saying the blessing every Friday night before dinner. This tradition had nothing to do with religion and everything to do with Estie's need to right the orbit of the world and align her family's place in it once a week. The ritualized movements, the striking of the match, the waving of her hands over the flames, the covering of her eyes with her fingers spread just enough to glimpse the light of the flames, the singing of the prayer, the balling up of her fists and rubbing them into the sockets of her eyes before opening them and looking at the world. Choreographed movements akin to a ceremonial observance of setting clocks that otherwise might cease to keep track of time as we know it. Even during times of stress and strife and, dare we say what was never said, depression, when Estie would take to her bed, she could be counted upon to make an appearance at the always shiny silver candlesticks, stiff, white candles standing sentry, ensuring all was put in order — striking match, waving hands, magical spell, rubbing eyes, the world as it should be. Order thus restored, even when no such thing had actually happened.

Petal had not assumed this candle-lighting tradition in her own life. Her own affiliation with Judaism, rife with resentments and complexities, held an insignificant place in the mosaic of her identity, or so she liked to believe. But that Friday just before Passover, finding herself alone with her sister for the first time in almost twenty years, she was overcome with a need to light the candles and welcome the Sabbath as much for herself as out of respect for Rosie's beliefs.

Rosie had inherited the candlesticks. In Estie's possession, they were always gleaming, but now they stood black with tarnish.

Petal couldn't find silver polish anywhere. In her classroom days, teaching basic chemistry of acids and bases was always a favourite. Hands-on, tangible experiments to demonstrate the effects of different household products on varied metals always garnered reactions of delight from the hardest to engage children. Given a teaspoon of white vinegar and some salt, tarnished pennies could be polished up to a warm glow that permeated far beneath the shiny surface of the coins. It was those kids — the ones who were hardest to reach — that made Petal want to teach, to do better, and then something so simple could light a spark. Today, for the first time in longer than she could remember, she wanted to do better for her sister. Not because she felt responsible to do so. Not because anyone else had asked or coerced her to, but because despite the passage of time and hurt and history, she loved her sister.

Salt and vinegar seemed too harsh and baking soda or toothpaste too abrasive for the delicate candlesticks, so she opted for the milder acid of ketchup. She banged the bottom of the sticky bottle until a small blob oozed onto the stainless steel surface of the sink. With a soft dishcloth, she rubbed ketchup into the candlesticks, up and down the swollen bulbs of corrugated silver, around the splayed brims at the tops, little by little restoring them to their former glory, the embossed grapevines and curlicues emerging from the blackness reminding her of Bubby. She ran the tap until the water steamed hot and submerged the silver pieces into the basin gently, burnishing away the residual stickiness of the ketchup. She dried and buffed the heirlooms till they shone like moonlight.

Petal found a small tray and a blue-and-white box of white Shabbes candles, the kind Bubby had always had. She wrapped the bases of two candles with strips of tinfoil and pushed them firmly into the holes at the top of the sparkling candlesticks just like her bubby had done each week. She searched the kitchen for matches but found none and decided to settle for the lighter she knew she had in her purse, which made her think about cigarettes. She wanted one. She thought about Benjamin drinking alone in the park, knowing full well that he would have gone home after hanging up with her. Drinking alone in the park in the afternoon was a scene he didn't have the stomach to play out in real life. She checked her phone. It was already after seven o'clock. Benjamin would be out for the evening with their friends by now.

Petal carried the tray of candles to Rosie's room and knocked gently on the open door. "Ro? Do you feel like waking up for a bit? We can make Shabbes and have some dinner."

The blankets stirred. Petal put the candlesticks on the dresser in the corner of the room where the drawers had barely enough room to open partway. She squeezed around the perimeter of the bed and adjusted a few pillows against the wall so Rosie could sit up.

"I know it must be hard to see straight let alone sit upright with all that junk in your system," she said awkwardly, trying to help Rosie pull up in the bed. "Not a lot of space in here, is there?"

Rosie pushed herself weakly into a sitting position against the heap of proffered cushions. Her heavy eyelids hovered at half-mast, lighting on the gleaming candlesticks. "You polished them," she said, her eyes now wide. "You made them so beautiful! How did you know? Did I tell you?"

"Did you tell me what? To polish the candlesticks?" Petal asked.

"Did they tell you? Were they mean?" she asked.

"Don't worry, Ro. You didn't tell me. You didn't forget. I just felt like doing it. I'm glad you like them. They remind me of Bubby."

"I think of her every time I light the candles," she said. Tears rolled down her face. "I don't get around to cleaning them often enough. But always for Pesach."

"It must have been my turn," Petal said, sitting next to her sister. "I've never done it before. It's high time I polished the family silver." She smiled. "I can't remember the last time I lit Shabbes candles. I'm really happy to be doing it with you. I'm happy to be with you, Ro."

"I'm happy you're here, Pet," Rosie said, wiping away tears and snot with the back of her hand.

"You want to get up to light the candles, Ro, or you want me to do it? I don't think I've forgotten."

"You do it," she said, pointing to the hooks draped with dozens of multicoloured scarves.

Petal took down a jade-coloured scarf and tied it underneath her hair at the back of her neck, pushing her frothy curls back behind her shoulders. She passed Rosie a pale-blue scarf with silver threads running through the weave, which Rosie expertly tied on her own head, tucking in stray strands of hair. She pulled the cigarette lighter from the back pocket of her jeans, suddenly self-conscious in front of Rosie. "You sure you want me to do it?"

Rosie nodded. "Wait! Your phone, Pet. You have to turn off your phone before we light candles. For Shabbes. For me."

Petal reached into her pocket and turned off her phone completely for the first time in longer than she could remember. Not silent or vibrate, but off. Then, as though to demonstrate to Rosie that it was no big deal, in fact her pleasure to do so, she put her phone into the top drawer of the dresser. Rosie smiled and relaxed into the pillows propped behind her.

Petal lit one candle, picked up the other candlestick, and tilted the unlit wick toward the lit flame. The two flames flickered in the dim bedroom. Softly, she waved her fingers over the flames like seaweed dancing in an ocean current. She lifted her hands and covered her eyes, spreading her fingers slightly apart to see the light of the candles. "*Baruch attah, Adonai,*" she sang tentatively, and then softly, hoarsely, Rosie chimed in, and they continued together, "*Eloheinu melech ha'olam, asher kidshanu, be'mitzvotav, ve'tzivanu lehadlik ner shel Shabbat. Amen.*"

Rose curled her hands into loose fists and pushed the backs of her knuckles into the sockets of her moist eyes, rolling them gently back and forth. Petal did the same. Order was not restored.

9.

PERHAPS, HAD RAIZEL Wolffe not been such a positive, cheerful person, she might have found fault in Schmuel Hirsch when they met. There was substantial fault to be found. He was socially awkward to the point of psychopathology. He was of questionable intelligence. If one were being kind, one might grant him at most a physical assessment of looking like all the rest, and if one were being critical, one might point out his pockmarked complexion, his rounded shoulders, his pigeon toes, his too-big ears, and his too-small eyes. Maybe if Raizel had been more savvy about the nature of dating and matchmaking in the Orthodox world, she would have understood that, much like in the secular world, common interests, values, rapport, and even chemistry were critical factors to consider when choosing a spouse. But she was naturally predisposed to see her world, whatever world that might be at any given time, through Rose-tinted lenses. What she saw in Schmuel Hirsch was what she believed she was meant to see: a future husband.

Raizel had no way of knowing that the backroom dealings of her introduction to Schmuel were not typical even in Orthodoxy, or that the rebbetzin from her seminary had gone out on a limb to facilitate what she thought of as a practice date. Had Rose been a fly on the wall of Raizel's destiny, she might have borne witness to the goings-on, and perhaps the outcome might have been different. Perhaps the spell Raizel was under might have been broken. Perhaps not.

"MRS. HIRSCH, I have terrific news," Rebbetzin Weiss said to Schmuel Hirsch's mother on a collect call from Yerushalayim to Toronto. "I have a date for your son, Schmuel!"

"A date? *Vos far* a date? *Nischt a shidduch auber* a date?"

"Mrs. Hirsch, all due respect, a match can only come from a meeting," Rebbetzin Weiss said, measuring her words carefully. "And, just between you and me, from this meeting it is unlikely we will have a wedding."

"So what's the point if not a wedding?" Mrs. Hirsch asked.

"Your boy, he's a good boy, a nice boy, but a scholar? No disrespect, Mrs. Hirsch, but I don't need to tell you that your son is not ... My husband, he's been working now three years with your Schmuel, and to be frank, he's concerned."

"Concerned? Is there something wrong? I know my Schmeilkeh is never going to be a rebbe, but concerned? B'ezrat Hashem, there is a girl for everybody, even the pauper and the imbecile ... not that my son is either, *chas ve'sholem!*"

"Mrs. Hirsch, your son is lonely. I've been looking high and low for a shidduch for him. My husband has been looking. But Mrs. Hirsch, the girls' families want boys who ... Look, I'm not telling you anything about your boy you haven't noticed yourself. He's a little bit ... different. He needs a girl who is a little bit different too. I'm not saying he won't find one b'ezrat Hashem eventually, but in the meantime, he needs to feel like all the other boys. They go on dates. He should also go on a few dates. Not every date needs to end with a promise. What harm can come from making him feel good about himself?"

"Rebbetzin Weiss, I know my Schmeil is more awkward than the rest," said Mrs. Hirsch. "I know my one and only son will never be a scholar. But my boy will be a caring, devoted husband to any girl who is lucky enough to get him!"

"Baruch Hashem! I couldn't agree more! In the meantime, I would like to send him on a date with a beautiful, outgoing, intelligent girl, handpicked by his sister, your daughter Schaindel."

"So *nu?* The girl has only one eye? A criminal record maybe?"

"*Chas ve'sholem!*" said Rebbetzin Weiss. "Heaven forbid, *kaiyn'nehora!* She's a friend of Schaindel. Sometimes we have girls from the seminary for Shabbes along with girls from the other seminary."

"The other seminary? Which other seminary? You teach also at another seminary? There's a seminary for *schvach*-minded girls, they should be blessed?"

"I teach also at the *ba'al tshuvah* seminary, so we have girls from both to dinner. It's very important that the girls who are just finding their way back to righteousness meet girls who have grown up in Orthodox families. It normalizes the lifestyle for them in a way that nothing else can."

"You want my Schmeil to go on a date with a *ba'alat tshuvah?* A girl who knows nothing? A girl from nowhere?"

"I'm not being rude, Mrs. Hirsch. I wouldn't suggest it if your daughter hadn't thought of it herself. The two girls met at our Shabbes table and were so taken with one another. They got along like sisters separated from birth! Raizel is a beautiful girl inside and out. She needs practice in Orthodox dating. Schmeil needs practice. It's a good opportunity for both of them. It was Schaindel who thought they should meet. I would never have thought of it on my own! Anyway, nothing will come of it. A girl from the secular world will have nothing in common with a shy, unsophisticated Orthodox boy. Mrs. Hirsch, I am not hiring a secretary to manage the overwhelming number of calls coming from the families of girls who want to meet your son. A date, I'm suggesting. Just a date. Maybe two. Not a marriage."

"All right, all right, so let him go. What harm could one or two dates be for my *nebedik* son," Mrs. Hirsch said to Rebbetzin Weiss. "If you give your hechsher, I can live with it."

But Raizel had not heard this conversation, and her secular upbringing notwithstanding, she was not nearly as sophisticated as Rebbetzin Weiss imagined. She was impressed by the grandeur of the hotel lobby at the King David where Schmuel Hirsch had arranged to meet her for their date. The art deco carved plaster mouldings, in greens and golds and deep blood reds, that ran along the vaulted ceiling beams and up the large, square pillars crowned with two rows of Corinthian curls struck her as classy. As did the marble floor, polished to a high gloss, and the Oriental carpets, which delineated intimate seating arrangements of plush, generous sofas and armchairs. This, despite the Rebbetzin Weiss's presumptions, was a far cry from the plastic-covered furniture in her bubby and zaideh's modest apartment, or the keg parties of her high school years.

Schmuel met Raizel at the entrance to the hotel. "Raizel?"

Raizel nodded demurely. Walking an uncomfortable pace ahead of the boy, past the elaborate flower arrangements on the grand piano, they found an empty spot in the lobby lounge. They seated themselves on two parallel sofas, flanking an unlit fireplace with a wrought iron screen and a mantle topped by a bronze bust of some late state elder. Above the fireplace, a painting of a man on a horse in a field, of which Raizel took note thinking it might provide a topic for conversation should they run out of things to speak about, which they did almost immediately.

Schmuel Hirsch, who was neither worldly enough nor experienced enough to recognize the complexities a girl like Raizel Wolffe presented to him and his family — a girl with no background, no family *yiches,* no circumstance worthy of even a boy like him — believed that Hashem had sent him no less than an angel. It was love at first sight, and all the rebbetzin's cautionary advice to him that this was a practice date, "until such a time as a proper girl could be found for him," vanished like yesterday's sunset.

Convinced of their destiny, Schmuel called from the payphone in the hotel lobby after his first date with Raizel. "Hello, Rebbetzin Weiss? It's me."

"Which me?" the rebbetzin asked, confused about what man might be calling her past ten o'clock at night. She grabbed at the neck of her housecoat, closing it tightly against her skin as though through the telephone her male caller might sense the exposure of her clavicle.

"Me. Schmeil Hirsch. You told me to call you after my date." Schmeil pulled the brim of his hat down.

"Oh. That me. Schmuel, you could have waited till tomorrow. Now it's a bit late."

"I'm sorry, rebbetzin, but you said I should call right away," Schmeil said, feeding another pierced token into the phone.

"So *nu?* It went well?" The rebbetzin assumed it hadn't gone well at all, but who was she to be the dark cloud. Let the boy come to his own conclusions and maybe learn from his mistakes.

"Rebbetzin Weiss, it was the best night of my life!"

And before she knew what she was saying, she said, "So you want maybe to go out again with this girl?"

And so it went, one date after another until the young couple had met five times in the lobby of the King David Hotel, a most unimaginative venue, but neither one knew any better. They hadn't a clue that the uncomfortable, cumbersome conversation was not the norm. They were unaware that venturing out to a restaurant or an activity or even for a walk were what people, even frum people, did on dates. Of the two of them, it is hard to say who was more insecure and inept — the girl who was desperate to avoid any hint of her former incarnation seeping into her current manifestation or the boy who nowadays would certainly be described as somewhere "on the spectrum."

Rose, desperately uninformed about the drama unfolding around her, about her, was excited, and excited Rose was intractable.

She phoned her sister on the kibbutz.

Petal, slightly irritated at having been pulled away from the Purim celebrations in the kibbutz dining room, stepped into the small closet near the entrance of the communal hall and picked up the dangling telephone receiver.

"*Allo?*"

"Pet, I need you to come to Yerushalayim!"

Rosie never called Petal.

"Is everything okay, Ro? What do you need?" she asked, closing the bifold door of the phone cubicle.

"Please, Pet, call me Raizel. It's my name."

"Okay, Raizel. Is everything all right?"

"Better than all right, Pet. Fantastic!" No surprise. Things were always fantastic with Rosie.

"Great! So why do I have to come to Jerusalem? You know I hate coming there." She bumped her fist gently against the plywood enclosure.

"I've met a wonderful boy! And I want you to come meet him," Rosie bubbled.

"Oh yeah?" Petal said.

"The rebbetzin made the shidduch. We've been on five dates already. Well, not exactly dates. Not like I used to, but I've met him five times."

"What's the rush? If you still think he's wonderful in a few months, I'll meet him."

"You don't understand the way it works. If he likes me, he might ask me to marry him. I'd like you to meet him, maybe give an opinion before he asks!"

"What the fuck are you talking about, Ro?" The hinge that connected her head to the back of her neck snapped open.

"Please don't swear. I don't like it when you swear."

"Oh, for God's sake! You're not even twenty years old! What on earth are you thinking about, marrying some guy you've met twice?" Petal cracked the flimsy door at its middle just enough to let the merriment of celebration leak into their conversation. She could hear the singing of Purim songs, and she didn't want to miss the performance of her kids.

"More than twice! I don't expect you to understand my world, I just need you to accept it and support me," Rosie said.

"Who fed you those lines?"

"Pet, if I marry him, you'll regret not meeting him before the wedding. Will you come?"

"Sure," Petal said. "I gotta go, Ro."

Petal cancelled her rendezvous with Raizel and Schmuel twice before actually making the trip. She had trouble forcing herself onto a bus to Jerusalem, which she thought of as returning to the scene of the crime.

Shula helped. "You know they say you need to get back up onto the horse. Jerusalem is your horse. You'll go. You'll see that there's nothing there to be afraid of. We've talked about hiding and using the kibbutz as a way of avoiding. It's not healthy."

"It's not the city itself," she told Shula. "It's a feeling of being trapped that I get going into the city. It's the bus and the station and the sense that there is no place on earth less hospitable to me. I know it's not rational. There is nothing wrong with Jerusalem. Just with me."

Shuki arranged a lift for her with someone from the kibbutz. She felt better knowing she would not have to take the bus or spend the night. Her driver, an almost mute kibbutznik, ate half a dozen hard-boiled eggs during the first hour of their early morning drive and burped loudly for the remainder of the journey. As much as she dreaded Jerusalem, she was rather relieved to get out of the sulfuric cloud of gas. It was a crisp Jerusalem day, and Petal had a brief recollection that it had been raining when she'd left for Tel Aviv just over a year before.

Petal had agreed to meet Rosie on neutral territory, in other words, outside the Old City, at the Montefiore windmill near Mishkenot She'ananim. Close enough to the Old City that Schmuel, concerned about being seen out and about with young ladies, agreed only reluctantly. Petal couldn't quite parse whether he wanted to be somewhere where he might be visible to people he might know or where he could be invisible. She decided it wasn't her problem.

"*Sham. Lechi le sham,*" said the gaseous driver, gesturing with his flattened hand like a traffic cop.

Petal circled the large windmill. Unless Rosie was playing another game, she wasn't there. Petal doubled her pace and circled a second time, just in case. Still no Rosie. She sat down on the pink-and-beige stone steps in front of the windmill and looked out across the valley to the corner wall of the Old City. Behind the wall, a minaret rose high in the distance, its moon-capped dome seeming to burst through the green copper roof of a church. *There it is*, Petal thought. *All the history of this fraught little city, spread out from here to there.*

Rosie appeared breathless and alone at the top of a staircase just beyond the windmill.

"I came all this way to not meet this guy?!" Petal accused before they had even exchanged greetings.

"He's coming, Pet!" she said, throwing her arms around her sister's neck. "And he's not just a guy! He's my *chossen!*"

"Your what?" she said, escaping Rosie's stranglehold.

"My chossen! My groom! Pet, I'm getting married!" She bounced in place as though her inclination was to jump up and down, but her newly acquired modesty prevented her feet from leaving the ground. Rosie twitched with excitement.

"Stop talking shit! You are not getting married!" Petal said.

"Say what you like, Pet. It doesn't change a thing," Rosie said. Then, unable to stand still, "Let's walk."

"I thought I was going to get to meet him before you got engaged," Petal said, trying to keep up.

"You cancelled twice," Rose chastised.

"How much can you possibly know about this guy three weeks later?"

Rosie dragged at Petal's arm. "You have to see the view from here!" she said, ignoring her sister's antipathy.

Jerusalem and its fucking views, Petal thought.

"Isn't it the most beautiful place you've ever been?" Rosie gushed.

Hills and valleys of green and gold, new and old and ancient, to their right, the city and beyond the desert and to the left, the terracotta roofed cottages of Yemin Moshe, the upscale dwellings that lined the hillside upon which they stood. Petal didn't want to admit to Rose or to herself that it was in fact magnificent, so instead she said, "So where is he?"

"Come, Pet!" Rosie said, grabbing Petal by the arm again and pulling her across the uneven stone pavement back to the stairs. "He'll come from this direction."

Petal released her arm from Rosie's clutch, and together they walked down endless flights of stone stairs flanked by alleyways where homes could be entered and cars could be parked. Down and down they kept going, Rosie skipping, Petal trudging, past cedars, bougainvillea, wisteria vines and cactuses, closed metal window grates and shutters painted goldenrod yellow, seafoam green, and dusty rose. Petal was working hard to notice, resisting her inclination to tune out.

"If I can't live in the Old City, this is my second choice of neighbourhood," Rose declared.

"Good luck with that," Petal replied.

"Why do you always have to be so negative? It's just a fantasy, Pet!"

"You have an expensive imagination."

AT THE BOTTOM of the stairs, a bridge bisected the Sultan's Pool, leading to the road on the other side of the valley that climbed up to the Jaffa Gate and one of the entrances to the Old City.

Running across the bridge was a young man in yeshiva bocher uniform: wispy facial hair, baggy black pants, partially untucked crumpled white shirt, long, streaming strings flying behind him, black fedora clutched to his head, jacket bunched in the crook of his other arm. Stopping just short of the sisters, the boy doubled over, panting.

Between gulps of air and heavy breathing, the sweaty youth sputtered, "Raizel! I'm so sorry I'm late. We were in a *shiur* and couldn't get away."

He looked only at Rosie, as though Petal were not there.

"Schmuel is a very serious student," Rose said to Petal. "You should feel honoured that he left a lesson to come meet you."

Petal looked at Rose expecting her to make introductions, but she didn't, so Petal jumped in.

"I take it you're Schmuel? I'm Petal," she said, offering an outstretched hand, forgetting where she was and to whom she was speaking.

"Good to meet you," the boy said, taking a small step backwards, avoiding the offered hand and shuffling his feet on the cobblestones.

"Schmuel is also from Toronto," Rosie jumped in, rattling off credentials and accomplishments, such as they were, as though he were there to interview for a job Petal was looking to fill. "He's been studying at yeshiva here in Yerushalayim for almost three years. His family is well known in the community, and his grand-father was a very well respected rabbi," Rosie continued, filling airspace with information that Petal couldn't help feel would have been entirely meaningless to her sister less than two years ear-lier: what neighbourhood his family lived in, which schools he attended, who his sister was and to whom she was married and at which shul his family davened. As though any of it meant any-thing to Petal.

What Petal saw was a greasy, sweaty, awkward Jew boy! All she could think was, *My sister, my Rosie, who dated the best looking, most popular, wildest boys all through high school and now this! This is what she has settled for! This is who she wants to marry! Marry! What the hell is she thinking!*

Petal wanted to flee. The world was closing in! She closed her eyes, trying to shut out her sister's affected singsong voice. She took three deep breaths and opened her eyes. Rosie was still talking.

Petal gritted her teeth and interrupted. "So, are you really planning to marry my sister?"

"Petal!" Rose shrieked. "You can't ask that!"

"Why, Ro? What's the big deal? You said you were engaged! Is it a secret?"

"No. It's not a secret," Rosie said, giving Schmuel a down-cast glance. "We're just waiting for his mother's *hechsher*, her blessing."

"We'll get her approval, Raizel. Don't worry. It's just ... you know ... taking a bit longer," Schmuel said.

"No rush," Petal said to Schmuel. Rosie replied with a sharp elbow to Petal's ribs.

"I have to get back to my studies," Schmuel said, tipping his head in the direction of the Old City. He bent his wrist, lifting one tentative palm from where it hung by his hip, bending his elbow only enough to create the gestalt of a wave. "Will I see you soon?" he asked.

Rosie blushed and giggled like she had never been pursued by a boy and gave a barely discernable nod. Schmuel lifted one foot from the pavement, as though he might fly directly across the valley, placed his free hand on his hat, and took off.

Petal watched him take flight and soar like a bird across the valley, perplexed by his seeming grace in motion. *For that I had to come all the way to Jerusalem?* she thought.

"Isn't he wonderful!" Rosie said.

"Hard for me to get a sense of the guy. He wouldn't even look at me," Petal said.

"Of course not!"

"And what does 'taking a bit longer' mean?"

"Because I'm not from a known family," Rosie said.

"Oh fuck, Ro! Seriously? This is the kind of shit you want to put up with in your life? You realize they are basically saying you aren't good enough!" Petal said, stomping her foot on the ground, unable to contain the insult she felt on her sister's behalf.

"Pet," Rosie said, "it's completely understandable. I'm not a known quantity. You know what an honour it is that a boy like Schmuel from a respected, righteous, and known family would even consider marrying a girl like me with no credentials or ancestry ... no yiches whatsoever." She held her hands to her heart as though she truly believed what she was saying.

"Bullshit, Ro!" Petal said, clomping up the stairs, the windmill fixed in her sights. Not stopping to catch her breath at the top, Petal passed the windmill, crossed the street, walked through a moist flowerbed, tripped on a concealed irrigation pipe, and collapsed on a circular patch of grass.

Rosie stopped shouting after Petal to slow down about halfway up the stairs. She followed Petal through the flowerbed, tripped on the same pipe, and landed on top of her sister. Rosie was panting and laughing with breathless hysteria in the way only Rosie could.

"Get off of me," Petal said, pushing at her sister.

"It's nicer across the street," Rosie said, rolling off Petal.

They crossed the road into the park, found a bird-shit-streaked bench under a tree, and sat down. It was a long time before either of them spoke.

"I hope the birds are away for the day," Rosie said to break the ice. Petal glared at the tree as though the tree were breaking her heart.

"What are you so mad about, Pet? I'd have thought you'd want me to be happy."

"They don't think you're good enough, Ro, and they never will," Petal said. "All our lives, we've been made to feel like less than everybody else — unworthy at worst or pathetic at best. Why would you willingly take that on?"

"I'm in love, Pet."

"But are you in love with Schmuel or God or Jerusalem or religion? It might be a good idea to figure that out before you do something you'll regret later."

"I won't regret it, Pet. You need to trust me. I know you think I'm flighty and impulsive, but I'm actually not a complete idiot. I'm not book-smart like you, but I know how I feel. I want you to be happy for me. I need you to be proud of me."

Petal plucked a leaf from a bush and rolled it between her thumb and forefinger, releasing the lavender oils and perfuming the air. "I don't think you're an idiot," she said, running her finger under her nose and breathing deeply while she tried to work out what she was really feeling.

When she got back to the kibbutz, Petal called her bubby.

"Mamaleh! So gut to hear your voice! What time is there?"
Estie always asked the time.

"Past midnight, Bubby. How are you?" Petal said, picking at
the peeling paint of the phone booth outside the kibbutz office.

"Gut, tanks gutness! More important, you? All's gut?" Petal
could hear the sound of her bubby pulling bobby pins out of her
nighttime hair curlers and dropping them into the porcelain sink.
Ping, ping, ping ... That pinging sound was the clearest indication that Bubby was all right. All right enough to put her thin,
pink hair into curlers before bed. All right enough to get up and
take the curlers out in the morning. Petal and Rosie used to laugh
behind her back because they could see no difference in the texture of Estie's hair no matter what she did. As she got older and
her hair got thinner and more transparent, and the girls could see
her scalp ever more clearly, it got less funny.

"I'm good, Bubby. I'm really good. Promise. I'm happy here."
She paused, looking up at the diffused sodium halo of light above.

"But? I know but when I hear but."

"But I'm worried about Rosie."

"It's not for you to worry for Rosie," Estie said. "Do I need to
remind what happens when you worry for your sister?"

"Bubby, she's talking about getting married. She wants to
marry a guy she barely knows!"

"A wedding is bad news?"

Petal didn't answer.

"Mamaleh, I was married already a year by your age. It's so
bad to get married young?"

"Did she tell you already?" Petal felt betrayed.

"Rosie called maybe a week ago," Estie said. "It's not so bad,
mine Pet. Everybody needs somebody. Soon by you."

"Does Zaideh feel the same way?" Petal felt she must be
dreaming. Tomorrow she would make the real call. Tonight, she

would sleep and try not to dream.

"Zaideh? He wants what we all want. He wants his girls to be settled and taken care from. She's young, but love doesn't ask how old. These calls are very expensive, bubaleh. I'll write in a letter. You'll write in a letter. You'll get used to that your sister will belong to someone else."

Estie's last sentence stung.

Petal had always been Rosie's voice of reason. Sometimes more and sometimes less successfully, she was able to talk Rosie out of making poor decisions, but since that very first day in the Old City, Petal felt she had become irrelevant to Rose, as though a vital bond had been severed and Rose could no longer hear the broadcast frequency of Petal's cautionary advice. But Petal was wrong.

After each date with Raizel, Schmeil would call Rebbetzin Weiss to report the success of the meeting, and Rebbetzin Weiss would do her duty and call Raizel to ask if she was interested in seeing him again. But when Schmeil called and said that he wanted to ask the girl to marry him, Rebbetzin Weiss invited the girl for lunch.

"I hear you are a very bright and devoted student, Raizel," Rebbetzin Weiss said, piling beige plates with mountains of brown food in her brown kitchen and guiding Raizel to the table covered in a shiny brown tablecloth. "Sit. Sit." She put a full plate down in front of the girl.

"Thank you. I'm trying," Raizel said silently cautioning herself not to talk too much. Talking too much wasn't modest. She took a small forkful of the brown food. "This is delicious."

"You know why I invited you for lunch, Raizel?" Rebbetzin Weiss said through a mouthful of food.

"I assume it has something to do with Schmuel Hirsch," she said cautiously, hiding the excitement she felt and hoping the rebbetzin couldn't hear her heart pounding.

"You see! This is why he's not the right boy for you!"

Raizel choked on a piece of overcooked meat.

"You are such a smart girl, and Schmuel, well, let's just say ... a yeshiva bocher doesn't always make for a rabbi."

"Does everybody have to be a rabbi?" Raizel said, overstepping a little.

"Of course not! But what will be with a boy like Schmuel? A girl like you, smart and beautiful, you can find a better match. I thought, because you and his sister are friends, it might be a good opportunity for you to practice dating in our tradition. Now you are practiced, the rebbetzin in charge of your seminary can start looking for appropriate *shidduchs* for you."

Your seminary. It was the way Rebbetzin Weiss said "your" that tweaked Raizel's radar. As though a neural pathway wedged deep inside her temporal lobe had been nudged awake, and with that nudge, Petal's suspicions were realized in Rosie's brain. It was a "your" that implied "not mine," other, separate, different. Rose had heard that "your" from teachers, friends, parents of friends — "your family is ..." — sentences that always smacked of pity and criticism and distinct undertones of superiority over poor Rose Wolffe the orphan, daughter of a disappearing mother and a nonexistent father, granddaughter of barely-coping-saddled-with-responsibility-beyond-their-capacity-Holocaust-survivor-wretched-of-the-earth old people. She had had to ignore that tone her whole life and recognized that it was her blessing to be able to do so with such apparent ease. Having Petal feel the hurt on her behalf had always been a powerful shield. But not this time. This time, she had been reborn as someone different, someone who didn't need anybody's thin veil of compassion varnishing scorn and advantage. This time, she was not poor Rose Wolffe, the sunny side of the Wolffe twins, she was Raizel, a woman of valour!

"*My* seminary? You mean not *your* seminary." Raizel felt the heat rising in her face, and, while her attempts to blend into

the brown and beige surroundings had been more or less successful to that point, her fair, freckled skin turned bright red and her
strawberry-blond hair took on the flash of fire when provoked.

"I like Schmuel, and he likes me. I think he is going to ask me
to marry him. I may be new to this world of *yours*," she said,
emphasizing the *yours*, "and I may not understand many things,
but I'm pretty sure the conventions regarding toying with the
emotions of another person apply in at least equal measure in
both worlds. You called me and asked me if I would like to meet
a boy. I did not call you. I expect that you will now behave with
integrity. I believe you call it *derech eretz?* I think you may even
find a commandment or two about it among the six hundred and
thirteen mitzvahs I am only just learning to follow."

Raizel got up from the table, leaving her brown slop virtually
untouched, reached a hand up on her way out to touch the mezuzah, kissed her fingers, and left.

Schmuel Hirsch, a kind, awkward, gawky young man of
marginal intelligence, had, through a series of well-intentioned
mishaps, fallen in what he believed was love with the wrong girl,
Raizel Wolffe. She was bright, beautiful, smart, gregarious, and,
under most circumstances, anyone could see that her infatuation
with Schmuel had more to do with the idea of marrying an Orthodox man than the actual man who wanted to marry her. But they
believed that, after half a dozen meetings, it was beshert. Their
self-proclaimed destiny for one another presented challenges for
their families and for the unlucky rebbetzin who had made the
shidduch in the first place. It was not exactly the ill-fated love
of Montague-Capulet infamy, but it would be no small feat for
Schmuel's mother to be swayed.

Rebbetzin Weiss called Mrs. Hirsch in Toronto.

Rosie called Petal from the first phone booth she passed on
her way back to the seminary and left a message for her at the

kibbutz. "Please tell Petal Wolffe that her sister called. Tell her I think she will be proud of me. Tell her she is as much my inner strength as Hashem. Tell her I love her."

Petal never got the message.

DESPITE REBBETZIN WEISS'S strong endorsement of the match and her implications that even with a lack of family background, this girl was better than any other Schmuel Hirsch could hope to marry, his mother needed persuading. Notwithstanding her undisclosed understanding that her son was not much of a catch and Estie and even Irving's conviction that there were far worse fates that could befall their granddaughter than marrying young and into Orthodoxy, agreement was complicated.

Der was less certain than Irving or Estie that this was a good idea. As always, Petal turned to him to share her own trepidation.

"We have to stop her, Der! At least you must realize that the shit she's spewing is just the latest of Rosie's 'possibilities.'"

"I'm not sure there is anything either of us can do beyond what we already have in voicing our apprehensions. Remember we let you make your own decision about staying in Israel. We all had serious concerns about that. But imagine if I had forced you to come home with me. Even if I believed it to be the better decision, not allowing you the freedom to choose would not have been the right thing."

"That was different, Der. I'm different from Rosie."

"You are indeed, but that doesn't mean you have never made questionable decisions or choices, ones I would have attempted to dissuade you from had I thought it would do any good."

"But marriage, Der! You should see him! He's not good enough for Rosie!"

"You need to let it go, Tig. Twitch has to live her life, and you can't control any of it. More importantly, you don't have to."

"I thought you'd be on my side, Der."

"You know I always am, but there are no sides here, just opinions. Of all the opinions, only two really matter, and they are not ours."

"But Bubby and Zaideh seem to think it's fine! You have to talk some sense into them."

"Only Rose and Schmuel can decide. All we can do is choose to accept and support their decision or not. In the long run, acceptance weighs much less than criticism or judgment. Only you can decide what you want to carry. Only you can decide what ties you down or lifts you up."

For all his brave talk with Petal, Der was not naive. He had some professional experience with the potentially fraught nature of Orthodox marriage agreements and an inkling that this particular arrangement presented additional complications.

Irving, Estie, and Der were invited for tea on a Sunday afternoon in late March to the home of the widow Hirsch. He tried to prepare himself for the meeting with Mrs. Hirsch. *It's not for me to say yea or nay. But it is my job to protect Twitch. But who am I, after all, to have an opinion. Of course, I am entitled to an opinion. Best just to make things as smooth as possible for Yitzchak and Estie.* Der thought these and other thoughts obsessively in Möbius loops of pre-emptive concern.

Estie fretted about what to wear. "I mustn't appear too flashy. But also, I should look like I tried. We wouldn't want she should think we don't care. Maybe I should wear the light-blue blouse with the flowers, or I could wear the pale-yellow cardigan with the pearl buttons. But what if it's cold? You can never be too sure of the weather this time of year. Should I wear maybe a hat? Does it make me look too old? I don't want to make too much attention that we are the grandparents. They shouldn't ask too many questions," she went on.

"Shh, Estelleh. What we wear isn't important. What we say, who we are, I have no doubt about that. I only hope Mrs. Hirsch is half the good woman you are and her son a mensch. Nothing else is important."

Mrs. Hirsch lived alone in a townhouse north of Steeles Avenue in the Orthodox enclave known as Chabad Gate, though the Hirsch family were not in fact followers of the Chabad rabbis.

"They can't be Chabad," Der explained to Irving and Estie as he made the right turn off Bathurst Street into the ultra-Orthodox subdivision. "A Lubavitcher family would never consider a marriage to a girl like Rosie. I'm sure they are more liberal in their beliefs," he reassured himself as much as his friends, but silently he wondered for the zillionth time why this match was in fact being considered.

Mrs. Hirsch, a small, round woman with thick ankles and a wig too dark for both her pale complexion and her age, greeted them at the door.

"Baruch Hashem! You found it! Welcome. Please come inside," she said, ushering them into the small, neat townhouse. "We used to have a bigger house." She motioned her guests to sit in the living room, decorated in a style reminiscent of a belle époque Paris bordello. "Now, *alleh ve'sholem* my dear departed husband, it's just me, but Baruch Hashem, my daughter lives only a few blocks. My other daughter, you know Schaindel, Raizel's friend ... she'll live with me when she comes back from Yerushalayim. Until she marries, God willing."

Mrs. Hirsch was a most gracious hostess. She had gone to some trouble to bake and prepare a tea worthy of respected visitors. Estie's open, naive nature eased the initial awkwardness.

"Such a beautiful home you have, Mrs. Hirsch," Estie said, picking up her teacup high enough to examine the underside. "Such fentsy china!"

"Thank you, Mrs. Wolffe. The Shabbes dishes for special guests, of course," Mrs. Hirsch replied cordially.

"Please, call me Estie," Estie said for the third or fourth time since their arrival. "After all, we're practically family."

"Family?" said Mrs. Hirsch, suddenly frosty. "No disrespect, because you seem like very nice people, but to be honest, your Raizel is not exactly the kind of girl I had hoped for my Schmuel."

"You've met our Rosie?" Estie asked.

"No, of course not. I'm here. She's in Yerushalayim," Mrs. Hirsch said.

"Because you said as though you knew her that you hoped for someone different," Estie said. "But of course, if you knew our Rosie, you wouldn't —"

"Shh, Estelleh," Irving, said waiting to hear more from Mrs. Hirsch.

Mrs. Hirsch inhaled a deep, asthmatic wheeze. "We are a respected family in the community," she said, her double chin inflating with superiority. "Raizel, a girl from, you'll pardon me, a secular family, isn't exactly ..."

Der cut Mrs. Hirsch off, hackles up in full animalistic protective mode. "Why did you invite us for tea, Mrs. Hirsch? It is doubtful that you were surprised by Irving's clean-shaven face and lack of *peyos* or by Estie's uncovered hair. Why are we here if not to discuss a marriage between our children?"

"It's just ... I thought ... what does she offer my boy?" Mrs. Hirsch stammered.

"You'll meet our Rosie, you'll know what she offers," Estie said, helping herself to another poppyseed cookie. "She's beautiful, smart, energetic, and loving like you've never known. And I tink she loves him, your son."

Mrs. Hirsch squirmed in her chair, tugging at her skirt, which had bunched at her robust *tuches*. "I have no doubt she's a lovely girl, but, as you know, I'm a widow with only one son. I must think about our future —"

This time it was Irving who interrupted. "Money?" he asked. "Are you asking about money?" Der put a steadying hand on Irving's shoulder, because as low-key and generally easygoing as Irving seemed, beneath the surface of his gentle exterior lay a dormant volcano, rarely catalyzed but potentially ferocious. "Mrs. Hirsch, with all due respect," he said, willing restraint upon himself, "we are a modest family. I am a tailor, and my wife is a bookkeeper. I assure you that our girls have never wanted for anything, but as your luck would have it, they are also not spoiled girls. Their expectations are as modest as their upbringing. Why is this so lucky for you? Well, the way I see it, if there was a girl from a more affluent family, perhaps a more religious affluent family, we would not be here in the first place. I think it is we who should maybe be asking what does your son have to offer our Rosie?" At this point, for the first, last, and only time since either Estie or Der had known him, Irving invoked a doctrine he knew well, from a time he made believe never existed. He fixed their hostess in a steely stare, hiked up the sleeve of his shirt just high enough to expose the number tattooed on his forearm, and continued in a voice so soft and gentle that those gathered needed to lean in to hear him. "Mrs. Hirsch, the commandment we of course all know well from the book of Exodus 22:22: 'You shall not mistreat any widow or fatherless child. If you do mistreat them, and they cry out to me, I will surely hear their cry, and my wrath will burn, and I will kill you with the sword.' I assure you, Mrs. Hirsch, this will be upheld by our family. Will your piousness take you as far as our humanity will take us? Will our fatherless children be allowed happiness? Believe me when I tell you, Mrs. Hirsch, you are neither the only one widowed in the room nor is your child the only fatherless one in this equation." Irving looked down at his own forearm, either to draw attention to it or because he was surprised he had played that card.

The silence that fell upon the room could have drowned the cries of all the widows and orphans on earth. Irving took a sip of his tea. Der exhaled the breath he had been unwittingly holding. Mrs. Hirsch cleared her throat, shoved two fingers under her wig, and scratched at her sweaty scalp. She got up and opened the window to let in some cooler air.

Estie spoke.

"Oy, Irving! Who knew you were such a scholar? You see, Mrs. Hirsch, our Rosie is not from such ignorant people as you tink."

Der cut her off, drawing upon the lingering gravitas from Irving's speech. "Mrs. Hirsch, if it's money to help pay for a wedding you want to discuss, that is why we are here. If it is whether we will be able to support your son and his future family, we have nothing left to discuss. If you are looking to a girl from a secular family for reasons other than what might be deemed aboveboard or perhaps kosher, you are misguided."

Mrs. Hirsch took the opportunity she was given. "Of course, I was speaking only of a wedding! A wedding is expensive, and as a widow, well, you can understand my concern."

"Of course," Der said, granting Mrs. Hirsch absolution for any real or perceived indiscretion. "And since we are all of humble means, we will no doubt all be in agreement that a *simcha* need not be lavish or ostentatious to be a worthy celebration."

"Of course," said Mrs. Hirsch.

SIX WEEKS LATER, under a chuppah sewn by Irving and embroidered by Estie, surrounded by their loved ones in Toronto, Schmuel Hirsch married Raizel Wolffe (nee Rose Wolffe).

Petal refused to acknowledge her feelings. Instead, she opted for disparagement. The blind, raucous enthusiasm of nuptial celebration for Raizel and Schlemeil (the Yiddish equivalent of "loser" she had taken to calling her new brother-in-law in the privacy of her own brain) was as unfamiliar to her as bacon to a rabbi. She was utterly overwhelmed by the merriment of it all and profoundly wounded by her alien status in Rosie's new life.

Petal attended the *aufruf* the Saturday before the wedding at a rundown ultra-Orthodox synagogue on Bathurst Street. The women were relegated to a screened-off antechamber full of unruly children and gossip. Petal couldn't understand the need for any women to be there at all. The religious proceedings were completely ignored by Rose, her mother-in-law to be, her future sisters-in-law, and every other woman who was chasing children or chatting.

Except at the wedding ceremony when the bride, the groom, and their families stood under the chuppah in the men's section of the hall, the partying was completely segregated, with the women looking on from behind a screened-off gallery adjacent to the main event. The men danced frenzied, swirling, aggressive horas around the groom, flinging him hither and thither with little regard for the fragility of even the most robust of human bodies, sweating themselves into states of tantric ecstasy. The women, though less euphoric, had significantly better food on their side of the hall. Raizel's new sisters-in-law and their throng of friends orchestrated an endless series of games and entertainments for the bride, which Petal thought patronizing and juvenile. Rose seemed utterly delighted by the maypole of coloured ribbons they danced around, getting tangled and twisted in the inelegant up and down weaving of the graceless women. She shrieked with delight, skipping over the rope of tied-together napkins that the young woman holding the opposite end instructed Petal to turn ever faster and faster. The games of monkey in the middle, hot potato, doggie doggie who's got your bone, and other cloying delights, all played using the bride's shoes as projectiles or treasures, made Petal squirm. *It's because they marry them off as children,* she silently disapproved.

The wedding was followed by seven nights of dinners and parties hosted by well-meaning friends and relatives of Schmeil's family. Rosie insisted Petal be at every event, where she was completely ignored. Estie was steadfast in accompanying Petal, despite being sanctioned by the bossy bride to "take a break if you need to." Petal was given no such dispensation. She dutifully attended one event after another where her sister was feted by bands of merrymaking women who all looked and dressed the same. Petal and Estie in equal measure stood out like sore thumbs and were invisible.

When Schmeil, Rosie, and Petal were on the plane returning to Israel, Petal peered across the row, past her married, wigged sister at the Orthodox man sitting next to her, his prayer book and hat resting on his lap, shuckling back and forth in his seat, putting the odds of their safe arrival entirely in the hands of God, and felt the full thrust of her own heartbreak and disbelief. *How did I become the outsider in this scenario?* But what she couldn't bring herself to articulate, even silently, was *Rosie doesn't need me anymore.*

Raizel and Schmeil were greeted at the airport by a mass of revellers and well-wishers from Yerushalayim who separated and surrounded them, women around Raizel, men around Schmeil, and whisked them away before Petal could even say goodbye.

PETAL WAS MORE than happy to return to her home on the kibbutz. Spring was spectacular in the valley, and every minute she had been away had felt like missing out on some agriculturally significant event: the first planting, the first harvest, livestock birthing, calves suckling, the earth-echoed life cycle.

Petal arrived late in the evening by bus. She dropped her bags on
the lawn in front of Shula and Shuki's home and climbed the plant-
lined stairs. Shula opened the door before Petal reached the top.

"Baruch ha'bah! Welcome home! We didn't know exactly
when you were coming, but I said to Shuki just this morning that
you should be back any second now! Didn't I, Shuki?"

Petal adored the way Shula and Shuki constantly asked one
another for confirmation. Shula threw her arms around Petal and
welcomed her into the small flat. Shuki was already putting water
on to boil and readying a tray for coffee — mugs, sugar, fresh milk
that smelled thick and sweet, and the ubiquitous cakes.

Petal collapsed on the pile of woven pillows of reds, oranges,
blues, and greens strewn across the rope-strung wooden bedframe
that served as a sofa.

"I'm so glad to be home! I think maybe I'll never leave again,"
she said, pulling her shoes off and flinging her feet up onto the
coffee table.

Shula shot Shuki a look.

"Is something wrong?" Petal asked.

"You must be exhausted. Tell us about the wedding!" Shula
said.

"Never mind the wedding," Petal said. "What's wrong?"

"Nothing is wrong," Shuki reassured. "We've been talking
while you were away."

Petal felt her heart sinking into her gut. The fatigue, jet lag,
and sense of dread turned her bowels to water, and she darted off
to the small toilet, emerging some minutes later a distinct shade
of pale green.

"Petal," Shula said, "nothing is wrong, but what's next? You've
been here for a year and a half now. You are welcome to stay as
long as you want, but only if this is your home, not your refuge.

And if it's your home, then you need to make some decisions. This isn't a conversation for tonight. Get some rest. Tomorrow we'll talk. There is nothing to worry about," Shula reassured.

But Petal was not reassured. She recognized the feeling of brewing panic too well to leave things as they were. She knew that there was too much potential danger she could find between the safety of the upstairs flat and her own room on the far side of the kibbutz. She couldn't leave. She needed to have the conversation. "If there's something we need to talk about, we need to talk about it now."

"We can talk, but no decisions tonight. We have time for decisions. Isn't that right, Shuki?" Shula said, Shuki nodding agreement throughout. They sat down on either side of Petal. Shula put an arm across Petal's shoulders, and Shuki held her hand. She was not reassured by their physical contact.

Shula looked deep into Petal's eyes. "You came to us when you were very vulnerable, and we're overjoyed to see how you've flourished here. You've become an important part of our community and of our family. *Nachon*, Shuki? We love you, and we know you love us. But, as you've learned, the biggest problem on kibbutz is gossip. Gossip is a terrible thing, but terrible or not, it's one of our realities. People have begun to talk."

Petal shook her head in disbelief. "Talk about what? What have I done?" She stood up, pulling away from their well-meaning embraces, and plunked herself in an adjacent chair, knees to chest, wrapped in her own protective embrace.

"You've done nothing. It's just that the kibbutz has rules about how long one can be a visitor. You're not a volunteer. You've learned Hebrew, so you are not part of the Ulpan. You have no official status here. That people are talking is their problem, but as one of our 'children,' our concerns are for your future. *Nachon*, Shuki?" Shuki nodded agreement.

"I'm happy here! Can't I just stay?" Petal felt the room receding. She felt herself detaching. She sat upright, put her bare feet flat on the cool floor, and forced herself back.

"You can, but there's a process. You have to apply to become a member and then be approved for membership. Sometimes it's easy. Sometimes it's not," Shuki explained. "You're well liked but young. On one hand, we need more young people. Right, Shula? On the other hand, what can we as a kibbutz offer young people like you? Our own children, born and raised on the kibbutz, are leaving. The lifestyle isn't relevant to them anymore."

"But it's relevant to me," Petal said. "If I want to be here, isn't that a good thing?"

"Yes, it's a wonderful thing, but it is a thing you need to be sure is real. You came to the kibbutz because you needed the safety of our cloistered, simple life. Der made that very clear to us. We were the port in your storm, and we had no idea what to expect. Der asked. We love him and trust him, so we said yes. Isn't that right, Shuki? We braced for the worst but have witnessed nothing but the best. You are so dear and precious to us." Shula reached out and took Petal's resistant hand and held it with both of her own.

Petal's tears rolled down her face in slow, heavy rivers. "I'm happy here," she repeated.

"Happy, but too exhausted for this conversation," Shuki said. "Sleep here tonight. You'll be up early from jet lag. We'll be up early because we're always up early, nachon, Shula?"

Shula began pulling the throw cushions from the couch and putting them onto the low-slung raffia armchairs. Shuki pulled bedding from a cupboard, and, despite her agitation, Petal fell into a deep sleep. She woke to the smell of strong coffee and the light of the sun rising in the window.

"*Boker tov!* You were so sound asleep I didn't want to wake you," Shuki said, bringing her a demitasse of Turkish coffee.

"Boker tov!" Shula said, bursting quickly through the door loaded down with mesh bags of bread, eggs, flour, cucumbers, tomatoes, oranges, avocados, and a dented aluminum milk can that made sloshing noises as it swung from its old handle with each of her steps.

"Shula, slow down! You'll slip, nachon, Petal? Where's the fire that you're in such a hurry?"

Petal's brow furrowed remembering their conversation from the night before.

"Don't think too much so early in the morning," Shuki mock scolded.

Petal hated her own transparency. "It's just I remembered my bag. I dropped it on the lawn last night," she said, trying to disguise her concern.

"Shuki took it to your room after you fell asleep, isn't that right? But I picked up your laundry and forgot to take it to your room after you left for Toronto, so if you want to shower here, you have clean clothes."

Petal smiled. She hadn't imagined the life she had built here. It was real. Her room. Her laundry. Nor had she fabricated her sense of contentment. This felt happy because it was happy.

"I'd like to apply to be a member," she said to their backs as they made order of Shula's packages in the tiny galley kitchen.

"Do you plan to go back to university anytime?" Shuki asked.

"I hadn't thought about it, really."

"Well, you need to think about it," he said, running a thick hand through his coxcomb. "At your age and stage, this will be one of your biggest problems, right, Shula?"

"If you become a member, it will be many years, maybe even decades, before you're allowed to go and study. More and more people want to get an education. Children born and raised on the kibbutz get first priority. Then members who want to study something that will benefit the collective. But it's not simple. I was turned down so many times when I wanted to study, we thought seriously about leaving the kibbutz." She pulled a knife from a drawer and spiral-peeled an orange in one long snake, pulled the fruit in half, popped a piece into her own mouth, and handed half to Petal.

Petal separated a segment of orange and bit down. "Things taste better here," she said, contemplating the sweet, tangy juice that splashed around her mouth. "That can't all be about the actual fruit. An orange is an orange."

"Not true," Shuki said, coming to the defence of agriculture. "What you know from growing up in Canada is not the same orange as we have here picked fresh."

"Yeah, but the orange is just the metaphor," Petal said, not wanting to repeat her proclamation of happiness. "You think I should go study before I try to become a member?"

"If studying is something you may want to do, doing it on your own terms is a much better idea. It's easy to become resentful in this insular little world of ours. Better to have options."

"What sort of options?" Petal asked, savouring her last segment of orange.

"What were you planning to study before you got side-tracked?" Shula asked, cracking eggs into a bowl.

"I hope you aren't making eggs for me," Petal said. She was not ready to eat, nor was she ready to talk about her Rosie-imposed derailment. "I think my stomach is still a bit unsettled."

"Cake for the weekend," Shula said, messily measuring ingredients into her batter. "You know that by now."

"I'm going to shower," Petal said, pleased to be back with her chicken people.

10.

PETAL HEARD THE toilet flush. Disoriented, she sat up and remembered she was at the crumbalow. She flopped out of bed to intercept Rosie on her way from the bathroom. *Keep her up. Keep her out of bed for a bit*, she thought.

"You're up!" Petal said.

Rosie was upright, but her glazed eyes made her level of consciousness unclear.

"You flushed. Is that allowed on Shabbat?"

"Cold water is okay," Rosie said, heading to her bedroom.

Petal sidestepped to block the doorway. "So can I do cold water laundry today?" Petal already knew the answer.

"No work on Shabbes. Day of rest. No electricity. No hot water. No work," Rosie slurred.

"Come to the kitchen and try have something to eat," Petal said, taking hold of Rosie's shoulders and gently guiding her to the kitchen.

"Not hungry. Headache."

"I know, but maybe just a little something. You liked the soup. It's still in the oven. I can give you just a little bit."

Rosie allowed Petal to steer her to the kitchen table.

Unsuccessfully trying to figure out which foil container was meant to be breakfast, Petal pulled the previous night's leftovers from the oven. She imagined that at some point, the chicken and potatoes had been done to perfection. Then Simcha must have left them in the oven for three of four more hours. By the time they had eaten it reheated at dinner the night before, it had resembled balsa wood, so Petal reasoned its texture was dry enough by morning to count as cereal. She put some meat and potatoes into two disposable bowls and moistened the desiccated leftovers with a bit of chicken soup.

"You gotta try to eat a bit," Petal said.

"I'm really not hungry, Pet. I need to sleep."

"Let's talk a bit."

"We can talk in bed," Rosie said.

Petal followed her, made her comfortable, then climbed across her to sit on the bed. "Remember when we were little and we used to climb into bed with Bubby and Zaideh?" Petal asked. "Remember how we used to play with the jiggly bits on the underside of Bubby's arms and ask her when we would get to have that? Like it was something we couldn't wait for?"

Rosie nodded and almost smiled. "I'm freezing, Pet. C'I have a blanket."

Petal got on her knees, reached for the fleece housecoat hanging on the back of the door, and draped it across her sister.

"Better?" she asked, adjusting the coverlet. "How on earth did you ever fit all your kids in this bed?" Petal asked.

"They weren't all little at the same time," Rosie said. "We weren't blessed with twins."

"You're kidding! Imagine having seven already and then twins!"

"Happens. Rabbi here had six then quadruplets," Rosie said, her teeth beginning to tap a quiet Morse code.

"Holy shit! That must be a nightmare!"

"No baby is ever bad news, Pet."

Not true, Petal thought. "Do you always feel that way, Ro? Or are there days when your kids drive you nuts?"

Rosie smiled, closed her eyes, and leaned her head back onto the stacked cushions.

"What's so funny?" Petal asked.

"You know."

"Because I said nuts? Because we always knew we were going to be crazy?" Petal said, reaching for her sister's hand under the fleece housecoat.

"I guess. I don't feel so good, Pet. Need'a sleep." Quivering, Rosie tugged at the bedclothes, trying to find a way in.

"You did really well. I'll give you your meds," Petal said, climbing over her sister to get the meds. Rosie was under the covers when Petal returned. She snapped back the lid on the compartment labelled "Saturday A.M." and placed the lorazepam directly under Rosie's tongue. "Later I want you to tell me about all your kids."

It made Petal sad she had no relationship with her nieces and nephews. She had tried to connect with the older ones when they were all still living in Israel, visiting them in Jerusalem, always arriving laden with small gifts and kosher sweets for the children, but they didn't know what to make of her. Though she conceded to dressing modestly when she visited out of respect, covering elbows, knees, and collarbones, she refused to pretend to be something she was most definitely not and didn't go out of her way to wear skirts or dresses that, even then, she didn't own. The two eldest girls, Sarah Batya and Leah Rochel, laughed and whispered about whether Petal was a man or a woman, miming breasts with their hands. They were little. They didn't know any better, but Petal found it irritating that Rosie was too amused to reprimand her girls for being rude. They spoke about her as though she wasn't there. Petal couldn't recall ever having had direct communication with any of her sister's children. There were neither coerced thank-yous for gifts received nor any forced hugs upon arrivals or departures. There were no expectations of any of the civil niceties that Petal and Rose had been raised with and that Petal believed, had they been her children, she would have insisted upon. Eventually, Petal stopped trying. She visited just enough to check in on Rosie, eventually arriving empty-handed and never on Shabbat so she wouldn't have to stay overnight. Rosie shared minimal news about the children, as though her relationship with Petal was something separate from the rest of her life. For a time, Petal hung on to a belief that their children would be close. When she realized she was probably never going to have any, she let go of her dashed expectations of any relationship with Rosie's kids. She tried never to touch the eight little holes in her heart, lest they become inflamed.

Petal took Rosie's pills to the bathroom and put them on the small windowsill. She gave the tub she had neglected to clean the night before a cursory wipe. *I guess that goes against the no work on Sabbath rule*, she thought, stopping herself. She put the sponge away, brushed her teeth, washed her face, and got dressed.

So now what do I do? she thought, quickly ruling out laundry, phoning Benjamin, watching television, tidying the basement, and a handful of other things she realized were forbidden. She wandered in and out of all the rooms several times, making mental plans for organizing and cleaning in the coming week. *I'll do laundry room by room. That way I won't get confused about what belongs to whom*, she thought, proud to have come up with this simple but practical plan. *Dr. Wolffe indeed*, she congratulated herself facetiously. She opened and closed each and every closet and drawer, finding various states of disarray from disorganized to complete chaos. A dresser drawer in the boys' room unearthed a box of what must have once upon a time been saved or hoarded candy that had dissolved into a sludge of rainbow stickiness, seeping through cardboard onto socks and underpants, which Shabbes or not required immediate attention. Petal threw away the gunk and tossed the gummy undergarments in a plastic bag she dropped at the top of the basement stairs. The drawer itself could wait.

She poked her head into Rosie's bedroom, got her *New Yorker*. There was a knock at the door.

"*Gut Shabbes!*" Heschy Glisserman said, rubbing his hands together.

"Come in," Petal said. "Is it cold out?"

"I'm just hungry. I get cold when I'm hungry," he said, going to the kitchen.

"Can I give you some lunch?" Petal asked.

"My wife will have my head if I don't show up for lunch at home very soon. I just wanted to check in." Heschy looked around. "You seem to have made order here."

"That was your wife. She's a *topha'at teva!*"

Heschy stared at her blankly.

"I meant it as a compliment," she apologized.

Heschy sat down across the table from her. "I don't speak Hebrew. A bit, but not enough to get by." Heschy scratched at the tinfoil covering of the table with his fingernail, leaving behind a small, embossed pattern. Petal wondered why that was allowed but writing on the Sabbath was forbidden.

"How can you discuss the Torah and Talmud? Isn't that what you do? Spend years studying and discussing?"

"That's a very good question. And, because we always like to answer a question with another question, I'll ask you one. Do you know that every word in Hebrew is derived from a three-letter root?" Petal nodded. "Did you know that there are two hundred or so roots in total?" Petal shook her head. That wasn't how she'd been taught in the Ulpan.

"Well, when we go to school, we learn the roots and their variations, and from that we learn to understand the texts. But spoken Hebrew, not so much. Maybe that's why we have to spend so much time discussing the meaning of things. Lots of room for interpretation." Heschy smiled.

"So first you learn to read and later you learn to understand?"

"I never really thought about it that way, but I guess that's true."

Petal scratched her head. "Have I told you about my doctoral thesis?"

"Not really," Heschy said, rocking back and forth in his chair.

"In non–English speaking cultures or countries, English is often the way out to a more prosperous life and is often taught by people who don't really speak it, as a rote subject, like math or Latin, with little emphasis on comprehension. As a teacher, I couldn't help noticing the effects of comprehension on literacy acquisition. When you teach your children to read in Hebrew, do they understand what they're reading, or is it just letters and sounds strung together with no meaning?"

"They get the meaning later," Heschy reassured. "At least some of them do. But at first, it's just memorizing sounds and rules and stringing them together."

"Interesting." Petal's neurons sparked. After all, fodder for academic publication was now her bread and butter.

"Who do you think is better educated in the frum world, boys or girls?" Heschy asked.

"Another answer with a question," Petal smiled. "I think I'm beginning to get the hang of this. But it's a silly question."

"Is it?" Heschy asked.

"Boys, of course!" Petal said.

"Wrong. Our girls are far better educated in all things other than liturgy. Our boys are taught to pray and read, discuss and interpret Torah, Mishna, and Talmud. Girls learn other things, and they learn at a more realistic pace," Heschy said.

"I thought that was the good part of Orthodoxy. No offence, but you know what I mean."

"None taken. It's a problem in Orthodox communities around the world. Our teaching methods are archaic and outdated. Why change something that's kept us going for two thousand years. Right?" He shrugged. "Except it's not working. The rates of functional illiteracy amongst Orthodox boys are disastrous."

"I'm shocked! If it's so bad, why not change it?"

"As I'm sure you can imagine, we go to a lot of trouble to close ourselves off from change. Many people are so afraid of change they refuse to see reality. Our education system caters to the best and the brightest. The ones who understand lessons taught in the same formulaic way by teachers who have never known any other way, they do great."

"Desert island kids," Petal said.

"What?"

"Desert island kids; the ones who left to their own devices on a deserted island would teach themselves to read and write with a stick in the sand," she explained.

"Exactly! For those boys, our system, which rushes them to read before most are ready to sit still, it works!" he said.

"So, what's the rush?" Petal asked.

"Prayer! Davening! Torah study!" Heschy threw his hands up in the air.

"I take it you're not a big supporter of the status quo?"

"No, because I see the fallout. That boy you saw yesterday in my car, he's our collateral damage. Him and many others like him. A good boy from a nice family, but he can't read."

"What do you mean he can't read? Do you mean in English or in Hebrew?" Petal asked.

"Both! Neither!" Heschy was turning red. Petal filled a paper cup with tap water and put it on the table in front of him.

Heschy gulped the water thirstily. "They didn't get it at age four or five when it was taught, so they missed the boat. So they learn to cover, to recite by heart, or they get labelled *schvach* — weak or stupid — but does anybody try to teach them better?"

Petal was baffled by the notion that illiteracy was a rampant problem in first-world Jewish circles.

Heschy got up to refill his cup at the sink.

"They don't learn to read properly in the small window of opportunity they have, so they remain functionally illiterate. The Orthodox world is not an easy one for adolescents."

"Is there an easy world for adolescents?" Petal asked.

"Good point, but Orthodoxy demands a higher degree of ... restraint than a secular life. It only works if we can engage our boys in something other than the temptations of the outside world and their own inner tumult. For the eager, focused students, it's a beautiful thing. It's a life of meaning and devotion. But imagine being a fifteen-, sixteen-, seventeen-year-old boy required to ... distract yourself through study and devotion to a higher power. Day in, day out — but you're only marginally literate, and the distraction relies almost entirely upon reading. There you are, not keeping up. Feeling frustrated and lost, losing any confidence you may have managed to hold on to. Where do you go? What do you do?"

Petal shrugged.

"Depression. Suicide. Drugs. Other trouble — that's where! But no one wants to talk about it! Boy, could we use someone like you."

"But no one wants to talk about it," Petal repeated.

"Our people are experts at pretending that if no one speaks about it, it doesn't exist," Heschy said, looking at his watch and making toward the door. "My wife's gonna kill me! I have to run.

I'll come back tomorrow. We can continue our discussion. By the way, how's Mrs. Hirsch?"

"I think she's going to be all right."

Petal hated the idea of spending hours lying in bed. It reminded her too much of depression, but there was nowhere to sit. She contemplated going to read in Schmeil's study but worried she wouldn't hear Rosie from the basement. *What could she need? She won't wake up unless I force her, and she won't eat unless I spoon-feed her*, Petal thought, suddenly hungry. She pulled the container marked *Shabbes lunch — cholent* from the warm oven.

There was another knock on the door. *Like Grand Central Station around here*, she thought as she shoved the container back into the oven.

"Der! You're just in time for lunch," Petal said, ushering Der into the kitchen. "Don't worry, it's kosher," she chided.

Der looked around at the tinfoil-covered surfaces. "It's for Pesach," Petal reassured. "She isn't creating a foil fortress to ward off aliens or anything."

"That's good to know. It was a fleeting thought, but one nonetheless. I have seen people cover their kitchens for Pesach before. I've also seen far more suspect uses of swaths of aluminum paper. Why is it that psychosis is so fond of foil?"

Petal shrugged.

"It's not as much of a mess as I was expecting," Der said, sitting at the table.

"It's better than it was. Heschy Glisserman's wife came and made some order. I'll do more cleaning and tidying during the week. She begged me not to do it on Shabbat or Chag." Petal took the lunchtime foil container back out of the oven.

"How is she?" Der asked.

"Drugged. Sleeping. I'd like to cut back on the sedatives a bit so she has more lucid time. Maybe get her to eat a little. She's frighteningly thin," Petal said, taking two paper plates from the large bag on the counter and dishing out brown meat and potato stew. "It's hard to imagine being thin on this heavy food. There's enough here for a small army." She placed two plates on the table.

"Be careful with the medication. It's a thin line between doped and psychotic. Should we wait and eat when she gets up?" Der asked.

"No, let's eat. Then I'll wake her." Petal stabbed at an uncooperative piece of meat with a plastic fork.

"It's actually tasty," Der said. "But the best cholent hands down was your zaideh's. It was so full of love ... and loss. Your zaideh didn't cook often, but when he did, he cooked passion. Like that Salman Rushdie novel where she cooks all her emotions into her chutneys."

"*Midnight's Children*. I was too young to understand Bubby and Zaideh and all they had been through."

"Nobody expected you to, Tiggaleh."

"I know, but even though I didn't understand or really have concrete information about their struggles and losses, I'm pretty sure that Rosie and I are who we are because of their tortured souls. Don't misunderstand, I'm not blaming. I know they did their best, but ..."

"They did better than their best. They faced their own worst nightmares repeatedly, and they didn't give in. They left their doors unlocked, literally and figuratively, to prove to themselves that the world, despite all evidence to the contrary, was a safe place. It almost killed them to give you girls the freedom to do what you wanted — to live the lives you chose — but ..." Der knew when to be quiet. He shook his head from side to side and concentrated on his lunch.

"The problem with Jewish food is that two weeks later you're hungry again," Petal said. "Let's wake Ro before we need to have our post-cholent naps."

"Will she let me in her room?" Der asked as Petal motioned him toward the bedroom.

"Less worthy men have been in her bedroom," Petal said, pushing open the bedroom door. "Ro? I have a special visitor for you."

Der stood as far back as the cramped space would allow, suppressing his instinct to climb onto the bed and hug his girl.

Petal pulled the covers off Rosie's head. Barely conscious, Rosie motioned toward the scarves on the hooks. Petal handed her one. Rosie's hands expertly covered her hair in the scarf before acknowledging Der.

"Der," she said, her eyes pink and wet like a rabbit's. "How come I never see you anymore? I miss you." She reached out as though to grasp his hand.

Der wasn't sure what to do. He sat uncomfortably on the edge of the bed. Petal wasn't sure what to do either. Der was family. Surely even a married woman could give her closest relative a hug. Petal got a chair from the kitchen and wedged it in the crevice between the wall and the bed. Der sat.

"I'll leave you two alone, if that's okay. Maybe go out and get a bit of fresh air?"

Der nodded approval.

"Sure," Rosie said.

Stepping outside, Petal felt as though she was leaving the airlock of a space capsule. *Give Benjamin a call, take a spin around the block, be back before long,* she thought between the door and the sidewalk, instinctively reaching in her pockets, patting herself down in search of her phone. *Shit! It's still in Rosie's dresser! No sweat. Pop back in. Get the phone. Start again.* But halfway up the driveway, she thought better of it. *Benjamin will understand my radio silence.*

The air felt clean and crisp. She stretched her arms out and up over her head, interlocking her fingers, pushing them skyward, stretching her shoulders and rolling her neck. An Orthodox man passed in the opposite direction, followed several paces behind by a haggard-looking woman carrying an infant and shepherding five other children in ascending sizes. Petal kept walking. Another mother with a large brood passed by. Petal looked back at them. Something inside her twitched.

The feeling was faint, niggling, but her sense she needed to get back to Rosie mounted. Petal turned around, at first maintaining her easy pace, then adopting her New York bus clip. Approaching the house, escalating dread coursed through her, heart pounding, stopping just short of panic, she burst through the door, shouting, "Is everything okay?"

"Fine," Der said from the kitchen. He was sitting with Rosie. She was moving food around a small plate.

Petal felt silly. Her unwarranted anxiety embarrassed her. She took a long moment to hang her coat and gather herself.

"Twitch was just telling me what a blessing it is that Schmeil and the children are able to be with his mother and sister," Der said.

"And having Pet here," Rosie said.

Petal stood behind Rosie, placed her hands on her sister's shoulders.

"I'm sorry, Pet. I'm so sorry."

"What for?" Petal applied a bit of gentle pressure, anchoring herself to Rose.

"For making you be here. I'm sure you have better things to do than babysit me."

"No. Nothing better," Petal said, looking intently at Der. "Remember when you came to be with me?" The comment was more for Rosie's sake than any sort of fond reminiscence. "That's what families do. How did you swing that?" she asked Der, suddenly aware for the first time of the disruption to his life she had caused. He stared blankly at her, not understanding. "When you came to save me in Israel. How did you come and stay for so long?"

"I was on sabbatical that year. It was an easy time for me to get away for six weeks. I was planning a trip to Israel anyhow," Der said, minimizing the disruption it must have been on his life. "Your bubby and zaideh were remarkable, resilient people." Der never failed to advocate on behalf of Irving and Estie. "They wanted to go, but I had connections and time. It made sense for me to go."

"You see, Ro, we might be crazy, but we have excellent timing!" Petal gently kneaded her sister's bony shoulders.

DER'S VISIT, HESCHY'S check-in, even her little panic attack the day before had broken the tedium of time in this vigil she was sitting. While Rosie slept, she alternated between lying in the bedroom and sitting uncomfortably in the kitchen. She marvelled repeatedly how a family of ten people lived in this tiny turmoil of a house. Where did they go? How did they spend their time? It was only Sunday, and she had agreed not to do any housework until Monday night at the earliest, but she thought she might lose her mind. She wished she had brought a stack of books with her. She thought longingly about the piles of books sitting next to her bed in New York; ones she had intended to read languidly during her time off. She looked around for reading material of any sort and found only children's books for the youngest of the lot. *Don't these people read? No internet, no computers, no indication of first-world, twenty-first-century connectivity whatsoever.*

In the basement, buried deep within the swamp of stuff, Petal unearthed an old television and VCR. She rummaged through the videotapes scattered haphazardly around the floor, discovering only unfamiliar children's content. None of the usual Disney or Barney but rather *Uncle Moishie's Succos* and *Hassidishe Tales*. She thought about watching a bit just see what they were about, just to pass some time, and then remembered the prohibition on electricity until after the holy days.

Petal rationalized that tidying up the toys a bit wasn't the same as cleaning. She separated Lego from Playmobil, Duplo, and puzzle pieces, attempting to organize each into an appropriate receptacle. Tea sets and dolls, a child-sized broom and kitchen, were all given a corner to rest in. It reminded her of setting up her classrooms, though it had been many years since she had taught kindergarten or primary grades. As she sorted the trash from the treasures, she took comfort in knowing that her nieces and nephews played and destroyed like any other children. How could she have presumed any different?

Every few hours, Petal woke Rosie up and tried to feed her from the overcooked offerings in the foil containers, the pickled herring and gefilte fish in the fridge or a piece of matzah with butter or jam. She forced Rosie to remain upright and conscious for as long as possible, eventually conceding defeat, doling out medication and letting Rosie crawl back under her covers. There were moments when Petal believed that the real Rosie was getting out from beneath the drugs and discombobulation of psychosis. When they made the blessings to welcome Passover, breaking matzah and reminiscing, Petal felt hopeful.

"Do you remember how deranged Bubby would get about the matzah crumbs?" Petal said. "She chased us around with the vacuum cleaner as though we were made entirely of matzah. Remember we chanted, 'Run, run as fast as you can! You can't catch me, I'm the matzah man!'"

Rosie smiled. "Was that me or you? Sometimes I can't remember what my own memories are."

"Me too," Petal said.

"We snuck the box of matzah over to Der's house so we could eat without Bubby nagging about the crumbs," Rosie remembered. "She loved the Passover jellies. She ate them until her teeth hurt from sugar. And she would slap her own hand for having no willpower." Rosie ran her fingers feebly over the back of her other hand.

"And Zaideh chastised her like a little girl: 'I told you would be sorry if you ate all the kendies,' wagging his finger at her. She couldn't resist sweets."

"Even in her bed," Rosie said.

"We found candy wrappers in her bed, and she would pretend she had no idea how they got there! I forgot all about that."

They laughed.

"And jelly beans," they said in unison.

"Like they grew there in the folds of her sheets," Petal added. "Remember we could never figure out why our Halloween loot would disappear so fast? And then when we got older, we hid it from the robbers in places Bubby would help us devise?"

"Let's not talk about Halloween, Pet."

"Why not, Ro?"

"It's not a Jewish holiday, Pet. Let's just not talk about it, okay?"

"Okay, Ro. We don't have to talk about it." *Fundamentalist*, Petal thought.

Late in the afternoon, while Rosie slept, Heschy Glisserman stopped in.

"I can't stay," he said, bouncing in the entry by the front door. "Seder soon. Simmy needs me home. Actually, she doesn't need me at all, but if I'm not there, it's hard for me to pretend I'm of any use to her, and it's hard for her to complain about how useless I am." He smiled. "I wanted to check in before we leave tomorrow night."

"Please come in, just for a few minutes. Honestly, I'm bored. I'm really not used to this degree of disconnection," Petal said.

Heschy looked over his shoulder toward the street, back at Petal, then back outside as though weighing his obligations. "A few minutes or Simmy will be asking the rabbi for a *get*," he said, bouncing into the kitchen. "She's sleeping a lot, your sister?"

"Yeah, I'm trying to force her to stay up, but as long as she's so drugged, it's too much to expect."

"One day at a time," he said.

"Can you sit for a minute? I'm sure your wife will understand you're doing a mitzvah, saving me from boredom."

Heschy sat in the kitchen. Petal filled two disposable cups with water and joined him at the table.

"Did you have a nice Seder last night?" she asked.

"There is no joy greater than having all my children around the table together," Heschy said.

"Can I ask you a question?" Petal said, looking down in case her forthrightness made Rabbi Glisserman uneasy.

"You know I love questions." He smirked.

"I don't have a lot of experience in the frum world, but I have enough to know that you're not the average ultra-Orthodox man. Most men from your community wouldn't give me, a secular unmarried woman, the time of day, let alone have a conversation, or ride in a car, or stop by to check in. Maybe I'm wrong, but what makes you seem so comfortable crossing into my world, even just at the edges?"

"Don't mistake effort for comfort or a willingness to meet partway as a crossing over," he said, unfurling the lip of the paper cup with his fingers. "In part, the work I do demands that I act without judgment. I couldn't be professionally effective if I didn't accept that good and right and legitimate are subjective. My truth is just that — mine. It doesn't diminish anyone else's, even if they are in direct conflict. Just because I believe my mandate is God-given doesn't make yours less worthy. Does that make sense?"

"I guess, but it seems divergent from, say, someone like Schmeil and his approach to the outside world," Petal said.

"Listen, Schmeil is not necessarily the norm, but like many others, he would like to pretend there is no secular world — no world beyond the boundaries of ours. It's easier that way."

"So you think the work you do forces you to acknowledge other paradigms?" Petal asked.

"Not exactly. I think I can do my work more effectively by understanding the draw the outside world might have to a floundering adolescent. If I pretend it's not there, I can't present our status quo as an engaging alternative. I need to validate the reality of temptations and the difficulty of resisting."

Petal thought carefully about what Heschy had said. "How did you even figure that out? I mean, it's kind of like a fish figuring out that it's in water without leaving the water."

"An interesting analogy and a valid question. The answer is that I got a parking ticket."

Petal took the bait. "So, what does a parking ticket have to do with an expanded worldview?" she sipped her water.

Heschy pushed his chair away from the table, leaned back, and stretched his legs out in front of him, crossing them at his ankles. "I got a parking ticket I didn't believe I deserved, so I decided to take it to traffic court instead of paying the fine. The hearing date was set for a Friday afternoon in winter. I had to go to city hall to change my court date. The woman at the desk wanted to know why I needed a different date, and I explained that as an Orthodox Jew, I was forbidden from travelling or working after sundown on Fridays. She said, 'You don't have to go to court personally. You can send someone in your place.'" Heschy stretched his arms out in front of him, crossed his wrists, clasped his fingers together, and stretched his locked arms above his head. "At that moment, I realized something I had never thought about before. Like suddenly I knew I was surrounded by water. In the whole world, I didn't know a single person I could call who wasn't also an Orthodox Jew. The diversity in my life was limited to degrees of Orthodoxy and rabbinic affiliations. I stood at that counter at city hall and looked around at all the people and realized I had never seen them before.

"I decided that Hashem wouldn't have given me eyes or ears or the ability to communicate if he didn't want me to see or hear or engage with the world, the whole world."

ON MONDAY NIGHT, Rosie seemed more present. Petal couldn't put her finger on exactly what had changed, but something subtle had happened. Rosie asked for food.

"Is there salad? I need something fresh," she said.

Petal's heart felt a small electrical impulse, like a carpet shock. Nothing big or earth-shattering, but a glint of possibility. The salad that had been delivered on Friday morning was far from fresh by Monday night, but Petal gave it to Rosie, and she ate it if not with gusto then at least with interest. Petal peeled an orange she found in the fridge and handed Rosie segments one at a time. Rosie chewed slowly as though she were contemplating each vesicle of fruit as it burst between her teeth.

"Now are we allowed to shower?" Petal asked, throwing away the dinner refuse.

"If you want. I'll wait. Tomorrow," Rosie said, deflating as though the fuel that had buoyed her had run out.

"I can wash your hair again if you want, Ro. Or we could shower together. Hydroterapies?"

"Nah. You go. I'll wait," Rosie said, heading for her bedroom.

"Schmeil's coming to visit tomorrow, Ro. I don't know what

time he's coming. If you bathe now, you'll be ready whenever he comes," Petal encouraged.

"Okay, Pet. You're right. I'll run a bath," Rosie said.

Petal followed Rosie to the bathroom. Rosie's energy was suddenly so diminished, Petal worried she might fall asleep and drown in the tub. Rosie didn't object when Petal sat on the edge of the bath and helped her step into the warm running water. She lay back and closed her eyes. Petal sprayed her head and shampooed her hair and helped her wash and dry and get ready for bed. She gave Rosie her nighttime pills and combed her long, flaxen hair, weaving it into a braid.

When Rosie was asleep, Petal showered. Before turning in for the night, she stripped the beds in the boys' room, gathered all the clothes from the floor, shoved everything into one of the pillowcases, grabbed the plastic bag of sticky socks and underwear from the top of the stairs, and headed down to the washing machine.

Petal woke in darkness to the sounds of wind-whipped windowpanes, cracking thunder, and Rosie screaming.

"*Be quiet! Enough!*" Rosie shouted. Petal leapt from bed and raced to the adjacent bedroom.

"What's wrong, Ro? What happened?"

Rosie was standing on her bed with the blankets draped over her like biblical robes.

"Tell them to stop screaming at me! I can't help it! Tell them I didn't do it!" Rosie pumped her fists at the air, stomping her feet on the too-soft, sinking mattress.

"It's just the thunder. You've had a bad dream. There's nobody here but us." Petal tried to keep her voice even, tranquil, but Rosie's agitation echoed in Petal's heartbeat. She was trembling and thrashing the bedclothes around her like the storm was right inside the room, tempest tossed, wind howling and whirling, thunder crashing.

"No! I won't! I will not wash with blood! Blood is unclean! Blood is unclean!" Rosie shrieked, covering her ears, at first with her hands then, collapsing to her knees, with pillows, pressing them on either side of her head, arms crossed — take cover, the sky is falling! *Drugs!* Petal thought. *I can't leave her like this! She might try to break the window or hurt herself.* Petal stood motionless. *Fuck me! I'm just like them. First thing I think of is to sedate her. But she's terrified! Should I restrain her, or do I just let her flail?*

Petal climbed onto the bed and wrapped her arms around Rosie's cushioned head, shoved her face between the pillows into Rosie's face, and talked to her sister in as soothing a voice as she could muster while her heart thumped drums of war in her chest.

"I know that you hear them talking to you. I believe that the voices are real to you. I know they are saying horrible things that you hear. I know that you hear them talking to you," Petal continued, her arms wrapped tight around her sister's head, her body as close as she could be, knees to knees, faces to faces, arms wrapped pretzel-like around pillows and head, helping to ward off invisible intruders. Crouched on the bed like an upright embryonic twin, Petal tried to anchor her sister in reality. "Come back to me, Ro. Listen to my words, Rosie."

After a time, exhausted from screaming and crying and fighting the demons, Rosie crumpled, taking Petal down with her, and the two of them lay on the bed in a fetal embrace, spooning and rocking back and forth. Rosie was calmer but still crying. Petal changed her refrain a little. "I know that you hear them, but they're not real. They are only real to you. They're just voices, not people. Only you can hear them," she continued, speaking into the back of her sister's head, an endless mantric flow of counterphobic voodoo, until she felt confident that Rosie was safe and she could step out for a minute.

Petal took a red Seconal from the dosette reserved for the

following night, then questioned the safety of another dose so close on the heels of the last. She put it back and instead brought some lorazepam from the pill bottle. "Open your mouth," she said, taking Rosie's chin between her fingers and gently pushing down to encourage unlatching of clenched teeth and lips. Rosie complied, too spent to resist. Petal tucked the pill under Rosie's tongue, digging in with her finger to ensure placement. She lay back down beside her sister, holding her until eventually Rosie drifted off to sleep as the thunder and lightning cracked and flashed more distant, the storm passing.

Petal slept fitfully and woke early feeling hungover and conflicted. Having done almost nothing for days, she felt more tired than when she was working around the clock to finish her dissertation. Petal wondered if she had done the right thing for her sister by drugging her. She tried to get back to sleep but had no luck, got out of bed, and stripped the three beds in the room where she was staying. As Petal pulled at the stale bedding, she heard a dull thud. A dog-eared copy of *Anne of Green Gables* that had apparently been hiding in one of her niece's beds lay on the floor. Petal picked up the book and turned it over in her hands as though it was a precious archaeological relic. *They read*, she thought with palpable relief. Petal tucked the book between the box spring and the mattress, bundled all the visible clothes into the bedding, and went to the basement.

When Schmeil arrived at just past nine o'clock, Petal was remaking the last of the beds. She had not yet folded all the washed clothes but had managed to make a good start on the boys' stuff stacked on their beds.

Schmeil called softly from the vestibule, "Hello? I can come in?"

Petal, finger raised to lips, met Schmeil at the front door. "Shh. Ro ... Raizel's still asleep. Rough night." She motioned him to the kitchen.

"It's okay that I come in?" Schmeil asked.

"It's your house!" Petal had never been so happy to see her brother-in-law. She was almost excited for his company. "Come in. Sit down. A cup of tea?"

Schmeil shook his head, more a vibration than a shake.

"Right," Petal said recalling the issue of leaven that had pre-occupied Schmeil the previous week.

They sat awkwardly across from one another, conversation stumbling to start.

"She's good?" Schmeil asked.

"I don't think I'd say good yet," Petal said.

"She's not good?" Schmeil said.

"She's having more good than bad moments each day, but last night was more bad than good." Petal was trying to be honest and positive but not so positive as to give false hope. She knew how literal Schmeil could be.

"Baruch Hashem!" Schmeil said.

Petal wasn't sure how to continue. Was his "thank God" an acknowledgement of the "more good than bad" or an indication of having ignored or misheard the "more bad than good"? Or was it simply a default response to whatever?

They sat together awkwardly.

Schmeil broke the silence.

"Thank you," he said, looking down at the table and rocking backward precariously on the rickety chair.

"Oh, stop it," Petal said, meaning both the seesawing and the thanking. "My sister! Of course!"

"No, I meant the house. I see you've been busy. Thank you."

"You're welcome. I just started last night," Petal said, suddenly self-conscious that Schmeil might think she had been working during the holy days.

"So much you were able to accomplish in such a short time. Usually, my Raizel ... well, not that our house is spotless, but ... she's a good mother, a good wife ..."

"Schmeil, I'm not here to judge. I'm here to help." Petal tried to reassure herself as much as him.

Again, they sat in silence.

This time, Petal broke the silence.

"I went down to the basement," she said, stopping to gauge Schmeil's response.

"Yes, it's a little messy right now. You know that's where ... that's where ..."

"Yes, about that ... would it be okay if I put the shelves back together?" Petal said.

"You don't have to do that. I can do it when I come back."

"I know I don't have to, but if I have time ... I have a lot of time to kill ..."

"Why not?"

Petal presumed the question was rhetorical.

More awkward silence filled the cramped space. Schmeil swayed back and front in his chair, looking anywhere but at Petal. Petal brushed matzah crumbs with one hand from the foil-covered table into the palm of her other hand. She stood up to throw the crumbs away.

"When do you think she'll wake up?" Schmeil asked, misinterpreting Petal's momentary departure from the table as significant. Petal wondered what time it was and for the first time in days thought about her phone, still in Rosie's bedroom dresser.

"We can wake her soon," and then, maybe to keep the conversation going, maybe because she was lonely, she said, "Can I ask you a question, Schmeil?"

"Why not?"

"I noticed on your study wall there's a portrait."

"That's one of our important rebbes," Schmeil said, raising a finger for emphasis.

"Yeah, that's what I figured, but that's not my question. My question is about graven images. I thought they were forbidden in Judaism."

"True," Schmeil said, looking a bit confused and rubbing his beard.

"So how can you have a portrait of a rabbi?" Petal barely cared about the actual answer. What she cared about was engaging with her brother-in-law. She wanted to connect with him on his terms, to see him as the person he was, not the person she had always presumed him to be. She had washed and folded his dirty laundry. She had cleaned his soap scum and pubic hair from the bathroom, but she was aware that to her he was still a caricature of a person largely of her own prejudiced invention. Unexpectedly, she wanted to see in him at least a little of what Rosie saw, and, in that moment, it occurred to her that she could only do that if she met him where he lived, both literally and figuratively. So here she was, asking him about religious laws and his beliefs. "If graven images are forbidden, why is a portrait allowed?"

Schmeil scratched his head, adjusted his kippah, stroked his beard, and rocked back and forth. After a time, he shrugged his shoulders. Petal wished he wouldn't behave quite so like a lampoon of a yeshiva bocher. It made it difficult for her to see anything other than the Nazi propaganda, anti-Semitic posters of Orthodoxy she had seen in museums and obviously, unintentionally, appropriated to some degree. She wished he would look her in the eye. She wanted him to stop swaying in his seat. She wanted to stop being such a judgmental ass. Then a small grin crossed Schmeil's lips, and his eyes glinted like a naughty schoolboy; he looked up at her and, pleased with himself, said, "You know, it barely even looks like him, so it's hardly what you might call a graven image."

Petal smiled back at him.

They woke Rosie. Petal took her cellphone from the dresser.

"I'll leave you two for a bit, if that's okay," Petal said, looking to both for permission. Rosie nodded a bleary-eyed confirmation. Schmeil bowed his head shyly. Petal construed acquiescence.

Petal grabbed her coat from the hook by the door and went out into the grungy day. The previous night's storm left tree branches strewn about, and it was clear that the heavens really had been shouting. She headed toward Bathurst Street. Petal pulled her phone from her pocket and turned it on for the first time in four and a half days. Just as she was thinking how nice the respite from electronic connection had been, her phone pinged to life with a string of anxiety-provoking rings one after the other, indicating many missed calls. "Fuck!" she said, feeling the weight of obligation descend heavily upon her. She scrolled through the calls. Of the twenty-three missed, thirteen were from Benjamin, one was from Der, one was from Dr. Farmer, and the rest were from miscellaneous friends checking in.

Without listening to the messages, she dialled Benjamin. "Sorry, sorry," she said.

"Hello, Canada! Welcome back!" Benjamin said. "I was so worried when I couldn't reach you. I didn't realize you would also have to be religious."

"Out of respect. I should have told you, but I didn't actually think about it till Rosie made me turn off my phone. How'd you figure it out?" Petal stepped into the middle of the road to avoid a large, water-filled pothole.

"Eventually, I found a number for Der and called him," Benjamin said.

"Oh, you clever boy! I wish you were here!" she said, feeling in her pockets for a perhaps forgotten cigarette. "How did you even find Der's name, let alone his number?"

"Oh, I'm quite a good detective!" he teased.

"Seriously." Petal was curious.

"I went to your apartment and found the number in your address book. I told you that you shouldn't keep the key above the door. You never know who might let themselves in. How's it going there?"

"I don't know," Petal said. "I thought better, but last night she freaked out, and I had to drug her down from an auditory hallucination. I'm bored and lonely, but I think maybe I'm helping." She was more asking than telling.

"I'm so pleased that you are bored and lonely," Benjamin said.

"Why would you say that?"

"Because I've booked a ticket. I'm coming to Toronto on Thursday night for the weekend. Didn't you listen to my messages?"

"What? I mean great, but ... I'm busy taking care of my sister. What are you going to do here?" Petal was thrown off by this sudden impending collision of her life with her sister's life.

"Should I not come?"

Petal didn't answer. A crew on a telephone pole working on downed wires distracted her.

"You don't want me to come? I can cancel my ticket. When I couldn't reach you, I was so worried something terrible had happened. My brain started spinning. I thought if something were in fact wrong, I would come to be with you. Then I got hold of Der, and he explained the turned-off phone, which, *duh* ... I should have been able to put two and two together. Anyhow, in my mind, I guess I was already ready to get on a plane and come save you from God knows what, and then Der suggested I come, so ..."

"Der suggested?"

"Pet, I don't have to come. Really, I can cancel. I just thought you might want some company. Der said you were bored and lonely with your sister asleep most of the time."

"No, it's a good idea," Petal said, jumping back onto the sidewalk to avoid a car racing toward her too fast. "I was just caught off guard. Sorry. I'm desperate for company! It might be a bit weird with Rosie, but I'm not going to worry about that. Don't cancel."

"So next question: how do you feel about me staying with Der? He invited me, and I said yes, but only if it's okay with you."

Petal turned right at Bathurst Street and headed north toward Lawrence Avenue.

"I can't think of anything I'd like more than you and Der having a chance to bond."

"Pet, I can't tell if you're being serious or sarcastic."

"That's not like you, Benjamin. I'm totally serious. I'm excited that you're coming. I'm happy you're going to stay with Der and meet my crazy sister. Bring me books from my apartment, please. I don't know how long I'm going to be here."

Petal strolled around Lawrence Plaza, remembering how as children she and Rosie had raided their zaideh's change drawer every Chanukah and gone to the plaza to buy gifts for Der and Bubby and Zaideh from a shop that sold cheap china figurines. So as not to be outdone by one another or play favourites amongst the adults in their lives, the girls bought everyone the same figurine twice each Chanukah. When Irving and Estie died, the windowsill of their apartment still had a lineup of blue porcelain horses, jade-green frogs, brightly coloured birds on branches, and various other small animals that had accumulated over the years. They were the only objects of pure sentiment that Estie held on to, though if Petal were honest with herself, she might have dismissed the idea that sentiment had saved the figurines and realized Estie actually liked the kitschy ornaments. That shop had disappeared eons ago, but Lawrence Plaza reminded Petal how proud they had been to give their grownups presents they had bought and wrapped all on their own. Doing so helped blur the scars of gifts promised but never given by their mother. Lawrence Plaza was their gateway to hard-won freedom and independence. "We're just going to the plaza," they said, and Estie was reassured even when they had no intention of going to the plaza. The plaza lay within the comfort zone. Nothing bad could happen at the plaza, at least in the fabricated world of Estie Wolffe.

Petal wandered for almost an hour, mustering up false sentimentality about this place she didn't actually feel attached to. She listened to her phone messages, finding Benjamin's escalating concern rather adorable. Der's message delivering Benjamin's desire to hear from her and the promise of a surprise, which she now presumed was his intention to come and visit. Dr. Farmer checking in to see how she was doing and leaving things open for their usual time slot. If he didn't hear from her, he would understand.

Petal checked the time: 11:45. *It's Tuesday*, she thought. In the offices at the west side of the plaza, she found a quiet, musty stairwell to make a call. She sat on the salt-stained stairs and dialled her therapist.

"Hello, Dr. Wolffe," Dr. Farmer said.

"Hey, thanks for being so flexible," she said.

"Not at all. Life gets complicated sometimes. How's your sister doing?"

Petal filled him in, stopping to let someone coming into the building pass her on the stairs and get far enough out of earshot to maintain some modicum of confidentiality — not so much for herself but for her sister. Hunkered down like a vagrant in a stairwell in Rosie's hood, Petal felt she owed her sister that.

"It's a precarious situation indeed. How are you managing?" the therapist asked.

"Okay, I guess. The strange thing is that if I dig deep and try to unearth my own primary emotions, it's not worry or fear I'm feeling. I see how much Rosie is suffering, but something inside me is pretty sure it's going to be okay in the end. Things with Rosie always are. I'm just worried that my own boredom, a nothingness of hour upon hour and day after day flatness, is a trigger for my own shit." But as she said it, Petal wished she hadn't made her sister's crisis about herself. Maybe they were less different than she thought.

"An appropriate concern," Dr. Farmer said. "I'm glad you'll be getting some company soon."

"I guess you just saw Benjamin," she said, uncertain how she felt about this borderline breach of confidentiality.

"Yes," he said, quickly moving past the disclosure. "If you need more support from me, all you need do is leave a message. I'll make myself available. I realize you think your job is to get your sister back to a healthy place. My job is to keep you in one."

"Thanks," Petal said, grateful to have him on her team.

Three quarters of an hour on the phone with Dr. Farmer had prolonged Petal's outing more than she was entirely comfortable. She hurried back to the crumbalow.

Rosie's screaming was audible as she reached the door.

"They take my things and hide them and then I think I'm crazy! I'm not crazy! They steal my things!" Rosie bellowed.

"Raizel, nobody is stealing from you!" Schmeil said, trying to reason with her.

Rosie was throwing the clean laundry, both folded and unfolded, around the boys' room as Petal came through the door. Petal looked at a sweating and distraught Schmeil. "How long has this been going on?" she stage-whispered.

"I don't know. She was fine when she woke up. We were talking. I gave her a few minutes of privacy to get dressed." Schmeil
was on the verge of tears.

"It's all right, Schmeil. Make sure she doesn't hurt herself.
I'll get the meds," Petal said, motioning toward Rosie, who
continued from room to room, rummaging in the piles of clean
clothes, screaming about her stolen property, about her dignity,
which they could not steal from her.

Armed with half a lorazepam, Petal got as close as she could
to Rosie the moving target and spoke serenely. "You must be very
frustrated, Ro. It's awful when others misplace your things. I'm
sure it'll turn up. We'll keep looking. I'll help you as soon as you
take this." She tried to put the pill into Rosie's mouth.

"It's a sin to steal, and yet they say I'm the sinful one. I'm not
unclean."

Petal got the pill in Rosie's mouth. Rose continued to circle
from one room to the next. Followed by her sister and husband,
Rose dug through the disarray she'd created on her previous pass,
shouting at her demons, crying, pulling at her hair underneath
her headscarf, clawing at her arms, until she stopped at her bed,
climbed under the covers, and fell asleep.

Petal and Schmeil collapsed in the kitchen.

"Do you have any idea what that was about?" Petal asked.

"She can't find her *sheitel*, you know, her wig. She said the
mean women stole it," Schmeil said elbows resting on knees, head
held firmly in hands, struggling to steady his breathing, unable to
control his weeping.

Petal pushed aside her impulse to put a comforting hand on
her brother-in-law's heaving back. "Does she have a sheitel?"

"Of course she does. Outside, she always wears a wig."

"Not that it really matters, but where do you suppose the wig
is?"

"I don't know! Maybe she took it to be washed and styled before yuntif."

"Is that something she would normally do?"

"This is not part of my world — what women do. I'm guessing."

"Guessing is good enough," Petal said. "Schmeil ... don't you think she should be in a hospital? I don't think she's safe."

"I don't know," he said, resting his head back in his hands as though the gravity of the situation was literally weighing too heavily upon him. "Rabbi Glisserman is away. Dr. Gold is away. There's nobody to ask, and I am not smart enough to know the answer." He was losing what little composure he had reclaimed.

"It's not a question of smart. We're both out of our depth here. That's why I'm thinking maybe we should put her in the hands of people who know better than us," Petal tried to persuade.

"Maybe we can call the hospital," Schmeil suggested, and Petal thought this was, at the very least, a good first step.

The hospital wouldn't do a phone consult and gave Petal the number for Telehealth. After giving a brief history, a rundown of the medications Rosie was on, and assurances that "the patient" was not in immediate danger, Petal was told to expect a call from an on-call physician. Not ten minutes later, her phone rang, and a very nice woman doctor with an Indian name and an upper-crusty Anglo-Indian accent called back. Petal repeated Rose's circumstance.

"You could take her to the nearest emergency room, or you can try increasing her lithium just a bit. She's currently on the lowest possible dose. Sometimes it is a matter of adjusting dosage. Normally, I wouldn't suggest doing that without her doctor's say-so, but you say her primary care psychiatrist is away on holiday. They will probably do the same at hospital. If you believe she is in danger or there is no change within next day or so, hospital is necessary," said the doctor.

"Dr. Gold said we might need to increase her dosage. If you're comfortable giving it a try, I'm okay with it too." Petal was looking to share the responsibility with Schmeil.

"I don't know anything," Schmeil said, pinching at his beard with his thumb and forefinger. "I suppose we could try and see ..."

"I'll call Der. Der has experience with these things," Petal said.

"Tiggaleh! I've been wondering when I might hear from you! Have you spoken with Benjamin?"

"Yes. I spoke with him. He told me he's coming. Der, I need your opinion on something."

"Anything," Der said.

Petal gave Der the condensed but complete version of events.

"It sounds as though an increase couldn't do any harm and might in fact make all the difference."

Petal still felt unsure.

"I'm calling Dr. Gold. I hate to bother him while he's away, but he did say I could call."

"*Vey iz mir!* All this time you have a way to call Dr. Gold, and you didn't tell me!" Schmeil was more relieved than angry.

"I forgot. I got sucked into the vortex of chaos," Petal apologized.

Dr. Gold agreed. "It's certainly worth trying. From what you say, your sister is experiencing some lucid time the past few days. Let's take that as indication that the medication is moving her in the right direction and bump her up."

Just to be certain, Petal called Dr. Farmer.

"It's hard for me to tell you what to do about your sister. I really don't have enough understanding of either the medical system up there or of your sister to make an informed suggestion, nor is it my place. What I can do is litmus test your state. If you feel the situation is putting you at risk or in an unmanageable position, then a pass off is in order. My concern must be you. It's the only part in this scenario where I feel I have any jurisdiction."

"I think I'm okay," she said.

"Think?"

Petal paused to take stock of her own well-being. "Think is as far as I'm willing to go, Doc. I think I'm handling things. In some ways, I actually feel good — tangibly useful. I think I've missed the hands-on world living in my academic ivory tower for so long. Am I certain I'm making exactly the right decisions for my sister? No, not at all! But is the cost my own mental health? I don't think so. I think this caregiver role might actually be good for me."

"Hmmm," said Dr. Farmer.

"Hmm indeed. I had no idea until I actually said it."

"Well then, Dr. Wolffe, you've got this. Call anytime."

"So, it's decided," Petal said to Schmeil at the door. "Tonight I'll double her dose. Tomorrow is a new day."

"B'ezrat Hashem, tomorrow will be a better day."

"B'ezrat Hashem," Petal said.

"I thought of bringing some of the children tomorrow, maybe, but I don't think it's the best idea," Schmeil said on his way out.

"Maybe not yet," Petal said.

ON WEDNESDAY MORNING, Schmeil arrived with a large brown paper bag clutched to his chest. "Lunch," he said, putting the bag in the kitchen. "I brought for all of us."

"That's great," Petal said, thinking the exact opposite. She had spent the previous evening throwing away masses of food left over from the weekend, cleaning the fridge and making room for the copious quantity of food that had been delivered in the late afternoon with a ring of the doorbell and an unaccompanied stack of foil containers. Throwing food away made Petal uncomfortable.

Growing up under Estie's roof, not a scrap of food went into the garbage. Even morsels left behind on plates were scraped into a container that was kept in the fridge, its contents repurposed once a week as part of a stew or sauce or soup, referred to by the girls as "spit stew," always their least favourite dinner regardless of the often-tasty results. But, like it or not, they had barely made a dent in all the food Simmy had brought, and, with fresh food arriving and science experiments beginning in foil petri dishes, throwing away was the only way to combat an eventual extraterrestrial takeover of the fridge.

Petal couldn't understand what made Schmeil's bagged lunch acceptable as opposed to the food that came from other kosher kitchens. She thought about asking but decided to leave it alone.

"Why don't you go wake Raizel?" Petal said, grabbing her coat. "I'll go for a walk and be back in time for lunch."

Having brought his own food, Schmeil stayed until late in the afternoon and, amazingly, Raizel was awake and coherent most of the visit.

"I think it worked!" he said to Petal on his way out. "She's so much better today. We spoke about the children. I think I should bring them tomorrow. Just the older girls. She misses them all."

"Whatever you think is best," Petal said, hoping all would go well and the children, whatever their ages, might be spared the trauma of seeing their mother in a psychotic state.

She put Rosie to bed around eight and spent a few more hours cleaning. She dusted in every room, washed all the floors, Windexed surfaces that hadn't been Windexed since before the dawn of time, and tried to make the house sparkle for the children. Just in case the visit didn't go well, at least it would go badly in a clean house.

I I.

IN THE AUTUMN, about six months after she'd returned from Rose and Schmeil's wedding, Petal moved from the kibbutz to an off-campus flat in Ramat Aviv a few blocks from Tel Aviv University. There, she was to begin studies at the Faculty of Education at Seminar Ha'Kibbutzim. Her plan was to complete an undergraduate degree then return to the kibbutz as a qualified teacher and make it her permanent home. In the meantime, Shula and Shuki made it clear she was welcome anytime for weekends and holidays and, of course, summers.

Despite her reticence about leaving the kibbutz and her apprehension about returning to student life, Petal felt good about having a plan. If she stayed the course, she could be done her bachelor of education by the spring of 1992 and be a classroom teacher on Ein Harod by the time school started the following fall. She could see the horizon, and it wasn't far off.

In line to register for classes, Petal tried desperately to look anywhere but at the guy standing in front of her. Fresh off post-army travels in the Far East, Cobi Ben Azra was like a hippie fantasy of beauty. His long, tight ringlets shone with the golden bleaching of months of carefree time spent in the sun and sea of some South Pacific paradise. He wore a too-small tie-dye T-shirt stretched tight across his broad shoulders and cut chest, climbing up his back and belly just enough to expose his toned and tanned midriff. His baggy harem pants of washed-out mauve would have been utterly ridiculous on most anyone, let alone a tall, thin

man, but on Cobi they worked. Perhaps it was his bare, dirty feet
that added an indescribable sexiness. Maybe it was that when
he stretched to yawn and his T-shirt rode up even higher, Petal
noticed the holes at his armpits that lent an air of "I'm really not
trying to look this good" to his dishevelment. Or it might have
been when he turned around to ask her a question, his dark eyes
shining, his broken front tooth just a little imperfect, he spoke to
her in Hebrew and referred to her as kibbutznikit, a moniker she
was proud to wear.

"Hey, kibbutznikit, at yodaat ulaiy im tzarich laasot stage
b'shana alef?"

Petal had no idea if they had to do placements in their first
year or not. She stumbled over her tongue to respond. Whatever
magic potion had Petal drooling had also set off a strong chemical
reaction in her that screamed, Trouble! Stand clear!

"Cobi Ben Azra," he said, pressing his palms together in Eastern greeting.

"Petal Wolffe," she said, much relieved that it was his turn at
the registration wicket.

Petal spent much of the day running the bureaucratic gauntlet
of registration, crossing the campus back and forth from surly
clerk to surly clerk to jump through flaming hoops of box tick-
ing, T-crossing and I-dotting. She returned to her new flat feeling
uneasy. Past experience and accrued therapy informed her need to
reach out to someone. She didn't want Shula to worry. Similarly,
she didn't want to call Der or Bubby or Zaideh and set them into
anxiety mode on her behalf.

She sat with her discomfort for a time, trying to tease apart the
threads of its essence. Was it the handsome boy who had spoken
to her? She rolled her thoughts around in her head. I'm present,
she reminded herself. I just need to talk to someone familiar.

Instinct swooped into her fissures. It had been some time since she felt like calling Rosie, so by the time she closed in on the decision it felt good, like a bridge between her previous resentments and her new, self-started adventure.

"Hello, *hello!* I can't hear you … hello? Can you hear me?" Rosie recited the ever-annoying refrains of Israeli telecom.

"I hear you, Ro! Can you hear me?"

"Now I can hear you! I can't believe it! I was just going to call you, Pet! Did you speak to Bubby? Do you already know?"

"Know what? Is everything okay?"

"Better than okay! I'm going to have a baby, Pet! I'm going to be a mother!"

Petal was struck mute.

"Pet? Can you hear me?"

"I heard you. I'm just a bit … surprised. That's quick, isn't it?"

"Quick? What do you mean? We've been married already six months! Petal! Just be happy for me!"

"If it's what you want, I'm happy for you!"

"I'm only a few weeks, but I already feel different! Like Hashem is inside of me in a whole new way."

"That's great, Ro."

"Maybe you'll come see me? I finally have boobs," she whispered. "That must be worth a visit?"

"Yeah, sure, Ro."

Irritable and angry, feelings more familiar than unsettled, Petal put down the phone without giving her sister her new phone number or filling her in on any of her own news. Pissed at Rosie was a good distraction, something she could process comfortably. *Only my sister can have boobs sculpted directly by the hand of God!* she thought.

There was a knock on her door. *Maybe God himself coming to tell me of the coming of my sister's messiah!* which was as likely as anything else since she knew no one in Tel Aviv.

"Hi, don't be scared," said Cobi.

"How do you know where I live? Did you follow me?" Petal's heart was thumping.

"Don't worry. I'm not creepy. Israel is a very small country. My mother is a cousin to Shuki. He told her to tell me to look out for the Canadian girl named Petal when I got to school. But with all the forms and lines, I didn't make the connection right away. You don't look Canadian. When I realized I had fucked up, I went back to the school and got your address from the office."

"They gave you my address?!"

"Yeah, why not?"

"Isn't that some sort of breach of confidentiality?"

Cobi laughed. "This is Israel! We don't stand on ceremony. We're in the same program. I asked, so they gave."

Petal shrugged. "Why not?"

"Can I come in?"

Petal moved aside and reluctantly let Cobi in.

He went straight to her tiny kitchenette, grabbed the kettle, filled it with water, lit the gas burner, and put it to boil. "You have coffee, yes?"

"Yes," Petal said taken aback by his ease and his chutzpah.

Cobi grabbed the two rickety chairs from the living room and put them on the small balcony. "We'll sit outside, okay?" he said, more telling than asking. He made coffee, helping himself to milk from the fridge and sugar from the cupboard. "You want some grapes?" he asked, reaching into her fridge as though it were his own, as though they were old friends.

And to her surprise, his affability disarmed her. "I don't have much food yet."

"We should go to the Shuk. We'll go on Friday," he said.

"Okay," she said.

And just like that, Cobi's world became her world. He introduced her to his friends and dragged her to pubs and parties.
He never let her choose not to participate, and deep down she
knew this was a good thing. She didn't understand what he could
possibly see in her. When they were alone, he made her feel like
she was the only person in the world, but in a group, he was a
magnet, attracting everybody around him, flirting, making everyone feel loved and special and important, which made Petal feel
less so.

They developed a friendship that could never be explained
or defined by vernacular conventions. It was wonderful and
complicated.

Petal had, by choice and necessity, remained celibate since she
had so inauspiciously left Jerusalem — a disclosure Cobi found
fascinating, when Petal eventually told him.

"No sex! At all? I like a challenge," he said.

"Be careful what you wish for. I only sleep with guys I hate,"
she said. The idea of a woman he couldn't have made Cobi believe
that Petal was his ultimate object of desire, a prize to be won.

"You know I'm going to marry you one day, Petal," he said at
regular intervals. But it was a long time before Petal could trust
her desires as libidinous rather than self-destructive, and Cobi
waited for her to be ready. In the meantime, he slept with other
women — a fact he never hid from her — and she was simultan-
eously jealous and relieved.

Rosie gave birth to her first baby in late spring. Petal was so
excited to be an auntie. Through the summer months, she made
the trek from the kibbutz to Jerusalem on several occasions, even
sleeping over a few times, erroneously hoping she might be helpful
to her sister. Rose's adopted community swooped in and replaced
any previous need she might have had for blood relatives. They all

knew how to take care of babies and deal with new-mom issues. Petal's feelings of alienation festered.

Irving and Esther came to meet their great-granddaughter Sarah Batya in late summer. Petal suggested they spend time with Rosie and her family alone in Jerusalem and come spend a few days with her at Ein Harod after. She wanted to neither rain on the parade nor march in it.

JUST BEFORE THE start of their second year of university, Petal agreed to move in with Cobi, "as roommates, just roommates!" They moved into a two-bedroom apartment on Har Tzion Boulevard in the crappy south Tel Aviv Shapira neighbourhood. The neighbourhood was being overtaken by illegal residents from Thailand, South Sudan, Ivory Coast, Ghana, and Ethiopia and was thought to be unsafe, but they liked it. They would tell anybody who suggested that it wasn't a good idea to be living in Shapira, with all the crime and drugs and danger, "The criminals work in your neighbourhoods and live in ours." They made friends with their neighbours from Thailand who cooked things that smelled alternately delicious or revolting, and they begged the junkie who slept in their stairwell to stop feeding the fucking street cats that were taking over the entrance to the building, adding to the lexicon of repulsive odours.

Cobi said, "If I close my eyes, I can imagine that I'm back in Mumbai." So they closed their eyes.

In summer, Petal returned to the kibbutz to work with the same children she had started with when she had first arrived at Ein Harod. Her summers soothed her soul and helped restore the confidence that Cobi's revolving door of girlfriends eroded in her.

"Sometimes I just want our place to be our place. I'm not like

you. I can't handle being at a party all the time!" Petal said. But
what she never said was "I love you."

"A few friends, that's all!"

"A few friends every day. And more than a few every night!"

"All you have to do is say you'll marry me and I will be only
yours," Cobi said, not because Petal asked him to stop charming
the pants off every girl he met but because he wanted what he
couldn't have.

"I can barely manage my own shit. If I marry you, I'll feel pos-
sessive. It's better this way," she said. But it was not.

When school and work and friends and life with Cobi got
too complicated, Petal left Tel Aviv for a few days of respite with
Shula and Shuki. They spoiled and pampered her with good food,
good company, and good advice.

"You can move. Right, Shula? She can move. Find another flat.
Find another roommate," Shuki advised when Petal complained
about how inconsiderate Cobi was as a roommate.

But Petal couldn't, much as she couldn't admit how she really
felt about Cobi. Shula understood at a more intuitive level. Her
counsel was different.

"Maybe it's time to explore some of your baggage. If you
unpack a little, you may find it possible to open your heart,"
Shula said about nothing and no one in particular.

Shula was an endless well of warmth and wisdom — until she
wasn't. Sometime around the end of the summer after third year,
Shula got bristly. Instead of her usual "Let me help," she said
things like, "I can't do everything for everybody!" or "Take some
initiative!" Instead of "How are you feeling?" she said, "If you
would only stop thinking everything is supposed to be easy!"

"I think she's mad at me," Petal told Cobi after returning from
each visit to the kibbutz.

"It hardly seems her style to not speak her mind, Pet," he tried to reassure her. "Have you asked her what's wrong?"

But when Petal finally asked Shuki if she had done something to offend Shula, his answer destroyed her.

"It's not you, *metuka*. She isn't well. Early-onset Alzheimer's," Shuki said, disintegrating.

Petal was overcome by shame that she had made this tragedy about herself. She returned to the kibbutz for the better part of the semester, ostensibly to be of help to Shula and Shuki as they learned to expect the unexpected and cope with her rapidly advancing dementia but also to manage what she recognized as her own downward spiral. The university was remarkably accommodating. Extenuating circumstances were the norm in a country where everybody did military reserve duty for up to sixty days a year on a schedule over which they had no control and what tomorrow might bring was never taken for granted. Petal's was far from the first accommodation ever needed.

Petal moved into Shuki and Shula's flat and took care of them with the tenderness of a devoted disciple. Shula declined rapidly, and Shuki's heart broke a little more each day. Petal couldn't help feeling that the care she was providing was helping no one but herself. The others were doomed. By the spring, it was clear that Shula could no longer be taken care of at home.

"The doctors say they have never seen it go so fast. My Shula was always in a hurry. I told her nothing was burning, but she never listened."

Shuki moved her into a care facility in Afula, where he took the bus through the blazing summer heat of the Jezreel Valley to visit her daily. There he would lie on the bed with Shula, ever more fetal, assuring her that whatever she needed to do was the right thing.

Some days, Petal went with him and stood feebly at the door to Shula's room, unable to leave but unable to enter. She felt she

was intruding on an experience too intimate to be shared. Petal
waited in the lobby for hours until Shuki was ready to go. As
Shula slipped into oblivion, Shuki became visibly more fragile
each day. On the rare days when Shuki travelled to Afula alone,
Petal stood at the bus stop at the bottom of the kibbutz road in
the evening, waiting to escort him back up the hill. Shuki reported
Shula's daily decline.

"Today she was cold. Can you imagine? In this heat she was
cold."

"The nurse gave her a haircut today. She's always kept her
hair short. She likes it that way."

"I think she's forgotten how to smile."

"No heroic measures. That's what they're saying is best. They
want me to sign. Is that the right thing?" he asked as though Petal
had any answers about anything.

By the end of the summer, it was clear it wouldn't be long.

"It's time," Shuki said.

"Time?" Petal didn't want to understand.

"It's time for you to come say goodbye and go back to your
life."

"This is my life, Shuki. She's my life," Petal said.

"She's my life. You have to live your own life."

The day before Yom Kippur, Shuki and Petal took the bus to
Afula.

"I'll wait here," Shuki said when they entered the lobby. "You
go and have some time alone with her."

More than anything, Petal didn't want to feel the agony she
was feeling, but despite herself, she couldn't ward off the crushing
in her chest, the dryness in her mouth, the burning beneath her
sternum, the painful stone in her gullet, or the ache in her heart.
It was too powerful. She was too powerless. It was grief, and grief
is a fierce overlord.

She climbed onto Shula's bed and lay beside her, her head on Shula's sparrow chest, her arms bent into the curve of Shula's side, and she whispered into Shula's ear. "I love you, Eema Shula. You didn't give me birth, but you gave me life. You taught me to speak. You demanded I feel. Damn you! I hope you're at peace. I'm not. I'm not ready." Petal lay there for a long time, crying, aching, trying to find the courage to say goodbye. "Rest, sweet Shula," she said, climbing off the bed.

Petal tried to collect herself in the hallway before returning to Shuki. She didn't want him to have to carry her grief along with his own. She calmed herself enough to head back to the lobby, but when she saw Shuki surrounded by his children and relatives, she was overcome, and instead of reaching out, she saw herself as an interloper and ran past him, straight to the bus stop.

Reach out, unpack, reach out, she repeated over and over in her head as the bus rumbled through the valley. She walked up the hill to Shuki and Shula's flat. She called her sister.

Rose answered. Petal could hear she was crying. For a brief moment, she thought, *My sister, my twin, she feels my suffering, our bond remains unbroken*, but the thought was interrupted.

"I lost the baby, Pet!" Rosie wailed. "I was pregnant, and I lost the baby! It's normal to miscarry with a first pregnancy, but a third? My body understands what it's supposed to do. Hashem is punishing me."

"I'm so sorry, Ro."

Petal packed her things and returned to Tel Aviv. At home, she climbed straight into Cobi's bed and begged him to make love to her, a request with which he willingly complied. She clung to him, and he protected her but, as was his way, not her alone. Petal leaned on Cobi and hated herself for needing him. Alternately, she withdrew and re-engaged depending upon circumstance, and he ebbed and flowed with her moods and needs. What she gave was enough for him. What she withheld he believed granted him amnesty.

Shuki died suddenly of a massive stroke only a few months after Shula. Cobi borrowed a car from a friend to drive them up to the kibbutz for the funeral. It was a ghastly day. The rain fell in blinding sheets through the darkened sky, slowing traffic to a crawl. Cobi could see Petal turning inward and tried his best to draw her out.

"Pet, talk to me."

"I have nothing to say."

"Should I tell you I love you?"

"Why does that matter?"

"Doesn't it?"

"Everybody I love dies. I'm a bad risk."

"I'm not sure that is just you. Why can't we be good together?"

"Not now. I can't do this now."

After graduation, they agreed that it was time for one of them to move out. It seemed like a good time for new beginnings. With both of them starting new teaching jobs, Petal believed she could find the strength to extricate herself from her complicated relationship with Cobi if not from the actual space they had shared for almost three years. It was a feeble separation. Petal stayed in the Har Tzion apartment as the neighbourhood decayed around her, and Cobi moved in and out and in and out again several times, depending upon whom he was sleeping with at the time. Petal filled his space with a revolving door of transient roommates and tried to be easygoing, but that was never her style.

She loved teaching at the primary school in Jaffa that served a mixed population of Israeli Arabs and Jews and the children of artists and hippies. She adored her students, and they worshipped her.

She threw herself into work, where she could sublimate loneliness as dedication, heartbreak as creativity, self-flagellation as hard work, long hours, commitment, martyrdom. She suppressed her own feelings and needs and absorbed those of her students, recognizing each of their special quirks, challenges, and gifts, teaching toward them. She was a gifted educator. She needed nothing else.

It was Chanukah. Petal and her colleagues were busy turning kilos of potatoes and onions into latkes for the school party the following day. She didn't mind the lingering smell of frying, which reminded her of Bubby's kitchen, so she volunteered her apartment. After many hours, some wine, and a few too many joints, Petal and her crew were punchy. Everything seemed uproariously hilarious, and for the first time in a long time, she felt relaxed, maybe even happy. They didn't finish frying latkes until late, and by the time her collaborators had degreased her kitchen and departed, Petal was too exhausted to shower. She climbed into bed smelling of potato pancakes, spent and content, and drifted peacefully to sleep.

Petal knew the sleep-disrupting ringing was Rose before she opened her eyes. Ironically, only Rosie called at ungodly hours. *You'd think that even without a functioning internal clock my sister could consult an actual clock! I'm not answering!* Petal thought, rolling over to reclaim sleep, but the ringing was relentless. The answering machine clicked on, only to be interrupted by a new series of palpitation-inducing rings.

"Ro, it's the middle of the night! Whatever it is, couldn't it wait till morning?" Petal said, succumbing to the telephone's insistence.

"I can't sleep. My heart is broken, Pet."

"Is everyone okay?"

"We're leaving Yerushalayim," Rosie sobbed.

Petal's mouth went dry, which surprised her. It wasn't news

she was expecting, but her autonomic physical response was one usually reserved for serious events, anxiety, trauma — but this? This wasn't about her.

"So many kids, the baby so fussy, colicky; we need to be closer to family and work opportunities. We're moving back to Toronto. Schmeil has a job waiting at the Chai Kosher Chicken processing plant. We need the money. We need family."

"Let's talk tomorrow, Ro," is what she said, but what she thought was, *Fuck you Rosie! You've forgotten that I'm your family!*

Petal tried to get back to sleep, but the satisfying aroma lingering in her apartment was overpowered by the oppressive phantom funk of kasha and bow ties.

ON A MORNING like every other morning, Der, wearing his slippers, pajamas, and heavy woollen bathrobe, opened his apartment door to pick up his newspaper. Instead of a newspaper, he found a folded sheet of cream-coloured stationery with a cabbage rose border containing a handwritten message he could not decipher without his glasses. Der went back inside, rested his spectacles on the end of his nose, immediately recognized Estie's neat, tiny European lettering, and read her note.

"My Irving is dead. It is time for me too. You are the best of friends. You are closer than blood. With all my love, E."

He crossed the hall in his pyjamas and robe and let himself into the always-unlocked apartment 2.

"Estie," he called as he crossed the very quiet threshold and shut the door behind himself. "Yitzchak?" He checked the kitchen. He pushed through the louvred half doors into the dining area, the polished silver candlesticks regally reflecting off the lacquered table surface from their white satin mat. He looked out onto the balcony facing the street, knowing full well he would find no one there. He crossed through the living room, past the plastic-coated brocade sofa and the two dusty-rose velveteen armchairs with their own form-fitting, see-through wrappers, stopping to straighten a wrinkle in the pink-and-green floral carpet. Der made his way past the girls' room, a place neither of them had spent more than a few nights since leaving almost eight years before, and stopped at the closed door of Irving and Estie's bedroom.

He knocked gently. "Estie? Yitzchak?" He knocked again a little bit louder. "Estie? Yitz?"

He turned the handle and opened the door silently.

Irving lay on his side, under the covers, facing the door, eyes closed as though he were asleep. Estie lay next to him, on top of the covers on her back, wearing the pale-pink raw silk suit he had made for her to wear to Rosie's wedding. Her thin hair was neatly combed. Her makeup was applied carefully. On the nightstand stood a half dozen empty pill bottles and a half-empty glass of water.

Der's heart dropped from his chest into his stomach and continued falling until it hit the floor, where his leaden feet seemed to be cemented. His body felt numb as his mind began to race. *The girls, call an ambulance, no don't, first, wait are they really, check, no don't touch, throw away the bottles, call Petal ...* He stumbled to Estie's side of the bed, willing his cumbersome feet forward. He gasped deeply, searching for air in the still room. He had forgotten to breathe. He sunk down on his haunches next to the bed and took hold of Estie's cold, dangling left hand.

Before Der called 911, he considered the circumstances. Estie had woken up, found that Yitzchak, the love of her life, her best friend and saviour, had passed peacefully in his sleep, and made the decision to join him. It was certainly a testament to the depth of love that they shared. Der concluded that whether she had had a hand in her own final destiny or not, it did not alter or diminish the truth that she'd loved him so profoundly that she could not live without him. The details could be of no good use to anybody, most especially the girls. He collected the pill bottles from the night table, took them across the hall to apartment 1A, and, along with Estie's note, buried them in his kitchen trash, which he sent down the garbage shoot directly to the incinerator.

Der struggled with his conscience. He knew how deprived Petal felt regarding family history, but this? Could this knowledge be of any use to her? "Your bubby committed suicide," he said out loud to himself several times, trying on different tones, variations in delivery, in words. But alas, there was no way he could find to make it sound any less horrible than it was. Der decided that he would add this detail to the list of secrets he held for the Wolffe family — at least for the time being.

He was the only one who knew the particulars of either Yitzchak or Estie's experiences during the Holocaust. And because of all he knew, he understood that for Estie to go on without Yitzchak was impossible and for the girls to be spared the truth of all these things was merciful. No one requested an autopsy. Both causes of death were recorded as cardiac failure, which Der believed was entirely accurate.

At the shiva, everybody was soothed and enchanted by the fable of true love, a fairy tale that Estie would have supported both whole- and brokenheartedly.

Petal returned to Israel almost as soon as shiva for Irving and Estie ended. She stayed only a few extra days to help Rose and Der go through the apartment. It was a relatively easy process, despite the inherent sadness. Neither Irving nor Estie had believed there was any benefit to sentimental attachment to objects or mementoes, so there were none of the usual things one hears about the deconstructing of lives of loved ones who pass. There were no boxes of old letters or photographs to be sorted through.

No faded artworks by children long grown. No diaries of secrets held close or ribbon-tied boxes of hidden treasures. Their memories were too painful to romanticize with yellowed stationery or dusty coffers. Petal, also unsentimental and unmaterialistic, wanted nothing from the apartment. Der practically forced her to take Estie's wedding ring and Irving's Timex with the articulated band. The watch needed a new battery.

"One day, you'll be glad you have something of theirs," he said, pushing the trinkets into her hand before leaving apartment 2 with her for the very last time. Petal held the ring and watch tightly in her fist until Der dropped her on the curb at the airport and she needed her hands to carry her bags. She slipped the ring on the index finger of her right hand and stretched the watch over it onto her wrist.

Raizel and Schmeil were very happy to take all the furnishings from apartment 2 to fill their new home, a small, rundown bungalow on Ledbury, secured with a down payment the provenance of which was a bit of a mystery.

Petal made the trip back to Israel on her own. The stewardess on her flight asked her to switch seats with the man sitting next to her to create a buffer of modesty for the Orthodox man who was in the adjacent seat. She complied only because it gave her an aisle rather than a middle seat, but mentally she hurled anti-Orthodox epithets at the religious man, scapegoating him for the resentment she felt toward Rosie and Rosie's family for not being with her, for leaving Israel, for choosing a life that was so without her.

Irving and Estie dead. Apartment 2 empty. Shula and Shuki dead. Their home on the kibbutz occupied by a young couple Petal didn't know. Rose and Schmeil living even further away than Jerusalem seemed, and Der no longer across the hall from anything that still mattered, there in apartment 1A — like half of a whole.

Petal felt homeless.

This feeling, likely grief not homelessness, shifted the tectonic plates of her universe, leaving a gaping crevice in her soul as long as the San Andreas Fault and as deep as the Grand Canyon. She upped her meds.

Cobi picked her up at the airport.

"Let's get married," Petal said as she hoisted her suitcase into the back of Cobi's tiny Peugeot.

"Don't say it if you don't mean it, Pet," he said, shifting his old beater into gear.

"I mean it. Let's get married." And at that moment, Petal believed she meant what she said.

Getting married in Israel was not simple. Petal went to the rabbinate to register their marriage and returned in a foul mood.

"Like we're living under Sharia law! The fucking rabbis control the institution of marriage in this country," Petal said. "They won't let us pick a date until they know when I menstruate. Then they need to know that I have verified the cleanliness of my hoo-ha with white cotton cloths I'm supposed to stick in my vagina. This notion of women being unclean is misogynist at best! You know that I have to go to marriage classes so the rebbetzin can tell me about sex and the sanctity of the marital bed? And after seven days of shoving cloths up my *knish* and them coming out unstained, I have to purify myself bathing in the fucking *mikvah* or they won't marry me! You know what else? They require verification that my lineage is Jewish. How the fuck should I know what my lineage is?"

"Just your mother," Cobi said, trying to calm Petal. "Wasn't she born in Israel? It'll be easy to find her birth certificate."

"Easy isn't the point. I won't be a hypocrite! I won't get married if I have to do it by their rules. I don't believe in any of that shit! I don't even believe in God! I won't be an outsider at my own wedding!"

"We could get married in Cyprus without the rabbis and their nonsense," Cobi offered, but it seemed like too much effort, and besides, Petal felt she had already missed too much work.

"We can do our own ceremony. It won't be legal, but does that matter?" he said.

"I don't know, Cobi. Does it matter? What's the difference between living together or pretending to be married?"

They had a small, symbolic wedding ceremony on the beach just south of Neve Tzedek, with a few close friends. They wore new white T-shirts, old blue jeans, and bare feet.

Cobi put Estie's ring on Petal's left hand. "With this ring, I commit to our union under the sun, in front of the water, on top of the earth, and outside of the rabbinate," he said to her.

She smiled. They hadn't agreed upon the last phrase. Petal put a ring they had bought together in the flea market on Cobi's left hand. "With this ring, I commit to our union under the sun, in front of the water, on top of the earth, and outside of the fucking rabbinate!"

They lay on blankets on the sand and ate watermelons with feta cheese. They drank warm beer and wine straight from the bottles. They danced to music from a crackly CD player. When the sun set, they all swam naked in the sea.

"Life's ironic," Petal said to Cobi as he cradled her in the silver water.

"How so?"

"I've spent my life being responsible, reliable, accountable — all the things my mother never could be. And here I am, participating in one of mankind's age-old heteronormative institutions in the most hippie-dippie way possible. I'm sure my mother would have loved this wedding!"

When their guests departed, they lay together on a blanket on the sand.

"This is our space," Cobi said.

"I need more than just this. I need more of you," Petal said. "I need a home."

Cobi held her close.

The opening of the "new" bus station in Neve Sha'anan, the neighbourhood adjacent to Shapira — a monstrosity more than thirty years in the making, which took less than three years to develop a reputation as not only a white elephant but also a den of Sodom and Gomorrah–proportioned iniquity — meant it was time to move anyhow.

Cobi was teaching at a south Tel Aviv high school, and Petal was still teaching at the primary school in Jaffa. They found a flat on the roof of an old, dilapidated building bordering the south end of Tel Aviv, where it butted up against the north side of Jaffa. After the wedding, they moved back in together to what was supposed to be a new home and a fresh start.

Though neither Cobi nor Petal was what anyone would describe as either domestically talented or aesthetically astute, they did their best to create a home. For a time, their roof became a gathering place for friends and colleagues who regularly occupied the collection of scavenged, mismatched chairs at the wobbly table. They cooked on the rusty hibachi, ate, drank, and enjoyed by the light of candles stuffed in wax-covered wine bottles. Merrymakers hung out till the wee hours many nights, sometimes falling asleep on the old Oriental carpets Cobi had bought from the Bukharan vendor at the Jaffa market. It reminded Petal of the life of Shula and Shuki's welcoming, bustling home, and there were things she loved about it, but it played against her natural propensities. When Petal had enough of the company, the socializing, the deficiency of attention, she retreated to their small bedroom while Cobi stayed and enjoyed the commune-like atmosphere of the rooftop. It worked for a while. Then winter came, the nights got too cool for the roof, the party moved indoors to their cramped flat, and there was nowhere for Petal to escape.

"I can't, Cobi. I need space. I need time alone," Petal said, never adding "with you" to her list of needs.

Cobi didn't begrudge her her desire for quiet or solitude, but he didn't share it. He made it clear to the hangers-on that the festivities were moving to another location, at least until the weather improved. And instead of staying home with his wife, Cobi followed the party. Petal hated being needy and begging or even asking for attention, so she stopped asking him to stay home. Instead, she slowly added bricks to her wall. And in the not asking, in the building of the wall, she stopped feeling much of anything; eventually, she stopped needing or even wanting what she couldn't hope to have. When they were alone and Cobi tried his magic to make Petal feel as though no one else mattered, her fortress became too impenetrable to be infiltrated by his inauthentic wizardry. Their coupledom lacked passion. Their sex was good but never great. Petal would close her eyes while he kissed her, and instead of fantasies of him or anyone else, she saw nothing. Petal was too devoid of emotion, and Cobi was too self-involved. They never even fought. They didn't care enough about anything shared to muster up the energy for conflict.

Petal and Cobi loved one another, but not enough, not in the same way. Cobi still flirted shamelessly and slept around. He barely tried to conceal it. Perhaps had he changed, she might not have had to shut him out. Perhaps had he not felt shut out, he might have changed. Eventually, their new home, a living metaphor of the two solitudes that coexisted on a porous Jaffa–Tel Aviv border, became a mirror of the lives they lived separately together.

To simulate real emotion, Petal picked fights with her sister from a distance.

"Oh, by the way, I got married," she mentioned casually on a call months after the wedding.

"You what? You didn't think to tell me, let alone invite me?" Rose was understandably hurt. Petal had known she would be.

"It's not as though you would have come!"

"That's not the point, Pet."

But Petal's world was losing its points. Rounding them down to harmless curves made them hurt less when they poked at her insides.

THE ATTACKS HAD begun more or less with the signing of the Oslo Accords in 1993, though there would be those that might argue no direct correlation between the unsuccessful peace negotiations and the rise of random, unpredictable suicide bombings within Israel's borders. All responsibility for the attacks was claimed by Hamas, Palestinian Islamic Jihad, the Popular Front for the Liberation of Palestine, and the Al-Aqsa Martyrs' Brigade. Between 1993 and 2000, there were twenty-five suicide bombings that claimed the lives of 171 people and injured 72 others. Between 2001 and 2003, the frequency of attacks soared to 110 bombings over three years, causing 641 injuries and 258 deaths. The escalation and dispersal across the country left the population feeling vulnerable in ways unfamiliar.

As teachers, Cobi and Petal were on the front lines. The level of collective anxiety was at fever pitch. Parents, Israelis who had grown up with the realities of wars and threats and military service and the need to soldier on and not give in, were crumbling. How could they let their children out of their sight with the arbitrariness of the unrelenting, unforeseeable strikes? Children and adolescents were shell-shocked, jumpy, and scared. No one wanted to take busses or be in crowds. The usually bustling street life of Tel Aviv came to a virtual standstill, with only the absolutely essential orders of daily life and business worth the risk. There was a communal looking over of shoulders that wreaked social instability and paranoia previously unknown in a country of stoics. Emigration reached an all-time high.

While the country burned itself from within with the cumulative pools of stomach acid that ate away at its social fortitude and fibre, Petal felt nothing. She watched as though in a dream, even while she helped organize trauma services for her students, coping workshops with psychologists and social workers for parents, professional development seminars for staff to learn how to manage this unfamiliar territory. The worse things got, the less she felt.

"Ask Petal" became an inside joke in the education community of Tel Aviv. Some of her colleagues had T-shirts printed with ASK PETAL because she could be counted on to handle the most difficult situations with a competence and serenity no one was feeling. Ask Petal to counsel the brother of a boy who was killed on a bus. Ask Petal to visit the home of a child who refused to leave the house. Ask Petal to speak at a public meeting about security precautions at school. Ask Petal to say the right thing to parents who were having trouble leaving their children. Ask Petal to hold their hands, validate their fears, never dismiss their anxieties, and guide them toward the fortitude they needed to go on. Between her regular teaching duties, visiting families in their homes, speaking at public events, learning about trauma management, and crisis counselling, she worked day and night.

The desk in her classroom accumulated a pile of pebbles with paintings of flowers, on each one a single petal of a flower painted reverentially in a different colour than the rest. The stones, left anonymously with the best of intentions by people whom Petal had helped in some way or another, became a morphing edifice honouring her courage and capability. Responsible, reliable, steady-as-a-rock Petal.

She had work and friends, accolades, achievements, a dwelling, and a spouse — all the perceived elements of a full, meaningful life. But Petal felt empty — or worse: she felt nothing. When she finally clued in to her own anesthesia in the face of everyone else's heightened awareness, Petal knew she was close to trouble. She had shut down. On January 5, 2003, two suicide bombers blew themselves up at the Tel Aviv Central Bus Station, killing twenty-three people. It was the third south Tel Aviv bombing in as many years. Petal barely flinched. She was the anti–Mrs. Dalloway. Death was at her party, and she couldn't react. Only she knew that the pile of painted stones on her desk had become markers on her own grave.

It was clear she needed to climb out of the hole before it swallowed her. She started planning.

TOWARD THE END of the school year, Petal asked Cobi to meet her for a drink at the café on the roof of the Esther Cinema Hotel overlooking Dizengoff Circle.

"I'm leaving," she told him.

"Me?"

"Everything. You. Israel. My so-called life. I need to cut bait."

"You're a star! You've been keeping it together for everyone," Cobi said.

"For everyone but me," Petal said. "Somewhere along the way, I disappeared from my own life."

"I'm going to miss you like crazy, Pet."

"No. You're not."

Petal stood up and walked to the railing of the patio. She needed to find some air. She gazed down at the past-its-prime fire and water fountain in the square below, lifting her eyes out over the rooftops toward the water, trying to feel the sea breeze that might be there.

Cobi followed. He stood near but not next to her.

"We've been doing this dance for so long it's become our normal," she said. "But this isn't normal. This isn't a marriage. This is barely a life."

Cobi raised his hand to reach out to Petal but stopped mid-air, as though resting his hand against a windowpane. "When are you going?"

"Next week. When school ends."

"You couldn't have just decided! Where are you going?" Cobi said with more passion than had passed between them for years.

Petal shrugged. "I thought you would notice the brochures, the applications, the stuff I've been busy with for months. I figured you didn't say anything because you didn't care."

Cobi looked away.

"New York," she said. "I'm going to do a doctorate at NYU."

"Will you come back?"

"No."

Though the facts of her sixteen years in Israel constituted the silhouette of a life, by the time she left, the details mattered little to her. She left for New York, all her worldly possessions packed into two duffel bags, and closed the door on a finished chapter.

She hoped to find lost pieces of herself and perhaps glean feeling from the collective trauma of post 9/11 New Yorkers.

12.

THURSDAY MORNING, ROSE woke early. She got up, brushed her teeth, washed her face, and got dressed unbidden for the first time in almost two weeks. She even looked for her sheitel, remembered that she had forgotten to pick it up from the *sheitelmacher* where she had taken it to be washed and styled before the holidays, twisted her long hair into a tight bun, and put on a pale-pink beret. Then she went to wake her sister.

"You okay, Ro?" Petal asked, eyes not yet fully open.

"I feel really good, Pet."

Petal looked at her sister, awake, dressed, a look of presence in her formerly vacant eyes, and promptly burst into tears.

"Don't cry, Pet. I'm okay."

"I've been so worried about you," she wept, pulling her sister by the hand onto the bed.

Schmeil arrived with the full entourage. "They insisted," he said.

Rose hugged and kissed them and excitedly suggested they all go to the park. Petal was stunned. She hadn't expected lithium to change yesterday's psychosis to ostensibly normal overnight. Had the crisis been averted?

Walking to the park, the older children took turns swinging the younger ones by their arms until Rose put an end to it, reminding them of some incident with a dislocated shoulder. Simcha Aron wrestled himself out of his father's grasp and took Petal by the hand, prompting Estie to escape her sister's grip and take Petal's other hand. Simcha Aron peeked around Petal's thighs and stuck his tongue out at his sister. Estie returned the gesture behind Petal's back. Front, back, back, front, tongue wagging, raspberry spitting, *nany nany poo poo* calling, and lots of giggling. Petal had no desire to stop the escalating taunts, which felt so suddenly normal.

"Tag! You're it!" Estie tapped Petal, running off into the playground.

"Come on, little one." She scooped the boy into her arms and ran after her niece.

Some of the others joined in, diverting Petal in her pursuit.

"Bet you can't catch me!"

"Try to get me!"

Petal put Simcha Aron down. "Come on," she said. "Help me catch them!"

Rose and Schmeil watched from a bench.

"You're it!" Petal caught Miriam Ruthie's flank and fled to the bench. "I'm not as young as I used to be," she said, breathlessly landing next to her sister.

"They like you," Schmeil said.

Petal's grin enveloped her face.

"You look like you just won something!" Rose laughed.

"I did," she said.

Sarah Batya deposited Simcha Aron on his mother's lap. With sandy hands, he fluffed Petal's hair.

"Oy gevalt! You're making Tante all dirty," Rose scolded.

"I like it," Petal said.

"It's going to make a mess in the clean house," Raizel said to Schmeil.

"Don't worry, Raizeleh. We can take shoes off at the door."

"We can take shoes off at the door," she repeated in what seemed to be agreement. "So tell them to stop accusing me of being dirty," she said, pointing at two Orthodox women in the park.

"They have no concern with you, Raizeleh," Schmeil said, oblivious to the encroaching paranoia.

But Petal felt the shift. She moved Simcha Aron to his father's lap.

"Come on, Ro. Let's go so we can put a mat outside the door." She guided Rosie out of the park.

Rose stopped to look at the electric company workers. "Look at them!"

"What about them?"

"Spies! You'll go to prison!" she shouted at the men.

"They're just fixing the wires that came down in the storm."

"They're connecting the women to my brain to shout at me. It's not safe anywhere, Pet!"

Petal yanked at her sister. "Come on, Ro. Let's get home."

In the few blocks home, Rosie's affect flattened like a balloon with a slow leak. "Think I overdid it," she said.

"You deserve a rest."

Petal gave her wilting sister a sedative and sat next to the bed until Rosie fell asleep. "Don't leave me," Rose cried out when Petal tried to quietly slip away.

Petal sat back down. "I'm here, Ro."

"I didn't think. It was too much. I'm taking the kids back," Schmeil apologized through the screen door.

"She needed to see her kids. See you tomorrow?"

"It's Shabbes then yuntif again. I'll come Sunday night."

WHILE ROSE SLEPT, Petal sat in the fluorescent light of the basement. If she turned the knob on the box with needle-nose pliers to the number nine, she could get reception-ish. Television was far too grand a name for this box she'd dubbed the channel nine.

"Pet?"

"I'm in the basement, Ro." But before Petal got up, Rosie came down.

"You're watching television?" she asked, surveying the neatly organized room.

Petal was embarrassed, as though she had been caught doing something unseemly. "Sorry, Ro. I was just passing the time."

"What are you sorry about?" Rosie plunked herself down on the mattress-cum-sofa and leaned in close. "What're you watching?"

"It's hard to tell with the crappy reception, and I didn't want to turn up the volume too loud."

"I didn't know we could get any channels," Rosie said, wrapping her fingers in her sister's fingers.

"Your kids don't watch any television? No computers or internet?"

"Only approved videotapes. It's an issue that's becoming harder to deal with, especially with older kids."

"I can imagine!" Petal said, not knowing where to even begin unpacking the myriad of complexities presented by a technology-free life in the twenty-first century. "How you feeling, Ro?"

"Better," she said, curling cat-like into Petal's lap. "I guess it's a happy-up-time thing."

"A what?"

"That's what we used to call it, me and Schmeil. I guess you wouldn't really know. There's this time around six or eight weeks after a baby is born, way longer for the colicky ones, where all they do is sleep and eat and poop. When they're awake, it's because they need something, so they're fussy. As they get bigger and stronger, they stay awake longer and longer without needing or wanting anything except attention and stimulation. That's what we would call happy-up-time. That's when you get to play with them and fall in love with them beyond primal instinct. They start to become real people."

Petal stroked Rosie's head, so calm and present in her lap. So much like Rosie. "So you just need to settle into longer periods of happy-up-time?" she said.

"I guess. You never wanted kids, Pet?"

Petal couldn't remember the last time Rose had asked about her life. Picking up their intertwined hands, she kissed Rosie's thumb.

"My life is so different than yours. I made decisions that were so different, I'm not sure I can even tell you about them in a way you'll understand or accept." Petal desperately wanted to tell her sister so many things she had kept to herself.

"You can tell me, Pet. I'm religious, not stupid. I'm the same person I always was. What's so terrible that I wouldn't understand?"

"I can tell you, but just like I try not to judge you or your choices, I need to be able to trust that you won't judge me."

"That's for Hashem to do. It is not for me to judge anyone. I know you don't believe in Hashem, but I do, which means I try to lead a righteous life. Part of that is following the laws and commandments, which for me includes accepting that you and other people I love and care about have different beliefs than I do. You've made choices that are no less right or valuable than the choices I've made, just different. I know I wasn't always the best at showing you. I was young and insecure. I was afraid of being judged by my chosen community, but I learned that 'Honour your father and mother' means everyone you love. It means I must honour you, Pet. I always have. The truth is, I'm pretty sure you spend much more energy judging my life choices than I have ever spent judging yours. I gave up hoping you would be proud of me long ago."

It wasn't much of a secret that she judged her sister's lifestyle and choices. But what really surprised her was that Rosie wanted her approval. Petal had always assumed she didn't rate in Rosie's eyes, and at that moment, she realized this was a heavy piece of baggage she had been carrying around most of her life. Since long before Rose had found religion. She was the ball and chain dragged to parties and sleepovers, the burden Rose had to bear. Mentally, she put the heavy bag down and let it go.

"I had an abortion," she said. "Just after my first year at university, Bubby and Zaideh came to visit Israel because you had given birth to Sarah Batya. Remember?" Rosie nodded. "I'd been celibate for two and a half years because for me, sex was a way of harming myself. Should I go on?" Rosie closed her eyes and nodded. "With Bubby and Zaideh around, I guess I felt safe in a way I hadn't even known I didn't before. They were staying on the kibbutz for a few days. I did something I never did in all my time on kibbutz. I went to a party in the volunteers' bar, down in the bomb shelter. It was July — I don't know if you remember how hot those bomb shelters could get in the summer. It was a sauna that smelled like stale beer and chocolate cake." She smiled, remembering the pungency of the heavy, sweet, funky air.

"I felt great! I had just finished a year of school. I was back on the kibbutz for the summer, working with my kids again. I was a new auntie, and I had fantasies that I would play an important role in my baby niece's life." Rosie gently squeezed her sister's hand. "Anyhow, I had a couple of beers and was dancing with some guy from Buenos Aires who was leaving the next day. We were sweating like pigs, and he was pawing at me, but his hands kept sliding off my sweaty skin, and I was laughing at how I was made of Teflon and nothing could stick to me. We left to go hang out by the pool, where compared to the underground bunker it felt breezy. The smell of manure from the cowsheds and the crisp greenness wafting from the eucalyptus trees ... it was familiar and sheltered, and I felt free and home all at the same time. We pulled off our clothes and went skinny-dipping. One thing inevitably led to another, and we had a roll in the grass. It was the first time I enjoyed sex." Petal paused, self-conscious.

"Go on, Pet. You were always such a good storyteller," Rosie said, still curled feline, her head in her sister's lap.

"There isn't much else to the story. By September, I figured out that my one night of indiscretion had gotten me into trouble in a different way. Turns out I wasn't Teflon. Something stuck. I had an abortion and took another long break from carnal pursuits. Are you shocked?"

"No. Sad, but not shocked. Did you think of having kids when you were married?" Rosie asked.

"Sometimes. We talked about it, but we both knew that the marriage wouldn't last. We didn't want to add children to an already complicated situation."

Rosie sat up, as though she had had enough of this particular conversation. "I like sex!" she said.

Petal smiled. "You always did!"

Rosie snapped the watchband on Petal's wrist. "Schmeil and I have great sex!"

Petal covered her ears. "TMI! Too much information!"

"Who's shocked now?" Rosie quipped. "My prudish sister."

"I was talking about sex with unknown partners. You're talking about your husband! I know him! I don't want to think about the two of you doing it!" Petal said, returning Rosie's watch snap with a light swat.

"Because that's not how you think about Orthodox people? Where do you think all the children come from?"

"Through the hole in the sheet," Petal said.

"Urban legend!" Rosie laughed and scanned the room. "You did a great job cleaning up down here! I usually make the kids do it. If it weren't Pesach, we could bake something."

"Are you hungry, Ro?" Petal said.

"Let's make something delicious for lunch!" Rosie jumped up and raced up the stairs, Petal flying behind.

"Oh, Petal!" Rosie exclaimed darting from room to room. "You've made it so organized I can do all the things I never get around to," she said, riffling through the clothes in the girls' closet. "I have to move what's too small to the little girls' room." She held up hangers with blouses and skirts, tossing them into different piles. "I'll move winter clothes to the back and spring clothes to the front." Rose pushed hangers to and fro.

Petal stood aside, unsure how to help or intervene. Leaving one room in a renewed state of chaos, Rosie moved to the next room, emptying drawers of freshly laundered, neatly folded clothes, which she unfolded, held up, and examined, assessing sizes of almost identical items, tossing them on beds into piles of indeterminate classification. Petal tried to fold as Rosie tossed, but she couldn't keep up with Rosie's momentum and indecision, which caused unfolding of refolded garments. Petal gave up.

In the boys' room, she pulled books off the small bookshelf and appeared to edit each book with a Magic Marker.

"Whatcha doing, Ro?" Petal asked, wondering if it was time to suggest a pill.

"I'm making the books kosher," Rosie said, continuing to pull picture books out, scribble in them, and drop them on the floor.

"How do you make the books kosher?"

"Like this," Rosie said, showing Petal how to change lowercase T sans serif to a hook-bottomed T with serif. "That way it's not a Christian 't.' And like this," she said, showing Petal how to draw skullcaps on the heads of boy illustrations and change girls dressed in pants into girls dressed in skirts or dresses, frantically turning pages and scribbling censored modesty into each book.

Did other Orthodox mothers alter the Ts in their children's books and re-dress the characters? Was this a fish writing an opera beneath the soapy sink water or was this crazy? Petal wondered.

Through the afternoon, Rosie continued to begin projects, get distracted, start something else, and leave a wake of disarray behind her. Initially, Petal was relieved that fun, frenetic Rosie was back. But after a few exhausting hours, Petal realized that even on the Rosie activity scale, which ran at a tempo typically more allegro than the average, and even within the parameters of an Orthodox paradigm Petal didn't understand, a frenny was underway.

"Ro, it's almost five o'clock, and we have guests coming for dinner. Maybe you should try and have a bit of a rest."

"We never have guests. Suddenly we have room for guests. Who's coming? The place is such a mess!"

Petal sighed. She hadn't anticipated Rosie being up to participating. "Der's coming with a friend of mine who's visiting from New York. His name is Benjamin."

"Who's Benjamin?" Rosie bounced. "Is he your boyfriend? Petal has a boyfriend, Petal has a boyfriend," Rosie chanted, childishly swaying to her rhythm.

"You're working yourself up," she said, putting her hands gently on Rosie's undulating shoulders, trying to quell the current that had taken hold. "Benjamin is a close friend. Not a boyfriend."

"Really?" Rose said.

"He's gay. Satisfied?"

"What on earth would satisfy me about a gay man?" She laughed. "Besides, I don't really believe in gay," Rosie said.

Channelling every ounce of compassion and maturity she had, Petal didn't say what she thought. Instead, she said, "I don't believe in God, but I would lay down my life for your right to

believe. Like you said, you love me anyhow. Let's pretend that
you didn't say that, and when Der and Benjamin get here, we'll
remember that by extension we all love one another."

"You always have to be so serious and complicate everything!"
Rosie said as though she were still the easygoing twin.

Petal tried to convince Rosie to take a nap.

"The house is a mess! We are so crammed in here, like sar-
dines, margarines. We don't usually have dinner guests. We have
to clean up, lean up!"

She tried folding clothes and quickly became overwhelmed
by the chaos she had created. "Told, hold, fold, bold, scold.
Told, scold, bold, not fold!" she repeated in various sequences
with escalating agitation. Petal returned the koshered books to
the boys' bookshelf. Rosie abandoned her laundry folding so she
could start cooking. Petal reminded her that it was Passover and
food had been brought.

"Because I failed. Because I'm not clean. My house is not
clean. I'm not good enough. I want you to be proud of me, Pet,"
she repeated, collapsing into a heap of tears and self-loathing on
the kitchen floor, on the border of red and blue.

Petal got the lorazepam. *I'll pop it myself, if she won't,* she
thought. She took a deep breath and joined Rosie on the kitchen
floor.

"Of course, I'm proud of you," Petal said.

"No, you aren't. You and all of them," Rosie said, casting
her arm across the room as though indicating a full house of
onlookers.

"Ro, are they talking to you now?"

"Who?" Rosie asked suspiciously.

"The women's voices. Can you hear them right now?" Petal
asked, uncertain what she was trying to achieve.

"Not right now, but they say awful things. Unlawful things."

"I know they hurt you. And I know that it all sounds real to you," she said, trying to validate some of her sister's perceptions without giving credence to her delusions. "Remember, happy-up-time? You've run out of happy-up-time. Time for a rest," she said, tucking the pill under Rosie's tongue without resistance.

"I'll just stay here," Rosie said, sliding down like a windless sail slipping its halyard.

Petal brought a blanket and pillow in pastel hues that clashed jarringly with the red and blue.

Der and Benjamin arrived just past six-thirty. Rosie was still asleep in the kitchen, so Petal cleared the bed in the front room so they could sit.

"How's it going?" Benjamin asked.

"Today was a bit of a shit show, but also good. She got up, got dressed, and had a whole bunch of lucid hours where it really felt like I was with Rosie. Then she totally spun out, like her motor shorted or something and it kept spinning faster and faster and ... well, you see where she ended up with the help of a horse tranquilizer."

"My poor Pet," Benjamin said.

"Tiggaleh ..." Der said squeezing the hand he held. "Remember, this only continues if you are managing."

"I'm managing. I felt like today was a breakthrough day. Until it wasn't, and then I drugged her." Petal forced a half smirk. "When she's her, when my Rosie comes through, I feel ... secure ... complete, in a way I didn't even know I missed. And then the crazy swoops in, and I feel the opposite of whole. Der, I never know what memories are real, but I think she reminds me of my mom. I've never made that connection before today. Is that weird?"

Der squeezed her hand again. "Tiggaleh ..."

"Am I right?"

Der had known the day would come when someone else would see it too, but how to respond eluded him for a moment. He turned to face Petal. "Whatever memories you retain of your mother are your truth. You were so young, and there was so much complexity. Layers of history and suffering strangled by desperate searching for safety and happiness."

"Don't hide behind those old refrains. I can't take it anymore. Just tell me if Rosie and Chavie are similar?"

"Similar, but not the same," he said.

Petal shook her head.

"I have often thought Rosie was like your mother at her best. They bear a striking physical resemblance to one another. When you were young, I sometimes had to blink to not superimpose Chavie's image onto Rosie. But Tig, you have also had moments when you reminded me of your mother — not at her best." Der looked away.

"Thank you. I've been needing to hear that for a very long time," Petal said.

Benjamin nudged Petal as Rosie appeared in the doorway, crumpled and groggy.

Der, Petal, and Benjamin jumped to attention as though their military commander had unexpectedly entered the barracks.

"That was quick," Petal said, thinking Rosie hadn't slept long enough. "Come meet Benjamin, my New York family."

Benjamin stepped forward, offering his hand to Rose.

"Come help me get chairs in the basement, Benjamin," Petal said, pulling him away, whispering, sotto voce, "She won't shake hands with a man."

HAD ANYONE OBSERVED, knowing nothing about anyone seated around the tinfoil table in the blue-and-red kitchen of the little square house, they might have thought nothing at all was amiss.

The conversation was lively but not manic. The food was a perfectly acceptable version of chicken schnitzel, mashed potatoes,
and slightly overcooked carrots, with baked apples and coconut
macaroons for dessert. They drank no wine nor other spirits,
which might have struck some as unusual but wouldn't raise eyebrows in many circles. Nor would it have been the first dinner
in the history of dinners served on paper plates with disposable
cutlery from foil takeout containers.

They told stories of how they had met and how they spent their
time, including the story about the twins who didn't share a birthday, the one about the displaced person who hadn't been through
the war, the tale of the accidental Zionist who lived sixteen years in
Israel and left it behind as though it had never happened, the yarn
about the man who was a successful New York writer who didn't
believe all the hype about his talent, and the anecdote of the wild
child who turned into a stand-up member of a religious community. It was, in fact, such a remarkably pleasant evening that by the
time the guests suggested for the second or third time that it was
time for them to go, it was near one o'clock in the morning.

"Don't go yet! It's not that late!" Rosie said for the second or
third time.

"Actually, it's pretty late." Petal sensed her sister's engine rev-
ving. "Time for our meds and then off to bed."

"Maybe we can all go for a walk or something tomorrow,"
Benjamin said, putting on his coat.

"Tiggaleh, Twitch, you have no idea how much good it has
done for an old man to spend time with his most treasured girlies." Der resisted the temptation to grab both the women into an
embrace. Instead, he kissed Petal on her head and let Benjamin
help him on with his coat.

"You'll come again tomorrow for dinner, won't you?" Rosie
said, her hands vibrating as though she suffered from tremors.

"Tomorrow is Shabbes," Petal reminded her.

"We can make Shabbes together!" Rosie said.

Rose and Petal watched from the front door as the two men left with a promise of returning the next evening for dinner. They climbed into the canary-yellow car parked in the driveway of the crumbalow and drove away.

"Der looks so much older," Rose said.

"Der is so much older," Petal replied.

"THAT WAS FUN! I can't remember a dinner without my family," Rosie said. Catching herself, she grabbed Petal's arm. "I mean the kids. Not you. I feel like a teenager with you! I'm not in the least bit tired. I still have loads of happy-up-time left!"

"Ro, you may not be tired, but I'm toast. I have to go to bed, and we both have to take our meds." Petal brought their pills.

"I don't think I need them anymore, Pet," Rosie said. "I feel really good!"

"You feel good because of the meds. You don't get to stop taking them when you feel good. Me too, Ro. I feel fine. But I know that I can't stop taking my meds just because I feel good today. Trust me on this one. I've been a pill popper for twenty-plus years, and stopping is never a good idea."

"You are not me, Pet. We have different problems. And my problems are fixed. I don't need to take any more pills."

"That's not the way it works," Petal said, getting irritated. "When Schmeil comes back and the two of you have a chance to speak with Dr. Gold, you can make that decision together. As long as I'm here, you take your pills." Petal handed Rosie a cup of water.

Rosie stamped her foot like a toddler.

"I'll leave if you don't take your meds," Petal threatened.

"Fine," Rosie agreed petulantly.

Together, they took their pills. "I'm really proud of you, Ro."
Rosie stuck her tongue out at her sister. They changed out of their
clothes and stood side by side at the bathroom sink to brush their
teeth, looking at one another in the medicine cabinet mirror.

"Remember Mr. Slipper?" Rosie said. "Why did I want to be
called Mr. Slipper?"

"Beats me," Petal said, too exhausted to contemplate the
workings of her sister's psyche. "Good night, Ro."

"Will you lie with me till I fall asleep, Pet?"

Petal wanted to say no. "Sure, Ro, I'll lie with you."

Petal slept a deep, psychedelic sleep crowded with colourful
characters invented by Fellini, Lewis Carroll, Tim Burton, and
the like, playing parts in sets designed by M.C. Escher and Antoni
Gaudi of nonsensical, rainbow-toned rooms and passageways
inaccessible by staircases that led nowhere. The chemicals in her
brain swirled around like oil and water in vibrant hues coming
together and separating, paisley patterns of implausible reality.
Petal woke with a start to the drumroll of her own racing heart,
franticly needing to escape the unbearable heat of the blankets.

She recognized this was the feeling of her medication not keeping up. Her stress was outweighing her chemical cocktail. The sky
outside was still dark. She was in Rosie's bed. Rosie was not.

Petal knew she hadn't slept enough. *Close your eyes*, she
thought to herself, and she did. *Don't check the time!* She breathed
slow and deep, allowing her thoughts to wash gently across her
mind, without penetration, without disruption of the delicate
chemistry at work in her brain. But try as she did to let sleep
reclaim her, she couldn't block out a tiny *squeak, squeak, squeak.*

"Crap!" she said, climbing out of bed. She went to pee. No
Rosie there. She looked in the girls' rooms and the kitchen. No
Rosie. Rosie was in the front room, standing on a squeaky step-
ladder, vigorously cleaning the picture window. In one hand, she

held a spray bottle of Windex, in the other a wadded-up bunch of damp paper towels she was rubbing in aggressive little circles on the glass.

"Whatcha doing?" Petal said.

"I didn't mean to wake you," Rosie said in a loud, breathy whisper. "I was trying to be quiet."

"How long have you been up?"

"I couldn't fall asleep. Then I figured out what I had to do, so I got up."

"What do you mean you figured out what you had to do?" Petal looked around the room. The beds had been stripped, and the curtains, such as they were, were nowhere in sight.

"If I just prove them wrong, then they won't have any reason to talk about me!" Rosie said with such eureka-like enthusiasm one might believe she had discovered, at the very least, a cure for cancer.

"So, you're cleaning. I get it. You know I already washed and changed all the beds. You don't have to redo it." But the more Petal said, the more she grasped that she was trying to confront irrational with rational. "I'm going back to bed, Ro. You do what you need to do. Maybe you'll try to get some sleep. You can finish in the morning."

Petal went back to the small bedroom and climbed into her niece's bed. *What harm could cleaning do?* she thought. *Except that was what set her off in the first place*, she rethought. Petal got out of bed and went back to Rosie.

"Ro," Petal said into the dim room.

Rosie started. "I thought you were going to sleep, little sheep."

"I am. I just want to be clear. What I said yesterday, about taking your pills ... that doesn't change no matter how much you clean. Okay?"

"Okey dokey, Pet. I'll take my pills, but you'll see. I'll make everything shine so bright that Hashem will tell me himself how clean it is instead of sending wicked witches to insult me."

Petal sighed, went to the bathroom, snagged one of Rosie's lorazepam, stuck it under her tongue, and slumped back to bed. Eventually, she fell back asleep.

THE UNMISTAKABLE SOUND of shattering glass launched Petal from bed. *Goddammit*, she thought. *Once, just once, I'd like to wake up normally!*

Rosie was standing on the small counter to the left of the kitchen sink.

"What happened?" Petal said, squinting into the light.

"I woke you again!" Rosie said, turning only her head toward her sister. "I'm sorry. Don't worry. Go back to bed."

"Cleaning?" Petal scrubbed her scalp with her fingertips, trying to wake.

"It's going great! I just dropped a glass accidentally. Don't walk without shoes! No shoes, bad news," she said, resuming her cleaning.

Petal checked the time on her phone. 8:30 a.m. Too early. She pulled her jeans on, wrapped her hoodie around her arms, and got her shoes from the front door. Shoving her feet into her sneakers, stepping on the backs, she could hear her bubby's ghost warning against the evils of tromping down the backs of your shoes. She swept up the broken glass from the kitchen floor, eyeing her sister's bony back through the thin fabric of her nightgown.

The counters and table had been stripped of their foil coverings. The sink was full of soapy water. "You uncovered the surfaces," she said to Rosie's back.

"I just wanted to clean them properly. I'll re-cover them. Can you wait to eat?" she said.

Petal nodded, pulling her phone from her pocket again. 8:45 a.m. She called Benjamin. "Good morning, sunshine," she said hoarsely.

"Good morning, princess! You sound less than rested."

"You could say that. Bit of a frenny going on. She's been up all night cleaning." Petal glanced around the room. Everything was in order: shelves dusted, floors scrubbed, beds made with tight hospital corners, smell of bleach and pine resin, windows clean — windows sparkling, in fact. "I think she went outside and washed the windows in the middle of the night," Petal said.

"Seriously? What do you think you should do? Should I come over?"

"Can you bring me coffee?" Petal needed to believe caffeine might miraculously present her with the answer to the question, *What next?*

"Coming up," Benjamin said.

"Benjamin, I think maybe she should be in hospital."

Back in the kitchen, Rosie was in the refrigerator; at least, most of her was. The kitchen floor was strewn with the contents previously contained therein.

"Did somebody throw away all my food?" Rosie's voice resonated from inside the fridge.

"Schmeil or Simmy Glisserman might have cleared some things out."

Rose pulled herself out of the box, hands on hips. "What kind of people go through someone else's refrigerator without their permission?"

Tucked behind one of Rosie's ears, posy-like, was a cluster of Q-tips. *Don't ask*, Petal thought.

"You should get dressed. Benjamin's coming over," Petal said, trying not to ripple the surface of her sister.

"I have things to do before Shabbes! I don't have time to get dressed!" Rosie ducked back into the fridge with the spray bottle of Windex and a boxing glove of paper towels.

"Suit yourself, Ro, but Benjamin is coming."

"Get me a cardigan and a *tichel!*" Rose commanded.

Petal got a sweater, which Rosie pulled over her nightgown, and a headscarf she tied, expertly avoiding her cotton swab bouquet.

"I'm going to brush my teeth. You want to join me?" Petal asked, but Rosie was deep in the fridge scrubbing and rubbing real and imaginary sludge and crud with exaggerated energy.

Petal was surprised to see Der. "Where's Benjamin?"

Der pointed Petal toward Benjamin, who was coming up the driveway with coffee in one hand and a paper bag in the other. "Go," Der said. "I'll cover for you."

Der went in. Petal joined her friend on the far side of Der's yellow convertible, a palpable celebration of a beautiful, sunny day. Benjamin handed the coffee and paper bag to Petal then reached into his jacket pocket and produced two cigarettes.

"M is for muffin, N is for nicotine!" Benjamin said.

"And they say the messiah hasn't come!" Petal slumped against the car. "How pathetic am I? My sister is in there in a state of major crazy, and I'm excited because you brought me coffee and a cigarette! I'm fucking Willy Wonka continuing the tour even as the children are lost, disfigured, or worse!"

"It's hardly the same thing. A pathetic muffin and minor stimulants are hardly a trip through candy land!" Benjamin said. "And your sister's madness isn't akin to those spoiled children's self-inflicted misadventure. Sorry, darling, your life is not Roald Dahl, it's Faulkner with a Sholom Aleichem amuse-bouche."

Petal smiled.

Benjamin lit both cigarettes and placed one between Petal's lips. She closed her eyes, inhaling deeply, sucking life force rather than nicotine. Petal savoured every haul of fetid smoke she drew into her lungs. She sipped her coffee and hid behind the car to eat her muffin, lest anyone see chametz consumed in the Hirsch driveway during Passover. "I feel like a teenager doing something illicit!" Petal squealed giddily.

"I wish I had known you as a teenager," Benjamin said, delighted that he could bring such glee to his generally earnest friend with one cigarette and a less-than-stellar baked good.

"We wouldn't have been friends. You would have been Rosie's friend."

"Are you kidding me? You think I hung out with the popular kids? I was a namby-pamby sissy. I was in the drama club, desperately trying to pass as 'artsy' instead of 'faggy.' We could have been great friends."

"I'm glad we're friends now. I don't know how much more sitting around 'the ward' I can manage on my own."

"That's why Der came. I told him what you said about the hospital. He wanted to see for himself," Benjamin said.

"How's that going? You and Der?" Petal asked.

"A match made in heaven. We have a theory that you and I clicked because my Der-ness allowed you to trust me."

"Your Der-ness?"

"You know, culture nerd, quasi-intellectual, destined to be single, 'confirmed bachelor,'" Benjamin said, making air quotes.

"Confirmed bachelor?"

"Der's term, hearkening back to the time when no one said *gay* in polite company."

"He said gay?" Petal asked.

"Only in reference to me being able to live 'out' in a way he never could," Benjamin said.

"Hmm," Petal said.

"What?"

"I guess somewhere along the way I mentally neutered him, like our plastic dolls, anatomically genderless. I never gave much thought to bloodlines or age or anything about Der other than he was just ours, forever and for always. When you say it, it's obvious, like I knew at some level, but it was another thing unspoken."

"He acknowledges that he made a choice to stay closeted. He said the shadows he would have had to lurk in were too dark for him."

"I'm almost jealous that you two bonded over this deep disclosure." Petal smirked.

"Significantly less deep than you might imagine. We are both jealous of the relationships you have with each of us."

"Lucky me," Petal said.

"You ready to return to the cuckoo's nest?" Benjamin said, taking Petal by the hand and guiding her reluctantly back to the house.

Rosie was putting everything back in the fridge while giving Der a running commentary. "I know you think Q-tips are overkill and a sign I'm crazy, but ask any frum woman what she does before Pesach! If I didn't use the Q-tips, it wouldn't be good enough for some people," she said with a paranoid scan of the room.

Der shot Petal a look. Petal raised her eyebrows.

"You are doing a stellar job. No one will have anything but praise for your efforts. Do you mind if Petal shows me the terrific job you did on the front room?" Der said as he edged Petal toward the boys' room.

"I need you all under my feet like a loch in kopf!" Rosie said, wrestling tinfoil onto the counters.

"What do you think, Der?" Petal asked shoulder to shoulder with the two men.

"There is no question she is floridly manic, but she appears contained. She's here at home, cleaning — albeit in overdrive — but by your own account the house was in need of a good cleaning. She doesn't appear to be doing herself or anybody else any harm, or doing anything she might regret later." Der turned his palms up and gave a small lift of his shoulders.

"So, you don't think she needs to be in a hospital?" Petal asked. "Even though she hasn't slept and is obviously still concerned about the voices?"

"Do I think all is well? No. She's not out of the woods yet. Medication takes time to be effective. But hospital is a whole other kettle of fish. Unless she's willing to go without coercion, admission would require a form. Do you think she would go to the hospital willingly?" Der asked.

"She doesn't think there's anything wrong with her. You're saying unless she's suicidal or violent, she just goes on like this indefinitely?"

"Unless she suddenly decides to go on a wild shopping spree or sleep eludes her for more than one night, I don't think anyone would admit her," Der said. "She's started on medication. It's not long enough to tell yet if it will be effective. Also, I hate to say it, but she's pleasant. Last night, she was positively charming."

"I kind of agree," Benjamin added. "If I didn't know any of the background, I'd think she was a bit loopy, but in a good way."

"That's what's always been so frustrating about Rosie. She's fun! And pretty. It sure makes crazy a whole lot harder to see." Petal plunked herself down on her nephew's bed. "So that's it,

I guess. I just hang in until the cavalry returns and hope for the best."

"Unless you can't," Der and Benjamin said in unison.

"If this is too much for you, I'll call Schmeil and put an end to it right now," Der said. "He can leave the kids with his mother for a few days, and he can come home and take care of his wife. You are not to be put at risk, Tiggaleh." His index finger was on guard.

"Der's right. I for one am not willing to sacrifice one sister for the sake of the other," Benjamin said.

"You two have been talking too much," Petal said.

"Yes," Der replied. "We had a plan. I assess Rosie, and Benjamin assesses you. What's your diagnosis, Benjamin?"

"I think Petal is of sound mind," he said, smiling at Petal. "But if you say the jig is up, we pull the plug and quit this popsicle stand."

Petal smirked. "If you think she's safe, I'm good. Knowing you guys are a call away is reassuring — my pillars," she said tucking her arms through theirs. "Go enjoy the day. Come for dinner around seven-thirty."

"I can stay with Rosie if you want to show Benjamin around. You can even have my car," Der said.

"That'd be nice, but I don't think so. At some point, she's probably going to crash, and I should be here. I hope that's okay, Benjamin?"

"I could happily just stay here and keep you company. I didn't come to Toronto to be a tourist."

"No, you go. We'll get ready for Shabbes, and you guys come back for dinner. We can hang all day tomorrow," she said, ushering them out.

Rose rushed outside past them. Petal followed. "Where to, Rosie?"

"Windows! Gotta do the back, Jack!" She scooted around the side of the house.

Petal followed Rose to the back of the house. She watched her climb a rickety ladder and zealously scour the windows, unfurling yard upon yard of paper towel and spraying pools of Windex.

"You can go inside. I don't need to be watched and judged all the time," Rosie said, aggressively scrubbing at a spot of bird shit.

"I'm just enjoying the weather," Petal lied as she stood guard.

"Who left this mess?" Rosie chastised the ether.

Petal collected the swamp of discarded paper towels and followed Rosie back inside.

Down on all fours, abrading the hardwood with a scrub brush and a solution of more bleach than water, stripping whatever varnish was left in the service of redemption, Rosie's fervour continued.

Rosie devoutly burnished every surface of the house with chemical cleansers and a hope of purification while Petal stood by, waiting to catch her if she fell from grace — or ladder, or chair, or countertop. Rosie was too busy eradicating the artwork from the walls in the entryway to take an afternoon call from Schmeil.

"Sorry, Schmeil, she's on a cleaning tear," Petal apologized to her brother-in-law.

"So, she's feeling good?" Schmeil said.

"Maybe too good. She's Hercules in the Augean stables. Putting her energy to good use."

"Who?" Schmeil asked.

"Never mind. How are the kids?"

"Baruch Hashem, all good."

"I'll try to get her to call you before Shabbes. Otherwise, we'll see you Sunday night?"

"B'ezrat Hashem, everything will come right by then."

"God willing," she said, clenching her fists, wanting desperately to believe.

Late in the afternoon, Petal followed Rose to the basement, where each toy was baptized in a bucket of bleach and water and laid out to dry on a carpet of old towels. Worried that Rosie might lose it by returning to the proverbial scene of the crime where the bookshelves still lay disassembled, Petal hovered. She pulled the door to Schmeil's study closed.

"Why did you close the door?"

"Schmeil asked us to stay out of his study," Petal lied again. "Ro, it's time to stop. Anyone would be happy to eat off any surface in your house! It's time to bathe before Shabbes."

"I'll shower after you," Rosie said.

"Don't you want to come shower with me? A little hydroterapies?"

"I'm okay to shower on my own now."

Upstairs, Petal turned the oven to 275 degrees and put the foil containers in to desiccate.

Showered and dressed, with the light of the evening sky beginning to wane, Petal went down to Rosie. "Your turn, Ro. Before Shabbes!"

"Gonna give the bathroom a quick scrub. Then a quick shower," she said, bounding up the stairs, Windex and bleach jugs in hand.

Petal stayed downstairs to reassemble the bookshelves. Putting the dismantled pieces back together, making order from chaos, was almost meditative. Reluctant to put too much import on this metaphoric righting of the keel, she couldn't help feeling that the reconstituted shelves, the books lined up in alphabetical order, represented tangible evidence that crisis was averted. Turning off the light, she closed the study door behind her and climbed out of the darkened basement.

At the top of the stairs, Petal smelled the acrid, ammonic air. "Jesus! It's toxic in here, Ro!" She rushed to open the front door and the small sliders at the bottom of the picture pane in the front room. "I'm literally choking on fumes! Are you still in the bathroom?" Petal opened the windows in the bedrooms. "Ro, it's almost sundown, and the guys will be here soon." Petal knocked on the bathroom door, coughing.

The door was locked. "Rosie! Open the door!" But she couldn't wait. Dread was suddenly encroaching, and with one hard yank on the ramshackle knob, the door swung open, releasing a gaseous vapour so fierce, Petal reflexively pulled the neckline of her T-shirt over her face. "Oh, Jesus!" she screamed. Rosie, still in her cardigan and nightgown, slumped over the edge of the bathtub. The tub was filled with a chemical brew, a milky blue pool of noxious soup. Empty plastic cleanser jugs, pills, and dosette boxes were scattered all around. Petal grabbed her sister by the armpits and pulled her to the front door. Rosie lay outside on the broken, chalk-covered stoop. Propping the screen door open with her body, she pulled her phone from her pocket and dialled 911.

"We're outside."

She answered the dispatcher's questions.

"I don't know if she swallowed chemicals."

"I don't think she's breathing."

"I don't know how long."

She wanted so badly to feel a pulse, but she wasn't sure.

The firefighters arrived moments before the ambulance, which arrived minutes before Der and Benjamin in the yellow convertible. Petal got into the ambulance. Her sister laid out on the stretcher, Petal tried desperately to disconnect from the world around her — human on hold — but instead she felt.

"North York General," the driver shouted.

"We'll follow," Der said.

Der and Benjamin stayed while the firefighters contained the contaminants at the house. It seemed that Rose had emptied all the cleaning solutions into the plugged bathtub, creating a chlorine gas chamber. It was unclear if she had also drunk the solution, taken pills, or simply been overcome by the vapours.

By the time Der and Benjamin reached the hospital, the details didn't matter.

Petal stood in the harsh fluorescent glare of the room at the far end of the emergency department, surrounded by machines and tubes and gunk-covered gauze, a tray of surgical tools scattered haphazardly, next to the barely convex, draped lump of her sister, clinging to the railing of the gurney. Der and Benjamin wrapped themselves around her. Der searched the room for air, gasping through his soul-sucking sobs. Benjamin held Petal so tight she cracked a little, oozing sadness and pain into him, and he absorbed it.

"She needed to be clean inside and out. She needed to prove she was worthy," Petal keened.

Clinging to the bedrail, she wished for numbness, willing every cell in her body to dilate so big, so wide, that matter might flow through without touching, without feeling, without causing ripple or ridge or wrinkle. To let go would mean collapse, and once down she may never get up.

Der had many questions, but only one mattered. "Does Schmeil know?"

"Shabbes. No phones." Petal's tremor shook the bed, metal on metal, a bell-like clanging. Peeling one of her hands from the rail, Benjamin took hold of Der's hand, and he steadied them in their immobile cluster.

"I'll go get him," Der said.

Benjamin nodded. Der put his blazer around Petal's quivering shoulders, cleaving to her with the motion. "I don't want to leave you, Tiggaleh," he sobbed.

"I'll go," Benjamin said impotently, because he didn't know where to go or who Schmeil was or how to drive a car, and he too wept.

"Maybe we should all go," Benjamin said.

"I can't leave her," Petal said.

"Stay with Tig, Benjamin," Der said, releasing his grip. "I'll get Schmeil."

For the third time in his life, Der went to deliver news of death in the Wolffe family, disrupting the family at Shabbes dinner. Schmeil knew as soon as he saw Der in the entry of Mrs. Hirsch's townhouse. He got in the car with no objection to driving on Sabbath. At the hospital, because he could not throw his arms around Petal, he folded Benjamin in an embrace so full of pain and sorrow that Benjamin felt the fissures in Schmeil's heart through his chest.

Petal needed him to know what she herself had no way of knowing. "It was an accident, Schmeil."

Sabbath and the holy days meant no funeral arrangements could be made until sundown on Sunday, and until that time, in accordance with Jewish law, Raizel's body needed to be watched. Schmeil insisted on staying until the Chevra Kadisha came and took her to prepare her for burial, and because Schmeil insisted on staying, Petal insisted on keeping him company and spelling him off when he needed to sleep, and because Petal insisted upon remaining, so too did Der and Benjamin. And so they sat until her passage was taken out of their hands.

13.

THE CHALK DRAWINGS had been cleaned away from the cracked cement step. In their place stood a cardboard washing station that included a bowl of water, a two-handled jug, and a roll of paper towels. Schmeil demonstrated the proper way to wash by pouring water over each hand three times, alternating between left and right. One by one, they washed the cemetery from their hands, the older siblings helping the younger. As each completed their symbolic cleansing, instinctively they gripped one another's damp palms. Linked, a human chain, they entered their house of mourning. Schmeil, Sarah Batya, Simcha Aron, Leah Rochel, Chava Malka, Avromi Yitzchak, Gittie Freidle, Miriam Ruthie, Estie, Petal, Der, and Benjamin, joined together centipede-like, snaking their way through bedrooms to basement. The kitchen was blocked. It was not for them to tend their corporeal needs during their time of mourning. The community would provide. Eleven mourners' chairs, their legs amputated below the knees, sat in a low row in the tidy basement. Schmeil had insisted there be enough chairs for all of the children, even the ones technically too young to sit shiva.

"Their mother, alleh ve'sholem, is dead," he said. "They should sit if they want."

Heschy Glisserman took care of the arrangements and didn't argue.

Simcha Aron climbed onto his father's lap. Gittie Freidle climbed onto Petal's lap.

"Not there," someone said to Benjamin as he sat down next to Petal in one of the stunted chairs.

"Loz ir," Schmeil intervened. "He's family. Sit, Benjamin. You too, Der."

Der let out a small, "Oy" as his aging knees creaked into position.

"Are you okay?" Petal and Benjamin asked.

"Is any of us okay?" he replied.

A parade of women brought paper plates with hard-boiled eggs and cooked-to-destruction vegetables. The community provided.

Prayers were said. A candle was lit. In silence they ate.

The men passed around tiny disposable shot glasses of schnapps.

"Give also to my sister-in-law," Schmeil said.

Petal toasted to life and drank shots with the bearded, ear-locked Jews, who likely had never before clinked glasses with a woman. Only her own awkwardness lingered beyond the first "L'chaim."

Three times a day, men came to pray with the mourners. Three times a day, women came to feed them. Heschy Glisserman organized a parade of rabbis to lead prayers. His wife commandeered the kitchen. Petal said Kaddish alongside Schmeil, the children, and Der. The community supported.

Visitors came and went repeating clichéd condolences.

"*Ha'Makom y'nachem et'chem b'toch sha'ar aveilei Tzion v'Yerushalayim.*"

"May the place comfort you among the other mourners of Zion and Jerusalem."

Am I comforted by this place? My sister's place?

"Why *Ha'Makom?* Why are we bidden be comforted by a place?" Petal asked no one in particular.

"It means Hashem," Avromi Yitzchak answered. "Hashem

is everywhere, so the place, no matter where, is where we find Adonai."

"Oh," said Petal. "Thanks."

Her oldest nephew smirked, barely able to disguise his pride of knowledge, his glee in his role of teacher, of rabbi.

"May her memory be a blessing," said the shiva callers.

And Petal agreed.

"We need to talk about her," Petal said to her brother-in-law.

He looked down at the carpet and shook his head slowly. "I want to." His words raked through his strangled gorge.

"Her memory can only be a blessing if we talk about her, tell her stories — all of them!" said Petal. "The good ones about the joy she brought to everyone and the bad ones about mental illness and suffering. The ones from her religious life and from her secular upbringing; they're all testament to the memory of her. I promise to tell you anything you ever want to know," Petal swore to Schmeil. "I'd like your permission to share memories with the children. I'll be respectful but truthful."

Schmeil nodded consent.

"I'm guessing there's a lot she never told you," Petal said. "I think it's important you know. Not to betray her confidences but to release you and the kids. Sometimes the truth hurts, but never as much as the weight of not knowing."

Schmeil dragged the back of his hand across his streaming eyes and gave another barely-there nod.

Between the waves of visitors, Petal talked to Schmeil about their childhood, about familial mental health, about intergenerational trauma, and about what she knew of grief.

"Our history's been repeating itself," she said. "Somewhere along the way, some kind of deep-seated damage was done. If anything good is to come of this tragedy, my sister's death needs to break the cycle of untold secrets and stories that have been eating away at our connective tissues, leaving us vulnerable to all manner of imagined shortcomings, insecurities, repressed emotions. We need to learn we are good enough, not perfect or unscarred, but enough. Your kids need to know they're worthy of happiness, respect, and love. They can only know that if they know the whole story. You know, like we say on Passover, how it's important to tell the wise son, the simple son, and the son who doesn't yet know how to ask."

"We tell also the contrary one the story of Passover," Schmeil said.

"None of your children are contrary, Schmeil. They might become so from time to time as they grieve and learn to live without their mother, but when that's the case, it doesn't mean we need to stop speaking about her."

AVROMI YITZCHAK AND Chava Malka escaped the crowd of visitors. Petal followed them. "Is this a private meeting, or can I join you?" she asked into the darkness of their father's study.

"Come in quick and close the door. We're hiding from all the people," Avromi Yitzchak said.

Petal closed the door and sat on the desk.

"You sit on the sofa," the boy said, jumping up with a crackle to make space next to his sister.

"I'm used to sitting on desks from being a teacher."

"You're a teacher?" Chava Malka asked.

"I was for a long time. Now I'm going to be a professor at a university."

"A lady professor!"

"Where I come from, there are lots of lady professors and doctors and anything they want to be. It's different. Your mameh and I weren't raised frum."

"We know," they said, "but she never really talked about that."

"Do you want to hear about it?"

The teens looked at one another, unsure.

"It's okay," Petal said. "It's not a secret. It's part of who she was. Before she was Raizel, before she was your mameh, she was Rosie, my twin sister."

"You were twins?"

Petal smiled in the dark to hide from her own sadness.

"We were. We are. I understand why that might be surprising," Petal said. "Your mameh was the most beautiful, most popular girl! By the time she was your age, Avromi Yitzchak, all the boys were in love with her. She got invited to all the parties. They all wanted to dance with her."

"You went to parties with boys?" Chava Malka asked.

"We did. I wasn't popular, but she always dragged me with her. She wanted to make sure I had fun."

"We don't have those kinds of parties," Avromi Yitzchak said.

"I know, but we did. In the world where your mother grew up, she was the best at parties, and boys, and fun. And when she decided to become frum, she tried to be the best at that too. She chose, and loved, and married your father with her whole heart. And when she became a mother, she devoted herself to loving all of you with the same energy and enthusiasm she gave to all the things that were most important to her."

"She was fun with us too," Chava Malka said. "We always had the best Purim costumes and the fanciest *sholoch monos*."

"Am I allowed to say things about her that are true, but maybe a little mean?" Avromi Yitzchak asked.

"You can say whatever you want, especially to me. I know she could be a bit much sometimes. Telling the truth and being mean aren't the same thing."

"Sometimes I was embarrassed by her," said the boy with a sob.

Petal wanted to squeeze between her niece and nephew and wrap herself around the boy, but she didn't. "Me too," she said.

"She was different than the other mothers," Chava Malka said.

"I'm sure she was," Petal said. "But that wasn't because she was a *chozeret te'shuva*. That was because she was Rosie — excitable, colourful, enthusiastic. That's honest, not mean."

ON THE THIRD day of shiva, Petal went to call Sarah Batya, Leah Rochel, and Miriam Ruthie for evening prayers and found them all asleep. *I'll leave them. Everyone will understand*, Petal thought as Estie bounded up the stairs and crashed through the bedroom door.

"Davening time!" Estie shouted as though beckoning the farm hands for chow.

"We'll be down soon. Ask Rabbi Glisserman to wait just a bit, please." Estie slammed the door and clomped back down to the basement.

Sitting on the edge of Leah Rochel's bed, Petal asked, "Are you up to coming down for prayers?"

"We don't really have a choice," Sarah Batya said, sitting up.

"I could make an excuse for you," Petal said. "I used to do that for your mother a lot."

"What kind of excuse?" Miriam Ruthie asked.

"I could say 'women's issues' or something."

"You can't say that!" the girls shrieked.

"It's not like I'd be giving details," Petal said.

"We don't talk about those things!"

"Everybody knows women get their periods, but we're not allowed to talk about it. I'm so sick of all the things we aren't allowed to —" Petal stopped.

"What were you going to say?" Sarah Batya asked.

"It doesn't matter."

"Yes, it does."

"I don't want to be disrespectful, but I'm just so sick and tired of all the things we aren't allowed to talk about. I don't just mean because I'm secular and you're Orthodox. I mean everything! Our bubby and zaideh loved us very much, but there was a lot of stuff we never talked about, like not having a mother or a father. It was something that we were just sad about in silence."

"How come?" Leah Rochel asked.

"I guess we felt ashamed," Petal said. "It was something that made us different from other kids. And it was painful. We knew without being told that it was too hard for our grandparents. That was the kind of family we grew up in: we didn't talk about stuff."

"Mameh didn't stop talking about stuff," Sarah Batya said. "She was always asking personal questions."

"That's because she loved you. She wasn't just being nosey," Petal said.

"I'm pretty sure she was just being nosey asking about my dates." Sarah Batya blushed.

"Sarah Batya is going to be engaged soon," Miriam Ruthie said.

Sarah Batya gave her sister a flick.

"You know, if I had had someone to ask me nosey questions, I might not have married the wrong man," Petal said.

"You were married?" the nieces exclaimed.

"Yes, but it wasn't a good marriage. It's not a secret. It's just a complicated story. Now's not the right time. I suppose the important part in the meantime is that I want you all to know what I didn't really know. A dead mother is no cause for shame. You are deserving and worthy of exactly what everyone else is."

"What's everyone else deserving of?" Leah Rochel said.

"Safety, security, success, respect, happiness, love."

"Those things aren't guaranteed," said Leah Rochel.

"No, they aren't. You have to work for them. But if you believe you don't deserve them because you're somehow less than everyone else, because your mother was sick, because she died, because whatever life has thrown at you through no fault of your own, because people whisper behind your back with pity, and you can't help noticing ..." Petal stopped.

"I don't think I will ever be happy again," Miriam Ruthie said.

"Happiness might be hard for a while, but you're lucky to have each other, and your father, and your bubby, and all your aunties, including me — even though I live a very different life than you do. Talking about it can help make the grief you'll always feel hurt a little less. Secrets and shame don't help."

"You think we'll always feel like this?" Sarah Batya asked.

"The shock goes away, but the love never does, so the missing lasts forever. In some ways, it gets worse," Petal said.

"It gets worse?" Miriam Ruthie cried.

"Maybe it's different for different people. For me, I know that I've spent a lot of time angry, wishing that the people I loved could be around to see me be successful, happy. But I've spent much more time, either consciously or subconsciously, resisting success, fighting happiness, to punish them for leaving me, to spare myself from searching in vain for approval. Who knows what? I think I'm only now learning to accept death as permanent."

"That's silly. Of course, it's permanent," said Leah Rochel.

"I know, but in a strange way, it's taken me my whole life to figure that out. There'll be times you'll feel sorry for yourselves. Times when you'll be angry with her, even though it wasn't her fault. Sometimes it'll hurt so much you'll think you're going to die. But, if you work at it, you'll remember the good stuff."

Petal lingered after her nieces went downstairs. She removed the contraband novel from beneath the mattress and tucked it under Leah Rochel's pillow.

SIMCHA ARON, GITTIE Freidle, and Estie were making believe in the play kitchen at the far end of the basement. "Can I play too?" Petal asked.

"I'm the mameh, Simcha Aron is the tateh, and Gittie Freidle is the girl, so you have to be the baby. You have to cry because I'm making dinner and it isn't ready yet," Estie commanded.

Petal lay on her back at the feet of the bossy six-year-old "Mameh" who banged plastic kitchen implements as though she were assembling an eighteen-wheel truck rather than an imaginary meal.

"You have to cry!" Estie said, and Petal did.

"Not quietly like that. Loud like a baby!"

Simcha Aron climbed on his tante, put his head on her chest, and shoved his thumb in his mouth. Gittie Freidle sat down next to them and stroked the tears on Petal's cheek.

"Are you guys still playing?" Estie asked.

"I'm much better at telling stories than I am at pretending. Would you like to hear some stories about your mameh when she was a little girl?" Petal asked.

"Uh-huh," Gittie Freidle said.

Simcha Aron popped his thumb out of his mouth, gave a definitive single nod of his head, and vacuum-sucked his thumb back into his mouth. Estie switched from fake cooking to fake floor mopping.

"Your mameh was the most fun in the whole wide world," Petal said, pulling up to sitting, manoeuvring her nephew into her lap. "She loved to play dress-up and put on shows."

Estie put down the mop and stood beside her aunt. Petal looked up at her niece.

"She always got lost when we went out. She would get so excited about stuff that sometimes she got in trouble. But it never stopped her from trying new things or taking risks."

"Did she get in trouble a lot?" asked Estie.

"Lots!" Petal smiled.

"Sometimes I get into trouble," Estie confessed.

Gittie Freidle laughed at her sister. "She cut the feet off her tights!"

"Why did you do that?" Petal asked.

"It was too hot!" said Estie.

"It seems to me like a sensible thing to do," Petal said.

Estie stuck her tongue out at her sister.

"She always does stuff," Gittie Freidle said.

"Don't you ever do anything wrong?" Petal asked.

Gittie Freidle blushed. "Not on purpose," she said.

"Your mameh never got into trouble on purpose. It just had a way of finding her. Like when she cut the feet off her tights."

"She did?" Gittie Freidle asked.

"She did," Petal replied.

"Did you ever get into trouble when you were little?" Estie asked.

"Not so much when I was little, but I got really good at it when I got older," Petal said to the delight of her nieces.

EACH DAY AFTER dark, when all the visitors had gone and the children were falling asleep where they landed, Petal, Der, and Benjamin left the shiva house and returned to apartment 1A.

"Tiggaleh, how are you?" Der asked each night, and each night Petal had a different answer.

"I'm numb."

"That's normal. I understand," Der said.

"I'm exhausted."

"As expected. Me too," Der said.

"I'm so sad."

"Of course you are," Der said.

"I miss her."

"That's forever. We both know that only too well," Der said.

"My heart hurts. Like my ribs are too tight."

"Oh, Tiggaleh, that too is normal," Der said.

They drank single malt and cried and laughed and told stories about Rosie and spoke nonsense that had no points. Benjamin made sure there were snacks to absorb the scotch. Oatmeal cookies and popcorn, their significance not lost on Petal even in grief.

"To the bitter end," she said.

"And then some, Pet," he replied.

They stayed up late talking each night until they could talk no more.

"Remember when she asked Bubby not to talk when she met our grade one teacher because she said Bubby talked funny?"

"She was so embarrassed when your zaideh pointed out that the teacher also had an accent. She hid in the closet so long, you had to bribe her out with treats!"

"Remember when we were about thirteen and we went downtown without permission? Estie would have never let us go! Then we ran into their friends, who said, 'We'll tell your bubby and zaideh we saw you.' Rosie made me call you and tell you some ridiculous lie."

"I knew you were lying, and you knew I knew you were lying, but we both knew we would tell the lie and protect Estie and Twitch."

"Like always," Petal said.

"Like always," Der said.

"I've got it," Benjamin said when he had run out of things to say.

"What?"

"Rice Krispie squares!" he said.

"Huh?"

"Edible Styrofoam!"

"Mmmm," Petal said as though it all made sense.

"Did I ever tell you about the time she made me play hide-and-seek in the pouring rain?"

"I don't think so," they said.

"Never mind, it's not such a good story," Petal said. "All of my relatives are dead. Does that free me from our collective history?"

"If only. Normally people try to hold on in grief, not untether," Der said.

"That's the first time you haven't told me I'm normal. I guess where family's concerned, I didn't win the normal lottery," Petal said.

"Get in line," Benjamin said.

"They aren't all dead, Tiggaleh."

"I didn't mean you."

"I'm talking about the children."

"I wonder if they'll keep me," Petal said.

"It's up to you to keep them."

"All these feelings are too hard."

"Remember how hard it is not to feel. Grief is the hardest feeling of them all, but you must feel it to get through it."

"He's right," Benjamin said. "Remember I told you how hard I resisted grief when Scott died and how hard it bit me in the ass? Let it drive for a while. It's the best insurance against a crash."

ON THE MORNING of the seventh day, they got up from sitting.

Once again holding hands, they made a line that stretched from one side of the street to the other. Followed closely by the community that had tended their needs through their period of initial mourning, they walked around the block.

Petal and Schmeil, separated by Gittie Freidle, stood in the centre.

"Why do we walk around the block at the end of shiva?"

"Because life goes on, and we need to rejoin it. Together, we give each other a little push forward," Schmeil said. "I have to for the children."

"I know you have a supportive community to help, and that gives me great comfort," Petal said, "but I'd also like to be a part of your lives. I know it's complicated. I live in my world and you in yours. They're miles apart physically and metaphysically, but I hope ... Schmeil, I will only ever honour my sister's memory and choices. I will only ever do right by the kids according to your wishes."

"I know."

DER DROVE PETAL and Benjamin to the airport.

Benjamin insisted on a stop at McDonald's on the way. "I'm having unkosher withdrawal."

"McDonald's?! Seriously, that's your antidote?" Petal was surprised.

"I'll just be a second," he said, hopping out of the car.

Minutes later, he returned and handed Petal a bag.

"I don't want anything."

"Just open it."

Petal unfurled the top of the bag and reached in. "A Quarter Pounder with Cheese?"

"There's more."

Petal pulled out a small red box of Sun-Maid raisins, a larger box of Smarties, and a roll of Tums. "I'm going to need the Tums."

"I still owe you U, V, W and Z. Something to look forward to," Benjamin said. "And don't think I haven't got a plan."

"I wouldn't dream of it," Petal said. "Did X stump you?"

Benjamin reached in his pocket and pulled out his small tin of coffee mints, shaking it around like a percussion instrument.

Petal smiled.

"What?" asked Der, who had only a vague idea of what was going on.

"Xanax," they said in unison.

They drove down Bathurst Street in relative silence, past Lakeshore Boulevard to the island airport terminal.

On the curb, Petal struggled to leave. "Heschy Glisserman asked me if I would consider doing some literacy work with the community here. He's going to try get funding. I'm going to try to get a research grant. It might be a way to step into their world without erasing myself."

"With or without a grant, I expect to see you both here soon and more often," Der said.

"I'll be back in a few weeks for the *shloshim*," Petal said.

Benjamin gave Der a hug. "Thank you," he said.

"I know my girl is safe. I know she is loved," Der said to him.

"For everything and for always," Der said, wrapping Petal in his embrace.

"Everyone I love dies, Der," Petal said losing the composure she had hoped to cling to.

"Yes, they do, Tiggaleh."

"What do I do, Der?"

"The best you can," he said, releasing her.

Der reached into his pocket and handed Petal a tiny plastic bag. "I didn't have time to wrap it."

Petal pulled open the Ziploc and dumped the tiny charm onto her palm: a silver daisy with a speck of rose gold in its centre.

GLOSSARY

Terms of Reference: Y = Yiddish, H = Hebrew, A = Arabic

A

Abba (H): Father.

Adonoi (Y) Adonai (H): Our Lord.

"Ain li lechem, Ain li mayim, Ain li shum davar." (H): "I have no bread, I have no water, I have nothing."

Alleh ve'sholem (Y) Alleh ve'shalom (H): Literally "go in peace," used like "rest in peace" when speaking of the dead.

Amhaoretz (Y) Amhaaretz (H): Literally "a man of the earth" but used to imply uneducated, unrefined, or ignorant.

"Ani cholah!" (H): "I'm sick!"

Aintibah (A): Heads up.

Asimon (sing.) Asimonim (pl.) (H): Token, specifically the old-style tokens with a hole in the middle used for public telephone booths in Israel.

Aufruf (Y): Jewish custom of a groom being called up in the synagogue for an *aliyah*, the recitation of a blessing over the Torah before his wedding day.

B

Ba'al tshuvah (m) Ba'alat tshuva (f) (H) (Y): Referring to someone who is born again into religious Jewish life.

Bar mitzvah: A Jewish rite of passage celebrated when a boy turns thirteen years old, welcoming him as an adult in the eyes of God and his community. A bat mitzvah is the same or similar rite of passage for a girl, celebrated when a girl is between twelve and thirteen years old. In Orthodoxy, girls are not bat mitzvahed, only boys are bar mitzvahed.

"*Baruch attah, Adonai, Eloheinu melech ha'olam, asher kidshanu,
be'mitzvotav, ve'tzivanu lehadlik ner shel Shabbat. Amen.*" (H):
Prayer over candles said to welcome in the Sabbath. "Blessed art
thou, o Lord our God, king of the universe, who has commanded us
to light candles for the Sabbath."

Baruch Hashem (H) (Y): God bless.

"*B'chol ofen ha tisah b'overbooking.*" (H): "In any case, the flight is
overbooked."

Beshert (H) (Y): Destined or destiny.

B'ezrat hashem (H) (Y): With God's help.

Bocher (Y): A male youth. A yeshiva bocher is a young man who studies
in a yeshiva.

Boker Tov (H): Good morning.

Bubbaleh (Y) (H): Literally, a small doll, but used as a term of affection
meaning dolly.

Bubby (Y): Grandmother. Also Bobba, Bubeh, depending on regional
pronunciation.

C

Chabad: A specific sect of Orthodox Judaism.

Chag (H): Holiday or holy day. In Yiddish, *yuntif*.

Challah (H) (Y): Braided egg bread used specifically for Sabbath and
holy days.

Chalutz (sing.) Chalutzim (pl.) (H) (Y): Pioneer, pioneers.

Chametz (H) (Y): Leaven, as in bread or bread products or other foods
forbidden during the eight days of Passover.

Chas ve'sholem (Y): Expression equal to "Heaven forefend."

Chaticha (H): Literally "a piece," referring to an attractive (young)
woman.

Chevra Kadisha: Organization of Jewish men and women who see to it
that the bodies of deceased Jews are prepared for burial according
to Jewish tradition and are protected from desecration, willful or
otherwise, until burial.

Chochem (Y): "Smart one," often used ironically or sarcastically as an
insult.

Cholent (Y): A traditional stew, generally of meat, beans, and potatoes, slow-cooked in the oven from before sundown on Friday night until lunchtime on Saturday, thus enabling a hot, cooked meal be served on Sabbath without overriding any religious laws.

Chossen (Y): Groom.

Chozeret Te'shuva (Y) (H): Literally "one who has returned to the answer," used in both Yiddish and Hebrew depending upon pronunciation. Meaning someone secular who has rediscovered or returned to religious Jewish life, like "born again."

Chuppah (H) (Y): Jewish wedding canopy.

D

Daven (Y): To pray.

Derech eretz (H) (Y): Literally "the way of the earth," used to mean "common decency."

"*Der professor is ayn lamdan.*" (Y): "The professor is a scholar."

"*Der professor raidst* English." (Y): "The professor speaks English."

"*Dos is mine tsifer*" (Y): "This is my number."

Drosh or drosha (Y): A verbal commentary on biblical or religious texts.

E

Eema (H): Mother.

"*Efshar la'azor? Tzricha mashehu?*" (H): "Can I help? Do you need something?"

Eshet chayil (H), Eshes chayil (Y): A Jewish woman of valour.

F

Far itst (Y): For now.

Farshteist (Y): To understand.

Farshteist du (Y): Do you understand?

Frum (Y): Orthodox.

"*Frytick, Shabbos, auber pesach, Zuntik, Muntic es bin yuntif. Dinstik, Mitvoch, unt Donerschtik er ken cumen un bazuchen. Demolt vider zaiyn Shabbos unt yuntif.*" (Y): "Friday, Saturday, then Passover, Sunday, Monday are holy days. Tuesday, Wednesday, and Thursday he can come and visit. Then again it's Sabbath and holy days."

G

Gatkes (Y): Underpants.

Geferlech (Y): Dangerous.

Gei (Y): Go!

Gei avek! (Y): Go away!

Genug (Y): Enough.

Get (Y) (H): A Jewish divorce that can only be sanctioned by a rabbi.

Gevalt (Y): Exclamation equal to "My gosh!"

Glatt kosher: Entirely kosher, as approved by a particular rabbinic body.

Gonoivim (Y): Thieves.

Goyish (Y): Non-Jewish, Gentile.

Grushim (H): Slang referring to *agurot*, the smallest coin denomination when currency was in lira.

"*Gut Shabbes. Gut yuntif.*" (Y): "Good Sabbath. Happy holiday."

H

Halacha (H) (Y): Jewish law.

Hashem (H) (Y): Literally "the Name." Used in place of God in order to uphold the commandment of not taking the Lord's name in vain.

Hassidishe (Y): Referring to the Hassidic sect of Orthodox Judaism.

Hatzot (H): Midnight.

"*Haut ver es iz phoon Saposkin aungekumen?*" (Y): "Did anyone by chance come from Saposkin?"

Hechsher (H) (Y): "Seal of approval," generally regarding the Jewish dietary laws about Kashrut or what is or is not kosher.

Hegdish (Y): Literally "an unholy place," used to mean a mess or a sty.

"*Hey, kibbutznikit, at yodaat ulaiy im tzarich laasot stage b'shana alef?*" (H): "Hey, girl from kibbutz, do you perhaps know if we are required to do a placement in our first year?"

Hora: Traditional Israeli circle folk dance.

I, J, K

"*Ich gayst, Heschy. Ich hoben a platz tsu ton. Gut yuntif*, Dr. Gold. *Zei gezunt.*" (Y): "I'm going, Heschy. I have a lot to do. Happy holiday, Dr. Gold. Be well."

Kaiyn'nehora (Y): Expression warding off the evil eye.

Kasha and bow ties: Buckwheat cooked with bow tie noodles.

Kasher (Y): To make kosher.

Kav (H): Line, as in bus line or route.

Kav Arba: Bus line #4.

Kibbutz (H): Collective farm.

Kibbutznik (sing.) Kibbutznikim (pl.) (H): Kibbutz member(s).

Kippah (H): Jewish ritual skullcap worn by men. *Yarmulke* is the Yiddish word for skullcap.

Kolnoah (H): Cinema.

Kotel (H): Literally a wall, but referring specifically to the Western Wall of the Ancient Temple in Jerusalem's Old City, deemed the holiest of places for Jewish people.

Kova tembel (H): Literally dunce cap. Ubiquitous bucket-style sunhat worn in the early days by pioneers in Israel.

Knafeh (A): Arabic confection made with cheese and syrup.

L

Levad (H): Alone. "*At levad?*" means "Are you (f) alone?"

Loch in kopf (Y): Literally "a hole in the head," as in "I need it like I need a hole in my head!"

Lool (H): Chicken coop.

L'Yam (H): To the beach.

"*Loz ir,*" (Y): "Leave him alone."

M

Ma alhimar (A): Great ass.

Machasheyfeh (Y): Witch.

Machbesah (H): Laundry.

Mamaleh (Y): "Little mother," a term of affection.

Mazel tov (H) (Y): Good luck or congratulations.

Mayim (H): Water.

Meshebairach (H, Y): Prayer for the ill and suffering.

Meshugas (Y): Craziness or nonsense.

Metuka (f) Motek (m) (H): Sweetie.

Mezuzah (H) (Y): A small parchment scroll inscribed with religious texts and attached in a case to the doorpost of a Jewish house as a sign of faith.

Minhag (H) (Y): Tradition, followed ritually, as opposed to law
    (Halacha); can change from place to place, from community to
    community.
Mishna: An authoritative collection of exegetical material embodying
    the oral tradition of Jewish law and forming the first part of the
    Talmud.
Mitbach (H): Kitchen.
Mitzvah (H) Mitzveh (Y): A commandment or good deed. There are
    613 God-given commandments in Judaism.
Mizrachi (H): Eastern or of Eastern descent.

N
Nachon (H): Right or correct.
Narishkeit (Y): Silly or unsophisticated, ignoramus.
Nazishe tenementen: Mix of English and Yiddish meaning Nazi
    tenements.
Nebedik (Y): Inadequate or nerdy.
Neshama (H) Neshoma (Y): Soul.

O
"*Od lo achalnu shum davar, v'shum davar od lo shatinu! Im ain cham-*
    pagne v'ain caviar, tnu lanu lechem ve'zaytim," (H): "We haven't
    eaten anything, nor have we had anything to drink. If there is no
    champagne or caviar, give us bread and olives."
Oy (Y): Exclamation. "Oh!"
"*Oy, mine Der! Du bist a chalutz gevoren!*" (Y): "Oh, my Der. You
    have become a pioneer!"

P, Q
Pesachdik (Y): "For Passover," referring to something that is kosher for
    Passover.
Peyot (H) Peyos (Y): Ear locks worn by Orthodox Jewish men to abide
    by one of the laws of Judaism.
Pish (Y): Slang for urinate.
Pomelo: A type of thick-skinned, grapefruit-like citrus fruit.

Purim: Jewish holiday celebrated in the month of Adar, which generally falls in February or March. The custom is to dress in costume and drink to excess until one is so drunk one doesn't recognize the Evil Hamman, the villain of the Purim story.

R

Rachmonos (Y): Compassion.

Rebbetzin (Y): The rabbi's wife.

Rugelach (Y): Typical croissant-like Ashkenazi pastry, usually flavoured with cinnamon and sugar or chocolate.

S

Sadeh (H): Field.

Schlemeil (Y): Hapless, loser.

"Schmeil, tsi ir hoben genug medesine?" (Y): "Schmeil, do you have enough medicine?"

Schvach (Y): Weak.

Schvartzinke (Y): Diminutive of Schvartz, meaning black. Used to refer to people of colour and darker skin tones.

Seforim (Y): Books, referring specifically to religious texts.

Shabbat (H) Shabbes (Y): Sabbath.

Shadchan (Y): Matchmaker.

"Sham. Lechi le sham." (H): "There. Go to there."

Shidduch (H) (Y): An arranged match between a man and a woman.

Shiksa (Y): A Gentile or non-Jewish woman. Often used in a derogatory manner.

Shiray sochnut (H): Zionist songs.

Shiur (H) (Y): Lesson.

Shiva (H) (Y): The seven days of formal mourning and visitation after a Jewish funeral.

Shloshim (H) (Y): Thirty days. The thirty-day period following burial (including shiva). During this time, a mourner is forbidden to marry or to attend a festive meal. Men do not shave or get haircuts during this time.

Sholoch monos (Y): Festive Purim baskets of food and drink and treats sent to family and friends.

Shtetl (Y): A small town inhabited by Jews, usually in Eastern Europe.
Shuk (H): Market. Shuk Ha'Carmel is the Carmel Market.
Shul (Y): Synagogue.
Simcha (H) (Y): Celebration or happiness.
Succot (H) Succos (Y): The Jewish feast of the tabernacle celebrated around the late summer/fall harvest.
"*S'vet gornisht helfen.*" (Y): "But nothing helped."

T
Talmud: The body of Jewish civil and ceremonial law and legend comprising the Mishnah and the Gemara.
Tateh (Y): Father.
Tichel (Y): Headscarf or women's head covering.
Topha'at teva (H): Phenomenon of nature.
Torah: Old Testament five books of Moses.
Tsnius (Y): Modesty, referring to modest dress required by religious law, particularly for married women.
Tsureh (Y): Trouble or problem.
"*Tsu achutzah! Chafetz chashud! Yalla, yalla, achutza!*" (H) (A): "Go outside! Suspicious object! [Arab slang] Go, go, outside!"
Tzitzit (H) Tzitzis (Y): Traditional garment worn by Orthodox Jewish men consisting of specially knotted ritual fringes or tassels.

U, V
Ulpan: Hebrew language course for newcomers.
"*Vey iz mir!*" (Y): Expression meaning literally "Woe is me!"
"*Vos far a prufeshiun is dos?*" (Yiddish mixed with English): "What kind of a profession is that?"
"*Vos far* a date? *Nischt a shidduch auber* a date?" (Mixed Yiddish and English): "What's with a date? Not a match, but a date?"
"*Vos hobn mir do?*" (Y): "What do we have here?"
"*Vos is dos?*" (Y): "What is this?"
"*Vos/Vus machts?*" (Y): "What's up?" or "What's doing?"
"*Vos machts, Rebbe? ... Yoh, mine froi un eiyr shvester.... Auber der chametz? Vos far der chametz?*" (Y): "What's up, Rabbi? ... Yes, my wife and her sister ... But the leaven? What about the leaven?"

W, X, Y

Yenta (Y): A gossip or busybody.

Yerushalyim (H) (Y): Jerusalem.

Yeshiva (H) (Y): Male institute of higher religious learning.

Yeshiva bocher (Y): A young man who studies in a yeshiva.

Yiches (Y): Status, as in family status or lineage.

Yom Kippur (Y, H): Jewish day of atonement.

Yom Toivim (pl.) (Y): Holy days, also referred to as yuntif (sing.).

Yom Tov (sing.) Yamim Tovim (pl.) (H): Holy day(s).

Z

Zaftig (Y): Luscious. Used in reference to what in English might be called a "Rubenesque" woman.

Zaideh (Y): Grandfather.

Zeiseh (Y): Sweet.

Zeiskeit (Y): Sweetie.

"*Zot'hee rotzah l'shanot tisa. Achotah lo higiya. Yaysh efsharoot?*" (H): "This one/she wants to change her flight. Her sister didn't arrive. Is there a possibility?"

ACKNOWLEDGEMENTS

I AM GRATEFUL to so many people for their contributions and support in the very long journey to the birth of this novel.

To my father, Vivian Rakoff (z"l), who allowed me to use him as a muse and to cannibalize his stories, experiences, and research to write this work of fiction. I'm heartbroken he didn't live to see it published.

To my brothers, David Rakoff (z"l) and Simon Rakoff, who have always told me I'm good enough and encouraged me to write. I love you forever and for always.

To the people who so generously shared their stories with me about the early years in Israel, I thank you for helping me construct a collage of real experiences to bring my fiction to life: Zelda Lootsteen (z"l), Peretz Lootsteen, Rina Arbiv (z"l), Rina Nemni, Ruth Golobik, Eli Boim, Avram and Malka Kuritzky, Ori and Rocha (z"l) Tzisling, Viola Machlouf.

Thank you to my many friends and relatives who mobilized their networks and brought me to the storytellers and drove me to locations: Ruth Yanovsky, Ayala Gerbi-Sharabi, Elana Gerbi, Iris Nemani, Claudia Skolnik, David Slater (z"l), Lisa Perlman.

For sharing their contemporary knowledge and experiences, I give thanks to Yocheved Zilber, Yael Shochat, and everyone from whom I gleaned information and knowledge through conversations over coffee, food, drink, and friendship.

To Erin and Joe Battat and Aliza Ben-Tal (z"l), who so generously provided me stellar accommodations for my research trip to

Israel, and to my brother Davey (z"l) for posthumously funding my travels.

Thanks to Greg Ioannou and Barbara Berson for all your publishing advice and guidance.

Thanks to Rhonda Tepper for being my trusted reader, and to everyone who read drafts along the way.

To my agent, Beverly Slopen, my editors, Marc Côté and Barry Jowett, Sarah Cooper, and the staff at Cormorant Books: none of it would be possible without you.

We acknowledge the sacred land on which Cormorant Books operates. It has been a site of human activity for 15,000 years. This land is the territory of the Huron-Wendat and Petun First Nations, the Seneca, and most recently, the Mississaugas of the Credit River. The territory was the subject of the Dish With One Spoon Wampum Belt Covenant, an agreement between the Iroquois Confederacy and Confederacy of the Ojibway and allied nations to peaceably share and steward the resources around the Great Lakes. Today, the meeting place of Toronto is still home to many Indigenous people from across Turtle Island. We are grateful to have the opportunity to work in the community, on this territory.

We are also mindful of broken covenants and the need to strive to make right with all our relations.